OUT OF THE RUBBLE

HEARTS OF NEPAL BOOK 3

RONALD BAGLIERE

For the children of Nepal

ACKNOWLEDGMENTS

This book would not have been possible without the support of my life partner, Linda Ortola, and my writing community here in Upstate New York. The community here is so supportive of writers and an invaluable source of encouragement, information and insights. Notably, is the support I received from the Romance Writers of America chapter of Central New York and my critique group, who provided comments and suggestions. The writers and authors in them are too many to count here, but I want to shine a light on a few of them as well as my two friends in Nepal who have vetted the writing to keep it as accurate as possible. First, a huge thanks to Martin Meiss, Mary Fancher, Debra Panebianco, Paul Baxter, Millisa Morrow and Julie Stuetzle for their comments and suggestions. To Binod and Sila Thapa, who lent their names for two of the major characters, and took the time to review sections of the book for me regarding Nepali culture and family life, I owe you so much more than words can say. For my editor, Charlee Bezilla, you have my gratitude for going through the manuscript and correcting all my little faux pas, and you additional suggestions to bring out the character's voices were so spot-on. And finally, to my beta readers; Sandra Jackson and Jann Block, thank you for taking the time to read and giving me your impressions.

NOTES FROM THE AUTHOR

Earthquakes happen all around the world. They're one of the most powerful destructive forces on Earth. When they happen in Third World countries, they're cataclysmic. The earthquakes that occurred in Nepal in 2015 left the country in tatters. They were both magnitude 7-plus quakes, the first of which (M_W 7.8) occurred in the Gorkha District on April 25, followed by two aftershocks of M_W 6.9 and M_W 6.7. The second quake occurred on May 12, in the Sindhupalchowk District (M_W 7.3), which is approximately eighty miles east of the first quake. Combined, these quakes destroyed 544,320 buildings and homes and took the lives of 8,790 Nepalis, orphaning uncounted children. Let that sink in a moment.

Now imagine yourself as a child faced with the loss of your parents and your entire family in this impoverished nation, living in a small, remote village in the mountains. Or perhaps you're living in the aging city of Kathmandu, whose buildings have collapsed, and you're alone, hungry, and scared. You don't know who to trust, where to go, or when the next tremor will rip the rest of your life away. You're scraping by, begging for handouts, when suddenly men come up to you, promising to take care of you, give you shelter and food, and help you find your parents. What do you do? Stay, and go silently into the night, or take a chance and go with them?

This is your choice, and so you make the decision to trust them, only to realize too late that their promises are empty lies and you're trapped in a dark world where every day is a lesson in survival, and getting by means closing your eyes and letting yourself be raped, beaten, or enslaved, with no escape unless by some miracle a hand reaches out and pulls you back.

When I was there in 2018 on a charity mission for the Sherpa, I witnessed the aftermath of these quakes in Kathmandu and in the mountains. You don't have to look far to find children fending for themselves in the streets of Kathmandu or living in unsafe buildings sitting on teetering foundations in the mountains. In spite of this, there are Angels out there who work the borders and cities to return these lost children to their families or to find them safe havens in new homes.

This novel attempts to shine a small light on the network of those on the front lines who work to curb the trafficking in this tiny country by those who would profit from man's inhumanity toward man. It also aims to show the resiliency of the Nepali people in the face of a national catastrophe. Sadly, not every home and shrine will be rebuilt, not every family will be restored, and not every Angel will succeed in saving a lost child, but like the story of the ridiculed man attempting to throw a thousand beached starfish back in the ocean:

To the starfish in his hand, it matters.

Namaste,

NOTHING IS PROMISED
The farmer grows the corn, but the bear eats it.

–Nepali Proverb

APRIL 25, 2015 — KATHMANDU, NEPAL

*I*t's a bright February morning as Mick weaves his rental car through snarled traffic on Ring Road. Beside him is Alan Forrester, High Trails' new expedition coordinator. They've just flown in from Pokhara for a logistics meeting with their new employee, Lincoln Webber and High Trails' Everest Base Camp guide, Binod Thapa. As Mick drives past the incessant beeping of darting vehicles, he glances at Alan, who's gawking out the window at the busy street lined with mobs of Nepalis. Sidewalk cafes put out pungent garlic and curry aromas, and a chorus of squawking radios blare Nepali music.

Mick looks at his watch, and from the corner of his eye, he sees Alan clutch his armrest. It's Alan's first tour of Nepal, and from the look of it, he's having a hard time getting his legs under him. "You'll get used to it," Mick says. "When we get there, we'll head in for the meeting, then get our room after. You hungry?"

"I could eat, I suppose," Alan says as they continue through the urban sprawl.

It's 7:35 a.m. Barring a major traffic jam, they'll arrive at the Crown Plaza Hotel for their meeting at 8:00. They're only a few minutes late. Not bad, considering their flight ran thirty minutes behind. He steers around a wheezing bus, zips down the road of failing macadam, and ten minutes later, he's turning onto Swayamblu Circle Road, heading for the hotel. "So, looking forward to getting up in the mountains?"

"I am," Alan says. He's quiet a moment and awkward silence permeates the space between them. Finally, he says, "I thought I knew traffic. But this...." He shakes his head.

"Yeah, it's a bit crazy," Mick answers as the hotel comes into view. He wends his way around a stopped car in the middle of the street. "You get used to it."

"I suppose," Alan says, but there's no conviction in his tone.

Mick speeds up and a minute later, they're turning into a drive flanking the five-story hotel. As he passes fragrant raised beds of edelweiss, anemones, and poppies, he hunts for a place to park.

Binod's motorbike is already here, parked in the large sweeping lot around the portico. Mick cocks a brow. Binod actually made it here ahead of him.

Five minutes later they're striding down the sidewalk to the front doors. The Plaza's sweeping masonry walls, prominent red metal roofs, and blue-tinted windows reflect the standard of luxury for Kathmandu's tourists. It's also the unofficial launching point for High Trails' Everest expeditions, not to mention that it's co-managed by Palisha Kc. She's a tiny, compact woman with vibrant brown eyes and a fetching smile. If there were any woman he could ever settle down with, it would be her. But she comes from a traditional Nepali family who frowns on taking up with foreigners. The fact that she's a widow, who by custom should be home and out of sight, only makes things worse. It leaves him in a heart-rending limbo of bottled-up love that should never be acted upon.

He follows Alan into the bright, airy interior and gestures to the broad hallway left of the reception desk. But his gaze strays to the office door behind the desk. It's open, but she's not inside. They cross a pale-blue oriental carpet and turn down the hall, passing muted tan walls. A coffered ceiling with hanging lights of polished brass extends down the corridor. The murmuring of a sanxian guitar, piped in from somewhere above, kisses his ears. At the end of the hall, an alcove leads to the hotel café. They stride past a couple of guests and go in. Binod and Lincoln Webber are sitting at a table by a window. They look up as he walks toward them.

"Hey, Binod," Mick says, glancing at his watch. "You're early. What the hell? Gonna turn into a regular American if you keep this up." He turns to Alan, explaining the concept of Nepali standard time, then introduces himself to Lincoln.

Lincoln pushes back from the table along with Binod and stands. The new American recruit Binod has spoken for is a tall redhead with a short-cropped beard and mustache. Above his deep blue eyes is a faint sickle-shaped scar that dives into a mop of curly hair. Under the collar of Lincoln's white cotton *tapālan* is a hint of a tattoo. Lincoln puts his hand out, and judging from his grip, Mick guesses he works out.

They all sit and pull menus toward them as a waiter comes around with a carafe of tea. As the man pours for them, he looks to Binod first. "What can I get for you?"

"I'm okay, thank you," he says.

Mick knits his brow. "You? Not hungry? You sick or something?" He reaches across the table toward Binod. "Give me your wrist. I want to check for a pulse."

Binod looks at him as if he's not sure what to say.

Mick grins and turns to Alan. "My friend has a bottomless stomach. Once, when we were at a teahouse on the Circuit, I think it was Jomsom...Jomsom, right, Binod?"

They both know where this is going. It's a joke between them he tells whenever he has a chance. Binod rolls his eyes and shrugs.

"Doesn't matter," Mick says. "Anyway, we just got off a fourteen-hour hike and you know meals on the Circuit, not a lot on the plate, so we're pretty hungry. Now I can put away my fair share, but Binod, he keeps going after I'm done. After his fifth helping, the owner, who's been watching his profits disappear, comes to our table and tells Binod if he makes that his last trip, our meal's on the house."

"I think you mistaken, Mick-ji. That was you," Binod says with a lilt in his voice.

Lincoln sits back, chuckling. Alan just grins. After the laughter settles down, Lincoln tags Binod on the arm. "You've been holding out on me, Bud."

Binod turns to Lincoln with a quizzical look on his face. "Holding out?"

"Yeah, keeping secrets," Lincoln says as the waiter stands by, waiting patiently.

Mick orders a plate of fried potatoes and onions, a stack of cakes with honey, and a double helping of toast. Lincoln, who's studying his menu, points to the selection of appetizers on the first page. "The Dehli

Chaat—is made with dahi vada or dahi bhalla?" he asks in Nepali.

"Dahi bhalla," the waiter answers.

Lincoln nods. "Okay. I take order of that. Extra hot chili, lots onions. Plain yogurt."

The waiter turns to Alan, who takes a last look at his menu. Frowning, he points to a picture of a breakfast entree of porridge, cakes, and eggs. "I'll have that." He passes the menu to the waiter, then suddenly puts his hand up. "You have toast and marmalade here?"

The waiter stares back, confused. "Marmalade?"

"Yes," Alan says. "It's like jam. Fruit preserves with peels."

The waiter glances at Mick with a hopeful look for help.

"*Phal sanrakshit karata hai,*" Mick says.

The waiter nods, then beams back at Alan. "Oh, yes, we have."

Alan smiles. "Good. I'll have another cup of whatever you're calling tea," he adds, raising his mug.

After the waiter leaves, Mick clears his throat, claps his hands, and eyes Lincoln. "Okay, you're probably wondering why we're not at a High Trails office, right?"

"Binod filled me in; something about liking to keep things light and friendly," Lincoln says, breaking back into English. He sits back with one arm on the table, panning the room.

Mick considers the American a moment. The guy is watchful, and there's a guarded air about him, as if he's hiding something. But Binod is vouching for him, and it doesn't hurt the guy's a doctor. Could come in handy down the road, not to mention he has an Ama Dablam summit under his belt. *The guy knows his stuff.* Finally, he says, "So, tell me a little about yourself."

"Not much to tell," Lincoln says, then shrugs and takes a sip of tea. "When I lived in the States, I served in a fire department as a paramedic for a couple years, then went and got a degree in emergency medicine. Bounced around after that, working ERs until a friend of mine talked me into a bit of alpine climbing. Thought he was nuts 'til I did it. Two years later, we landed here."

"I assume you went for Everest?" Alan says.

Lincoln sets his mug on the table, absently turns it around, and looks off. "That was the plan. Never got to it, though."

"That's too bad," Alan says. "What happened?"

"Bunch of things."

"So Ama Dablam was a training summit?" Mick asks.

Lincoln shrugs as the waiter brings more tea. "Sort of."

When Mick looks up, he sees Palisha coming behind the waiter with their order. His heart thumps. "Namaste, Polly! How are you?" he says. He drinks in her beaming smile, the soft crinkles around her large brown eyes, and the slight tilt of her regal tan face. Her thick jet hair is pulled back with a floral pin, and a subtle scent of jasmine wafts around her.

"Namaste, Mick," she says. She holds him in a knowing gaze before setting the platter of food on the table beside them.

For the first time, he notices the flower-print satin blouse hanging off her shoulders. The top button is undone and a thin gold necklace peeks out from underneath. "I looked for you when I came in, but you weren't in your office."

"No, I was busy in the kitchen," she says. Her gaze strays past him. "Namaste. Hello, Binod. How are you?"

"I am very good, thank you," he says, nodding politely. "And how are you?"

"I am very good also," she replies, then looks to Alan and Lincoln. "Namaste, good morning."

"Morning," Lincoln and Alan say in unison. Lincoln adds, "Something smells good."

"I hope so!" Palisha says, favoring them with a charming smile. "So, you are all staying with us?"

"Just Alan and myself," Mick says. He picks up his mug and sips, then eyes Alan and Lincoln. "Palisha here co-manages the hotel. She's the best hostess in all of Nepal, isn't that right, Binod?"

"Oh, yes," Binod says, flashing a broad grin.

Palisha waves off the compliment. "Do not listen to them. They are just looking for extras," she says to Lincoln and Alan, then turns to the platter on the table beside her. She picks up the bowl of porridge. "So, who gets this?"

"That would be me," Alan says, reaching to take the bowl from her.

"And the Dehli Chaat is mine," Lincoln puts in.

Palisha passes their plates out as Mick unwraps his silverware. When everyone is served, she turns to him. "Can we talk over there a minute?"

"Sure." He gets up and follows her out of earshot. "What's up?"

"So, we will have dinner tonight, yes?"

"Of course!" He wonders why she has to ask.

"Good." She peers around him, then leans in close, and in Nepali, whispers, "I have a gift for you that I think you'll like."

When she pulls back with an innocent smile, his body fizzes. The thought of sitting on the couch talking all snuggled up sends a wave of anticipation rushing through him. He tries to control himself, but it's not easy. "Really?"

She nods. The way she's looking at him is maddening.

"What time?"

She hesitates, looks around them again, then turns back and says, "Six, maybe?"

"Sure."

"Good. Oh, one thing. My sink is clogged, so maybe you can fix it for me sometime this afternoon?"

"I'll need tools."

"No problem," she says, slipping her key into his hand. "Go see Rajan downstairs. He will give you what you need."

"I'll head over right after we're done here."

"Okay, put your bags at the reception desk and I will have them taken up." She backs away and waves to the rest of them. "Okay, I leave you to your meeting now."

After she leaves, Mick digs into his breakfast. But he feels Lincoln's furtive gaze flick at him from time to time. At length, he sits back and wipes his mouth. "So, Lincoln, where were we?"

"Ama Dablam," Alan puts in. "What was that like? I heard it's quite a climb."

Lincoln takes a bite, swallows, and shrugs. "It wasn't easy."

Alan nods as he pours honey on his porridge. "When did you do it?"

Mick watches Lincoln's face tighten and his gaze go inward. *There's more to this man than what I've been told.*

Lincoln takes a bite, wipes his mouth, and says curtly, "2011."

I don't remember reading that in the resume. "You were on the mountain in 2011?"

Lincoln looks away, and it's clear he isn't comfortable with the direction this conversation is going.

Alan wrinkles his brow and sets his spoon down. "I heard there was a storm that year?"

Lincoln sips his tea. "Yup."

Mick sits back, realizing the man was on the mountain when the storm hit. *Shit. I wonder....*

"Christ! That must've been a hell of a ride," Alan says.

Lincoln's expression darkens as he takes another sip of tea. "It was."

Alan leans forward as Mick nudges the Brit's leg under the table to give him a hint to shut up, but Alan pushes on. "Where were you at the time?"

Lincoln stiffens and sets his mug down. "Camp 3."

Binod turns to Mick, and there's an anxious look on the Nepali's face.

Suddenly the air goes out of the room. It takes but a second for Mick to add things up. While most people know the story of Patterson, Kincaid, and Madden on Everest, not many know about the four men on Ama Dablam who were caught in the storm. One of them fell to his death and was more than likely a friend to the man across the table.

Alan's glance sweeps over them as if he's being left out on a secret. "What?"

Lincoln clears his throat and stares coldly at Alan. "Not what! Who! People died, okay? Can we please move on?"

"Yes, let's," says Mick. "We have a lot to cover for the upcoming season and next year, not to mention our next group, which will be here next week."

After the meeting breaks up, Mick collects a pipe wrench, a plumbing snake, pipe dope, and a pair of pliers (probably more than he needs) from Rajan and heads to Palisha's apartment. It's just outside the old Chamati neighborhood near the Bishnumati River. As he drives, his thoughts fixate on the evening ahead and where things might lead. What started out five years ago as a casual friendship has moved into new territory and he's unsure where it will go.

He turns onto Museum Marg and drives into the dense residential mishmash of two- and three-story masonry. There are no sidewalks here, just a string of railroad timber curbs laid down in front of the houses. Motorbikes weave back and forth ahead, beep-beeping incessantly in the stop-and-go mid-morning traffic. It's heading toward noon and people are swarming in and out of houses or gathering in groups on street corners. The ubiquitous tang of the muddy river downwind mingles with the smoke of his cigar and the pungent odor trailing off the garbage truck ahead. He tosses his cigar in his coffee cup and rolls the window up, shutting out the stink.

Fifteen minutes later, the residential sprawl is behind him and he's at a T- intersection, making a right. He follows the snaking brown river a half kilometer before making another right into the driveway of Riverside Apartments. The four-story L-shaped masonry and concrete building, built shortly after the 1934 quake, sits back from the road, flanked by a row of acacia and rhododendron. A Tibetan Cherry stands out front on a sheared lawn, its spindled and crooked branches laden with white blossoms. Hugging the front entrance is a bed of purple asters.

He parks out front. The lot is nearly empty this time of day; most of the tenants are at work. Grabbing his bag of tools, he hoofs it to the front door under a sun playing peek-a-boo with the clouds. The narrow lobby welcomes him into cool, deep shadows. As he pushes the call button for the elevator, he catches a whiff of ginger and faint Nepali music drifting down the hall. The elevator dings, and the door slides back. It's a tight fit inside the claustrophobic car, but he endures it rather than climb the two flights of creaky metal stairs to the third floor.

Palisha's apartment is to the left down the hall. He pulls her key out, walks to her door, and enters, taking in the subtle floral fragrance saturating the sunlit room. Shucking his boots at the door, he heads into her tiny galley kitchen with his tools. A plunger stands on the floor next to the sink cabinet and a bottle of dish soap and a dirty breakfast bowl, spoon, and cup sit by the sink above. He takes a look at the brown water lingering in the basin, considers a plan of action, and pulls the snake out, but first he needs to deal with the copious amount of tea he put down at his meeting.

As he unzips in the tiny bathroom off the kitchen next to the bedroom, he notices a clear plastic bottle on the vanity. It's none of his business, but when he's done, he picks it up and reads the label.

LVL Personal Lubricant.

He's perplexed for a moment, but then it hits him. Of course she would. Men aren't the only ones who think such things. He smiles, wondering if she thinks of him when she uses it. It's an image he's never considered before, and one he's quite sure he won't forget.

He should feel guilty for having such thoughts, for invading her intimate life, but he's not a monk and the bottle was left out in plain sight, he tells himself. Setting it down, he heads back to the kitchen to take care of the stubborn drain. After five minutes of fighting with the snake, he decides the trap has to be taken apart, but for that he'll need something to collect water in. He rummages around in the surrounding cabinets for a large pot, then gets back on the floor, digging sludge out of the U-shaped pipe with his finger. When he feels a faint tremor run through the building, he frowns and stops what he's doing. Then another tremor comes, more like a jolt this time.

He jerks up, banging his head on the cabinet frame. The floor is shaking underneath him now. For a second he freezes, then he's on his feet running to the living room. The walls are listing back and forth, the hanging tapestry fluttering wildly. A zigzagging crack is running down the exterior wall, and an ominous groan follows. The window shatters and a shower of glass bursts into the room.

Get out!

Stumbling into the hall, he races to the stairwell behind another tenant. The treads shift back and forth like a sieve sifting flour as he runs down. Dust and chunks of plaster rain from the ceiling. Another powerful jolt reels him sideways, throwing him into the railing. The Nepali in front of him tumbles down the stairs, hitting the landing with a thunk. Twenty feet below, the first floor yawns up at him. His breath catches. Something hurts. Coughing, he scrambles down into the mounting gray haze flooding the shaft. A loud bang jolts the floor above. The twisting steel staircase shivers below. Another explosion of shattering glass, and then a loud *pop, pop, pop*. Gripping the rail, he lurches ahead, descending the rocking treads to the landing. The fallen Nepali is struggling to his hands and knees. He pulls him up, sees a deep gash splitting the man's brow. A stream of blood is running from it down the side of the Nepali's narrow face. Draping the man's arm over his shoulder, he darts ahead. Then another jolt rams the building, knocking him backward onto the stair. When he looks up, the exterior wall before him is peeling away. Sunlight pours in, revealing a rolling landscape outside. Thick dirty clouds blanket the Chamati neighborhood beyond. Birds are arcing wildly across the sky above it.

A voice in his head yells, *Go, go, go!* He pulls himself and the Nepali up. The man is dazed, dead weight under his arm as he rushes headlong down the faltering stairs, socked feet slipping and sliding. Then all at once, he's outside, stumbling ahead breathlessly with the Nepali on the seesawing macadam. How he got here, he doesn't remember, and he doesn't care to think about it. Just get as far as he can into open space, away from the crumbling building.

People ahead are running every which way, calling out for each other, crying, screaming. Children are bawling. Then a booming thump hits the ground behind him, lifting his feet and sending him and the Nepali crashing to the ground. He half expects his life to end. But when the deathblow doesn't come, he closes his eyes. Catching his breath, he finally rolls over, clambers to his hands and knees, and sucks another gulp of air into his burning lungs. Wiping his brow, he looks back. The end of the building is shorn off into a towering mishmash of brick and broken concrete. Underneath it somewhere is his rental car. As he stares at the destruction, he suddenly realizes the ground is still.

His heart thuds, and he waits for another jolt. When it doesn't come, he sighs, and for the first time, realizes how fortunate he is. He glances at the Nepali beside him. The man is on his side panting and pushing himself up with one hand planted on the pavement. A lackluster gaze clouds the man's dark brown eyes. His tan face and short black hair are chalked with gritty white dust and streaked with blood and sweat.

Mick waves a hand. "Lie back down," he says in Nepali. "It's okay." With an effort, he gets up and sweeps his gaze over the eerie, silent world, absorbing the wreckage and the ruined land around him. On the other side of the river, a thick dirty haze hangs over the city, and here and there, plumes of smoke rise into a cloudless pale sky. To his right, the acacia and rhododendron are partially uprooted, listing every which way at sharp angles. The Tibetan Cherry out front is lying on its side, half-buried in rubble. Behind him, voices are coming on. He turns to see several Nepali men rushing up to the man he brought out from the building.

One of them steps beside him, reaches out, and taps him on the arm, then averts his gaze downward. "You bleeding," he says in stilted English.

Mick looks down and sees a broad wedge of

wicked glass poking through a spreading dark red stain on the side of his shirt. *Shit, that's not good.* He looks back up at the Nepali, whose concerned face is now wavering in and out of focus, and as the world spins, Palisha's face flashes before him.

2

JANUARY 26, 2015, FOUR
MONTHS EARLIER —
KATHMANDU, NEPAL

*M*ick peers out the window of the Cessna as it taxies to a stop outside Kathmandu's domestic terminal. It hardly seems possible his good friend, Frank Kincaid, is dead. Across the aisle, Frank's significant other, Sarah Madden, is looking ahead, subdued, while she strokes a gold locket around her neck. She moved from the States last year to spend the rest of her life with the man she'd fallen in love with three years ago on the mountain. But now she's going back home, and she hasn't said a dozen words since he picked her up this morning from her teahouse and walked her down the lane behind the tiny mountain airstrip. He hurts for her and for himself. He'd known Frank for over twenty years and considered him a great friend. The mountains won't be the same without him. The man did so much to provide a better life for the people who'd taken in his family after they fled a war-torn country so many years ago.

Unbuckling his seat belt, he gathers his daypack as the flight attendant lowers the air-stair down in the back. Sarah is gathering her things as well. She glances over at him with a thin smile and gets up to follow Terry Andersen off the plane. The tall, silver-haired expedition owner, who'd known Frank since he started the company forty years ago, had flown in from New Zealand for the funeral puja. He'd be connecting with his flight back to Christchurch in the afternoon. Sarah would be staying overnight and heading to the States first thing in the morning.

Mick reaches out and tags her arm holding her pack. "Here, let me get that for you."

"Thanks," she says, handing it to him, then moves ahead, waiting to deplane.

He follows her, wanting to say something, do something, anything, to lift the heavy weight they're carrying in their hearts. But there's nothing there. He sighs. The empty feeling inside him is familiar territory. He wants to pretend it's all a bad dream, wants to be Mick again.

Sarah and Terry wait for him outside, and when he steps down onto the tarmac, they walk under bright sunshine to the stuffy two-story terminal. For a Monday morning, it's unusually busy inside the antiquated building. Foreign nationals and Nepali guides are milling around in the crowded dingy passenger hall waiting on flights to the mountains. The three of them weave through the throng to the baggage claim, and when they come to a cart of off-loaded luggage from their flight, Terry turns and puts his hand out to Mick.

"Well, I guess this is good-bye for now. Take care of yourself, Mick."

He shakes the man's hand. "Have a safe trip home. Best to the missus."

"Thanks." Terry smiles, then turns to Sarah hesitantly, as if not knowing if he should pull her into a hug. Finally, he extends his hand. "I wish ya well. If ya need anything at all, ring me up, ya hear."

"Thanks, I'll be sure to do that," Sarah answers, shaking his hand. "Have a safe flight."

They watch him grab his bag and wave to him as he marches away toward the international terminal. Finally, Mick says, "Well, let's grab our taxi. You want to do lunch out or head straight to the hotel?"

"I think I want to go to the hotel. Maybe do lunch after we get settled?"

He nods and they walk outside to hail a cab. The ride in the sub-compact car into the dense, sprawling, smog-ridden city is stop and go. Traffic is heavy on New Road, which leads to Dubar Square in the old part of the city—and he's uncomfortable. The cabbie seems to be trying to find every bump and pothole, and no matter how he sits in the back seat, he can't straighten his legs. Sarah looks back from the front seat and her expression is one of apology. He shakes his head, gesturing for her not to worry. It's not the first time he's been stuffed into a tight space.

Finally, the cab pulls up to their hotel. It's an unpretentious brick and pale stucco building with a narrow court leading around the side to an entry vestibule flanked by a tired acacia that's seen better days. He pays the cabbie and they find their way inside. The dated lobby is furnished with a pair of vinyl-upholstered chaises. A faded oak coffee table and a tallboy cabinet converted into a continental breakfast bar stand at the end of the room. A heady scent of Champa permeates the stuffy air. Presently, a small group of tourists is checking in. He sets his bag and Sarah's down by a potted rubber tree over in the corner that appears to not have been watered for some time.

Sarah finds a seat on one of the chaises and pulls her phone out, stares at the screen, and then types away. When he steps next to her, she looks up. "So, where do you want to catch a bite once we're done here?"

"I was thinking maybe we'd wander into Thamel. There's a nice little café I know of that makes something I think you'd love."

She cocks a brow and a hint of a smile appears on her lips. "Oh, what would that be?"

It's good to see her smile. He wags a finger at her. "You'll find out."

"Okay, be that way." Her phone buzzes in her hand, and she looks down at it. "My son says to say hi."

"Tell him I said hi back, and he better be treating my EBC leader right or he'll be answering to me."

"I'll do that," she answers, then glances over her shoulder at the reception desk. "Ah, they're done. Time to check in."

An hour later, they step out of the hotel and head into the old part of the city. It greets them with a cacophony of beeping horns, ringing bicycle bells, storekeepers hawking their goods, and a confluence of Nepali and foreign chatter. The warm gentle breeze wafting around them on the crowded street carries the murmur of reedy flutes and squawking radios. As they weave through the swarming throng of city denizens and tourists, the aroma of garlic and curry drifts out of street-side cafés. His stomach grumbles.

The place he's leading Sarah to is located down a broad lane off the main street a hundred feet ahead. When he comes to it, they turn onto the cobblestone lane and walk into a mall-like atmosphere. Unlike the hodgepodge conglomeration of markets, shops, and restaurants along the main thoroughfare, the storefronts here are modern and orderly. Trash finds its way into decorative dark green receptacles and the potted ferns, pale lilies, and rosy gardenias are well tended. It's also less crowded.

"Wow," Sarah says, ogling the shops as they walk.

"Frank never brought you here?" Mick asks, surprised, but he's not astonished. Frank wasn't much on upscale, modern things.

"No, the stinker." She drifts over to a storefront window and looks through it at a shelf of neatly arranged singing bowls and brass Buddha statues.

He waits until she's seen her fill, then gestures her to an open door ahead under a sign that says *Rhododendron Café.* "We're going up to the second floor," he says, ushering her inside. "Watch your step, the stair is a little steep."

At the top landing, they enter an airy reception space that flows into an open floor plan with paddle fans spinning overhead. Pots of tall leafy ferns and lilies are scattered about the dining area that hums with mingled conversations and a vibrant Nepali tune piped in from above. He scans over the occupied bar-height mahogany tables while Sarah pans the room with an appreciative gaze.

"What do you think?" he says, turning to her.

"I like it," she answers as the receptionist heads toward them.

"Could we have that table over in the corner?" Mick says in Nepali to the smiling, short-statured woman whose long black hair is pulled into a thick braid. As she leads them to their table, he leans down and whispers into her ear to bring them two tall glasses of the house specialty. When he looks up, Sarah is side-eyeing him.

"What are you up to?" she asks.

He shrugs, flashing her his best innocent smile. "Nothing."

They take their seats and peruse their menus, which are aimed at western tourists, and in this case, American tourists. While he's looking at the selections, he's sneaking peeks at Sarah, wondering if he should bring up her going back home. He feels like anything he says is inadequate or worse yet, flippant and stupid.

At last, he clears his throat. "So, what looks good?"

"I'm thinking a cheeseburger and fries. I haven't had one of them in six months. You?"

"Ditto," he says, setting his menu aside.

"So, where are you off to after I leave?" she says, leaning back in her chair.

He pauses. Until yesterday, he'd debated whether to go back to Pokhara and try to busy himself with work, anything to take his mind off the last four months. But the truth is, he doesn't want to be alone. Should he drop in on Palisha? Yet, how can he burden her with so much death, so many broken lives, and the pain he carries for people he cares about? It doesn't seem fair, but now that it comes to it, he finds himself wanting to hear her soothing voice tell him, *I am here for you, tell me everything.*

Finally, he says, "Gonna see a friend on the other side of town, I think."

"I'll be doing that as soon as I get home," Sarah says as the waiter brings Mick's surprise over. The woman sets down two tall glasses of thick chocolate cream poured over ice, topped with whipped cream, shaved chocolate, and drizzled caramel syrup. Sarah looks up, her eyes wide as the waitress sets straws down beside them. "Oh, my God!"

The waitress smiles, then pulls out a small pad and pen from her apron. "What I get for you?"

Sarah pulls her menu over, gives it a last look, then in Nepali, says, "I'll have the cheeseburger and fries."

"Me too," Mick adds in Nepali, watching Sarah with a grin as she stabs her straw in the shake and sucks a drink. After the waitress heads off with their order, he switches back to English. "Well?"

"I love it!"

"Thought you would. They make the best shakes in town." He picks up his drink, sucks a gulp, and wipes his mouth with the back of his hand. When he sets the glass back down, Sarah is snickering. "What?"

"You missed a spot. You have whipped cream on your nose."

"Oh!" He wipes it off and they go quiet a moment.

Finally, Sarah says, "So, do you have anyone special in your life?"

The comment catches him off guard, and he hesitates. He knows what she's getting at. A woman. Palisha is close to what she's hinting at, but they're just best friends. Except he can't deny he loves her, and if circumstances were different, it might be more. At last he says, "Not really. I almost got married years ago, but it didn't work out."

"What happened? That is, if you want to talk about it."

"She died," he says, shrugging as the memory of Vivian surges forward. He hasn't thought about her in a long time, mainly because he doesn't want to relive the week he spent in the hospital watching her struggle for her life.

"I'm sorry," Sarah says as the waitress brings their meals over.

"It's okay. Don't worry about it."

Sarah nods, and he sees her gaze go inward. He wonders if she's thinking of her husband, who died on the Everest all those years ago, or maybe she's thinking of Frank. They eat in awkward silence, and he's uncertain where to go in this emotional minefield. Everything seems to lead back to loss and grief. At length, he sets his burger down and blurts out, "I do have someone I care about, and if things were different...."

"Oh?"

"Her name is Palisha. She co-manages a hotel in town with another woman. She's a Nepali widow, and her family's very traditional."

Sarah looks up in surprise and sits back with a speculative expression on her face. At last she says, "I get it." She wipes her mouth with her napkin and he can see her turning something over in her head. "She's a grown woman, right...around your age?"

"Yeah."

"Well, it seems to me, customs and status aside, she can make up her own mind. Have you told her how you feel?"

"Not really. I never saw the sense in it," he answers, surprised at himself for bringing Palisha up. *Stop talking, Mick.*

"Well, you'll never know, unless you say something. I take it she's on her own, not with family?"

"Yeah."

"Then I think she's quite capable of making her own decisions. Say something—tell her! She might be having the same feelings. Don't take that choice away from her. That's not fair to you or to her."

He knows Sarah is right, but she doesn't know how difficult traditional Nepali families can make it for family members who stray from their own. Palisha has finally started making her way back to her family after years of alienation for striking out on her own. To put her in a position of making a choice between him and her family after fighting to get back in their good graces for the last ten years is not only presumptuous, but cruel. But he doesn't want to argue with Sarah. "You're right. I'll think on it."

"I hope so," she says, and drags a fry through a dab of ketchup on her plate. "You're a good man. She could do a lot worse."

Lincoln bolts up in bed. Another nightmare! He can still see Collins falling, falling: falling head over heels from the vertical slope five feet away from Camp 3. What should have been a glorious day after summiting the mountain had turned into a disaster.

He rips the blanket away and gets up in the little room swathed in heavy shadow. Beside him on a nightstand, red numbers bleed out into the darkness from his LED alarm clock. 5:34 a.m. Another hour before he needs to be up for work, but there's no going back to sleep now.

He runs his fingers through his hair, shaking away the nightmare, and goes into the bathroom down the hall. The tiled room is basic: a porcelain sink, a hose on the wall used as a shower, and an eastern toilet on the floor. A plastic pail sits in the corner with a roll of toilet paper hanging on a crooked wire over it. He turns on the faucet, cups cold water in his hands, and splashes his face. Looks in the mirror and sees a man he barely recognizes these days.

What is he still doing here, halfway around the world? Yet he can't seem to uproot himself and move on. He thinks of home back in the States. *Not yet*, a voice whispers in his brain. Then where? What is he searching for? He thought he'd found it when he first came here in 2011. Now he hasn't a clue, except he doesn't belong back home. He sighs, traipses back into the bedroom, and looks out the window at the approaching dawn. The city sleeps below, save for the faint crowing of a rooster in the surrounding Kalimati neighborhood. He moved here shortly after coming down from the mountain, intending to stay only a few months until he figured things out. Almost three years later, he's no closer to it. The one plus is that he's made a few good friends. Among them are Binod and Sila, who live in the upper flat across the street from him with their son, Arjun, and their daughter, Sunita.

Binod is a real go-getter, working two jobs, one of which is guiding in the mountains for an outfit called High Trails. The other is at his brother-in-law's shop in Thamel. Binod's wife, Sila, is a nurse, and she's a delight. A ready smile always graces her tan heart-shaped face whenever their paths cross. At present, she's very pregnant.

He smiles as he thinks of how attentive Binod is around her. Although their marriage was arranged, there's no doubt they love each other. Every action between them conveys an adoration and respect that spills over to their children. Arjun is a sturdy-built boy: a rambunctious thing, kinetic, curious, and perpetually moving. Yet he's obedient to his parents' gentle directions and polite to a fault. His thirteen-year-old sister, Sunita, is her brother's antithesis: quiet and thoughtful with dark eyes that look at the world in a searching, absorptive way. Lincoln's mother had that same look, a deep soulful gaze that translated into her paintings of the rural countryside around their Central New York home back in the States. He sees a budding artist in Sunita that needs encouragement. The young girl has told him her birthday is coming up soon. Perhaps he'll hunt for an artist's pad and pencils for her.

Again, he hears the rooster crow and he comes to himself. A run out in the fresh air would do him good. He changes into a fresh t-shirt and shorts, slips into his sneakers, and is out the door jogging into the misty haze of the deserted street. It's a comfortable morning with a breeze carrying the remnants of last night's rain. In the distance, the shush of traffic on Ring Road whispers over the aging two- and three-story buildings, houses, and apartments. He turns north toward the park and rouses a dog that barks at him from an upper porch. A muffled reprimand follows from somewhere inside.

His usual route is a three-mile loop around the park (four times around), then back through the maze of streets that make up this section of the city. His feet slap the gritty pavement and sweat beads on his brow. His rambling thoughts dissolve into the pounding rhythm of the run, and it isn't long until the cascading rush of endorphins takes over, delivering a liberating high.

When he gets back, his mind is clear, but he knows it's only temporary. The demons of his past will be back, if not tonight then tomorrow or the next day or the day after that. They like to remind him of the part he played in the deaths of his parents and of his friend Collins on the mountain every opportunity they get. At least he has his job at Tripureshwor Transportation (thanks to Binod) to keep him busy so he doesn't spiral down into the guilt that haunts him.

He strips out of his clothes, showers, and throws his uniform on, then heads back out to his Honda Aviator. It's a six-mile, forty-five-minute ride by cab through the congested metropolis to his job. For this reason, he gave up on cabs shortly after he started at the company and opted for his two-stroke motorbike. He pulls his helmet on and starts the bike up as Binod pops out of his apartment building.

A moment later, Binod rides over to him. "Namaste, Lin-ji, how are you?" he says. Binod has a hard time pronouncing Lincoln's name, but Lincoln doesn't mind.

"Tired. Woke early. Could not sleep," Lincoln says, answering in Nepali. He's getting more proficient with the language, but he still has trouble with it even after living here for so long. "And you?"

"Very good, thank you," Binod says, pulling a pair of reflective sunglasses from his pocket. He puts them on and taps Lincoln on the arm. "I would like you to come for dinner tonight. If you want to, of course."

Lincoln is surprised at the sudden invitation. Up until now, things have been casual between them, a favor here and there, friendly conversation and sharing a bit about their lives. He shrugs. "Sure. What time you want me come?"

"Maybe six?"

Depending on where his dispatcher sends him on deliveries, he should be able to make it. "Okay. What I bring?"

"Whatever you want," Binod answers, inserting the cord of his ear buds into his phone. He smiles, then revs his bike and is off riding down the road.

3

JANUARY 26, 2015— KATHMANDU, NEPAL

*B*inod turns his motorbike onto the narrow street where he lives and motors past a group of boys playing soccer in an abandoned lot. He's invited Lincoln to dinner tonight and he's anxious and excited about it. He's never entertained an American before. He wonders how it will go as he pulls in front of the narrow three-story concrete building he lives in.

Walking his bike inside the front hallway, he leans it on its kickstand and hikes up the flight of stairs to his flat. When he opens the door, Arjun and Sunita are there to greet him.

He kicks off his shoes, gives his son a quick hug, and heads for the kitchen as Arjun flees ahead. Sunita slips back to whatever she was doing in the living room. His wife, Sila, is at the kitchen sink with her back toward him when he enters. It's her day off from the hospital, and her hair is loose and flowing over her casual red sari.

"How was work?" she asks over her shoulder.

Binod grabs a bottle of aloe vera juice from the refrigerator. "Very good. I invited Lin-ji to dinner tonight."

Sila turns with widened eyes and looks up at the clock on the wall. It's pushing four o'clock. "Binod?"

"What? We talked about it, remember?"

"I know, but...okay. I will need to go shopping, though. What time did you tell him?"

"Six."

She rolls her eyes and sighs. "What does he like to eat? I don't know much about American cooking," she says, gathering her hair into a loose knot.

Binod uncaps the bottle of aloe vera, sits, and takes a drink. "He'll eat whatever you make, I'm sure. Don't worry." Except he is worried. He wants every-thing to be perfect. He sweeps his gaze around the tiny kitchen. There are dishes waiting to be washed on the counter, and a pair of plastic airplanes on the table.

"Arjun, put your toys in your room." Then he turns and calls to his daughter, "Sunni, come here and help your mother with the dishes."

"I'm still playing with them," Arjun protests.

"I said, put them away. We have company coming over."

Arjun frowns, then says, "Who?"

"Lin-ji, across the street."

Arjun's frown disappears into a wondrous smile. "Really? When?"

Binod softens his tone. "Soon, put your toys away." He watches his son gather the planes up and run into the other room, then turns back to Sila. "How did Madrid do today? Did they win?"

"I don't know. I was busy. I think maybe it was a tie," she says. "I need money."

Binod digs his wallet and cell phone out of his pocket. He snatches a pair of thousand rupee notes from it and puts them in her outstretched hand. "Sunni, I said now!"

Arjun runs back into the kitchen and stops with a thud behind his mother, who's pulling down a canvas bag from the shelf. "Can I go?"

"Fine. Go change your shirt," Sila says over her shoulder. "Hurry up. Don't make your āmā late."

The boy scampers off as she sets the bag on the table. "Are you guiding for Mick next month?"

Binod picks up his cell phone and scrolls through his messages. "I don't know. We're still sorting things out."

"I need to know so I can plan."

He looks up. "Don't worry. I'll let you know," he says as Sunita comes into the room. His daughter darts a curious glance back and forth between them.

"Where are you going?" she says to her mother.

37

"Shopping, we're having company for dinner tonight."

"Who?"

"Lin-ji, across the street," Sila says.

Sunita's eyes brighten and a demure smile crosses her lips. She looks away quickly, hiding her reaction to the mention of Lincoln's name. Binod and Sila exchange knowing looks. They're both aware that Sunni is (*what's the word?*) crushing on the American. It doesn't bother Binod, though. Sunni is young and infatuated, as many young girls are at her age. *She'll get over it.*

Arjun comes rushing back wearing a bright yellow t-shirt with the words *Everest Base Camp* printed across the front. It's one of his son's favorites, and he dons it every time they have guests. Sila looks him over and tucks a lock of curly dark hair around his ear.

Behind him, Binod hears Sunita pick up where her mother left off with the dishes. There's a subtle bounce in Sunita's scrubbing—a click-clacking of plates that's not lost on Binod or her mother. Sila flashes Binod a grin, then pats Arjun on the shoulder. "Okay, let's go."

He looks after his wife, watching her sari sway back and forth on her pear-shaped rounded body. At nearly eight months pregnant, the baby is riding low on her hips. He loves how the growing unborn child radiates and beautifies her. She thinks it's a girl. He's hoping for another son, and he's already picked a name for him.

"When is he coming over?" Sunita asks, breaking into his musing.

Binod comes to himself. "At six," he says, stepping to her side. She plunks a cup into the sudsy water and avoids eye contact as she washes it. When she sets it down in the drainer he picks it up and taps her arm. "You missed a spot. Slow down, Sunni, you'll have plenty of time to change before he gets here."

She freezes, then looks up as if she's just caught him peeking in her dresser drawers. For a moment he isn't sure if she's going to run out of the room or break down and cry. But she just takes the cup from him and washes it again.

He leaves her to finish up her chore and puts his bottle of aloe vera back in the refrigerator. Walking into the living room, he looks things over to make sure the space is presentable for their guest. While Sila is an excellent housekeeper, he takes it upon himself to make sure Lincoln will be comfortable. He restacks the pile of magazines on the coffee table, straightens the picture Sunita drew of the *Yamuna* on the wall, and refolds the blanket draped over the back of the couch. As he does, he notices a drawing pad and pencils strewn on the floor near the window.

He picks the pad up and looks at the picture she drew of the shadowed buildings outside their living room window. A vibrant red and orange sunset is drawn in the background. She's smudged the colors to create a fuzzy haze that bleeds over the rooftops, giving the drawing a muted, peaceful essence. He smiles. His daughter is talented. He collects her pencils and sets them with the pad on the coffee table for her to put away when she's done with the dishes. Satisfied everything is in order, he turns to the TV and picks up the remote. Scrolling down the menu, he turns the channel to the news, hoping to catch the New Madrid score.

"I'm done," Sunita announces, padding into the room.

"Okay, put your drawing away," he answers, distracted by the reporter on the screen. It's a segment about the Sherpa on Everest. Although he's heard multiple reports over the last year regarding the demands of the Sherpa after the avalanche that took the lives of sixteen of their brothers on the *Icefall*, things are still evolving. He turns up the volume.

While he isn't a mountain guide on any of the Himalayan high peaks, whatever is happening there is sure to affect him. Mick says he shouldn't worry, but Mick doesn't know that underneath all the uproar and rhetoric is a growing gap between the old Sherpa guard and the next generation.

~

Lincoln shows up a few minutes after 6:00 p.m. with his daypack in hand. Binod lets him in as Arjun runs into the room. The American kicks off his boots, sets them next to the door, and pulls a large bottle of *chhaang* from his sack and offers it to him.

"Namaste, Binod. Thank you for invite me your home. Thought I bring refreshment," Lincoln says in Nepali.

"Come, come," Binod says, taking the bottle. He holds it in front of him and forces a smile. He doesn't drink alcohol but it's a gift, and a gift from a guest can never be turned away. He ushers Lincoln into the living room with Arjun trailing behind. After motioning Lincoln to sit, he dashes off to the kitchen with the bottle, leaving his son with the American.

Sila turns around from where she's standing by the stove when he rushes in. "Is he here?"

"Yes," Binod says, setting the bottle down on the counter. He opens the refrigerator and paws around the shelves.

"What are you looking for?" Sila says.

"An appetizer. He brought a bottle of chhaang," Binod answers, glancing back at her.

"Chhaang?" Sila's eyes widen and she darts over beside him. In a low voice, she says, "We don't drink."

"I know, but he brought it as a gift," Binod says, running his hands through his hair. He looks up at her, then back to the refrigerator. It's too late to go back to the store. "What are we going to do?"

41

Sila taps his arm. "I know!" She goes to the cupboard, opens the door, and takes down two drinking bowls. Giving them to him, she adds, "Go back and attend him. I'll be there in a minute."

"What do you have in mind?"

"Don't worry," she says, patting his shoulder.

Binod shuts the refrigerator, considering, then starts for the living room. "Wait! Americans like their drinks cold." He turns back, opens the freezer door, drops a couple of ice cubes in Lincoln's bowl, and runs out.

Arjun is sitting on Lincoln's lap, peppering him with questions about the mountains, when he comes around the corner. "Arjun, go to your room and play."

The boy looks up, and the excited expression on his face sours.

"He not bother, certainly," Lincoln says. "We talk concern Everest. Please, let stay."

Binod appreciates Lincoln's efforts with Nepali even if his words are a bit off. "You're doing good with your Nepali," he says, opening the bottle and pouring their drinks. "If it's easier, we can speak English."

"No, is okay. This your fine home, so I want stay in Nepali," Lincoln says, tousling the boy's hair. "Something smell good. What is?"

"Lamb sekuwa and some kind of salad. I hope you'll like it."

"Of course," Lincoln answers, appearing quite comfortable with the boy on his lap.

Binod wonders if he should insist on Arjun going to his room, but Lincoln seems to enjoy having him there. At last, Binod says, "Arjun, go sit and be quiet, okay?"

The boy flashes a victorious smile, hops down from Lincoln's lap, and scampers over to the couch. Lincoln winks at him, leans forward, and takes up his drinking bowl. A peculiar smile comes over his face when he sees the ice in it.

Oh, no! Did I make a mistake?

"Thank you," Lincoln says and holds his bowl up to Binod. "To fine host." They clink their bowls together, and as Binod takes a sip, he furtively watches his guest, worrying he might have offended him. But Lincoln drains the bowl, smacks his lips, and sets it down beside him. "That go down good after long day drive on road...and who we have here?" he says, looking up.

Binod turns to see his daughter standing in the hallway. She's in her finest red sari that has gold embroidery on the hems and sleeves, and her hair is drawn back into a thick braid like her mother wears. A dab of red tika dots her forehead, and her hands are lavished in flowery henna artwork. The flushed look she's giving Lincoln is furtive and anxious. When Lincoln smiles at her, she dashes away toward the kitchen.

43

"She's very shy sometimes," Binod says into the stilted silence. *Why can't I think of something interesting to say?*

"Is okay," Lincoln says. "I like that when her age."

Binod takes a drink. "So you and Arjun talked about Everest. You want to go sometime? I guide Everest Base Camp. I can take you."

Lincoln tosses Arjun a lopsided grin, then turns back to Binod. "I've already been there."

"He climbed Ama Dablam," Arjun blurts out.

Binod looks back at Lincoln in astonishment. "Really? When?"

Lincoln nods and sets his bowl down on the floor. "Back in 2011."

The revelation startles Binod. Everyone in the guiding business knows what happened on the mountain that year. The rescue of the American on Everest by the two famed mountaineers is legend. He pauses, wondering if Lincoln was part of it. Finally, he says, "There was a storm that year. You were on Ama Dablam when it happened?"

"Yeah," Lincoln says, and his face darkens.

Binod hesitates, suddenly remembering people also died in the storm. Were they friends of Lincoln? He bows his head, staring at the floor, and fidgets, wondering where to go from here. When he looks up, Sila is walking into the room with a tray of snacks.

"I hope you're hungry," she says, and Binod breathes a sigh, grateful for her interruption.

44

Lincoln brightens and stands to greet her. "I am. How you?"

"I'm very good, thank you," Sila says as Sunita comes in carrying a folding tray table. She snaps it open and sets it between her father and Lincoln, then steps back. Arjun jumps off the couch and hurries over, looking at the tray hopefully.

Binod stares his son down. "Wait!" Then he takes the tray from his wife.

Lincoln appraises Binod's wife, taking in her blossoming body under her flowing sari. "Baby getting big. Will not be long now."

A diffident smile crosses Sila's face. "I know."

They all look at each other a moment and silence spreads throughout the room. Finally, Binod gestures to the tray. Lincoln plucks a wafer off it and sniffs, then tilts his head. "Is thyme I inspect?"

"Ajwain," Sila corrects, glancing at Binod as Lincoln pops it in his mouth. She looks on anxiously as their guest chews.

"Tastes like oregano," Lincoln remarks.

Binod trades smiles with his wife. "You like?"

"Is good," Lincoln says, helping himself to another. He shoots a furtive glance at Arjun, who's waiting patiently beside his father. Looking back at Binod, Lincoln gestures to another piece. "I think someone waiting."

Binod lowers the tray and the boy snatches a couple wafers and runs back to the couch. From the corner of his eye, Binod sees Sunita standing off to one side, darting glances at Lincoln.

Lincoln turns to Sunita. "So, what you want for birthday?"

Sunita fidgets. "I don't know. Maybe a Harry Potter book," she says in a quiet voice.

"That quite a book, I told. So, how old will you will be?" Lincoln says.

"Fourteen."

"I'm seven," Arjun pipes up.

Lincoln laughs. "Go on twenty, I bet."

Sila takes a seat next to her son, folds her legs under her, and puts her arm around the boy. Looking down at him with a wide smile, she says, "That's what he thinks." They're all quiet a moment, then she looks up at Lincoln. "So Lin-ji, what brought you to Nepal?"

Lincoln sits back down and takes up his bowl. "I came climb mountains, but umm..." He furrows his brow as if looking for words, then continues, "I find I like stay here, nice people, very kind, so I do."

"You're from the United States, right?" When Lincoln nods, she goes on, "Where in the States?"

"I was born New York."

"Oh, that's a big city. What's it like there?"

"I not live in city. In, umm...." Again he pauses. "Middle State."

"Ahh!" Sila says. "And you climb mountains there, too?"

Lincoln pauses, and Binod is about to change the subject when Lincoln gives her a lopsided smile. "No. I umm...I doctor there."

Silas's eyes grow large and she looks at Binod. "You never told me that," she says to him.

Binod shrugs. "I didn't know."

Sila turns back to Lincoln. "How come you drive trucks then? I could get you a job in the hospital. They're looking."

Lincoln shakes his head. "Thanks, but umm...I like what I do. Maybe sometime in future, I do not know," he says and picks another wafer off the tray. "I like," he continues, and pops it in his mouth. He turns the conversation onto Binod and Sila then, asking about their family and how they met.

Binod tells him he was born north of the city in a mountain village called Ichok, and that he has a sister who still lives there with her husband, and a brother. His parents are very traditional, and his and Sila's marriage was arranged when they were Sunita's age. But as for his daughter and son, he's letting them choose for themselves. It's time to embrace the modern ways...to a point, of course. Tradition will always be important, but change is necessary if they're to grow as a nation. It just won't happen fast because Nepal values its history and its ways of doing things.

Lincoln listens attentively, asking questions about their faith and politics. Then he gestures to the picture of Yamuna on the wall over the couch. "What goddess name?"

"Yamuna! She's life energy, the daughter of Lord Surya and goddess of kindness, humanity, and beauty," Sila says, and with a beaming smile, she adds, "Sunita drew it."

Lincoln turns to Sunita with a fathomless look in his deep blue eyes. "You drew?"

"Yes," the girl answers just above a whisper. Her eyes go downward, unwilling to meet Lincoln's dumbfounded gaze. But the flickering smile on her young face betrays her basking in his approving attention.

He stands up to get a better look at the drawing, studies the intricate detail of the ruby-studded golden headdress and the red and white flower lei around the neck of the reposed goddess. "It very, very good," he mutters, then turns to Binod. "She very talented. Does she have more I look at? I very much like see after dinner."

"She has plenty more," Binod answers, as pride wells up in him.

When Lincoln sits down, Sila says, "She's going to be a great artist someday." Then she wrinkles her brow and leans forward. "But what about you, Lin-ji? Tell us about your parents. They must miss you being away so long."

Lincoln clears his throat. "My parents die when I

young. My umm..." he pauses, "mother-sister, bring me up."

"Oh, I'm so sorry," Sila says.

"Is okay."

Again silence smothers the room. Finally, Binod gets up and says to Sila, "Dinner is ready, right?" When she nods, he gestures toward the hall, inviting Lincoln to join him. "Well, we should eat."

4

JANUARY 26, 2015—
KATHMANDU, NEPAL

*P*alisha is busy checking a guest into the hotel when she looks up to see Mick standing off to the side. Her heart quickens and she squashes the tiny gasp in her throat as she takes in the half smile on his face. But his shoulders are drooped and his dark eyes have a faraway look, as if he's lost in thought. The sober, long expression on his large round face doesn't surprise her, though. The last time she saw him was a week before he left for the mountains to attend the funeral of a good friend he's known for many years. She runs the guest's credit card through the card reader and waits for the acceptance reply. When it comes through, she pushes the invoice with the room key card to the guest and has him sign in. Once the guest is on his way, Mick steps up to the desk, and for a moment he just looks at her.

At last, he says, "Hi."

"How did it go?" she asks. It's a rhetorical question, but what else is there to say?

Mick shrugs. "It was a nice send-off. Lots of friends and people from the village showed up."

Palisha holds him in her gaze, sensing he wants company. "Want to talk about it?"

"If you have time later. I don't want to get in the way here."

"You are not in the way. Let me get Namu to run the desk and we can go down to the café for tea."

"If you're sure?"

"It is no problem," she says and picks up the phone to call her co-manager, Namu. When she answers, Palisha breaks into Nepali. "Can you come up front? Kesab is busy with a guest and I need to be away from the desk for a bit."

"Okay," Namu says and hangs up.

"My partner will be right down," she says to Mick, slipping back to English. "You look tired."

"It's been a long couple weeks," he replies, tilting his head to the side to stretch his thick neck. His beard has bushed out since she last saw him, and it needs a trim. The short-sleeved button-down shirt he wears looks like it's been lived in for more than a few days. He clears his throat. "Anyway, how have you been?"

"I have been good. Keeping busy, as always. You

know how it is with us Nepali, always a holiday to observe and celebrate."

Mick chuckles. "Ain't that the truth? Sometimes I wonder how you keep track of all of them."

"Mick!" They both turn to see Namu heading toward them. "How are you?" she says in English.

"I'm good. And you?"

"I am very good. So, you are getting ready for upcoming trekking season?"

"Getting there," Mick says, but Palisha knows it's a lie. Trekking is the last thing on Mick's mind. "How's business?"

Namu shrugs. "It is okay. It will be much better, once you start bringing tourist in for the mountains." She glances at Palisha, then says, "So, you are staying with us here tonight?"

"Yeah, sure," Mick says, but there's a flash of hesitancy in the reply. They all go quiet and an awkward moment fills the space between them.

Finally, Palisha pastes a smile on. "We are going down to the café for tea and to catch up. Kesab should be back shortly."

The friendly expression on Namu's face brightens, and she winks at Palisha. "Of course. Enjoy!"

Palisha starts down the hall, knowing her partner will interrogate her later. She can see and hear Namu now in her mind plying her with questions, chief among them: is there something going on between you two? She smiles, wishing it were true. To be honest, she's been toying with the idea of having him over to her apartment, but she's also worried word might get back to her father. She's spent almost five years working to find peace between them after she left home to follow her heart and get an education. To make a life for herself after losing her husband all those years ago.

When they get to the café, she waits for Mick to pick a table and follows him to one in the far corner, away from everyone in the room. He pulls out a chair for her and when she's seated, sits across from her. Flashing a tight smile, he says, "Namu is certainly looking forward to the season. I guess I can't blame her after last year's disaster on the mountain."

"Namu is always looking forward to something," Palisha says, trying to keep her tone light, then returns his smile as the waiter comes to the table. She looks to Mick to order for them, and after he does, she waits for the waiter to leave and breaks into Nepali. "Are you okay?"

"I suppose. Actually, I don't know," Mick says. He picks up his napkin-wrapped silverware and peels the tissue away. "My friends are all moving away or DYING. I just wonder what I'm doing here right now. Maybe I should call it a day and move home to Germany. Find something else to do."

Her heart thuds, and it's all she can do to keep from pleading with him not to go. "What does your heart say?"

He looks up. "Huh, good question." He pauses, looking out the window beside them. She sees him run his tongue around the inside of his mouth and swallow. Finally, he mutters, "I just know I'd miss you if I go."

Palisha closes her eyes as her heart races. Suddenly, she realizes she likes Mick way more than she should. He's kind, honest, generous, and outgoing to a fault. What's more, he makes her laugh, and when he looks at her, he sees her; makes her feel respected, valued, and pretty. The problem is, there's no way her parents would accept Mick in her life: a solitary life, save for her sons, that has left her alone for far too long. No matter how she looks at it, anything more than friendship between her and Mick will not end well. *But*...her heart says, and it's that *but* that won't let go of the fantasy that's played over and over in her head every single night for the last year.

"I would miss you, too," she finally says.

He offers her a tiny smile as the waiter comes with their tea. After the young man leaves, Mick doctors his up with cream and takes a sip. She watches him, wondering what he's thinking. If he were to leave now, she would lose whatever chance, albeit slim, of ever finding out what could become of them. *Maybe it's time to take a chance*, she thinks, and her body tenses up and her palms dampen. Her father's face flashes before her, followed by both of her sons.

Finally, her heart drumming, she says, "Would you like to have dinner with me tonight?"

Mick's face lights up. "I would like that very much."

"Good," she says, and looks down to conceal the anxious excitement rolling through her, because what she has in mind is not what he's probably thinking. She takes a deep breath and screws up her courage. She's never been a forward person, and what she's about to suggest is so out of her character she wonders if something has come into her body and taken over. At last, she says in a low, deferential tone, "What can I make for you?"

She forces herself to look up and finds Mick staring back in astonishment. "You mean dinner at your place?"

"Yes, if that's okay?" she says and holds her breath, waiting to hear his answer.

"Of course it's okay!" he says, and the delight on his face sends jolts of relief coursing through her, mixed with palpating fear, joy, and anticipation.

Mick looks into the bathroom mirror of his hotel room. What had started as a gloomy day has suddenly turned into one of unexpected surprise, and he's feeling like a teenaged boy getting ready for his first date. He knows tonight's dinner with Palisha is nothing more than two good friends spending time together, but there's a tiny part deep down that wonders *what if*. Why, after all this time, has she gone out on a limb to invite him into her home for dinner? He knows what a big chance she's taking. If it were to get out to her parents that she's invited him into her home, the two of them alone—friends or not—what it would mean? Part of him wonders why, yet he can't help but be excited about this new turn in their friendship.

A voice inside whispers, *maybe something more will come of it*, but he squashes it. She comes from a traditional family, and she has two boys she loves more than anything. It's foolish to think she'd even consider anything more than friendship, except for the whispering voice in his ear.

Stop going there.

He appraises his trim work on his beard, tilting his head this way and that. He looks pretty good, he tells himself, then doles out cologne he bought in Thamel and splashes his face. It's one of the popular new colognes the storekeeper suggested, and it has a breezy, tangy scent that reminds him of a fresh-cut apple. He hopes he hasn't put on too much—and that she'll like it. Sniffing the scent, he goes out to change into the new shirt and pants he bought.

On the dresser is her address. It's a twenty-minute drive to her apartment building overlooking the Bishnumati River. He glances at the alarm clock on the bedside table. It's a quarter after five. Again, his heart thumps and he takes a deep breath.

Settle. It's just dinner! Okay, with a woman—in her apartment—alone.

He fumbles with the buttons on his shirt, which is a little snug, and pulls the bottle of wine from the bar-sized refrigerator in the room. It's a fruity red he knows she'll like, and it should go well with the lamb kabobs she's preparing. He stuffs it into his daypack along with the cheese and crackers he picked up, steps into his pants and shoes, and heads for the door.

Ten minutes later, he's driving down Museum Marg. The cigar in the cup beside him is calling for him. He ignores it, taps his thumb on the wheel, and checks his watch. He's going to be ten minutes early. Should he wait in the lot until it's time? This is maddening. *It's not a date*, he keeps telling himself.

When he arrives, he sits in his car. The lot is full and the sun has ducked behind a bank of clouds. In the yard, a couple of boys are kicking a soccer ball around near a row of acacia and rhododendron trees. He shuts the engine off, grabs his daypack, and gets out. The three-story brick apartment building with a metal red gable roof is laid out in an L-shaped configuration. Beds of marigold and another flower he has no name for hug its foundation. Inside, he finds a narrow hall in shadow. He pushes the button for the elevator adjacent an open door leading to the stairwell and waits for the door to slide open.

Palisha's apartment is on the third floor, number 305, and it's a one-minute clunky ride up in the close-quartered car. He's glad to be out of it when the door opens. Turning left, he wanders down the corridor, checking numbers as he goes. Here and there noise from a TV or a radio trickles out. The aroma of curried meats and seasoned vegetables mingles with the outgassing of freshly painted walls. Finally, he comes to her door. He lifts his hand to knock, hesitates, then raps on it. A moment later, he hears her call from the other side. When the door opens, he's speechless.

Palisha has changed into a flowing silky red and gold sari and has made herself up, tastefully accenting the lids of her animated dark brown eyes and lashes. Her thick black hair, bound with a floral tie, is draped around one slender shoulder. A fresh dab of red tika graces her forehead, and there's a soft, downy velvetiness to her face he's never seen before.

"Come in," she says. "Did you have trouble finding me?"

"No, not at all," he says, and takes off his boots. There's a heavenly aroma of kabobs coming from the kitchen and a soft sarangi aria playing in the background. He hardly notices either of them, though, because of the faint scent of her jasmine perfume. Digging into his pack for the wine, he adds, "Something smells good."

"I hope you like," she says as he hands her the

bottle. "Oh, what is this? You did not have to. You are so kind."

"It's just a little something to sip on at dinner," he says. They stare at each other a moment, and he's having a difficult time tearing his gaze away. He wants to take her in his arms and hold her, breathe her in and feel her warm body tight to his. Wants to be wrapped up in love and forget about the last four months. "Is there anything I can help with?"

"Oh no," she says, shaking her head. "You go sit and I will get us a couple of glasses." She starts for the other room, and over her shoulder, adds, "If you want I can put some different music on."

"No, not at all. This is nice," he says, finding a place on her sectional. He sweeps his gaze over the muted tan walls. They're bare, save for a family picture (he guesses) on the far wall and a large colorful mandala tapestry hanging over the sectional. A broad coffee table sits in front of him with a couple of magazines on it, and a brass lamp sits over in the corner. Beside the lamp is a sliding glass door leading out to a deck facing the river, and across from him is a black lacquered TV cabinet stacked with books. Tiny framed photos of more family are scattered on its shelves, along with a statue of Lakshmi and a pair of golden Buddhas. One thing the room doesn't lack is candles. They're scattered in dishes everywhere, on the shelves, the tables, and the hardwood floor. Presently, none of them are lit.

She comes back with their wine, hands him a glass, and sits beside him with her legs folded underneath her. "I hope you are hungry," she says, then sips her wine.

"Been looking forward to your cooking all day," he replies, and takes a gulp. He swallows, trying to quell the battle of nerves raging in his stomach. She's inches away from him and her attentive gaze is taking his breath away. "I like your place."

"Ahh, it is not much," she says. She's quiet a moment as the plucking notes of the sarangi guitar fills the space around them. "Are you sure I can not put some different music on? I have other CDs maybe you would like."

"No, this is fine," he says. Suddenly, he doesn't know what to say or how to act, and it confuses him because he's always been able to be himself around her. He shifts in his seat, feeling awkward and unsure of himself, then averts his attention to his wine. "So, how was your day?"

"It was good," she says. "We were busy today. I think maybe we are going to have a good summer. Already, people are coming for the mountains. When is your next trek?"

"In a couple weeks." He takes another sip of wine, and from the corner of his eye, he sees her gaze go inward as she runs her fingers around the rim of her glass. Whatever is going on between them, he thinks she feels it too. He wonders if maybe she thinks his coming here was a mistake.

At last she says, "You will be staying with us, then?"

"Of course. You're my headquarters," he says, turning back to her.

Her pixie nose crinkles and a soft melodic giggle dribbles from her lips, blending with the notes of the sarangi guitar. "You are so funny."

He shrugs. "I don't know about that."

They go quiet again and listen to the music for a while. But his mind is racing. He's trying to grapple with whether to risk stepping over the threshold of friendship with her. But then, he tells himself, how could it ever be anything more than heartache? He sighs, and he's just about to ask her if she feels nervous, when she says, "Are you okay?"

"Yes. Why?"

"You seem anxious. Does it bother you to be alone with me?"

"No, no...not at all. I just..." It's a lie. He's plenty nervous. He shrugs again. "I just haven't been alone with a woman in a long time, and I—I'm worried."

"About what?"

"That something might happen between us that would ruin our friendship."

"Oh..." She laughs, and it's a light, breezy laugh. Then she looks at him gravely, and the enigmatic expression on her face says maybe yes, maybe no, and he's at a loss of what to do. She puts her hand on his cheek and says, "Do not worry, Mick, we will always be friends, no matter what. Let us go and you eat now. You must be hungry."

As Mick takes a seat at the table, Palisha asks if he wants more wine as she dishes up a plate for Mick. She's anxious as she sets it on the table before him, then takes a seat, and folds her hands in her lap.

Mick looks over at her with a puzzled expression. "You're not going to eat?"

"I will later," she says.

Mick frowns, deepening the creases around his eyes. "No, you'll eat with me! This is your home, and you're not a servant. Get yourself a plate and join me. I insist."

She drops her gaze, feeling self-conscious. But it's his custom for everyone to eat together. Getting up, she takes a plate down from the cupboard, plucks a kabob off the platter, and adds a spoonful of rice with some chili marinade on her plate. When she sits across from him, he glances at her dish and up at her as if to say, *That's it? Just one kabob?*

She ignores the look, tamps down the butterflies in her stomach, and says, "So, tell me about the ceremony for your friend, Frank, is it?"

Mick takes a bite and swallows. "Yes. The lama did a mountaineering puja for him."

"Oh, how nice," she says, picking up her kabob. Nibbling a bite, she sets it down and dabs her mouth with a napkin. Mick has already polished off one of his kabobs and is working on a second. "You said a lot of friends showed up?"

"Yes," Mick says. He takes a drink of wine and clears his throat. "Most of the village, all his climbing Sherpas, and a bunch of competitors. One of them came all the way from New Zealand."

"Wow. He must have been liked," Palisha says, watching him. The way he's tearing into his dinner gladdens her. She hasn't cooked for a man in a long time. More than that, he's starting to be Mick again, instead of the tongue-tied man on her couch twenty minutes ago. As for herself, she's barely holding it together. "But what about family? No wife, children? Parents?"

"Well, he did have a wife, so to speak," he says, picking up another kabob. "They weren't married—not legally—but they considered themselves so."

"It must be hard for her, being there all alone now," Palisha says, spooning marinade onto her rice.

"Oh, no. Sarah, his significant other, went home this morning," Mick says, mixing marinade into his rice with his fingers.

Palisha blinks and looks up. "Oh...She does not live here?"

"Yes, and no," he says, scooping up a bite of rice. "Sarah gave up her life back in the States last year to come live with Frank. She was working on her permanent visa when he passed. Didn't I ever tell you about Frank?"

"No."

"Huh...Well, he did a lot of charity work for the Sherpa, improvements on the school, repairs on people's houses and such. He was loved by all, her the most," he says, dropping his gaze. He's quiet a moment, and she wonders what he's thinking. Then, he says, "It's a damned shame. You wait your whole life, finally find the one person that's the right one, and then lose them. It's not fair."

He shakes his head, and she knows exactly how he's feeling, because the one person she's waited for her whole life is sitting right in front of her, and she can't have him the way she wants. She watches him pay attention to his meal for a couple minutes, then says, "He sounds like a good man."

Mick nods, finishes his last kabob, and sits back, his gaze far away. "He was, and he'll be missed."

"I am sorry, Mick. It is very hard to lose someone you care about."

"Yeah. I've known Frank for over twenty years. The two of us did a lot of tramping together before I gave up the mountain to push paper." He nods toward his empty plate. "That was outstanding."

"Oh, thank you. You want more?"

"No, I'm good."

Wrong, Mick. Nothing's good, and you're right, it's not fair.

5

FEBRUARY 27, 2015

*L*incoln rides into the Tripureshwor Transportation lot and parks his bike. It's been a long week and he's glad for Friday. It's also payday, though he really doesn't need the money. He's plenty well off. He dismounts the bike, pulls his helmet off and hooks it over the handlebars, then heads into the building through an open overhead garage door. Housed in an expansive old two-story brick building with parged and patched walls, Tripureshwor Transportation delivers everything from construction supplies to appliances and furniture.

Lincoln's early for work this morning, so he joins some of his crewmembers standing inside the cavernous truck bay. He's gotten to know most of them over the last year, and for the most part, he likes them. One of them, a lean Nepali with a hatchet-sculpted face, moves over to make room for him. His name is Sameer and he's well into his fifties. He offers a toothy smile, and like Binod, he has a hard time with Lincoln's name.

"Lin-ji!" he says. "Payday today!"

"Yes, it is," replies Lincoln. "How are you?"

"Very fine, thank you," he says. "You have idea for tonight?"

Lincoln shrugs. "I might go out for dinner and a drink. Not sure yet. What's your plans for the weekend?"

"Oh...don't know yet. Maybe see...umm...wonder-children."

Lincoln knows he means grandchildren, but he doesn't correct him. He looks around the circle of men. Three of them are immersed in what sounds like a political conversation. A couple of others are passing a cigarette around and casting glances at the comings and goings on in the street. The tourists are out and about, and more than a few of the women are wearing shorts.

Another Nepali, Gopal, a chunky man with a pencil mustache, comes in from outside and joins them. As far as Lincoln can tell, the man and Sameer are close friends, and he wonders if they're related in some way. Gopal is around Lincoln's age and always has a smile on his plump face. Not today, though.

Sameer turns to the man and breaks into Nepali.

"Gopal, how's your father? Has he gotten any better?"

Gopal shakes his head. "No. The tests came back. He has cancer."

"Cancer! Oh, no!" Sameer says. "That's terrible. Can they do anything?"

Gopal shakes his head. "No. It's spread to his lungs. There's not much hope. He's going to die."

"Oh, I'm so sorry," says Sameer as a cigarette comes around to him. He waves it off. "How long does he have?"

"They're not sure. Maybe six months, maybe less," Gopal says, taking the cigarette. He takes a drag and shrugs. "My mother refuses to believe it."

"She's been married to him a long time," Sameer says. "I shall have to get over to see him. I hope he's not in pain."

Gopal passes the cigarette to the man next to him and glances at Lincoln. "Namaste Leancone."

Lincoln dips his head and says in Nepali, "Namaste Gopal. I sorry hear, too."

"Thank you," Gopal says.

One of the Nepalis watching the tourists turns and elbows Gopal. The man nods to a tall, leggy blonde wearing shorts. She's an American or maybe a Brit, Lincoln thinks, and she looks to be in her late twenties. The Nepali says, "Gopal, look over there. Not hard to look at, huh?"

Gopal turns and follows the man's gaze through the open garage door, but says nothing.

The Nepali next to Gopal cracks a leering grin. "She'd probably kill you."

The comment brings a round of laughter from the other Nepalis looking on, except for Sameer, who's watching Gopal with sympathetic eyes.

One of the Nepalis says, "I wouldn't mind finding out."

The horn announcing time to start work blares overhead, and Sameer says, "We better get to it."

It's a busy night at the Brahman Buddhist Bar in the center of the old city. People are gathered around tall tables near the walls or standing in clusters around the dimly lit room. Energetic Nepali music pulses through the air, inciting the women patrons to sway and dance. Many of them are tourists and, Lincoln's guessing, Americans. He has no interest in picking any of them up tonight, and he pays them little attention as he sits at the bar nursing his vodka neat.

Setting the tumbler down on the bar, he turns it around and around, thinking about this morning. He doesn't know Gopal very well, but he feels for him, or more to the point, for himself. In his mind's eye, he can see his aunt, who took care of him after the accident. She was the only thing between him and foster care, and instead of being grateful for her, he resented having to take care of her after she was diagnosed with ovarian cancer at fifty-seven. He picks the drink up and downs the remaining gulp, pushing the glass ahead for another. It's number four, and he's sensing the numbing effects of the alcohol taking over.

It's rare for him to sink into his past and remember all that happened back then. It's too painful and what's more, it's condemning. He leans forward, plants his elbows on the bar, and steeples his hands together with his head cradled between them.

"Headache?"

He looks up to see a striking brunette standing beside him. She has a credit card in one hand and an empty glass in the other. Her flashing blue eyes are staring down at him, and a non-committal smile is painted on her lips. She's definitely American.

"Oh, just thinking is all," he says, tossing back a lazy smile. "Thanks for asking."

She nods and peers down the crowded bar. Lincoln sweeps a quick glance over her tight-fitting sweater and jeans. She's tall, and by all means, athletic. She's also putting out a delightful fruity scent, which he's trying to ignore. When she steps back with a sigh, he averts his gaze.

"Can't believe they only have one bartender in here. By the time I get a refill, I'll be dead," she mutters.

"Yeah, they pack 'em in here pretty good on Friday nights," Lincoln says.

She turns with a raised brow and gazes back, startled. He gets this uncertain, gaping look often from tourists whenever he says things like that, as if they're trying to figure out if they heard him right. At last she says, "Sounds like you've been here before?"

"A few times." He sees the bartender free up and whistles, calling down to him in Nepali. "Another for me, and what always she wants."

The brunette is gawking back, and her lips form a big "O." "No! You live here?"

He nods as she orders a rum and Coke. "Couple years."

She mulls his answer over. Finally, she says, "What brought you here?"

What she really means is, why would you live here? "I assume the same as you: the mountains. You coming or going?"

"Just got back."

"Everest Base Camp?"

She nods as the bartender sets their drinks in front of them. When she offers the man her card, he says, "Already paid for."

Lincoln speaks up. "I got it."

She flashes Lincoln a tight smile. "Thanks."

"No problem." They both go quiet, and Lincoln expects her to go back to her friends. He's about to say, "enjoy the rest of your stay," when she speaks up.

"I'm Nicole, but my friends call me Nikki," she says and puts her hand out to him.

Her fingers are long, and she has a firm grip as they shake. "Lincoln, nice to meet you. You can call me Link."

"I got that from your shirt," she says, pointing to the stitched monogram above his breast pocket. "So, Link, what do you do here?"

He takes his tumbler up and sips. "I drive a truck, delivering stuff. And what do you do, back in the States...I assume you live there?"

"Portland, Oregon, and I'm a travel agent," she says, then takes a sip of her drink.

"Nice town," Lincoln says.

"You've been there?"

"I stopped in for a while when I made my way west." He pauses, wary of where things might go from here. He doesn't want to get into a conversation about him. "So...how were the mountains?"

"They were great," she says, and for the first time, she really smiles, and he has to catch his breath. "I loved Namche."

"Namche's nice," he answers. "Did you get all the way to Base Camp?"

"I did, and it was fantastic."

She looks around for what Lincoln assumes is an empty bar stool, but they're all taken. Suddenly, he finds himself teetering between his original thought of having a few drinks to forget about the memories

Gopal stirred up or following this rabbit hole and seeing where it ends. At last he says, "Want to get a table? Oh, wait a minute, you're here with friends."

"They're just people I hiked with. And yes, let's," she says and turns away, panning the room. "Ahh... there's one over there."

He collects his drink and follows her to a table near the back of the room, away from the noisy crowd. They sit and talk about the mountains and her life back in the States, and as the conversation goes on, it's quite apparent to Lincoln from the way she's looking at him that she's interested in more than just talking. He's seen the look she's giving him before. It's a look of someone appraising a sports car and wondering what it would be like to take a spin in it. But she's also keeping her distance and avoiding any innuendo that might heat things up. She's telling him about going to the Monkey Temple and to Dubar Square, remarking on the architecture, the insanity of the traffic, and the crowds. She asks him how he deals with driving in that craziness every day. Then suddenly, she says, "I bet you know a lot of places the tourists don't go."

He shrugs. "I know a few, but I don't know about tourists not seeing them. It's more like having the time to see them. Most people don't hang around long after they get back from their tours."

"I've got a lot of time," she says. She leans forward, her deep blue eyes fixed on him, and there's an eager expression on her face. "Maybe you could take me around."

He has no plans for the weekend other than going over to Binod's sometime to give Sunita her birthday gift, which he forgot to give her a couple weeks ago. "Sure. You want to go tomorrow?"

"I'd love to," she answers, and her face lights up. "What time do you want me to be ready?"

"I don't know, noon maybe, if that works for you?"

"Noon works perfect." She pulls her phone from her back pocket and wakes it up. "What's your number? I'll send you where I'm staying."

He reels off his number, watching her type it into her phone. He won't be going back to her room tonight. Part of him is glad of this, despite the uncomfortable tightness in his jeans. When his phone chirps, he takes it out and looks at the message. She's staying at the Eco, a popular hotel in Thamel all the expedition companies recommend to their clients. It's also going on 11:00 p.m., and he's feeling a little tipsy.

"Can I get you another drink?" he asks, hoping she'll refuse.

Maybe she picks up on the lackluster way he says it, because she shakes her head. "No, that's okay. I should be getting back to my hotel."

They get up and head for the door. The Eco isn't far away, a five-minute walk, and the streets in the old section of town are still busy, so he's confident she'll get back safely. "I'll see you at noon tomorrow," he says. "You want me to text you when I'm on my way?"

"Sure, I'd like that," she says as he opens the door for her.

For a minute they look at each other, and he feels the uncertain awkwardness of how to say good-bye. He's certain she's feeling it, too. Should he move toward her for a hug or just put out his hand?

She smiles, tells him to drive safe, and walks away, making the decision for him.

Lincoln's cabbie pulls up outside the lane to the Eco Thamel and Nicole is waiting for him. She's dressed in a cream-colored button-down blouse and jeans. The top two buttons of her blouse are undone, revealing a thin silver necklace with a cross. Her shoulder-length dark hair is pulled back into a ponytail, and her lids are shadowed in pastel blue, accenting the deep blue of her eyes. There's also a hint of pink gloss on her lips.

He opens the back door from inside the compact cab, and she slides in next to him with her camera. She's like a breath of fresh air, and she offers him a wide smile as she shuts the door. Lincoln takes a whiff of her jasmine cologne and smiles back. They have a good day for sightseeing. The sky is clear, save for a few puffy clouds, and the temps are in the seventies.

"Hey there," she says.

"Hi, yourself," he replies, conscious of how close she is to him in the cramped back seat. He tries to keep his gaze from drifting down to the open part of her blouse, which is providing him an ample view of one of her breasts.

"So, where are we going?" she asks, leaning into him. Her tone is bubbly and excited.

"Patan Durbar Square," he says, enjoying the pressure of her body against him. "It's in Lalitpur. There's lots to see there. I think you'll like it. I thought we'd do lunch there first, then walk around. I hope you're hungry."

"Starved. I got up late this morning and didn't have a chance to get breakfast. How far is...Lala-whatever it is from here?" she says, darting a glance out the window.

"Not far, maybe fifteen, twenty minutes, de-pending."

She tosses him another smile and they both go quiet as the cab weaves in and out of traffic. When they finally get to Patan, it's about quarter-to-one, and the square is teaming with tourists taking in the sights and locals observing one of the numerous Hindi holi-days of which there is no lack of throughout the year. Lincoln pays the cabbie and they get out and head for a café he's fond of. It's located on the third floor of one of the ornate brick and timber-framed buildings surrounding them.

Nicole pans her gaze over the ancient architecture of flaming rust-colored brick that rises up layer by layer like a tiered cake with broad overhanging skirted roofs at each level. The skyline with its ascending stacked tiled roofs reaching for the heavens is reminiscent of an image in a science fiction novel Lincoln read years ago. It's like a colony of square-topped mushrooms.

He leads her into the building and they climb a narrow staircase to the third floor. The receptionist meets them and takes them out to the veranda, where they choose a table near the railing and take their seats. He orders tea for both of them and looks on as she drinks in the ambience of the World Heritage Site. Finally, she turns and says, "Amazing!"

"Yes, it is," he replies, and turns to his menu. He knows what he wants, but it doesn't hurt to look. "Are you adventurous when it comes to food?"

"Define 'adventurous,'" she answers.

He looks over the top of his menu and sees her perusing hers. "Spicy," he says.

"As in heat?"

"Yes."

She looks up from her perusing. "Sure, as long as it's not atomic hot."

"No, nothing like that." He turns his menu

around and points to the Dehli Chaat selection. "You might like this. They make the best Dehli Chaat in all Nepal."

"Okay." She sets her menu down, pushes it aside, and takes her phone out. "Smile." She takes a picture of him, then turns the screen toward him so he can see.

He's not a fan of having his picture taken because he doesn't think he's all that attractive, even though he doesn't seem to have any trouble with the ladies. He shakes his head. The picture on the phone shows a quirky, awkward smile on his face that also seems too large on the screen, but he doesn't say anything. "So, tell me about your job. I've always wondered what else a travel agent does besides arranging trips for people."

She shrugs, tells him about the required research that's involved. "As a travel agent, you need to know as much about where you're sending people as the locals who live there. And then there's dealing with alliances between hotels, airlines, cruise lines, and the like that have to be nurtured and maintained. The one big perk is the enormous discounts I get for traveling to the destinations they serve."

The waiter comes with their teas, and Lincoln orders for them. When the woman leaves, Nicole leans forward and says, "What about you? You don't talk much about yourself."

"All part of the mystery," he says and grins, then sips his tea.

She rolls her eyes and it crinkles her nose, making her even more beautiful, if that's possible. "Come on, talk to me. Where'd you live in the States, and what did you do before you came to Nepal?"

She's staring back, her penetrating gaze intent on finding out about him, and he knows he has to give it up, so he says, "I grew up in upstate New York, and once upon a time, I was an EMT." He leaves out that he's also a doctor.

"An EMT!" she says. "Huh, I never would've guessed it."

He doesn't know if he should take that as a compliment or a slight. "Why's that?" he says, leaning back in his chair.

"I don't know, you seem like a woodsy type, someone who likes living off the land."

"Like a logger?" he says.

She averts her eyes. "Sorry."

Now it's his turn to lean forward. He puts his hand on hers. "It's okay. Not to worry. I'm sure a lot of people get that impression about me." He turns his gaze toward the bustling square below. "So, what do you think? Quite a place, isn't it?"

He feels her hand wrap around his. "Yes, it is. This whole city is amazing. I can't imagine living here. What's it like?"

"Well, it's crazy most of the time, but for the most

part, I've found myself more at home here than any-place I've ever lived."

"It sounds like you've been around a lot."

"I've lived my share of places, if that's what you mean."

"Never settled down?"

"Not really. Ahh, our lunch is coming." And he's glad for the interruption, because the direction the conversation is taking isn't where he wants to go. Once they're alone again, he says, "We'll go to the Bhimsen and Vishwanath Temples first, then the royal palace after. There's also a museum that ex-hibits the history of the square and the lives of the royal family who once lived here that you might like to see."

"Sounds wonderful," she says.

They dig into their lunches, and as they do, Lin-coln thinks about how quickly Nicole had disarmed him and put him on the verge of revealing things he rarely told even himself. It's not like he's ashamed or embarrassed of his past (well, not exactly true) but he just finds himself un-interesting and he doesn't want to bore this woman he's hoping to spend some quality time with later tonight.

After lunch he takes her out to the square and they go through the temples, looking at the artifacts and having light conversation about the things they've seen. After that, it's the museum, which she really enjoys. They spend the rest of the afternoon reading the plaques under the exhibits, and as the minutes pass, she grows closer and closer to him, touching his shoulder and arms. By the time they're heading for the cab to take them back to Thamel, she's holding his hand. He suggests they go to dinner at a place a friend of Binod owns. It's a modern restaurant that caters to tourists, serving American and western cuisine he knows she'll like.

He's also anticipating what the evening might bring, but he's not counting on it either. In fact, part of him feels a bit guilty about taking advantage of her wide-eyed wonder of the city. She's flying high, care-free with excitement, and more than likely, not thinking clearly about where things might lead. Or maybe she is. Still, he doesn't want her to think he's here for only one thing, and he tries to tell himself he isn't, because he doesn't like to think of himself as a player out for his own ends.

He hails a cab and fifteen minutes later they're taking an elevator up to the restaurant. The place is busy tonight, and Indian music flows from the speakers hanging from the bamboo ceiling. In the corner is a small stage, and on it is a drum set and a pair of guitars sitting upright on their stands. A keyboard is off to the left. He points to a table near a small dance floor beside the stage and they walk to it, hand in hand.

"They make a great burrito here," he says as he pulls a chair out for her.

She takes a seat and looks around. "What time does the band come on?"

"I don't know," he answers, taking the seat across from her. When the waiter approaches, he asks, "You want a drink?"

"I'd love one," she replies. She looks up at the waiter. "Do you have wine here?"

"Yes. We have Merots, Zins, Cabs, and Pinot," the waiter says.

"I'll have a pinot," she says.

Lincoln nods. "Me, too."

"Wait, let's get a bottle," Nicole says, and reaches into her jeans pocket and pulls out a pair of thousand-rupee notes.

"Put your money away," Lincoln says. "My treat."

She smiles, and the way she's doing it is putting visions in Lincoln's head of the two of them naked in bed. He forces the thought away and sends the waiter off to get their wine. When he looks back, she's still smiling.

"Thank you for taking me around. I had a great time today," she says and picks up her menu.

"You're welcome." He watches her peruse the dinner selections a minute. "So, what do you think?

83

You want to try a burrito, or is there something else in there you want?"

"Hmm...how's their penne?"

He's never had it, so he's not sure, but he has to believe it's good. Everything he's had here has been excellent. "I don't know. Try it and see."

"I think I will."

The waiter brings their bottle back with a pair of glasses, and they give the man their orders. When they're alone, she takes a sip and sits quietly across from him, staring back. The look in her eyes is suddenly enigmatic, hard to read. It's the same look he got last night after she left him outside the Brahman Buddha with a simple good-bye and walked away as if they'd just passed in the street. He realizes then that he's been getting ahead of himself, and he resolves to not think about what might or might not happen.

Yeah, good luck with that.

She takes another sip of wine and the enigmatic look in her eyes turns critical. "I want to know more about you. How come you gave up being an EMT? Did something happen?"

Her question startles him. Then again, everything about her is startling. "Nothing happened. I just wanted to see more of the world."

"So you just up and left?"

He takes a gulp of wine. "Yup."

She cocks her brow. "No family, friends?"

"No one close. I have some cousins in Arizona somewhere." He watches her consider his answer. It's hard to tell whether she believes him. Normally, he wouldn't care one way or the other, but now he does. "I know, I sound vague and maybe a little evasive, but really, my life isn't all that interesting. To be honest, I'm amazed I'm sitting across from a beautiful woman right now."

Her critical expression melts. "Thank you, and you're plenty interesting. I like you, Link. You're hands-off, unlike a lot of guys I know, and I might add, very attractive," she rebuts, and extends her hand over the table to him. "Don't sell yourself short." The way she says it is so sincere and sweet, he hasn't the nerve to tarnish the great time he's had with her with some random tryst.

It's near midnight when the cab pulls up to the lane leading to her hotel. The music from the band is still ringing in his ears. He's had a great time with Nicole, and he's about to say goodnight when she turns to him with a bubbly smile. "Want to come up?"

It's the four (or is it five?) glasses of wine during dinner that's doing the talking for her. He'd settled on being a gentleman and just walking her to her room, but she's so damned beautiful in that low-cut button-down blouse. He smiles. "Sure."

She opens the car door and they get out. He pays the cabbie and they stroll back under the stars to the hotel courtyard, which is lit in soft golden pools of light coming down from tiny spotlights peeking out from behind leafy vines draped over the second-floor railings. A couple of hotel guests sit at a metal patio table talking near a knee-high brick wall surrounding a ring of yellow lilies and red dahlias. In the center of the flowers sits a statue of a Buddha on a brick pedestal.

Nicole leads him across the courtyard to an alcove with a flight of stairs. Her room is on the fourth floor. When they get to it, she fumbles with the key, unlocks the door, and hits the light. Lincoln looks around. The hotel has upgraded the rooms. The walls have been repainted, overhead lights replaced with decorative sconces, double beds changed out for queens, and the curtains have been replaced with vertical blinds. There's even a couch with a coffee table and a portable bar with a small refrigerator.

"Have a seat, I'll be right out," she says, and goes into the bathroom.

He plops down on the couch, snags one of the hotel magazines off the coffee table, and leafs through it. A minute later, she opens the door and kicks off her shoes. She's unbuttoned another button of her blouse and let her hair down. He feels his breath catch and his heart quickens as she walks past him, tapping away on her phone. She sets it on the dresser, turns her back to him, and bends forward, giving him a view.

Okay!

"Any requests?" she says, peering back at him from around her hip. She smiles an innocent smile, but he knows there's nothing innocent about it.

"I don't know, whatever you want. I'm good with it all."

She straightens up, and Bob Seger is suddenly belting out "Midnight Rider." "I'm getting a drink. You want one?" she says, stepping over to the bar.

He thinks maybe it's not a good idea for her to have another drink, but it's not like he's her husband. "I think I'll pass."

"Oh, come on, don't wimp out on me now," she replies, holding up a bottle in each hand. She looks at the bottle in her right hand. "I have rum..." she says, then turns to the other, "...and tequila."

He hesitates. "Okay, just a small shot of rum."

She pours a double shot of tequila for herself, then his rum, which is also a double, and sits almost on top of him when she brings their drinks over. She raises her cup to her lips. "Bottoms up!" She downs the double in one gulp. "Whooh, love tequila! So, I had a great time today. Thank you for taking me around."

It's the second time she's thanked him, but he lets it go. "Pleasure was mine," he replies and sips his rum.

They talk for a while about her trip and her plans for the next couple weeks doing research for her company. She tells him she's going to check out Pokhara and then the Chitwan game reserve down south. As they talk, she's nestling closer and closer, and her hand is finding its way onto his thigh higher and higher. By the time Seger's "Turn the Page" comes on, she's just about taken complete inventory of him.

"Let's dance," she says suddenly, hopping up.

Lincoln isn't much on dancing, unless you call it going round and round in circles. But she's insistent, so he gets up and joins her in the center of the room. When he puts his arms around her, she arches her back and presses her body into him. Face to face, he inhales the intoxicating blend of her fruity perfume and the alcohol on her breath. Even though she's had more than enough wine and tequila, he's surprised at her firm hold on him, and it isn't long until her hands are roaming up and down his back. At the rate she's going, he'll lose it before the dance is over.

Mercifully, the song ends and he pulls back, aware of the erection in his pants. He wonders if she notices it.

She glances down, then back up, and there's a predatory hunger in her gaze and a crooked smile on her lips. She moves her warm, damp body into him, grinds her pelvis against his erection, rolls her tongue around the inside of her upper lip. "Maybe we should let him out, what do you think?"

A minute later they're clawing at each other, tearing off clothes, and before he knows it, she's pushing him onto the bed and climbing on top, straddling him. She's naked, wet and ready, and when she reaches between her legs and guides him inside, he closes his eyes and sinks into the euphoria of being engulfed by this beautiful woman. For the next few moments they're like a machine thrusting back and forth, and when he looks up he sees her eyes rolled up under her lids. She's getting close, he can feel it, and so is he. He reaches up and palms her breasts. Her nipples are hard and erect as she rocks back and forth. Then all at once, she bends forward and pins his wrists to the bed, and her lips are all over his mouth.

Suddenly, his body goes stiff and he feels trapped and breathless. He's confused why he feels this way, and then a memory of being pinned in the back seat of his parents' car flashes before him. His mother's lifeless body is thrown back onto him from where she sat in front. There's a gaping rent in her head, and the spatter of blood and pieces of brain are strewn across his lap. He panics. He has to get out, get away.

He pushes Nicole off him with all his strength, almost sending her flying off the bed. When he regains control and sits up, her beautiful countenance is bunched up in a puzzled, hurt expression, and there's steely anger in her eyes. It's as if he just slapped her across her face. He eyes her, and it's like they're a couple of feral cats squaring off in an alley. At last he sighs. "I'm sorry. I—"

"What?" she snaps back. When he can't make words to answer her, she gets up and grabs her blouse off the floor. "I don't know what the hell's wrong with you, but I asked you back here to have a little fun, not to deal with your shit, whatever that is. I get enough of that at home. Christ!"

He rolls over and sits up on the opposite side of the bed with his back facing her. "I should go," he mutters.

"Yes, you should," she replies.

He hears her picking up clothes off the floor, then a moment later, the slamming of the bathroom door. He runs his hands through his hair, confused and dumbfounded. *What the hell's wrong with me?* Then again, no one's ever restrained him before. At length, he gets up and gets dressed and goes to the bathroom door.

"I'm leaving now."

There's no answer, not that he expects one.

"Sorry," he adds, then turns away and leaves the room, pulling the door shut behind him. He stands there a moment, embarrassed, regretting his reaction and feeling like a shit until he hears the click of the lock engaged on the other side, driving home the point that he fucked up.

MARCH 13, 2015

*B*inod pulls his bike over and goes into the Playful Panda Café for a cup of spiced tea to go. He's just dropped Arjun off for school, and he's on his way to work. Outside the small café, a ring of men are lingering in animated conversation, discussing the prospects for the Reds' upcoming soccer season. He's tempted to join in, but he's already running late.

As he waits in line, he thinks about Sila. He keeps close tabs on her now that she's getting close to having the baby. While it's true she works at the hospital, and if she goes into labor, there's no better place for her to be, he still worries. More than that, he wants to be there when her time comes. And then, there's the future. Between working in his brother-in-law's shop in Thamel, guiding expeditions for Mick in the mountains, and Sila working at the hospital, they've been making ends meet. But soon, there will be another mouth to feed, and with Sila not working for a while, things are going to be tight financially. He wonders if maybe he should pick up another job, perhaps driving cab on the weekends until Sila's back to work. There is, of course, the option of having Sila's sister, Roshika, come to baby-sit, but that would be a last resort. He likes Roshika well enough, but she's nosy and opinionated. The last thing he needs is to come home to squabbling sisters.

He steps up, gives his order to the cashier, and ten minutes later, he's motoring down New Road into Thamel. Traffic is heavy this morning on the main arterial running past the old section of the city. People are out in force, crossing the busy highway, threading through oncoming cars, buses, and motorbikes. A bony old bull is walking down the middle of the road ahead, heedless to all going on around him. Binod turns off the arterial onto one of the narrow streets leading into the tourist section of town. The buildings are old here and serviced with a mishmash of tangled wiring and outdated sewers, like much of Kathmandu, but it's a different world than the rest of the city. This is where the tourists flock, and he feels their presence everywhere; from their masses on the streets scouring the ancient avenues searching for treasures and souvenirs to the pretentious offerings of the shops—like his brother-in-law's—and finally the restaurants and cafés catering to tourists' tastes for Italian, Mexican, and American cuisine. Mingled in with all this is the ubiquitous essence of his country's history and its culture that's been embedded and steeped into him since he was a little boy. Sometimes the old city, which he loves, feels like a distant cousin, lingering on the edge of a proud and independent family.

He drives down the street and pulls into an alley, parks his bike, and removes his helmet. His brother-in-law's bike is already there. Dibaker arrives early every morning to open up. Binod checks his phone for messages. Seeing none, he walks around the building and goes into the Singing Bowl. The store exudes the heady aroma of Champa incense. Already, there's a customer inside perusing the shelves on the wall that's stacked with singing bowls and Buddha figurines. Dibaker is hovering nearby, ready to be of assistance. It's important to make that first sale because it portends the success of the rest of the day. When he sees Binod, Dibaker gestures him over to a pair of boxes with a wave of his hand. There's merchandise to put on display.

Binod pulls back the top flap of one of the boxes. It's packed to the brim with an assortment of tapālans and tie-dye shirts. He pulls them out one by one and hangs them on a rack near the cash register. By the time he's finished, it's going on 10:00 a.m. and he's ready for another cup of tea. He collapses the empty boxes and sets them to the side, then tells Dibaker he's stepping out for a minute. As he heads down the busy street, he checks his messages again. Nothing. He tells himself to settle down, stop worrying, but it's hard. The last time Sila went into labor, Arjun was breeched and had to be turned around. It was, as the Americans like to say, *touch-and-go* for a while. He steps into the little teashop a block down from the Singing Bowl and orders a masala tea for himself and a ginseng for Dibaker to go. As he waits for the girl to fill his order, another customer comes in. She looks like an American from what he can tell. Tall, athletically built with shoulder-length brunette hair. She's wearing a lavender-colored fleece with an insignia on it that says *Enterprise Travel Agency*. When she passes him, he gets a good whiff of a tangy, fruity essence from her and a guarded, thin smile. A moment later, she's perusing the assortment of pastries behind the glass-enclosed cabinet beside him. He tries not to stare, but she has the most intense blue eyes he's ever seen.

She darts a glance back at him and smiles again, then moves further into the shop, inspecting varieties of tea on the shelves. The girl behind the counter sets his order in front of him and he pays for it. As he walks out, he feels the American's gaze looking back at him, and he wonders if she caught him checking her out.

~

Binod rings a sale up for a customer and bags her purchase. It's going on 3:00 p.m. and sales have been brisk. Dibaker is in back doing paperwork, and there are a dozen other customers in the store fingering merchandise on the shelves. He hands the woman her purchase and as he goes to see if he can help someone else, his phone pings in his pocket. He takes it out and when he reads the message, his heart thumps. Sila's water has broken and she's been admitted to the hospital. He runs in back and tells Dibaker he has to go.

The ride to the hospital is at least twenty minutes on a good day, but not today. Everybody is out, and a truck ahead is slowing traffic to a crawl. He looks for a path around it, but motorbikes weaving back and forth are blocking his way. He closes his eyes, taking a breath and trying to stay calm. The nurse who called him said it would be a while before she'd go into heavy labor, and to take his time. But Sila isn't her wife. He laughs at himself for the absurd thought and tries to push the memory of Arjun's difficult and dangerous birth out of his mind.

Everything will be okay, he keeps telling himself as he motors ahead and mingles with the bikes trying to find their way around the truck. He looks at his watch. It's almost 3:30. At the rate he's going, he won't get there until 3:45 at the earliest. *Of all days for this to happen,* he mutters under his breath. And then, just like that, the tangled mess ahead thins out and he's on his way. He glances up at the hazy tan sky and thanks Lakshmi for her blessing, then bears down on the throttle.

Thirty minutes later, Binod is in Sila's room staring out the window at the sprawling city. She's lying in bed beside him hooked up to a fetal monitor to keep track of the baby. He doesn't remember Sila being monitored like this the last time and he asks the midwife if there's anything to be worried about. The tiny woman, Faria, gives him a reassuring smile and tells him it's standard procedure when a woman has had a prior difficult delivery.

"There's nothing to worry about," Faria says. "Her contractions are just starting."

The beeping sounds coming from the monitor reel out in a steady, incessant rhythm, and with each beep that echoes the baby's heart rate, Binod's heart answers in return. He forces a smile and looks down at Sila, who's looking up at him with an easy, contented expression, as if it's just another day. He wonders how she can be so calm and he wishes he could tap into her peaceful acceptance and belief that everything's going to be okay.

Faria speaks up, "I'll check back in another hour to see how you're doing."

Binod watches her leave, then says, "I called your sister and she's going to pick the kids up from school."

"I know, she told me," Sila says and pats his hand. "Sit, please. You're making me nervous. Everything's going to be okay, you'll see."

Maybe, but he won't breathe right until the baby is born and she's all right. He nods and pulls a chair by the window up to her bedside. The monitor across from him beeps away on its stand. Its screen shows a series of rolling graphs and flashing numbers. He assumes the top two graphs and numbers represent her and the baby's heart rates. What the last graph and numbers are about, he doesn't know. Presently, the needle scribbling the line is hovering around fifteen on the scale. Whatever that means.

Sila says, "How was work?"

He turns back to her, dumbfounded that she would ask such a question. "It was fine."

"You were busy today?" she says.

"Yes. Very busy. You're sure you're okay?"

"I'm fine, don't worry about me," she says. "It's not like it's my first time."

Except last time, I almost lost you.... "I'm not worried. I'm just making sure."

She pats his hand and he knows she doesn't believe him. They fall quiet, and the monitor fills the space around them for the next ten minutes until he sees her wince. He jerks up as the beeping races for a second, then settles down. Sila draws a quick breath and says, "Someone's making themselves known."

"Are you okay?"

"Of course. It was just a tiny contraction." She points to the monitor. "See the lower number? That's the strength of it."

He looks over and sees short spikes on the graph, then follows the line crossing the tip of it back to the scale on the left that runs from zero on the bottom to one hundred at the top. The contraction measured twenty-five. "Does it ever get to one hundred?" he asks.

She nods. "But not always. High enough, though! What's important is the top two numbers. By the way, what time is it?"

"I don't know, why?"

"I want to time my contractions."

"Oh." He pulls out his phone. "5:25."

"Okay," she says. She bends forward, pins her palms on the mattress, and tries to shift herself back.

"Here, let me help," Binod says, and he gets up and lifts her into a more comfortable position. "How's that?"

"Better, thanks." She reaches behind her, punches her pillow. "Have you called your parents yet?"

"Not yet. You know how my mother is. She'll be asking why you're in the hospital when you should be home having the baby the old-fashioned way. I don't want to get into an argument with her." He's about to say more when his phone buzzes. He looks at the number. It's Mick. He answers in English, "Can I call you back later? We are having a baby right now."

"Oh, wow!" Mick says. "Absolutely. Hey, what hospital?"

"Patan Hospital."

"Got it, and congrats, Binod."

It's a bit early for congratulations, but Binod doesn't say anything. "Thank you. I will talk to you later," he says, and ends the call.

"Who was that?" Sila asks.

"Mick."

"Oh." She taps his hand again. "I think we're going to be here awhile. You should get something to eat, and maybe bring me back something to read? And some tika."

"Are you sure?"

"Positive, go. I'll be fine. My mother will be up soon to see me, so I won't be alone long."

He gets up, reluctant to leave her, but he knows she's right. It's going to be awhile.

It's going on sixteen hours since Sila was admitted to the hospital. Binod nibbles a fingernail and walks to the open archway to peer down the hall his wife works in. He's no stranger here, but today is different in a way he can't articulate. It feels as if an invisible hand is gently holding him at arm's length from the people Sila calls friends.

He takes a gulp of aloe vera juice, caps his bottle, and shuffles back into Sila's room to join her family who are gathered around the bed. Sila's father is at work and Binod knows that even if he were able to come, he would still defer to Sila's mother, Sumi, to manage things with their daughter. Having babies is women's work, or so he's said on occasion.

In the corner of the room, a TV babbles. Sila's mother turns away from the bed and walks to him. Unlike Sila's brothers and sisters, who prefer western clothing, Sumi is in a black and ruby-colored sari. A long golden shawl is wrapped around her generous body.

"Are you okay?" Sumi asks in Nepali.

"Oh, yes. I just thought I heard Faria," Binod replies, forcing a smile.

Sumi considers him with a knowing gaze that tells him she's seeing right through him. "She's fine. Don't worry."

"Oh, I'm not worried."

"Hmm...then why are you pacing around like a caged tiger?" Sumi says.

"I'm not pacing," Binod retorts, strutting to a chair by the window. He plops down on the hard seat and mindlessly scrolls down incoming tweets on his phone.

But Sumi follows him. "Of course you are. You've

been up since yesterday morning. And that chair is so uncomfortable. Why don't you go to the waiting room? There's a couch you can lie down on. If there's any news, I'll come get you."

"No, it's all right," says Binod. He stretches his tired neck muscles and averts his gaze from his mother-in-law, who's looking at him like a doting parent. "I'm all right, really," he says. When Sila has another contraction, he jumps up and rushes to her bedside. Sila's face contorts, and her eyes squeeze together tight until it passes.

Once Sila gets her breath back, she says, "This baby's being a brat."

Everyone smiles. Sumi says, "It won't be long, I think."

Another ping diverts Binod's attention. He's expecting a text from his brother-in-law. He glances down at his phone. It's a text from Dibaker.

Dibaker Nath:
Hi, any news yet?

Binod Thapa:
Not yet. Are you coming up?

Dibaker Nath:
Yes, as soon as we get the kids off to the baby-sitter.

Binod Thapa:
Ok. We're on the fourth floor, room 4225.

"Knock, knock."

Binod turns around to see Faria sweep in. "Hello," she says. "Okay, I need to check on Sila here, so I need you all to step out, okay? In fact, why don't you all go down to the waiting room?"

But the waiting room is the last place Binod wants to be. Even though Faria has told him the baby isn't breeched, he can't help remembering the last time. He watches Sila's family shuffle out, and casting one last look at his wife, he reluctantly follows.

The waiting room is around the corner, down the hall. When they go in, Binod sees Mick stuffed into one of the modest blue upholstered chairs lined up against the wall. Beside Mick is a vase of budding red roses. Mick shoves his phone in his pocket and gets up with the vase. In English, he says, "How's she doing?"

"She is doing fine. You did not need to come up, and what are these?"

"Are you kidding me? How long have I known you, huh?" Mick says. He hands the vase to Binod, then turns to the rest of Sila's family. "Namaste!"

Sumi takes the vase of flowers from Binod, appraising the bouquet, and says in English, "Oh, very pretty. You have help with these?"

"A little," Mick says and shrugs. He turns back to

Binod. "So, what's the status? Has the little one made an appearance?"

"Not yet," Sumi says.

Mick takes a seat. "She must be exhausted?"

Binod introduces Mick to everyone as his phone pings in his pocket. He ignores it and casts a glance back at the open archway. "She is tired, yes."

"And by the looks of it, so are you," Mick says.

Sumi takes a seat on the couch kitty-corner from them and says, "He been up all night with her." To Binod, she says, "Come sit."

There's no use arguing with Sumi, and Binod knows it, so he sits and listens as she questions Mick about his affairs, wanting to know where he lives, if he has family, and what exactly he does at the expedition company her son-in-law works for. Binod wishes she would be less intrusive, but that's how Sumi is. Like her daughter, she's an inquisitive woman, and Mick doesn't seem to mind answering her questions.

After some time, everyone runs out of things to say. They listen to the sounds of the hospital staff going back and forth in the hall and the occasional squawking of an overhead speaker paging a doctor. Binod is grateful for the silence and tips his head back, resting it on the wall.

Finally, Mick looks over and says, "Amelia has to sit the season out. Her father needs a kidney and she wants to donate hers to him. Do you know of anyone who might be interested in filling in for her?"

Binod immediately thinks of Lincoln. "I might. Let me ask around."

"Thanks," Mick says as Faria comes to the open archway with a broad smile.

Binod looks up, and suddenly his heart drums.

"You have a son," she says in Nepali.

Binod puts his hands together as the room explodes with gleeful cries. "Thank you, thank you," he says. He turns to Mick, and in English says, "I have another son. I knew it would be a boy. That is what I said to myself."

"Well, what are ya waitin' for? Go see the little guy," Mick says, nodding toward the door.

"Yes, yes, of course. I will be back soon if you—"

"Don't you worry about me," Mick says. "I'll keep just fine, now go already."

Binod bows quickly to him, then follows Faria into the busy corridor. Behind him, he hears a parade of clicking heels on the polished terrazzo floor. Sila's family is right behind him. As they stride along, he can hear them jabbering about how they can't wait to see the baby. The hospital staff looks up as he passes and turns approving glances his way. He's doing all he can not to break into a dead run.

Faria turns down the maternity corridor and comes to a halt in front of a small alcove. As everyone gathers around her, she turns to Binod. "Go on down. Everyone else, wait here."

Binod marches down the hall and when he comes

to Sila's door, he stops. Through the glass pane, he sees her lying in bed under a soft yellow light. At last, he pushes the door open and steps into the shadowed room. When Sila sees him she works the controller on the bed, propping herself up. Their son is swaddled in her arms, and the Buddha smile tugging at her lip is one he's seen many times during their marriage; a look steeped in the mysterious ways of a woman. As he gazes back at her and their dark-haired child, his chest swells with pride and relief.

Their son yawns and opens his eyes, and as he does, Binod senses once again, as he had with Arjun and Sunita, the ancient tides of the past and the emerging ripples of the future collide. It overwhelms him, and for a moment he can't move. Finally, he comes to himself and steps up to the bed.

"He's beautiful," he says, running the back of his finger over the baby's cheek. He turns his gaze back onto Sila, loving her more than he thought possible. His phone pings in his pocket.

"You want to hold him?" Sila says.

"Very much," Binod replies. He takes his son into his arms and inhales the baby's saffron scent, watches his son stare up at him, holding him with a palpable embrace that shuts out the room. Binod smiles, drifts over to the window, and looks out on the city. As he stands soaking up the ambiance of his perfect world, a break opens in the cloud cover and through it, a bright spray of golden sunlight shines down.

7

MARCH 21, 2015

*T*oday is Palisha's monthly visit to her parents in Lalitpur, and she's anxious as she drives along the F103 highway that skirts the city's southwest rim. Even though she's a woman in her mid-forties, educated and on her own, she's still a widow in her father's eyes, and widows should be home with their parents and out of sight. And he doesn't let her forget that. She wonders if she'll ever really be seen in his eyes. Even after all this time, he still can't forgive her for wanting more in life than just being a specter, drifting from one room to another in the sprawling estate in the upper-caste neighborhood of Kathmandu.

She turns off the highway onto a dusty road with no name that wriggles through the humble neighborhoods huddling around the upscale section of town.

It's a Saturday, so the kids are out on the streets and fields running around and playing. Some of them turn to look at her as she passes by. She waves back, offering them a smile. It seems like a lifetime ago her sons were their age, and she suddenly remembers watching them from the rooftop deck of her father's mansion as they kicked a soccer ball on the mani-cured grass below. Sometimes it feels like a dream that's ended too quickly, leaving her to gasp at wak-ing, wondering if she's imagined it all. That her life has fast-forwarded, skipping over all the could've-beens and should've-beens to drop her off in a life she'd never have recognized growing up in the privi-leged world of her parents.

She takes the one-lane bridge over the brown wa-ters of the Bishnumati River and follows the road into the upper-caste neighborhoods of her childhood. As she winds around the roads, the houses grow larger and the yards more ornate, with flowering bushes, trees, and gardens. Further along, these yards are walled off by tall brick enclosures with wrought iron gates. Even the power lines on the service poles passing by are neatly arranged, unlike the tangled messes in much of the city.

At length, she comes to her parents' home. She pulls up in front and parks, takes a deep breath, and looks in the rearview mirror. She's wearing a white sari, in the tradition of what's expected of a widow in her father's home, and she feels conspicuous as she gets out of the car. She knows that here in this neighborhood, she's no more than a ghost, avoided at all costs, lest she bring bad luck on anyone who comes across her. She hurries across the street to the front gate. It's locked, but she knows the combination to the electronic keypad. She enters it and the gate sweeps open onto the herringbone brick walkway that leads to the broad circular concrete front porch. Here, she removes her shoes and sets them next to a line of other footwear beside the door, then rings the bell. She's a bit late, but no one will mind. In fact, it's almost expected of her.

When her mother opens the door, Palisha tips her head in reverence. "Namaste, Āmā."

Her mother smiles and looks her over. "Namaste Polly. Your father is out just now, but will be back soon," she says. "How was the drive in?"

"It was good," Palisha says, hearing her Aunt Usha's reedy voice and another woman talking in the other room. "The gardens look nice. You've been working hard."

"Ahh...it's nothing," her mother says, casting her gaze over the blanket of red, yellow, and orange blossoms springing up amongst the backdrop of ornamental grasses and budding rhododendrons. "Come, let's go sit. Your aunt is here, and so is a friend of mine. Her name is Gita. You will like her."

Palisha steps inside and follows her mother around the corner into the living room. Her mother

refers to this room as the Receiving Room. It's lav-
ishly furnished with red velvet-upholstered chairs
and a large divan set against the interior mahogany-
paneled wall. A marble-topped coffee table sits on an
oriental carpet in front of it. On the table is a silver
platter with a teapot and a tray of rice cookies. Palisha greets her aunt, who's siting at one end of the
divan with her legs folded under her bright red sari,
then takes a seat on the other end.

Her aunt nods, and there's a judging look in her
dark eyes and round face. She lowers her lids halfway
as she considers Palisha. "Nice to see you again. You
should come by more often."

Palisha bites back the urge to tell her aunt the
road goes both ways and averts her gaze to the broad
picture window across from her that looks out over
the gardens. "Yes, I should," she says, then turns back
to Usha and smiles. "How's my uncle? He's good, I
assume?" It's no secret that Usha and her husband
are at odds with each other, and that he's been away
from home a lot the last year.

Usha's mouth turns down. The rumor of her husband carrying on with one of his employees has been
making its rounds and it's well known it's reached her
aunt's ears. Palisha sees her mother's disapproving
glance from the corner of her eye.

As her mother pours tea, she says, "Gita, this is
my daughter, Palisha."

"Namaste," the woman says from where she sits across the room.

Palisha turns to the woman, takes the cup her mother hands her, and smiles. "Nice to meet you. You're new here?"

"Yes, we moved in down the street a few months ago. I met your mother while I was out walking."

"We both share the appreciation of a nice garden," Palisha's mother puts in.

Palisha takes a sip of tea, enjoying the ginger essence rising from the cup. "My mother has a way with flowers."

"Yes, she does," Gita says, then leans forward with a sympathetic gaze. "When did you lose your husband?"

"Oh, it was years ago, during the Maoist war."

"Such a terrible time," Gita says. "The monarchy in ruins." She sighs, shaking her head, and as silence fills the room Palisha finds herself in Gita's gaze. There's a discerning look in the woman's sharp gray eyes, as if she's trying to figure something out. Finally she leans forward and says, "So you don't live at home?"

Palisha glances at her mother and sees her draw a breath. "No, I live north of here."

"By yourself?" Gita asks, as if she can't believe a widow would live on her own.

"Yes, I quite like it," Palisha says, and her comment is quickly punctuated by a rattle of a cup on a saucer.

"How do you support yourself?" Gita says.

The woman's line of questioning is leading into an area that isn't talked about in the house, but Palisha isn't going to lie or be made to feel like a pariah. "I have my inheritance, and I work," she says.

The woman's jaw drops in astonishment. "Really! Doing what?"

"I manage a hotel with another woman." Suddenly, all the air leaves the room, and although Palisha can't see her mother's face, she's quite sure her mother is doing all she can to hold it together. *I'm sorry, Āmā, but this is my life and I will not apologize for being me. Time to change the subject.*

But before she can say anything, Gita says, "What got you interested in doing that?"

The way Gita says it, it's as if it's servants' work and below someone of Palisha's status. *Really? And what's wrong with that, exactly?* She takes a sip of her tea, which is growing colder by the minute, and says, "I've always liked providing hospitality to people, so it came naturally. And I get to meet lots of interesting tourists from all over."

From the corner of her eye, she sees Usha shift in her seat and roll her eyes. "I bet you do," her aunt says. She's about to say more when they all hear the front door open.

Palisha's mother jumps up. "Amir, is that you?"

"Yes. Is that Palisha's car out front?" he calls from the foyer.

"Yes, Bubā," Palisha says, getting to her feet. She sets her tea on the coffee table and walks out to see her father removing his Dhaka topi. He folds it and sets it on the console by the door, then lays a trembling, bony hand on her head and looks her over as if he's inspecting a prospective purchase.

Finally, he says, "You are losing weight. You need to take better care of yourself, Polly." It's as close as she will get to an affectionate embrace from him.

"Yes, Bubā, but I feel just fine," she answers and smiles up at his thinning mottled brown face. Her father is getting older and there are fewer dark hairs on his head and more creases around his deep-set dark eyes. But what really bothers her is the tremor in his hands that seems worse every time she sees him.

He nods and says, "Very well, have it your way. You never listen to me anyway." But there's a glint in his piercing gaze, and she knows he tries hard to embrace a few of the progressive movements in Nepal toward women and widows. He's made progress over the last few years, but old traditions are hard to break, so for now he honors the truce they made five years ago not to ask how she's doing in her new life, and she plays her role as a widow when she comes into his house by wearing the white sari and abstaining from make-up, jewelry, and even tika.

He takes his leave of her, greets his wife, then

goes into his office down the hall. He's an important man in the district, holding the office of Commissioner of Human Affairs, and his work consumes him. She doesn't expect to see him until dinner. Sometimes she wonders if he's really just hiding from her in there, pretending to work, but she doesn't press him about it. Maybe it's easier that way. Yet, she yearns for the time when she was just a girl and he'd come up and take her onto his lap and tell her stories about the old times, when life was simpler.

She goes back into the living room and sits, thinking about her father. She wonders if he's seen a doctor about that tremor and determines to ask her mother when they're alone. For now, she watches her mother, Gita, and Usha talking about their kids. Gita's son is in university, studying to be a doctor. He's going to marry a young woman from an esteemed family as soon as he graduates this spring. It's going to be a huge affair, four hundred guests are invited, and everyone is excited about it. Perhaps, Usha and her mother would like to be invited. As for Palisha, being a widow means she will not be invited. Not that she's interested in attending.

As the women prattle on, Palisha's thoughts drift from her father to Mick and their time together last night. She can still feel his arms around her as they sat on her couch listening to music and sipping wine. How she wanted to kiss him, to give herself to him completely, but she knows once she crosses that line, there's no going back. Their friendship will be forever changed, and it scares her because she knows she'll want more, and that she can never have it. Not and remain in her family, that is. Still, she's fantasized from time to time recently what it would be like if she were to give everything up, but the thing that always brings her back to reality is her sons. Even though they're away in England with their wives at university and she doesn't see them much, she knows eventually they'll be back and she can't imagine not being near them or the grandchildren that will eventually come.

There's no happy ending here for her. The deck, as Mick has said more than once, is stacked against them. Yet they can't help playing this game of solitaire they can never win. At best, they can only steal moments, dreaming of what could have been had they come from different worlds, and if they dare, entangle their bodies that scream for each other. Right now, she wishes she could wrap herself around him and hold on with all her might.

"Palisha, Palisha," her mother says. "Say good-bye to your Aunt Usha and Gita."

Palisha starts and looks up. "Oh, sorry. I guess I was daydreaming." She gets up, gives her aunt a perfunctory embrace, and wishes Gita a good rest-of-the-afternoon, then watches the women pad out of the room. She sits back down, folds her legs under her, and stares out the large picture window, glad to be out from under their watchful eyes. Now it's only her and her mother, and her thoughts go back to her father's tremor. Her mother doesn't like talking about unpleasant things, and she's sure she'll make some excuse to avoid Palisha's questions. But she needs to know, so when her mother walks back into the room, she looks up and says, "Dad's tremor is getting worse. Have you noticed?"

Her mother sits beside her and is quiet a moment, then says, "Yes, it's being taken care of, though. Have you heard from Milan and Nugah lately? How are they doing with their studies?"

"My boys are doing fine." Palisha holds her mother in her gaze, determined not to let her wiggle out of telling her what she wants to know. "What do you mean, 'it's being taken care of'?"

"Just what I said," answers her mother.

"So, he's seeing a doctor?"

Her mother looks out the window and Palisha sees her jaw tremble. Finally, she says, "Yes."

"And, what does the doctor say?"

Her mother turns back to her. "I don't know. You know your father. He keeps things to himself."

"But you suspect something, right?"

"Yes." Her mother sighs, staring down at her hands folded in her lap. "Your grandfather, you probably don't remember him very well. You were little when he died, but he had the same problem. Back then we called it 'the shakes.' I think today it's called—"

"Parkinson's," Palisha says, and the gaze in her mother's eyes tunnels inward. Palisha doesn't know a lot about the disease, but she knows it gets worse, and knowing her father, it will embarrass him and likely mean his time as Commissioner will be coming to an end. This will crush him. He loves his job and he's devoted his life to it. "Is he taking anything for it?"

"I think so, but again—"

"Yes, he doesn't talk about it." Palisha reaches over and puts her hand over her mother's hands. "We'll say no more about it."

Her mother nods, and for the first time in as long as Palisha can remember, her mother cries. "Oh, Āmā, come here," she says, and holds her mother tight against her. It's been a long time since she felt her mother's arms around her and despite the reason for it, she can't help relishing the rare moment. At last, she says, "I love you, Āmā."

Her mother pulls back, wiping her eyes. "I love you too, Polly. We should start dinner for your father and brother."

"Oh, Ramesh is coming?"

"Yes. He has some business with your father, I don't know what it is."

"What about Renu?" Palisha says, hoping to see her sister-in-law. She hasn't had a chance to see her since her niece, Aadarasha, returned home from a year away in Paris studying art history. Aadarasha is the rebel of the family who's taken up the modern, progressive ways, pushing for women's rights in the male-dominated world of Nepal. And she also holds a sweet spot in her grandfather's heart. Palisha has no doubt Aadarasha was responsible for softening her father's intransigence toward her defying his insistence she live the life of a secluded widow.

Her mother shakes her head. "No, she's off to her mother's for a few days to help with her ailing father."

"Oh, what's wrong with Hari?"

"He's been having heart trouble, I hear," her mother says, getting up. She puts her hand out to Palisha. "Come, let's make dinner for your father and brother."

Palisha pulls into the lot outside her apartment building. It's late, and the bright full moon is shining down from a star-spattered sky. She's exhausted. Visiting her parents is like being under a microscope, where everything she does is watched with a judging eye. But today at least was tolerable, and if she were honest, it was a giant step forward with her mother. She gets out of her car and hurries into the building. She doesn't want to be caught out in her white sari; it would bring curious and condemning glances from some of the tenants who, she's sure, observe the traditional ways.

Once inside her apartment, she takes a deep breath and leans back against the door, thinking about her mother. She tries to imagine what she's going through. She's been married to a man who has been larger than life in their family for over forty years, has depended on him for everything she has and loves. What will happen when that all goes away? While it's true that her father could live a good many years with the disease, there's no guarantee, and then what? Her mother will be a widow, and Palisha knows all too well what that means. Who will take her in and care for her? Ramesh? Maybe, maybe not, meaning it will be up to Palisha: a widow looking after another widow.

She forces the thought away and goes to her room to change out of the widow's robe into something... something what? More alive? It's late, but she needs to feel pretty again. She paws through her closet and pulls her red sari with silver embroidery out and puts it on, then goes to her dresser and digs out her jewelry and the necklace Mick gave her for her birthday. It's become a touchstone for her, keeping her glued to the present. She adds a pair of gold hoop earrings, then walks out into the empty room. In her mind's eye, she can see Mick sitting on the couch looking back at her, and in her ears she hears his voice complimenting her eyes, her face, her smile and most of all, her heart.

She lights a pair of candles and an incense stick and slides a CD into the stereo. It's a CD that Mick favors, a blind Italian tenor named Andrea Bocelli. Picking up the remote, she navigates to "The Prayer" and hits play. The room fills with the sounds of violins followed by the man's rich, tender voice, and she sways as the notes dance around her. She wishes Mick were with her right now, wishes they were dancing to this beautiful aria, but he's back in Pokhara, and it's late.

By the time the song is over, her face is damp with tears for all that can never be between them. She hits replay and the song repeats, and she closes her eyes as the words "let this be our prayer" pierce her heart. Suddenly, she can take it no more and she reaches for her phone. She scrolls to his number, hesitates, then hits send and waits, breathless, until he picks up. His voice is like air rushing into her lungs and she gasps, breathing in its life-sustaining energy.

"Hi Mick," she says in Nepali.

"Polly!" His voice rises on the other end. "What a nice surprise. How did things go today? You went to see your parents, right?"

"Yes, it went well. How was your day?"

"It was good, too. I've been thinking of you all day."

"Really?" she says. She wants to ask him if he's missed her, but she doesn't want to look needy.

"Yes, of course," he says, then pauses a second.

She nibbles a fingernail, wondering if she's over-stepped. Finally, he says, "Is everything okay?"

"Oh, yes. I was just thinking of you and wanted to say hi."

Another pause. "Uh-huh. Talk to me. What's wrong?"

She chews her lip and laughs nervously. "Nothing!"

"Polly, this is me, Mick, remember? I know you well enough by now. There's something on your mind. What is it?"

Her eyes blur. "I just miss you and wish you were here. It's been a long day, and I just found out my father might have Parkinson's. I'm sorry, I shouldn't have called and bothered you."

"Hey, stop. You're not bothering me at all. In fact, I can't think of anything I'd rather be doing right now than talking with my best friend. I wish I were there to hold you, God knows I could use your arms around me."

Palisha wipes her eyes. "When do you think you'll be back in Kathmandu?"

"I was planning on next Friday, but you know what? I think Tuesday is looking better. Can you get some time off this week?"

"Probably. What do you have in mind?"

"I was thinking maybe a trip up to the mountains. Have you ever been to Lukla? It's pretty up there this time of year with the trees coming into bloom. We could get a room at a teahouse, hike a trail or two."

Palisha's heart jumps at the thought and she bursts into a big smile. A couple days all by themselves with no prying eyes to report back any impropriety. And then it sinks in: a room for the two of them...overnight. Up until now, it had just been holding each other and dancing around and a couple of stolen kisses. Is she ready to go beyond that? But how can she say no to this man she adores?

"I'd love it."

"Great! I'll make the arrangements. Remember, we're hiking, so you don't need to do dressy. Pack appropriately, sweetheart."

He called me sweetheart! "Of course. I'm so excited. I can't wait."

"Me either. Now, I need to get online and get us a flight. Sleep well, and I'll see you Tuesday, sometime in the afternoon."

He hangs up and her heart is singing.

8

MARCH 24, 2015 —
KATHMANDU AND LUKLA

*M*ick pulls up in front of Palisha's apartment building at 6:13 a.m. and parks. He's booked them a flight to Lukla at nine this morning, and he's running a bit late. He hopes Palisha is all set to go. The domestic airport isn't known for expediency of meeting flight schedules. He gets out of his rental car and is about to head for the front door when it opens and she comes out, dragging a small carry-on piece of luggage. He should've mentioned she'd need a daypack, but they can purchase one in the village and transfer everything they need for their hikes.

What holds his attention most, though, is the pastel-blue tapālan and embroidered blue jeans she's wearing. The embroidered lapels of her top are parted, revealing a hint of cleavage, and it fits her like glove, bringing out the color of her soft tan complexion. She's left her silky dark brown hair loose so it's flowing over her shoulders. There's a big smile on her face as she comes to the car.

"Namaste!" she says, furtively panning her gaze over the parking lot. He knows she's looking to see if anyone's out and milling around. He hates that they have to conceal their relationship for appearances, but that's the price they have to pay and will keep paying if this relationship continues to grow. But she's happy to see him, and that's all that matters right now, so he refrains from the powerful urge to hug her and opens the tiny trunk of the compact car. There's no room in the back seat for her things because he's loaded it with their sleeping bags and all the essentials they'll need for the next four days.

"Are you ready for a great time?" he asks in Nepali.

"I can't wait. I've never flown before."

"No? It's an experience, especially flying into Lukla. Okay, let's get going. We don't want to miss our flight."

She goes around and opens her door, and when she gets in, she peers back at the sleeping bags. When she turns a diffident gaze on him, he knows she understands they won't be sleeping together, at least not in the way he would like or maybe the way she imagined. What she doesn't know is that the bags can be zipped together, but he's not going to bring that up.

He pulls out of the lot, and they fall into comfortable conversation about where they're going. He tells her what his hiking plans are for them during the next couple days. "My idea is, hike to Namche, and if there's time and the weather agrees, walk the rim trail out of the village and catch a glimpse of Everest."

That brings a smile to her face as he pulls into the airport loop road. The lot is filling up as cars arrive for early morning flights. He's lucky this morning and they find a spot right near the front of the domestic terminal. He parks and grabs a luggage cart out front and loads their gear up. When they get inside, he checks them in. Their flight is running a little behind. Palisha is wide-eyed, looking around, and he's basking in her wonderment. He can hardly wait to see her expression when the mountains are right in front of her.

"Let's get a cup of tea," he says.

"Okay," she answers, and suddenly her hand is sliding into his. It's a bold move, even here where nobody knows them, and a combination of euphoria tempered with trepidation runs through him as they make their way through the waiting travelers to the terminal teashop.

I have to be careful with her heart. She doesn't deserve to be hurt. Did I make a mistake taking her away like this? But we're here, and she's so happy. He chews his lip. *She deserves this. Don't take away the joy she's feeling right now. Let it be!*

As they wait in line to order their drinks, he turns his gaze on her and holds it there. He can't stop looking at this woman who's making his heart race. "Would you like something to eat?" he says. What he wants to say is: "You make me so happy. I wish...." But he slams the brakes on this musing, knowing it could never happen. It's too heavy, and today is supposed be for her.

She looks up at him, and the look in her eyes is searching, like that of a shy bride on her wedding day. "I don't know. Are you getting something?"

He wags a playful finger, knowing her answer depends on his. "I asked you first," he says, trying to curb her from being so deferential to his wants and needs.

"Okay, maybe a cookie—one of the chocolate ones?"

The people in front of them move off and they step up to the counter and give the clerk their orders. While they wait, he points to the panel of full-height windows at the back of the building that look out over the runways. At present, there's a large jet taxing along one of them, getting ready to take off. Palisha watches as it pirouettes around and comes to a stop, then glances back at him. He knows she wants to get a better look, so he nods to a line of chairs by the windows. "Go, I'll bring our stuff over."

An hour later, they're sitting in a nineteen-seat Cessna waiting to take off. Palisha's gaze is fixed on her window, looking out over the airfield. She's like a child on Christmas morning; every new sight is a feast for her insatiable curiosity. He's having the time of his life watching her.

The pilot calls back in English and tells the attendant sitting behind them to prepare for takeoff. The engines rev, and the noise from the props drowns the conversations around them. Palisha's eyes grow large as the plane hurls down the runway and lifts off. It's easy to see she's exhilarated with this new experience, and even though he's flown hundreds of times over the last twenty-five years, her reactions are making it feel brand new.

The plane banks north and the mountains come into view over the clouds. He reaches across the aisle, taps her arm, and points to a distant summit peeping over the Lhotse ridge.

"Everest," he says. "Maybe we'll get a better look when we get to Namche."

She bends her head closer to the window, then turns back to him. "It looks different than the pictures I've seen."

"Well, we're far away," he says, and sits back for the fifty-minute flight to the mountain village. As he sits, doubts about his suggesting this trip creep back into him. *But she also agreed to it*, he reminds himself. And they're both adults, well into their forties. Certainly, she's able to make up her own mind about what she wants and what she doesn't. But he still feels like he's circling round and round between what he wants and what's the right thing to do.

~

"Attendant, prepare for landing," the pilot says as the tree-topped ridge below slides by. The plane dips, then drops quickly in altitude and swings north toward the tiny airstrip nesting on the mountainside. Mick watches Palisha, whose face is glued to her window. He wonders if she's thinking: just where is this airport? There's nothing but a variegated green slope. But she doesn't look back until after they land.

"Well, your first flight—what do you think?" he says.

There's a huge smile on her face as the plane rushes down the five-hundred-meter runway toward the terminal. "I loved it."

Her excitement is contagious and it squashes the doubt he's been wrestling with the last two hours. "Great, then you'll love the take-off from here," he says, as the plane pulls onto the apron outside the terminal. "Okay, collect your pack and when the attendant opens the door, move quickly and head for the gate outside."

Twenty minutes later they're walking down the lane through the village. Palisha is stopping at almost every shop to peruse the clothing and jewelry. She's enamored with the village and the mountains. As he looks on, he's wondering how Lotti will receive Palisha. He's known the old woman who runs the Juniper Hotel for almost twenty years, and she's everyone's mom. He calls for Palisha and they head down the alley between the buildings to the tiny courtyard before the hotel. As usual, the courtyard is cluttered. Stacked firewood is piled up against the wall beside the door and pots of flowers are scattered on the stone pavers. They drop their packs outside and he opens the door. Down the hall, he hears the murmur of guests talking in English, Nepali, Chinese, and another language he's not sure of.

The sound of dishes clacking is coming from behind the door beside him. He pushes it open to see the tiny Tibetan matriarch, whose back is turned to him. She's stacking plates. "Hey Lotti, what's good for lunch?" he says in English.

The woman wheels around. "Mick! What you doing back here so soon?"

"No one told you?"

"No, no one tell me anything," she says, then marches up to him and looks him over. "You losing weight."

Mick chuckles, glances back at Palisha. "Oh, I don't think so. If anything I've put on a few." He smiles, drawing a breath. *Well, here goes nothing.* "Hey, I'd like you to meet my good friend, Palisha Kc. Palisha, this is Lotti. She runs the Juniper here, among other things," he says, giving Lotti a wink.

Anyone who knows the old Sherpa woman knows she has high standards for those she loves and isn't afraid to hold them to it.

"Oh," the old matriarch says and steps aside, taking a good look at his companion. At last, Lotti glances back at him, then bowing to Palisha, says, "Hi and welcome to Juniper. This first time to mountains?"

"Yes, and namaste, Lotti," Palisha says in English, then dips her head and presses her palms together. "So very good to meet you."

They all stand there a moment in awkward silence and Mick can see the old matriarch adding things up in her head. Finally, he nods to the stacked dishes on the table. "So, are we too late for lunch?"

"Oh, no," Lotti says. "What you want?"

He turns to Palisha, who shrugs. *Okay.* "How about a Thermos of butter tea, a platter of momos, and a couple servings of your famous Dal Bhat?"

"No problem," Lotti says, then gestures toward the kitchen door. "You go check in and get seat. I bring lunch out when done."

After they eat, Mick leads Palisha into the village to find a daypack, hiking poles, and a CamelBak. But what starts out as a quick errand soon turns into a foray into the roadside shops to peruse the assortment of handcrafted jewelry (which she's helpless to ignore) and other items such as colorful Tibetan scarves, gold thread hats, fur-lined boots, and festive native dresses. By the time they're done, it's mid-afternoon and he's shopped out.

"What do say we grab a mug of tea?" he says in English, pointing to a small wood-framed café with a porch jutting into the lane.

"Sure," she says.

He takes the bag with her latest jewelry purchase, slips it into her new daypack, and starts off with her beside him. As they walk under streaming prayer flags, he points out the mountain ahead, peaking over a series of gable roofs. "That's Kusum Kangguru."

"Did you climb it?"

"No, a friend of mine did. He's back in the States now, I think, or maybe Canada, I'm not sure. Are you having fun?"

"Oh, yes." She taps him on the arm, and when he turns to her, he finds himself in her wistful gaze. "Thank you."

"For what?"

"For this," she says, sweeping her hand toward the mountains.

"You're welcome," he says.

She reaches down and takes his hand. "You are the best friend I ever had."

He smiles as the words sink into him. Of all the

things she's said to him since he's known her, this simple statement means more than all his possessions, and he's quite certain he'd give them all up for her if she asked him to. He squeezes her hand, humbled by her confession. He wants the world to stop, for them to exist in this moment forever. At last, he says, "And I'll always be your friend, no matter what. Come on, let's get our tea."

They walk to the little café and find a seat at a table on the porch. After they order from a little Sherpa man, they look out on the lane, watching the tourists mill about the shops. Down the road, a man is leading a team of donkeys toward the Sagarmatha gate that goes to the trail into the park. Birds are wheeling overhead in the cool breeze buffeting the village.

Palisha says, "What got you interested in climbing?"

It's a question he's heard before, and he's always had a stock answer ready to reply. But looking back at her, that answer clangs in his head. It's trite and glossy, like an advertisement in a magazine someone passes over looking for a story to read. The truth is, he didn't come here to climb, but had ended up here by running aimlessly away from a world that had taken Vivian from him. What he didn't expect was the powerful draw of the mountains on his wounded heart.

"Mick, did you hear me?" Palisha asks. "You do

not have to answer if you do not want to."

He starts and comes to himself. "Oh, sorry. No, it's okay," he says. "It wasn't so much what got me interested, but instead the reason I was here to begin with. I was engaged years ago when I lived in Germany, and she died in a car accident. I tried to move on afterward, but I couldn't. Everything where I lived reminded me of her, and I had to get out, so I ran, I guess, until I ended up here. It was just a stop on the way to where I don't know, until I saw the mountains. They captivated me. I was never a very religious man but I believed in God, and in our bible, it says He lives in the mountains. I had questions, so I went up to find answers."

"And did you find the answers you were looking for?"

"No. But I did find peace, and a lot of friends... and you."

After they get back to the Juniper, Mick rolls their sleeping bags out on the opposing twin beds. Behind him Palisha is putting her purchases away. As he rolls the bags, he senses her looking on. They're alone in a bedroom a hundred miles away from her life back in Kathmandu, and he's quite sure the implications aren't lost on her. He tosses her pillow on top of her bag and turns back, almost bumping into her. For a moment they stand face to face, and it's hard to breathe. She's wearing an inviting smile and her pixie nose is flared just a little, and he knows that if he were to lean in for a kiss, she would accept it and return it. Finally, he says, "I think we're all set. Let's go down for dinner."

"Yes, I am starved. Shopping is hard work."

"More than you know," he says, then pats her cheek and opens the door.

It's not too busy in the dining room when they enter, maybe a dozen or so guests sitting at the tables lining the perimeter of the room. He points to one in the far corner next to a window that looks out over the mist-laden mount to the south. A beam of golden sunlight is spraying the treetops climbing up through the haze clinging to the slope.

They take their seats and peruse the menu. The Juniper's simple fare is geared toward the foreign travelers coming to the mountains: flatbread cheese pizza, spiced French fries, vegetable and meat momos, noodles with tomato sauce, and the like. He asks her if she wants to order something else and she tells him whatever he wants.

He hides a frown. "You know, it's not always what I want."

"I know," she says, looking up, and there's a mischievous expression on her face. "And I am. You are wanting me to make my own choice right now, and I have decided I do not want to."

Mick throws his head back in laughter. "That's pretty good."

She grins and looks back at the menu. "So, are we ordering off this menu or are you going to ask for something else?"

"We'll go off the menu."

"Good." She points to the pizza. "I will have that...and some French fries," she says, setting the menu aside, then looks around the room. "Is there a bathroom down here?"

"Yes, down the hall."

She gets up as the waiter comes to their table, leaving him to order for her. Once he's alone, he looks out the window and his thoughts drift back to the moment between them in their room. All he can think of is what might happen later tonight once the lights are out and it's just the two of them behind closed doors, because he isn't sure he can resist her if it happens again.

"So your friend, how come you not tell me about her before?"

He starts and looks back to see Lotti standing at the end of the table. "Oh, Lotti. I didn't hear you come up. I guess it just slipped my mind."

"Hmm...I think you keep a secret," she says, and she gives him one of her trademark looks, the ones that bore into him, letting him know she's seeing through the bullshit. "I think she more than just a friend."

"No, just a friend," he says, and smiles. But he's feeling like a mouse under the intent gaze of house cat.

The gaze narrows on him. "Then how come you only have one room?"

"I thought it would be easier."

"For who, me or you?" Again, the look comes back and he knows he's trapped. "Surely you can afford two rooms."

He's toast, and he knows it, but he can't let her know it. He returns his best professorial gaze at the old Sherpa mom. "Lotti."

"Okay, I say no more. None of my business," she says as Palisha comes back in and heads their way. Then she leans in close and whispers in Lhasa, "Very nice girl, very pretty. You did good."

Palisha stabs her pole into the soft earth and looks up at a sky so blue it blinds her. The last two days have been wondrous. Never has she felt so alive. She didn't know air could taste so good or that the world was so beautiful. Sure, she's seen pictures, but being here in this land of mountains with towering trees and sparkling rivers is totally different. It's like stepping out of a dream. She feels like a bird, let out of a cage after having been sequestered so long, either in her father's mansion or in the chaos of Kathmandu. She turns back to Mick, who's standing behind her.

Today they're going to Namche, which is on a mount overlooking the Dudh Koshi River they've been following the last half hour. She takes a drink from her CamelBak and looks ahead to a pair of high gossamer bridges stretching above the river from one side of a towering hill to another that rises even higher. Pulling her phone out, she takes a picture.

Mick points to them and says, "Hillary Bridges. We'll be crossing the higher one. The lower one is abandoned."

She feels her eyes widen and a wave of unease rushes through her. "Truly?" she asks.

"You'll be okay," he says. "They're very safe." His tone is matter-of-fact, as if it's nothing more than walking the trail they're on.

Says the mountain climber. She pastes a smile on her face. She doesn't want him to see how afraid she is. But she trusts him, so she plods ahead on the rising rock path, trying to ignore the oncoming peril over the deep river gorge. Twenty minutes later, she's standing on a concrete pad, looking over the river valley far below. But what has her attention is the chain link and metal slatted bridge swaying in the breeze before her.

"Here, let me take your picture," Mick says. "Give me your phone and go stand over there by the post."

She considers his suggestion as she battles a war of anxiety against the fierce independence she's waged over the last ten years to step out of her comfort zones. *Stop being a 'fraidy cat. You can do this!* She gives him her phone, steels herself, and goes over to pose for him. "How is this?" she says, tilting her head playfully as she leans back against the thick masonry post.

"That's great." He takes a couple more pictures and hands her back her phone. "Now, walking across is like walking on a bed. Springy! So you time your steps like this," he says, mimicking a bounce. "You'll get the hang of it quick, you'll see."

We'll see about that. "Okay, I am ready." She blows out a breath and steps onto the bridge. It feels solid under her feet for a while, then just like Mick said, she feels the give and bounce as she walks. And when Mick comes behind her, it bounces more, but she's getting used to it and by the time she's across, she's got the rhythm down pretty well.

"See, that wasn't so hard," he says, joining her. He points to the rocky trail ahead that runs under the trees on the steep face of the mount, and grins. "Now, the real work starts."

But as far as she's concerned, the worst is behind her and she starts off fearless and energized. It's like a game to her, planning each step, each placement of her poles in the ground as she picks her course up the mountain. She's in her own world and by the time she comes to the last switchback, the game has drifted into a spiritual journey, a healing balm, and she begins to understand what Mick tried to convey to her back in Lukla on the porch of the little café. She knows she'll never be the same, and she has him to thank for it. He's opened her eyes, and she decides that later on, she'll open his, even though she knows what it could mean. It scares her to think about it, but it scares her more never to know what it would feel like to sleep in his arms and feel the warmth of his body pressed to hers. She smiles, but it's a grim smile, permeated with the sadness of what will never be between them. But she'll know him at least once.

"Come on, hurry up," she says in Nepali, looking down on him from the top of the switchback. There's a flat level space nearby with a rubble wall and a small building off to the side. A few tourists are milling about.

"I'm coming, speedy," he says, hopping over a large stone and stepping up on a bulging tree root. His face is glistening with sweat, and she sees him run his arm over his brow, wiping it away. A minute later he's beside her, stabbing his pole in the ground and sucking water from his CamelBak. He blows out a breath. "You're a regular cat, coming up this mountain."

She reaches in her pocket and pulls out a tissue, wipes his face. "Did I go too fast for you?"

"No, not at all. I have to hit the head over there. I'll be right back."

She watches him plod over to the little building, knowing he wasn't truthful, and admonishes herself. This is supposed to be a shared experience, not a race. When he comes back, they sit on the wall and munch trail mix. Mick tells her the rest of the way isn't bad: no switchbacks, a steady, easy slope. They'll be in Namche in an hour or so. They'll get to their teahouse, unpack, and relax until dinner. Then maybe some more shopping and if she's interested, maybe they'll stop in the small theatre there and see the movie *Into Thin Air*, which plays every evening. Later, if they want, they can walk up to the fields above the village and look at the stars, which are spectacular, or they can do something else.

She's already decided what that something else is, but she'll make time to see the stars as well.

They arrive in the mountain settlement a little after 3:30 p.m. The village is busy. Early-bird tourists are steadily arriving ahead of the yearly pilgrimage of the masses heading for Everest Base Camp. She stands outside on the stone terrace as Mick gets them checked in. The sprawling masonry teahouse with large overhanging eaves is situated on the west side, midway up the terraced landscape on the mount

Mick calls the Namche Hill. She looks over the red, blue, yellow, and green roofs to the river valley far below, contemplating her decision, then turns and goes inside.

"All set," Mick says, holding the key up.

They walk down a short hallway, then out the back door and up a short wooden stairway set against the wall of the two-story split-level building. At the top, they step onto an adjoining rooftop. The floor below it runs back into the grassy hill, its masonry walls half-buried in the earth. Palisha follows Mick across the roof to their room, which looks west out over the roof. Inside, the room is spacious and there's even an attached bathroom with a western shower and toilet. She slips out of her pack and sits on one of the twin beds, watching him unpack their sleeping bags, and wonders if the beds could be pushed together. They've been sleeping in separate beds up to now, so when she stays put when he brings her bag over so he can spread it out, he freezes. He fixes her with a startled gaze that says, "Are you sure?"

She stares back, holding her breath, and nods. "If you want."

He's quiet a moment, then swallows, and says, "Yes, very much."

"Then you shall have me, but not now." She gets up and puts her hand to his chest, feels his beating heart. "I want to see the stars with you later on, and the movie you told me about."

"Of course. If you change your mind—"

"I will not. I do not know if it is wrong, or what it will mean for us, but I know how I feel, and it is been too long. If you change your mind, I understand, too."

"Let's just play it one minute at a time, then," Mick says.

"Yes, let us," she says, and gets up on her tiptoes and brushes his cheek with a kiss. "I need to get changed."

"I'll finish up here. You want to go for a walk, see what's out there?"

"Sure." She bends down and digs a fresh top and bra from her pack, along with a brush, deodorant, and a hair tie. "I will be right back." As she shuts the bathroom door, she hears him moving furniture. This is really going to happen: them...together...tonight! It's been so long since she's made love, she's almost forgotten what it feels like, but more than that, she doesn't want to disappoint him. She wants to be pretty for him, wants it to be perfect. Maybe she can find something more becoming than the tops she bought in Lukla, something frilly and alluring, yet not too suggestive.

She strips out of her top and bra, looks herself over. Her body is no longer taut and there are tiny rolls here and there she hasn't noticed before, not to mention a little sag in her breasts. Maybe he won't notice. It'll be dark, after all. She sighs, puts her fresh bra and shirt on, brushes her hair and ties it back.

When she opens the door, the twin beds are pushed together under a thick comforter. Mick looks up from where he sits at the end of the bed. He's zipping their sleeping bags together.

They exchange knowing glances. "You ready?" he asks.

"I think so. That looks nice."

"I think it'll work," he says. He pulls the sleeping bag zipper all the way up, stands, and a minute later they're heading into town to peruse the shops. As she walks along the crowded lanes with him, American rock and country music pours out along with Eastern and Nepali. Children run around chasing chickens or playing hide and seek in the alleyways.

She steps into a shop bearing colorful tapālans and when he isn't looking, she buys a floral printed top with a daring neckline she plans on wearing under the stars later that night. A small vial of patchouli follows. By the time she's gotten everything she wants, it's dinnertime, so they head back. When they get there, she tells him to go in and get a table, then makes an excuse to go to their room.

Fifteen minutes later, she's back wearing her new top and lightly scented with the oil. She's also let her hair down. When Mick sees her walking toward their table, he smiles. "Wow, when did you get that new top?"

"Oh, a little while ago. You like it?"

"Of course I do," he says, getting up. He comes

around and pulls a chair out for her. He's selected a table on the terrace where she stood earlier looking out over the village. "I thought maybe we'd eat out here and enjoy the sunset."

"You always know what I want," she says.

"I don't know about that. You want tea?"

"Yes, thank you." She watches him pour and sees him breathe in deep. *Good, he likes.* "So, after dinner we are going to see the movie you were telling me about?"

"If you want, or we could just skip it and go wait for the stars."

She considers his answer, though she's already made up her mind. "Let us go see the stars."

"Okay, that's what we'll do," he says as the waiter comes to the table.

Two hours later, she's strolling hand-in-hand with Mick up the main street toward the top of the village. It's getting near dusk, and the sun behind them is a bright orange ball sinking into the dark hills beyond. Already, the stars are pricking the darkening sky and the quarter moon is directly above and riding high.

Mick has been quiet for the last fifteen minutes and she can see he's thinking about something, most likely about what's going to happen tonight. To be honest, so has she. She wonders if she made a mistake, if she misread him, and whether he's just being kind so as not to embarrass her. After all, she's never approached a man like this before. Never even considered it.

"You are quiet. Are you okay?"

"Oh, yes. I'm just tired."

"We do not need to do this. We can go back."

"Nonsense. I'll be okay."

She looks up as they come to the end of the lane. "The stars are coming out."

"Yes they are," he says beside her. "I think we're gonna have quite a show tonight."

"I can not wait." She looks around at the tall grasses shivering in the cool zephyrs buffeting the hill. "So, where do we sit?"

"Anywhere you want. Pick a spot."

She looks around and when she sees a boulder some ways down the path, she says, "How about over there on that rock?"

"Lead on," he says, and when they get to it, he helps her up and sits beside her. "Comfortable?" She nods and leans into him, and his arm wraps around her. "When I was a kid, my father would take me and my brother out at night and show us the stars and planets. I knew all of them in our part of the world. Not so much here, but that one over there is Mars and the one over there is Venus."

"What about that one over there?"

"Hmm...Ursa Major, I think, but don't hold me to it."

"Do you miss home...in Germany?"

"Not really. I think of it once in a while, more often than before."

"You said once you were thinking of going back."

She feels him shrug beside her. "Yeah, it crossed my mind."

"What changed?"

He turns to her and searches her with his dark eyes that see through the walls she's erected over the years. When he looks at her like this, she's powerless. "You. You changed it. I can't imagine being halfway around the world away from you." He turns away, then turns back. "I know what we said back in our room, but I don't want that. I don't want to wake up tomorrow morning regretting it. I just want to hold you close, feel you next to me. Is that wrong? Do you hate me?"

"No, I could never hate you." What she wants to say is, *I love you*, but she can't, not now, maybe someday when it won't matter what anyone thinks. She sinks into the cocoon of his arms. For too long she's been alone, fighting to create a new life, to find her footing between the traditional and the ever-changing progressive worlds she straddles. But the reality is she hasn't been living at all, but instead existing in a trap of her own making. She closes her eyes as tears gather, knowing the only escape is to gnaw off a part of her, but doing it will leave her forever scarred. Yet she can't help herself for wanting more, to always be near him. It's like she's a proverbial moth whose fragile wings flutter around Mick's bright light, wanting to touch and hold his luminescence that feeds her starving spirit.

He's quiet a moment. "Are you okay?"

"Yes...no. You deserve better than this."

"Better than what?"

She bites her lip, knowing what she has to say, but she doesn't want to say it because she's afraid of what he'll say back. "This. Us! Sneaking off to be with each other. This is not a life, not for you."

"Why don't you let me decide what's right for me?"

Her heart pounds, and she wants to stop, to accept his answer and extricate herself from the terrifying ledge she's suddenly led them to. "You say that now, but later, maybe not. And I could not bear it."

He reaches down and lifts her trembling chin with his finger. "I'll tell you what I couldn't bear. Not having you in my life. I—"

She reaches up and puts a finger to his lips. She knows what he's about to say, because she feels the same way, and she can't bear to hear the word that will crush her. "No, do not say it, please."

He falls silent, until at last he says, "So, what do you want to do?"

"I do not know. But I need you in my life."

9

APRIL 3, 2015 — KATHMANDU

*L*incoln downshifts and turns left onto the arterial leading into the heart of the city. He's delivering a load of cabinets and furniture to a new office building in Bishal Bazar. Even after two years of driving on the opposite side of the road, he still has a hard time getting used to it. Beside him is Sameer, who's riding shotgun and smoking a cigarette. Lincoln rolls his window down to air out the aging, stuffy cab only to get slammed with a choking cloud of diesel exhaust.

He scrunches his nose and turns to Sameer, who's looking at the passing buildings. "Hey, mind put that out? I congest to death in here," he says in Nepali.

Sameer looks back and smiles. "Oh, sorry," he says and flicks the butt on the floor. As he mashes it with his foot, he points ahead to an upcoming traffic circle. "Take the first left, it's shorter and less traffic."

Lincoln nods, downshifts—grinding gears—and steers the clunky box truck over to the far left lane of the busy arterial as motorbikes buzz by. "So, how Gopal father? You go see, talk him yet?"

"Ahh, yes. He's doing okay, but he's very weak and has lost so much weight. It's such a shame for his family. They're such good people."

"You know long time?"

Sameer nods. "Yes, since we were kids. Sudip and I went to school together. I don't see him much since he retired. He used to work for Tripureshwor Transportation, too, before you came. It doesn't seem possible he'll be gone. I'll miss him."

Lincoln looks into his driver-side rearview mirror and merges into traffic, darting across the large circular intersection. It's go first and ask permission later at these circles, otherwise you end up trapped interminably in the unrelenting onslaught. Sameer sticks his arm out of his window, casually waving off a car that's crowding in on them. There's a loud beep, followed by a couple more that fade away as Lincoln pushes the accelerator down.

Sameer looks over at him and shrugs with the universal "too-bad-for-you-mister-car-driver" look on his thin, smiling face. He's quiet a minute as they chug toward a depressed section of town, then says, "You want to stop and get something to eat?"

"What, no eat this morning?" Lincoln says.

"I was running late," says Sameer.

Lincoln's hungry himself despite almost being gassed to death back on the arterial. "Sure. Why not? You know place?"

"Yes, not too far ahead on the right."

Lincoln chuckles, suddenly understanding why Sameer wanted to take this supposed shortcut. He motors ahead until Sameer gestures him to pull over and park next a long one-story brick building with a timber-framed porch. The Nepali cracks his door, checks for oncoming traffic, then gets out and waits for Lincoln to follow him.

Inside, the store is lined with shelves displaying canned goods, crackers, candy, and the like. Down one of the long aisles, Lincoln sees a man and a young girl perusing a display of chips and cookies. When the man looks his way, Lincoln turns and joins Sameer, who's inspecting breakfast sandwiches on the front counter. The selection is minimal: egg and cheese biscuit or egg, cheese, and mystery meat biscuit. Lincoln chooses the egg and cheese, Sameer the latter and a to-go black tea.

As they wait for the clerk to ring them up, the man and the girl come up behind them. Lincoln steps to the side to make room for them and when they move up, he gets a closer look at the two of them. The man is a tall Nepali with deep-set suspicious eyes that barely stray from the girl, and he has a protective hand riding on her back. He's at least in his forties, and he's dressed in a cream-colored cashmere sweater. A Rolex watch circles his caramel-colored wrist and a large gold ring with a sapphire stone sits on his middle finger. But what's bothering Lincoln is the all-too-familiar way he's acting toward the young girl by his side, as if he's a jealous boyfriend.

Lincoln averts his gaze, but not enough so that he can't see the girl, who's maybe thirteen or fourteen. Up close, he realizes how inappropriately she's dressed. The shift she's wearing is short and skimpy, with lots of leg showing. What's more, her face is made up and she's wearing high-heeled shoes. He turns and offers her a friendly smile. Dark brown eyes look back dully as she pulls a lock of long black hair over her narrow shoulders, returning a Mona Lisa smile that reminds him of a wounded, frightened animal. Lincoln wants to ask her if she's okay, is everything all right, but before he can open his mouth the clerk asks him if that's all he wants. Lincoln looks back and hands the clerk his money, then reluctantly follows Sameer out to their truck.

As he shuts the door, he turns to Sameer. "You see girl in there?"

Sameer, who's unwrapping his biscuit sandwich, glances at him. "What girl?"

"Girl who stand beside me. She look scared, and dress is daring."

Sameer holds him in his gaze a moment. "Oh, you mean the prostitute."

"Prostitute!" Lincoln can't believe his ears. "What mean? She just child!"

"I know. It's very sad," Sameer says, and bites into his sandwich. The way he says it, as if it's an accepted fact that no one can do anything about, dumbfounds Lincoln. As Sameer chews, he adds, "A lot of girls who have no family turn to it. There's no place else to go. The orphanages won't take her even if she could escape. And even if she could, she probably wouldn't at this point. I see what you're feeling, Linji, but that's how it is. It's how they survive, same as everywhere, no?"

Lincoln can't wrap his mind around that, and suddenly he thinks of Sunita. The thought of Binod's precious beautiful child ever being drawn into *that* girl's world is so disturbing it leaves him speechless, as if he's just been punched in the stomach. He stares out the window, wanting to run back into the store and rip that girl away from that piece of shit hovering over her, but he knows Sameer's probably right. Even if he were to get the girl away from the man, she'd more than likely end up right back where she is.

All afternoon at work, the vision of the girl in the store has stuck in Lincoln's head. He can't get the look in her eyes out of his mind, as if it's been burned into his retinas. He pulls his bike into the drive out-side his apartment building and wheels it inside the hall. He's been invited over to Binod's tonight to see the baby. Bishal, he thinks Binod called him.

He walks up to his apartment and changes out of his uniform, takes a quick shower, and gets dressed. He should eat, but he's not hungry. Instead, he grabs the artist's pad and colored pencils he bought for Sunita and wraps them in some gift paper (pink with little blue, yellow, and purple balloons) he picked up a day ago. As he ties the ribbon around the gift, he looks at the card he bought for her. It's plain, no writing on it, with a picture of a red flower he doesn't know the name of. He hopes she'll like it. But what to write in it? He's never been good at sentimental things, and he's never given a birthday card to anyone before—well, not to a young girl on the verge of be-coming a woman, anyway. He sits and opens it up, thinking about what to write, then just scribbles, *HAPPY BIRTHDAY to a talented, beautiful girl* and signs it, *LINK*.

Ten minutes later he's walking across the street, and as he comes to their front door, he realizes he forgot a gift for the baby. He rolls his eyes. There's no time to run out and get something now, so he goes in and climbs the stairs to Binod's apartment. When the door opens and Binod lets him in, Arjun comes run-ning up.

"Link, I drew a picture for you," the boy says, showing him a crayon drawing of a cone-shaped mountain. "It's Ama Dablam."

Lincoln takes it from him and looks it over as Binod stands by. "I see," Lincoln says in Nepali. "Thank you."

Binod says, "He's been waiting all afternoon for you. Okay, Arjun, let Lin-ji get his shoes off." He shoos his son away, then turns back and puts his hand out toward the gift in Lincoln's hand.

"Oh, this for Sunni," Lincoln says, and from the corner of his eye he sees Sunita looking on from the archway. She's wearing a pretty purple sari and her hair is loose around her shoulders. For a second the memory of the girl in the store is superimposed over her. Lincoln blinks the unwanted vision away. "I forget bring gift for infant, Binod. Sorry."

"Oh, don't worry. It's okay," Binod says as Lincoln slips out of his shoes. "Sila's in the bedroom nursing Bishal. She'll be out in a little bit. Can I get you anything? I have chhaang or soda if you like."

"Soda, fine. Thank you."

Binod turns to get their refreshments and when he sees his daughter, he says, "Lin-ji brought you a gift."

Sunita's eyes light up. "For me?"

"Yes, for birthday," Lincoln says. He goes to her and holds it out.

Sunita looks down at it, her gaze fixed on the

bright red bow and the envelope tucked underneath the ribbon, then takes it over to the couch and sits with it on her lap. Lincoln watches her pull the card out and open the envelope with her name written across it in his scrawled script. With deft fingers she pulls the card out and studies the flower on top as if it were the most beautiful thing in the world, then opens it.

"What does it say?" she asks, turning her eyes up at him.

He's forgotten she can't read English, and he laughs at himself. "It say Happy Birthday, to..." He looks for the right words in Nepali, but they escape him. "Umm...capable, handsome girl."

The beaming smile on her face touches his heart as she thanks him. A second later, she looks down to conceal the blush rising on her cheeks. It's quite apparent to Lincoln as he looks on with Arjun beside him that if the card were the only thing he'd given her, it would've been enough. He's also keenly aware she has a crush on him. She doesn't know he thinks of her like a daughter, so he needs to be careful so she doesn't get the wrong impression. He points to the gift. "Open it."

Hesitantly, she unties the bow, sets it with the ribbon beside her as if it was a treasure in itself, then painstakingly unwraps the paper from around the pad and pencils. For a minute, she stares at them, then finally looks up. "I love," she says. "Thank you so much, thank you."

Arjun nestles in closer to get a better look, but she shoos him away. Nobody is going to touch the pad and pencils he's given her, or for that matter, the gift wrapping and the bow and ribbon. She tucks the card into the pad, protecting it from her brother's curious fingers, and takes the gift and wrappings out of the room. Lincoln ruffles Arjun's curly hair as they look after her. "I think she like," Lincoln says.

Arjun shrugs, says, "Maybe for my birthday, you'll get me paper and colored pencils?"

Lincoln smiles down at him. "Sure. Now show me more your drawings." The boy rushes out of the room as his parents return with the baby. Lincoln steps forward to get a look at the child, whose eyes are closed as he lies in the soft powder-blue blanket in Sila's arms. His mother's gaze is fixed on her son, drinking in the yawn spreading across his contented cherubic face.

Finally she looks up at Lincoln. "What do you think?"

There's only one answer to this question. Again, he searches for the word. "He very handsome," Lincoln says, caressing the sandy-brown fuzz on the child's head. From force of habit working as an ER doctor, he sweeps his critical gaze over the baby. The child is by all accounts healthy. "Bishal, his name?"

"Yes," Binod says, handing Lincoln his soda. "I

name him after my father. We're going to a naming ceremony soon at my parents' home in Ichok up north. Maybe you would like to come."

Lincoln is flattered, but he thinks maybe it's better to stay put in Kathmandu. Besides, he has a job he needs to be at. "Oh, thank you," he says, "but no. My job. I hope you understand."

"Oh, okay," says Binod, but Lincoln can see the slight disappointment on his face. He gestures to a chair. "Let's sit. You want something to eat?"

"No, no, it okay," Lincoln says, and takes a seat. To Sila, he says, "Binod tell me Arjun breech. How..." Once more words escape him. "...transport go?"

Sila giggles. "You mean delivery? It went fine."

"Good, good. Binod worry."

"Yes," she answers, and smiles at her husband as she sits on the couch across from him. As if on cue, Arjun runs back into the room with drawings to show Lincoln. Sunita comes in behind him and takes a seat on the couch next to her mother.

Binod puts his hand up to Arjun, stopping him. "Not now!"

"Oh, I ask see," Lincoln interjects. He smiles at the boy. "Arjun, give minute, okay?" The boy frowns, but drops down and sits on the floor beside Lincoln. To Binod, Lincoln says, "So, you go on trek soon?"

"Yes, to Everest Base Camp on April 28," Binod says, then his face lights up as if he's just remembered something he forgot. "Hey, High Trails, the company I work for, has an opening for a guide. I don't know if you'd be interested, but I could get you in. The pay is good."

Lincoln blinks at the suggestion. He likes his job at Tripureshwor Transportation well enough, and the pay isn't an issue either way. But he can't deny he's attracted to the idea, as long as it doesn't involve climbing. That he'll not do again. "Is steady work? My boss, not like yours."

"Oh, yes, it's steady if you want it to be. So, you're interested?"

"Maybe," Lincoln says. "Is application I need fill out?"

"I'll ask. My boss, Mick-ji, will like you. He's a good man."

"Okay," Lincoln says. "Why not? Don't hurt to ask." Binod stares back as if he doesn't understand what he's just said. "Umm...never mind."

As Lincoln lies in bed that night, he thinks about the job Binod told him about at High Trails. It's tempting, so long as it's not climbing. To be honest, he has to admit that he's been thinking about getting out of the city, but something always seems to hold him back. As if there's something here waiting for him to discover. He punches his pillow and puts his hands behind his head, lacing his fingers together. Is this opportunity what has held him here in Kat? Is there unfinished business in the mountains? There's nothing to keep him from moving on, except a few friends, and of course Binod's family, which he's begun to consider more and more as his own family.

He thinks of Collins and that terrible day on the mountain. Why hadn't he been more aware of his friend's failing health and paid more attention to where Collins was that night during the storm? The excuse his other climbing companions had tried to pound into him, about everyone just trying to survive, rings hollow in his ears. He should've been saving Collins instead of sitting huddled up inside their tent on the precarious ledge overlooking the Sagarmatha Valley two thousand feet below. And then there's the *accident* with his parents that he played a part in, and the death of a patient he should've been able to prevent. Maybe it's best, he thinks, that he leaves before someone else he's grown to care about like Binod and Sila, or God forbid, Sunita and Arjun, dies because of something he might or might not do. It wouldn't mean he'd never see them again; he isn't leaving the country.

He gets up and pulls his laptop down off the dresser and boots it up. When his home page comes up, he types High Trails into the search window and waits for the site to load. Clicking on the "about" page, he reads about the owner, Karl Ballinger, and the history of the outfit, which started in 1984 as a small independent expedition company in Germany. Next, he clicks their lists of treks and climbing adventures in the Swiss Alps and Himalayan mountains. The bread and butter of the outfit is mountain summits, but they do a good business with their treks to EBC, the Annapurna Circuit, and the Annapurna Sanctuary. Not that any of those treks are without some degree of danger. Just last year there'd been a freak blizzard on the Circuit that cost a lot of people their lives. Then again, the blizzard that hit Ama Dablam had been called a freak storm too.

He taps his fingers on the laptop, debating, then clicks over to the staff page. Binod told him the boss he works under is Mick Hanson, so he scrolls down until he comes to the man's bio. Hanson is a large, burly, bearded man with friendly dark eyes and a bulbous nose. He's a strange combination of John Goodman and the character Norm Peterson from *Cheers*—except for the beard. He also has an impressive climbing resume from when he was younger: Everest, Lhotse, Nuptse, and a dozen other peaks in the Himalayas. The rest of the bio talks about his affiliations with Trekking Agencies Association of Nepal (T.A.A.N.), International Climbing and Mountaineering Federation (U.I.A.A.), Austrian Alpine Club (A.A.C.), etc., and his education from Humboldt University in Berlin.

There's also a job application page on the site.

Lincoln clicks on it. The application requires a resume with experience, preferably on a peak of six thousand meters, as well as tool climbing experience and basic first aid. Well, he's got the medical part covered, and also the six-thousand-meter peak under his belt—but tool climbing not so much. Then again, he won't be applying for a mountain guiding expedition position.

10

APRIL 11, 2015 —
KATHMANDU AND ICHOK

The rumble of thunder wakes Binod out of a sound sleep. He burrows his face into his pillow, opens his eyes, and looks toward the alarm clock on his bedside table. 6:43 a.m. He turns away and stretches his arm out toward Sila, but she's not there. He thinks she's probably feeding the baby and getting the kids up. They have a long drive ahead of them today to Ichok. And what is this thunder? It never rains in April; well, hardly ever.

At length, he rolls over and lies back, looking at the ceiling. They're going to see his parents today for the baby's naming ceremony, then they'll stay a few days before coming back for work. Arjun and Sunita won't come back right away, though. The children don't see their grandparents often, and there won't be many more times they will, so he's taken them out of school for a couple weeks.

He sighs, knowing he should get up there and see his mother and father more often, but spending time with them is always a struggle to find balance between the old ways and the new without getting into arguments. The saving grace is that his brother and sister, along with his extended family, will be there this weekend to buffer things, so as long as he goes along with his parents' whims (providing they're within reason), there shouldn't be any problems.

He gets up and runs a hand through his hair, then shuffles down the hall barefoot to the kitchen. When he walks in, Arjun and Sunita look up from eating breakfast. He goes past them to the refrigerator and takes out a bottle of aloe vera juice.

"Where's your mother and the baby?" he says to them as he uncaps the bottle.

Sunita takes a bite of her porridge. "Batharuma."

He yawns and goes to the kitchen window. It's drizzling outside, but in the distance he sees a clearing in the clouds. With luck the clearing will open up and they'll have sunshine for their ride to Ichok, but he isn't betting on it.

"After you're done eating, you need to get dressed," he says to them as Sila comes in with the baby on her arm. He tousles Arjun's hair, and the boy looks up at him worshipfully.

Sila slips past him and lays the baby in the bassinet. "You want something to eat?" she says.

"No. I'm fine." He comes beside her and gazes down at his son, who's smiling and wiggling around. "He has your eyes."

Sila looks up. "I don't know, maybe. But there's one thing he does have."

"What's that?"

She smiles. "Your impatience. He wants what he wants, when he wants it."

"Hmm..." Binod eyes her, then strokes the child's cheek and says, "I don't hear you complain."

She rolls her eyes and groans. "Go get dressed."

With his family packed in the rental van, Binod sets out on the road to Ichok with Sila's family following behind. The five-hour ride on the winding gravel and dirt road is one he's made many times over the years, but it's never to be disrespected. His father has told him more than once the road is a lesson in patience. A virtue he'd need as he grew into a man and had a family of his own. Never has his father been more right in anything. One small mistake where the road clings to the cliff, and they'll all go careening hundreds of meters down the steep, sloping hillside into the raging waters of the Trisuli River.

Just now, he's at such a place. He keeps to the leeward side as far as practical from the ragged edge overlooking the river gorge below, and puts in a CD with old Nepali folk songs to take their minds off the harrowing yet striking spectacle. The road bends sharply to the left as he comes to the blind corner. To his dismay, he meets a bus going the opposite direction.

Everyone comes to a stop.

There's no passing each other here, and seeing how the bus takes precedence, it means he'll have to back up to a passable stretch of road. He opens the van door and signals to Sila's father, who's following him, to back up. Prabin sticks his head out from the driver's side window, assessing the situation, then nods.

As the family caravan inches backward, the pinging of pebbles can be heard tumbling over the edge. No one says a word as they creep backward, save the singer on the CD. Although this tenuous situation is nothing new to Binod, he nonetheless grips the wheel tight, whitening his knuckles. Fortunately the rain gave up a long way back, and the road is dry. He glances at Sila. Her gaze is riveted on his passenger side window and her grasp on their newborn son, tight to her breast, is fierce. Arjun plays in back while Sunita draws, both of them oblivious to the danger outside their window.

The road behind them veers to the right and opens up enough to be passable. The rule of thumb is larger vehicles command the interior passable portion of the road away from the cliff edge, so with the help of Prabin, who's gotten out of his car and is standing behind them, Binod maneuvers the van over as far as he can. The bus creeps ahead with its mirrors pulled in tight to the side, and for the next three minutes the two vehicles brush past each other, centimeters apart.

Once they're clear of the bus, Binod starts forward, and sixty minutes later they're back into drizzling rain. But the cliff-hugging road has been left far behind, replaced by a countrified road that runs through a forested landscape. He looks off through his window as Sila sleeps beside him and sees glimpses of the river peeking through the low-hanging branches. He's home again, and suddenly he realizes he feels like a stranger here. It quite bothers him, because so much of his childhood existed in this world. A world far apart from the life he's chosen.

He glances over at his newborn son, who's also asleep in the soft cashmere sling around his mother's shoulder, then looks back in the mirror at Arjun and Sunita. His daughter, who's reading, has only seen her grandparents a dozen or so times, Arjun even less, and for all practical purposes, this will probably be the only time his newborn son will see them. His father Bishal is getting on, and Aaista is battling kidney problems. He frowns at the thought of his parents passing away alone in a cruel bed within the dark confines of the old family house. Still, what can he do? He's tried numerous times to convince his father to move to the city, but he refuses. *This is our home,* his father has said. *I will die here with your mother.* And that was that. But it doesn't stop the pang of guilt Binod feels every time he comes home.

At last, the sweeping arc of the road straightens, and the house comes into view. Pulling off the road, he drives through tall rangy grass up to the front porch of the old homestead and parks. For a moment he sits looking at the wood-framed house. The roof seems to stoop a little more each time he sees it.

As Prabin pulls up alongside with Sila's family, Binod comes to himself and turns the van off. "We're here," he says, rousing Sila.

She blinks and yawns, then checks on the sleeping baby in the sling. Seemingly satisfied, she turns toward the children in the back, who've nodded off. "Arjun, Sunni, wake up, we're here."

The children rub their eyes, then stare out the back passenger side window. Arjun leans forward, points, and cries, "Dādī!"

Sila swats his hand. "Do not point like that. Use your hand like this," she says, showing him how to lay his palm out and gesture toward what he wants to show. Sila turns back to Binod as his mother and father step out onto the porch. "You look troubled," she says. "Are you okay?"

"Yes, I'm fine," says Binod, but he's not. He stares at the frail, wrinkled, and pockmarked man who stands stiff-shouldered, supporting himself with an old wooden cane on the porch. The years haven't been kind to his father and it troubles Binod to see the strong, resilient man in such a poor state. Bishal has been the quiet centerpiece of the family for forty years. Binod bites down the guilt of being absent from him and his mother so much and opens the door. Purposefully, he strides up to his parents and bends his head low with palms pressed together.

"Namaste, Bubā, Āmā."

His father lays a hand on his head. "Binod, it's good to see you. How's my son?"

"I am very good, Bubā," Binod says, rising to see his father's careworn face looking down. The once vibrant dark brown eyes, dimmed by the slow march of time, take in a son who's gone off to make a life in the big city. Binod turns to his mother then, who's looking on in her bright red and yellow sari. Her brittle long black hair, which is streaked with white, is bound in a thick braid. How thin she looks to him, too thin, he thinks.

His father leans forward, licks chapped lips, and studies his son critically. "Your Āmā, she has missed you."

"And I've missed you both, too. It's good to be home," Binod says, feeling his mother's accusing glare. He draws a breath and adds, "Where's Galen?"

"He's in Thakre on business. He'll be home tonight. Kedar will come in the morning with Anika,"

169

Aaista says, and turns to Sila, who's standing back a pace with the baby cradled in the sling around her neck. Arjun stands fidgeting beside her. Sunni is standing tall and straight with her head dipped. The rest of Sila's family wait by the car out of respect. Aaista waves Sila forward.

Binod smiles, glad to be out of his mother's gaze, and says, "Āmā and Bubā, you have another *pōlyānda*."

Sila steps beside Binod. "Namaste Bishal, Aaista. It is good to see you again," she says, and pulls back the edge of her sling to reveal the dark-haired child.

Bishal puts out his hand and touches the child, and as he does, Binod sees the old patriarch and the baby connect on an ethereal bridge spanning the generations. Finally Bishal looks up from the deep well of the baby's gaze and glances at Sila.

"Shashthi is strong with this one. I can feel it," he says, then thumps his cane on the ground, as if to satisfy himself with his declaration. "And this one," he says, turning to Arjun, "has sprung up like a sapling. Come here. Let me look at you. How old are you, boy?"

Arjun glances up at his mother, then back to his grandfather, and steps forward. "Seven."

"Hmm...already?" says Bishal, smiling down. Then he eyes Sunita almost like an afterthought. "And what about you?"

"I'm fourteen now, Hajurabubā," Sunita says, keeping her gaze downward.

"Do you still draw?"

"Yes, Hajurabubā."

Bishal nods, then turns back to his grandson, gazing at him as if he were a prize bull. "What about you, boy? Do you draw, too?"

Arjun smiles. "Oh, yes."

"And what things do you draw?" Bishal asks, leaning forward on his cane.

"All kinds of things," Arjun says, suddenly brightening under his grandfather's rapt attention. "I can show you?"

"I can't wait," Bishal says and lays his hand on Arjun's head. To Binod, he says, "You're doing a good job with them."

"Thank you," Binod says. "It's not hard. They're good children." He looks back to Sila's parents and sisters, who've gathered around behind him. "You remember Sila's mother and father."

"Of course we do," Bishal says, tucking his cane under his arm and pressing his palms together. "Where are my manners? Namaste, Prabin, Sumi. You're looking well."

"And you also," Prabin says, coming forward to return the greeting.

"And how was the trip?" Bishal says. "Not too tiring, I hope?"

"Not at all."

Bishal glances at Aaista, then reaches down beside him and takes up a small plate with tiny flowers and tika smeared on it. Running a bony finger through the red paste, he dabs it on Binod's forehead, then does likewise to Sila. Afterward, he snatches two small white blossoms and sets one on Binod's head, then the other on Sila's. Stepping back, he smiles and says, "Welcome all. Come, take some tea and cakes with us and rest your weary feet."

The village priest arrives at the family's front door with his leather-bound mantra books early the following morning amid a rare downpour. The rain hasn't deterred preparations for the Nwaran ceremony, though. The house is a hive of activity: Aaista and Binod's sister, Anika, are busy in the kitchen putting together the festive meal to follow the ceremony while Sila's mother and sisters clean and purify the house with the blessed water from *Varuna*.

As hosts, Bishal and Galen meet the bony old priest at the door and let him in. Gokul Sharma has been a friend and a central part of the Thapa family since before Binod was born. The man shakes the rain from his Dhaka topi and greets Binod's father and brother, then turns his gaze toward the jasmine-scented room.

Galen takes Gokul's jacket and sets it on the

couch near the door as Bishal leads the man to Binod and Sila.

"Namaste," Binod says when the old priest is before him. He presses his palms together and dips his head to the man. "So good to see you. It's been a long time."

"Yes, a very long time. You're looking well. And your wife, she grows more beautiful every year," Gokul says, then reaches out a finger and nudges aside the sling shrouding the sleeping child in Sila's arms. "What a good-looking son you have."

"Thank you," Sila says as her mother and father join them. "You remember my father, Prabin, and my mother, Sumi?"

"Oh yes," Gokul says, offering them a broad smile.

Prabin and Sumi press their palms together and dip their heads. Prabin says, "Namaste. Thank you for honoring us here today. Can we get you some tea?"

"Oh, that will not be necessary," says Gokul. "Perhaps after the puja." He looks around. "Where are we having it?"

"We've set up a *mandap* out back," Binod says, and he leads Gokul through the house to a terraced courtyard where he and his brother have erected a canvas-covered ceremonial shelter. Inside is a low table facing east on a simple tan carpet covering the slate floor.

Gokul eyes the table that's dressed in a white cotton cloth. Several brass bowls filled with turmeric, cardamom, and camphor sit on it along with a slew of red, blue, and green candles. Incense sticks surround a long-necked *Kalasa* vase. A bell metal plate is set at one end beside a small ceramic bowl of tika.

Gokul sets his books on the table and sits down, folding his spindly legs under him. He opens one of his tattered books and motions to Binod that he's ready to begin.

Binod, Sila, and the baby, along with Binod's brother, mother, and father, take their seats around the table. Sila and the baby are to Gokul's left, and Binod to the right. Bishal, Aaista, Galen, and Kedar sit across from them. The remainder of the extended family gather around behind them, some snapping photos with their phones.

When everyone is settled, Gokul recites the long litany of mantras to invoke Varuna to bless the water in the vase. As he speaks, Binod lights the candles and his father sets the cedarwood incense aflame. A thin spiraling ribbon of resinous smoke rises, and a moment later, as if in answer, Varuna thunders above, sending a volley of rain pounding on the canvas cover.

Gokul looks up from his reading and smiles, as if interpreting the rain as a good sign, then returns to reading the mantras. As he reads, he draws the bowl of bright red vermillion powder to him and dips his thumb in it. Leaning to Sila, he has her pull back the soft red sheath around the baby's face. After marking the child's forehead with a red dot, he continues his reading, asking the God of Water to bless the child and the parents.

When he finishes, he sets the book aside and spreads his astrological charts in front of him along with a small leather-bound journal. To Binod, he says, "What is the day of his birth?"

"March 14."

"And the time?" Gokul asks, opening his journal and taking out a pencil.

"1:42 in the afternoon."

Gokul sets his pencil beside him and traces his long, gnarled finger over the much-used yellow chart of scrawls written around a colorful astrology wheel. As his finger flicks back and forth over the chart, he confers with the small brown journal he's set beside him. Binod looks on, anxious to hear what Gokul will say. Finally, the old priest looks up and takes out a small, folded slip of paper from his pocket and writes the child's name on it. Folding it back up, he hands it to Binod.

When Binod sees what Gokul has written, he's elated. The name is perfect.

"According to his sign," Gokul says, "I deem him to be a light, a source of radiance, a spiritual illumination, therefore I name him Aadeep."

Sila bends her head down and kisses the child,

and when she looks up with a beaming smile, Binod knows she's as pleased as he is. She lifts the child from her sling and gives him to Gokul. The old man whispers into the baby's ear, then picks up the bell metal plate and bites it near the baby's ear. Afterward, he holds it before the child's face, reflecting the daylight onto the baby's forehead.

"The puja is done," Gokul announces, handing the child back to Sila, and then he adds, "Have you a calling name for the child?"

Binod turns to his father and holds him in his gaze. At last he says, "Yes, we name him Bishal, after my Bubā."

On Sunday morning the family gathers outside, and Binod watches Arjun showing his grandfather his drawings. All day yesterday, Arjun was busy with his pencil on a pad of paper his aunt Anika found for him. His son, who's sitting cross-legged on the grass, is soaking in his grandfather's attention, rapt in everything Bishal is saying. The boy is so impressionable at this age, believing whatever anyone whom he looks up to says. And Bishal is more than ready to teach him. Binod wonders how much he'll have to undo once Arjun is back home. He wants his son to respect girls, his sister especially.

As for Sunita, she's buried in a book she's

brought with her. *Harry Potter*, he thinks it is. His daughter is barely acknowledged by her grandfather, and while he knows that's just the way it is with his father, he can't help but feel upset about it. At least his mother pays attention to Sunni, but he's quite sure it's because she's filling the girl's head with notions about how she's supposed to act as a young Nepali girl growing into womanhood. He wonders if his mother is thinking about who would be a good husband for his daughter, and it will only be a matter of time until she corners Binod about it. Though his marriage to Sila was arranged over ten years ago, it was different back then. He and Sila grew up in the same village and knew each other, and what's more important, they liked each other. But Sunita lives in Kathmandu and things are different there. The traditional ways are fading into new, progressive ways. Women are taking charge of their lives, going to college, working outside the home, even living by themselves. He has to admit, it has taken him time to get used to it, but now that he has, he sees it as a better way. His daughter is thriving, branching out, and exploring the world around her. And, he reminds himself, she's thinking about boys.

He turns to Sila, who's sitting beside him, nursing the baby. "Maybe we should bring Sunita home with us, what do you think?"

Sila looks up. "Why? She doesn't see her grandparents very much, and she might not see them again."

"I know. I just wonder because my father ignores her and my mother...well, you know."

Sila is quiet a minute, then says, "I know, but it's only for two weeks. And Sunni should be exposed to some of the old ways so she can see and make up her own mind."

"I suppose you're right. I just...never mind."

"It'll be okay," Sila says. She switches the baby in the sling over to her other breast. "Besides, her aunt is here, and you know her; she'll make sure Sunni isn't run over by your mother."

Binod nods. "Do you ever miss home here?"

"Sometimes. What about you?"

He shrugs. "I guess." He looks off toward the grove of rhododendron trees bordering the back of the yard, and memories flood his mind. "We used to play over there when we were kids. Do you remember?"

Sila smiles. "Yes, you weren't very good at UNO."

"I think you were cheating," Binod says, looking at her sideways. He pauses, remembering their wedding day and how beautiful she looked in her red sari and the marigold lei that was draped over her neck, then asks, "Was there anyone else you liked back then?"

"What do you mean?" she says, looking back hard at him.

"You know, someone you wanted to be with, but couldn't?"

"Oh." Her brows suddenly fly up. "No! You were always on my mind. Why do you ask that?"

"I just wonder sometimes. We...you never had a choice, and..."

"That was the way it was back then," she says, then lays her hand on his arm. "But I loved you from the very first time I saw you."

"Truly?"

"Yes," she answers emphatically. "It never crossed my mind to look at anyone else, even if I could."

It soothes his heart to hear this and he looks back at her, loving her ever more. "For me, it was the same. You were the only one I saw."

The baby gurgles in her arms and she lifts him from her breast and hands him to Binod. "Your son is messy," she says, wiping herself. "I'll put him down for a nap before we leave."

Binod stares down at his son, and their gazes connect. Sometimes when he looks at him, it's like staring into a deep well of eternity. It was the same way with Sunita. Arjun, not so much. The boy, even as a baby, always had his eyes elsewhere, thirsting for something new to look at. He gives the child back to Sila. "I hope your parents made it home safe."

"I'm sure they did. My father had a good time with your bubā."

"They had a lot to talk about. And your āmā and mine were cackling like hens."

Sila smiles. "I think she was trying to keep your āmā's mind off us."

"Yes. I'm glad there hasn't been one of her and bubā's lectures."

"What time do you want to leave?"

"Couple hours, after I see Galen to say good-bye. Okay, I better get at it. Be back soon."

Binod walks back from his brother's house, deep in thought. Galen has just told him their mother needs a new kidney, but because of her age and lack of money, they won't be able to get it. Even if he and Galen pool all their money, it won't be enough. The cold hard truth is, she won't live past this year. Suddenly he feels ashamed for wanting to get back home so he can avoid the inevitable conversation about adhering to the old ways. He stops at the edge of the property, gazing at the house that's slowly falling apart year by year. It seems like an age ago that this was his world. What will his father do once she's gone? They've been married for over forty years. Suddenly, his throat tightens and he wants to hug his mother, hold her tight, and never let her go.

Arjun is running around the yard, chasing a chicken. Everyone else is inside. He takes a deep breath and marches to the porch. Inside, everyone is talking. Sunita is sitting on the couch, reading her book. Sila looks up from where she sits next to the stone fireplace. When she sees him, her brow furrows. She knows there's something wrong. He smiles, pushing back the news Galen has told him, and sits beside his daughter.

"How's the book?" he asks, but his gaze is on his mother, who's sitting across from him next to his father.

"It's good," she answers.

His mother makes a face, as if Sunita is wasting her time, and says, "She's had her head in it ever since she got here. Hopefully, she'll make time for us."

Meaning her, Binod thinks. He turns to Sunita. "Don't live in that thing, okay? You don't see your hajura'āmā very often."

"I won't." She holds the book up to him, showing him she's three-quarters through it. "I'm almost done."

"Do you want something to eat before you leave?" his mother says. "I can make something for you."

But he isn't hungry and he couldn't eat even if he wanted to. "No, it's okay. I should get the van packed." He's fighting tears as he loads them in the back seat of the van, and resolves himself to come back more often from now on until....

When he turns around to go back in, he finds Sila standing behind him. "What's wrong?"

"Not now. I'll tell you on the way home."

"Okay." But there's a worried look on her face. She can always tell when he's upset.

Twenty minutes later, he and Sila are outside on the porch saying their good-byes. He bends down before Arjun, takes him into his arms, and tells him to be a good boy and that he'll see him in two weeks, then he gets up and hugs Sunita tight. "Make sure your brother doesn't tire your Baṛagārō, okay?"

"Yes, Bubā."

"Remember, keep your nose out of the book, okay?"

Sunita nods.

He squeezes her to him, then steps back, puts his palms together, and faces his parents, who stand by watching. Again, he wants to reach out and drag his mother into his arms, but if he does, she'll know he knows and there'll be tears he couldn't bear: not now. "Okay, I guess it's time to go. We'll be back in two weeks."

His father steps up to him. "Drive safe, okay? Don't worry about the children. They'll be fine."

"I know. Namaste Āmā. I'll see you soon." After Sila says her good-byes, he turns away, but it takes all his strength.

11

APRIL 25, 2015

incoln comes to a stop outside his apartment building and wipes the sweat off his brow. He's just come back from his morning run through the neighborhood. He quit his job at Tripureshwor Transportation three days ago. It wasn't anything he aspired to anyway: just something to keep him busy while he tries to figure out life. But back to the mountains again? Why are they drawing him back? Except, if he's truthful about it, they were the only place he's ever felt connected to anything, until *that day* of course, when everything went wrong. He chews his lips. He's gone over this again and again since he sent his resume to the company. Is he trying to face the memory of Ama Dablam, to find a way to live with not paying attention and letting Collins fall to his death? Or is it something else? All his life, since his parents died, he's never found a place to belong. Everything he's done—firefighting, working as an EMT, becoming a doctor—has never turned out the way he thought it would. None of it lit a fire in his heart.

He sighs and goes up to his apartment to shower and change. He's supposed to meet Binod in twenty minutes to ride in for their meeting-slash-interview with Mick Hanson at the Crown Plaza Hotel. The interview part is more of a get to-know-you meeting before they go over the logistics of his first gig at Everest Base Camp. EBC is a popular tourist adventure, not too hard for most people, providing they pay attention to their bodies. He's not exactly anxious about meeting Mick, but he's wondering how it'll go. From what Binod has told him, Mick is pretty relaxed, but Lincoln's seen these types of people before. They treat you one way, and think another.

He checks his phone for messages, then strips out of his running clothes. The place needs picking up, and there are dishes to do and laundry is overflowing in the basket on the couch. It'll have to wait. He tosses his t-shirt in the basket and steps into the bathroom. It'll be a cold shower this morning because he doesn't have time to wait for the antiquated water heater on the roof to warm things up.

Fifteen minutes later, he's opening his laptop to review High Trails one last time, then checks himself in the dresser mirror. He's picked out a white cotton tapālan. Not too dressy, but not too laid-back either. His best pair of jeans completes the look of subtle confidence. He combs his hair, grabs his wallet and helmet, then checks his cash situation. He'll be riding tandem with Binod this morning, so a buff to go over his mouth during the ride is also in order.

When he opens the front door of the building, Binod is waiting for him on his bike. "Namaste," he says.

"And you, too," Lincoln answers in Nepali. He puts his helmet on, gets on the bike behind Binod, and a minute later they're zipping down the street. Traffic is light this morning in the Kalimati neighborhood and Lincoln sits back, his knees clutching the narrow vinyl seat, enjoying the ride. To his right, the sun is lighting up the brick façades of the passing buildings in oranges and golds.

They motor along for a bit, until Binod leans back and glances over his shoulder. In English, he yells into the wind, "You want to stop my apartment after we get back? There's game on. We can watch."

"Sure," Lincoln hollers back. He's not much on soccer, but hanging out alone all afternoon in his cluttered apartment isn't appealing. Besides, he can go over anything he might forget to ask Mick about while they watch the game.

They turn onto Ring Road and merge into the swarm of bikes sweeping past a tourist bus that's chugging along. Even though traffic is heavy, they're moving at a good clip. Five minutes later, Binod raises his arm toward the hotel. It's just down the road, and they're early.

Lincoln turns to see the hotel's reflective dark windows gleaming in the morning sun. The U-shaped building with a prominent red metal roof is set back a few hundred yards from the road. It towers over the jumbled sea of old brick and wood-framed buildings gathered helter-skelter along the arterial. Binod veers to the outside lane, and a minute later they're turning onto the drive flanking the hotel.

They park across from a broad white portico that stretches over the drop-off lane and head into the spacious two-story lobby. On the right is a long wood-paneled reception desk (bamboo, Lincoln thinks) with a cream-colored counter. A pair of uncomfortable looking black vinyl chairs flank each end of a couch of the same material on their left. He follows Binod past them, down a long corridor to the hotel café. There, a hostess shows them to a table near the window. They take their seats and Lincoln is about to open his menu when Binod taps him on the arm. He looks up to see the High Trails expedition coordinator and another man heading their way. He gets up as Binod's boss calls out.

"Hey, Binod," Mick says, and glances at his watch. "You're early. What the hell? Gonna turn into a regular American if you keep this up." He turns to the man beside him, explaining something about

Nepali standard time, then introduces himself and the other man, whose name is Alan. He's thin and wiry, and he speaks with a hint of a British accent (or so Lincoln thinks). They shake hands and they all sit. Mick is exactly as the bio on High Trails' website portrays him, save that he's a little larger around the chest and stomach. It's obvious the man doesn't climb anymore, at least not Everest or any of the other eight-thousand-meter peaks. But the wide smile and alert dark eyes are the same, and he has a firm grip when they shake. Alan, not so much.

The waiter comes around with a carafe of tea. He looks to Binod first. "What can I get for you?"

"I'm okay, thank you," Binod says.

Mick frowns. "You? Not hungry? You sick or something?" He puts his hand out. "Give me your wrist. I want to check for a pulse."

Binod looks back at Mick as if he isn't sure what to say. Mick grins and turns to Alan and tells him some outlandish tale about Binod gorging on a buffet.

Lincoln sits back, chuckling. "You've been holding out on me, Bud."

Binod turns to him. "Holding out?"

"Yeah, keeping secrets," Lincoln says as the waiter stands by.

As Mick orders, Lincoln studies his menu. When the waiter looks to him, he points to an appetizer. "The Dehli Chaat—is made with dahi vada or dahi bhalla?"

"Dahi bhalla," the waiter answers.

"Okay. I take order of that. Extra hot chili, lots onions. Plain yogurt."

The waiter turns to Alan, who points to a picture on his menu. "I'll have that," he says, then puts his hand up. "You have toast and marmalade here?"

The waiter stares back. "Marmalade?"

"Yes," Alan says. "It's like jam. Fruit preserves with peels."

The waiter glances at Mick, who translates in Nepali.

The waiter nods, then beams back at Alan. "Oh, yes, we have."

"Good. I'll have another cup of whatever you're calling tea," Alan adds, raising his mug.

After the waiter leaves, Mick clears his throat, claps his hands. "Okay, you're probably wondering why we're not at a High Trails office, right?"

"Binod filled me in; something about liking to keep things light and friendly," Lincoln says, and sits back with one arm on the table, noticing a woman who looks an awful lot like...*what was her name... Nicole, that's it*, at the far end of the room. The last thing he wants is to run into her again.

He looks back to Mick, considering him, and collects himself.

Finally, Mick says, "So, tell me a little bit about yourself."

"Not much to tell," Lincoln says. He shrugs, takes

a sip of tea, and gives an abridged version of his life over the last two and a half years.

"I assume you went for Everest?" Alan says.

Lincoln sets his mug on the table. He doesn't want to get into what happened on Ama Dablam. "That was the plan. Never got to it, though."

"That's too bad," Alan says. "What happened?"

Lincoln sees the Nicole lookalike get up from her chair and watches her head toward him. *Okay, this ought to be interesting.* He braces himself for an unpleasant encounter. "Bunch of things."

"So Ama Dablam was a training summit?" Mick says.

The approaching woman isn't Nicole, though. Lincoln relaxes, then shrugs as the waiter brings more tea. "Sort of."

Behind the waiter is a petite Nepali woman with effervescent brown eyes and a warm smile. Mick's face changes, as if he's just seen an angel. "Namaste, Polly! How are you?" he says.

She tells him she's all right, but Lincoln sees her affectionate gaze on the man. It isn't hard to tell there's more going on between them. She smiles, then looks past Mick. "Namaste. Hello, Binod. How are you?"

"I am very good, thank you," Binod says. "And how are you?"

"I am very good also," she says, then turns to Lincoln. "Namaste, good morning."

"Morning," Lincoln says, and Alan joins him in unison. Lincoln breathes in the spicy aroma of the Dehli Chaat and says, "Something smells good."

"I hope so!" she says, favoring him with a charming smile. She sweeps her gaze over them. "So, you are all staying with us?"

"Just Alan and myself," Mick says. He picks up his mug and sips, then turns to Lincoln. "Palisha here co-manages the hotel. She's the best hostess in all of Nepal, isn't that right, Binod?"

"Oh, yes," Binod agrees.

Palisha waves off the compliment. "Do not listen to them. They are just looking for extras," she says, then turns to the platter on the table beside her. She passes their plates out and when everyone is served, she turns to Mick and leans in, whispering something in his ear.

He gets up and follows her out of earshot. As Lincoln unwraps his silverware, he furtively glances at them as they chat. They're inches apart, and when she pulls back there's an innocent smile on her face. A moment later she walks away.

"So, Lincoln, where were we?" Mick says, coming back to the table. He's trying to hide a smile and failing at it as he digs into his breakfast.

"Ama Dablam," Alan says. "What was that like? I heard it's quite a climb."

Lincoln swallows and shrugs. He was hoping the subject was forgotten. "It wasn't easy."

Alan nods, pours honey on his porridge. "When did you do it?"

Lincoln sees Mick from the corner of his eye, watching him. "2011." The minute he says it, he wants to take it back.

"You were on the mountain in 2011?" Mick asks, and his face pales.

Fuck, here we go. Lincoln looks away and feels his gut tighten.

Alan says, "I heard there was a storm that year?"

Collins's face flashes before Lincoln, and the visceral anger that comes with it surprises him. "Yup."

"Christ! That must've been a hell of a ride," Alan says.

Lincoln looks up, trying to keep his cool, and takes another sip of tea. "It was."

Alan leans forward. "Where were you at the time?"

Lincoln clanks his mug down, wanting to tell the man to shut up. "Camp 3."

Binod and Mick suddenly stir in their chairs.

Alan's glance sweeps over them as if he's being left out on some secret. Finally, he says, "What?"

God damn it! Lincoln clears his throat and stares coldly at Alan. "Not what! Who! People died, okay? Can we please move on?"

"Yes, let's," says Mick. "We have a lot to cover for the upcoming season and next year, not to mention our next group, which will be here next week."

~

After the meeting, Lincoln walks out with Binod and they talk about the upcoming trek as they head for Binod's bike. They'll be leading a diverse group from the States, Britain, New Zealand, and Germany. A few of them are arriving tomorrow, and he, Binod, and Alan will go to Thamel to welcome them. Lincoln hops on back of the bike and they're off. As they weave through traffic, he thinks about Alan. While the man is versed in all the details of leading a trek, he seems out of his element, and to be honest, out of shape. The thing that caught Lincoln's attention most was the Brit's not reading people, not knowing how to observe and listen to unsaid words and actions; a shortcoming he learned about himself the hard way on Ama Dablam. Missing the cues on what was going on with Collins on the mountain had cost his friend his life. He'll never let that happen again.

His opinion of Mick hasn't changed either, but overall he likes the man. The High Trails coordinator certainly likes to rib people, and Lincoln isn't sure if the man was being sarcastic or really meant what he said. Also, Mick is observant. Lincoln caught the man eyeing him with a furtive gaze more than once when they were eating, especially after it came out he was on Ama Dablam during the 2011 storm. The wheels were definitely turning behind the man's ever-ready smile after he heard that. Obviously, a man in his position knew all about what happened on the mountain that year.

When they pull up to Binod's building, it's going on 11:00. The neighborhood is quiet. Kids are off to school and a lot of people are at work. A bony old man who lives in Binod's apartment building is sitting outside gumming a cigarette and enjoying the sunshine. As they bring the bike up to the porch, the man turns his wrinkled, sunbaked face up to them and offers a toothless smile. Lincoln has seen him before, usually early in the morning when he goes out for his run. He returns the smile as Binod wheels the bike inside.

When they walk into Binod's apartment, they hear the baby crying in the other room along with Sila's soothing voice. Little Bishal is not having it, though, and his bawling only gets louder. Binod looks at Lincoln with a sheepish expression, but Lincoln smiles and shakes his head. "Do not worry," he says in Nepali. "Is okay. I doctor, hear many baby cry. Good for them. Strengthen lung."

Binod smiles. "Be right back," he says, then goes around the corner into the hall that leads to the kitchen.

While he's gone, Lincoln drifts over to the couch to take another look at Sunita's painting. He's amazed at the level of detail she put into it. The lavender-hued goddess looking back at him has bright, all-seeing, dark eyes that almost seem real, as if they could blink at any moment. Sunita is talented, indeed.

Binod comes back with a couple of drinking bowls. He hands one to Lincoln and grabs the remote. "The match comes on at 11:30, so we're just in time. Do you want something to eat? We have some chips."

Lincoln shakes his head. Ever since he's become a regular guest in their home, Binod and Sila have been making sure to keep American snacks and chhaang available, despite his telling them not to go to the trouble. "No, I okay, not hungry," he says, and takes a seat in the chair across from the TV, which seems to have become designated for him.

He sips his drink while Binod scrolls through the channels, then asks, "So when kids come home?"

Binod looks up from scrolling. "We're going to get them tomorrow."

"I bet they having much enjoyment with grand-parents."

"Oh, yes," Binod says, averting his eyes back to the television.

But the way Binod says it strikes Lincoln cross-ways. The tone in Binod's answer is all wrong. He wonders if he should ask if everything is okay. He doesn't want to be nosy, except he considers Binod and Sila his friends. At last he says, "How old your mom and dad?"

"My buba is sixty-seven, and my āmā is fifty-nine."

Sila comes around the corner. "Oh, Namaste Lin-ji. I didn't know you were here." She turns to Binod. "Your son's being a brat."

Binod looks up from the TV, but he doesn't say anything.

Lincoln says, "Like his father," and smiles.

Sila glances at the TV, which is showing a soccer field behind a pair of announcers. "I'm going to make lunch. Are you hungry?"

"Oh, no," Lincoln says. "I still full from breakfast this morning."

"What about you, Binod? You want something to eat?" she says, and as she does, the floor suddenly jilts a little under their feet, and the lamp on the table shifts. A moment later another jolt sends the pictures on the walls swinging to one side.

Lincoln straightens along with Binod, and their eyes widen. "Earthquake!" Lincoln cries out. "Get the baby. Get outside, quick!"

Binod jumps to his feet and runs out of the room, which is shaking back and forth now. Glass shatters in the window and knick-knacks and magazines fly off the tables. Lincoln runs over to Sila, grabs her hand, and pushes her toward the door as Binod rushes over with the baby. As they hurry into the hall, another jolt shoves Lincoln's shoulder into the wall. He runs ahead and grabs the stair railing as dust and pieces of plaster rain down. In front of him, Sila is shrieking as she staggers down the stairs. The baby is bawling in Binod's arms behind him. The racking walls sway, and large cracks are opening in the plaster. Chucks of debris are crashing down, exploding on the floor below. The wailing of cracking wood and breaking glass reverberates all around him.

"Hurry, hurry!" Lincoln shouts as the stairs shift and twist beneath their feet. Another jolt hits the building and it groans. Lincoln can feel the impending collapse coming as Sila steps over the fallen motorbike and stumbles out the door. Lincoln turns back to Binod, ushers him and the screaming baby past him. "Go, go!" he yells as another jolt slams him into the wall. Binod slips and tumbles down the last few steps on his back, shielding his son as he goes, then scrambles to his feet and staggers over the bike and through the door.

The hallway is now a hazy, dim tunnel of raining dust and debris. Lincoln wipes the grit from his face and squints into the filtered light shining through the door below, then jumps down the last six stairs, taking them two at a time. As he clambers over the bike, he feels the building tremble and then hears the *pop, pop, pop* of beams and studs. The sound rings in his ears as he lurches outside.

Ahead, the rolling macadam is thrusting parked cars off its back like children's toys. Sila and Binod stand in the middle of the street, clutched together with the baby tucked between them. Power poles are swaying back and forth, their tangled lines swinging like jump ropes. People are running everywhere, yelling, screaming, crying. No one knows where to go, where to stand, where not to stand. Then another wave ripples through the neighborhood, and with it comes the death-cries of crashing concrete, masonry, glass, and timbers. Overhead, birds wheel in the thick, ashen clouds of rising dust that dim the noon sun.

A moment later, the ground swells down the street from him, and a large gaping crack opens up, knifing through the macadam, sucking down everything in its path. Lincoln sees a car roll into it as he ambles toward Binod and Sila, who are looking on with terror. And then, just like that, the ground goes still. Lincoln comes to a stop, waiting for the next jolt, the next wave to come rolling through, but it doesn't come.

An eerie silence follows, as if the earth is taking a deep breath after a long run, and then comes the cacophony of distraught voices from people who've lost everything they own, except their lives.

12

APRIL 25, 2015

*P*alisha is trembling, and her legs are like jelly. She's standing outside the hotel in the parking lot among the rattled guests who are milling around aimlessly. Everywhere she looks there's chaos and damaged buildings. Many of the buildings have collapsed or are teetering to one side. Her hotel has withstood the earthquake, but whether it's safe to go inside, she doesn't know.

In the distance, she hears sirens blaring with the rise and fall of frightened voices all around her. Everyone is terrified, waiting for the next jolt to come. She tries to think, but her head is a solid block of confusion. Then suddenly, her phone chimes in her pocket. She flinches, then pulls it out to sees her parents' number flashing on the screen. When she answers, her father's ragged voice streams out.

"Are you all right, are you all right?" he says.

"Yes, Bubā, I'm okay," she says. It's almost unheard of for her father to be rattled. There's an audible sigh on the other end, and for the first time since she can remember, he's really worried about her.

"I was so concerned about you. If anything...."

He doesn't finish, but he doesn't have to. She knows what he's thinking and it touches her deep inside. She has yearned to hear concern like this from him for a long time. Finally, she says, "What about you and Āmā? Are you okay?"

"Yes, we're fine," he says, and his tone lets her know he's regaining control of himself. "Just a little shaken."

"And Ramesh?"

"Yes, he's good also. Where are you?"

"Outside the hotel. It's crazy here, Bubā. So much destruction," she says, covering her ears to block out the whine of sirens coming down the road. Then, suddenly, Mick's face flashes before her and her heart nearly stops. *Oh, no...no...no!* "Bubā, I need to call you back."

"What's wrong?"

"I'll call you back, I promise." She ends the call and scrolls down to Mick's number. Her fingers are shaking so badly she can hardly make them work. Finally, she hits the send icon and waits...and waits...and waits, until at last his voicemail comes on. She leaves a brief, frightened message, begging him to call her back, then hangs up and bends over, trying to contain the scream that's lodged in her throat. Has she sent him to his death for a damned sink? Her thoughts fly everywhere, trying to make sense of the unconscionable possibility she might've lost the best friend she's ever had... no, he's more than a best friend. Outside of her family and her children, he's her everything, her life, and she imagines...no, she refuses to believe he's gone forever.

She straightens up and gazes around, trying to think of what to do. She needs to get to her apartment to ascertain her fears are for nothing, that the building is fine and he's busy fixing her sink inside and didn't hear her call, or perhaps he lost his phone, or maybe the call never made it to him. It's irrational, and she knows it, but she clings to that thought, holding onto the insane hope. But deep down there's another reason—one reason that digs into her, that threatens to carve an irreparable hole in her life, and it's gripping her, strangling her.

Her co-manager Namu comes up to her. "Are you all right? You're not hurt, are you?"

Palisha shakes her head. "It's my friend, Mick. I asked him to fix the sink in my apartment. I tried to call him, but he didn't answer. If I...."

"Oh, no, you mustn't believe that," Namu says. "And besides, you don't know. He might be all right. The earthquake might not have done anything there."

But the feigned look of assurance on her friend's face betrays her.

"I've got to get to my apartment," Palisha says, sweeping her gaze over the parking lot, looking for her car.

Namu puts an arm around her. "I don't think that's possible right now. The roads are impassable from what I can see, and I don't think the police would let you go through, even if you could get out. Why don't you come sit with me? He might call, you don't know."

Palisha wants to believe that, but all she can think of is Mick lying unconscious or (she can't say the word) dead underneath a pile of rubble. She follows Namu over to the parked cars away from the building and they sit, looking out at the dazed and confused people. She's never felt so helpless, so scared. She stares at her phone, begging it to ring, to bring Mick back to her. All she can think of is a world without him in it, and her mind is reeling, spinning around and around, always returning to her asking Mick to fix her sink. She wants to rewind it all, go back and unsay it.

The sirens blare, coming closer, but their wailing, like Namu's attempts to comfort her, is like a bug droning in her ears. She pretends to listen to her associate, nodding at appropriate places. But Namu's words are like molasses, syrupy and thick. She stares down at her phone, feeling disconnected from the world, as if she's been lifted up into the ether and she's looking down dispassionately at the vast landscape of broken buildings whose guts have been vomited out upon each other.

When she feels a hand on her arm, she looks up. She's not sure how long she's been sitting here, looking into the dark abyss of this new reality. Namu is staring back, as if she's just asked her a question and is waiting for an answer. Palisha is about to ask her to repeat herself when a deafening boom strafes the air, echoing over the city. Everyone jumps and heads turn toward it. In the distance, a thick cloud of smoke is rising, staining the azure sky.

It's coming from the old part of the city. Namu's eyes bulge. "Oh, no! I hope that's not Dubar Square!"

Palisha doesn't say anything as they watch the cloud disperse. What is there to say? She has become numb inside, empty among the sea of stunned humanity. It takes a moment before she realizes her phone is ringing. She looks down as sudden hope flies into her heart, then sees it's her father again.

"Hello," she says flatly.

"Why haven't you called back? Your āmā is worried about you," her father says, and his tone is no longer worried, but annoyed and demanding.

"I'm sorry, I forgot, Bubā." She pauses, collecting what little resolve she has. "Things are crazy here."

"Humph...crazy here, too!" he says. "Here's your āmā."

"Polly, are you okay?" her mother asks. "What's going on there? Your brother says everything north of the city is in ruins. Isn't that where your hotel is?"

"Yes, Āmā, but—"

Then the ground trembles under her feet.

Mick opens his eyes and blinks. He's disoriented. Where is he? Everything is hazy, and hushed voices are talking all around him. At first, he thinks he's lying outside looking up at the stars and moon, but then he realizes it's not the night sky. He's in a tent, and lying next to him is another man, an injured Nepali. Further away, under the spray of lantern light, there are more injured, and scattered around them are uniformed men; medics, it looks like. Suddenly, he realizes he's in some kind of field hospital. Why is he here? What happened? He's at a loss to answer the question, and then an image flashes before him: a peeling wall. *The earthquake.*

He jerks his head up, and his breath is ripped away. Suddenly he's dizzy and his stomach flips. He swallows the bitter bile rushing into his mouth and winces.

One of the medics turns around. "Hey, careful," he says in English and hurries over to help him lie back down. As the man pulls the blanket back over him, he adds, "You need to be careful, you'll break your stitches."

Stitches? What stitches? Mick runs his hand under the coverlet. He's bare to the waist. There's a large bandage on his left side. Suddenly another wave of nausea comes and he can't hold it back. He turns and vomits on the ground. As his body heaves, a blinding, searing pain shoots through him, stealing his breath. He's never experienced anything like it. He lies back, gasping, then panting as the medic's dark face goes in and out of focus, circling in front of him. When at last the pain subsides, he closes his eyes and tries to collect his thoughts. He doesn't remember getting hurt. Then again, he doesn't remember much of anything after fleeing the building.

"Just breathe," the medic says. His voice is soothing but firm.

Mick hears him unwrapping something and opens his eyes to see him placing a clear plastic bag with some liquid on the pole above him. He follows the tubing running out of the bag down to his arm and notices the IV inserted into the top of his hand.

"This will make you feel better," the medic says, flicking the tube with his finger.

Mick watches the man a moment, then casts another glance around him, eyeing the pair of lanterns pushing away the darkness. "What time is it?"

"A little after ten," the medic says.

Ten? He lies with that thought a moment, turning

it over in his head until Palisha's face flashes before him. His eyes pop. *Jesus, she must be going nuts.* Then another thought rushes in and the world tilts on its side. No, he won't believe it. Not again! He can't have lost another woman he's fallen in love with. He taps the medic on the leg. "Where's my phone? I need it."

"I don't know where your phone is," the medic says, bending back down. He pats his shoulder. "Now you need to rest, okay? You've sustained a deep cut to your abdomen."

The words swim in his head. They're meaningless. He has to know she's alive, that she's okay. "I need my phone. There's someone I need to get a hold of...now!"

The medic looks back and frowns. "Okay, let me see if someone found it. But you lie still, okay?"

Mick breathes a sigh as the man leaves, but the comfort of the man going to find his phone doesn't last long. His mind is spinning, going all sorts of directions: first to Palisha, then to Binod and Sila, to Alan, then back to Palisha. As their faces spin around him, his eyes get heavy and darkness fills in. Where's the medic with his phone? It feels like hours since he disappeared.

When Mick opens his eyes again, sunlight is pouring into the tent, and there's a lot of commotion going on outside. The injury to his side is reminding him it's still there, but the pain isn't like before and (thank God) there's no nausea. He turns his head to see the Nepali beside him. He looks familiar. Then he realizes it's the man he rescued from the apartment building.

Everything floods back, and with it, the horrific thought of losing Palisha and everyone he cares about. He can't endure it, won't endure it. He needs to know or he'll go crazy. He braces himself for the pain that's sure to come when he sits up, then notices his pants folded nearby. He ransacks the pockets, and when he feels the phone, he snatches it out and waits breathlessly while it powers up. When the screen lights, there are seven missed calls, six of them from Palisha. Two are voicemails. He clicks on one.

"Mick, Mick...Are you all right? Please call me back!"

The next message is even more harried. "Mick, please, if you're okay, please call me back. I'm so scared. If anything's happened to you, I'll never forgive myself. Just please, call me back."

He closes his eyes, lets out a breath. *She's alive!* He hits reply and listens to the ringing on the other end. When she picks up, her voice is ragged, and he can tell she's been crying.

APRIL 26, 2015

Lincoln marches toward the latrine across the park that's down from what was once his apartment building. It's mid-afternoon, he's hungry, and it's hot. Save for four hours of sleep and two short meal breaks during the last twenty-four hours, he's been tending to the injured, helping erect tents, and unloading trucks bearing food, medical supplies, blankets, and cots, and when he wasn't doing that, he was working the brigade lines removing rubble and wreckage in the search for survivors. This has stirred memories. He's been here before, not here or to this extent, but in this world of life and death, blood and bone. Now that he's back in it, he discovers the reasons he loved it and hated it, why a saved life always had him coming back for more, and how death could whittle his heart down.

He pulls the flap of the latrine tent back, holds his breath, and does his business, then heads back to the streets. As he weaves through the maze of tents, he stops to watch children blissfully playing in a small clearing. Some of them have just lost their parents, with no place to go. Until now this bleak reality of what it means to be an orphan in Nepal has never crossed his mind. Growing up as an orphan in America, he was lucky to have an aunt who took him in and an enormous trust fund to see him through the rest of his life.

But this isn't America and these kids don't have an aunt or a trust fund waiting for them when they come of age. Here, Sameer had told him, kids without family are either shuttled to antiquated, over-populated orphanages or they end up on the streets begging, or worse yet...whisked away by opportunistic men who sell them on the black market; and woe be it if you're a young girl coming of age. This sobering thought has been waxing on his mind for the last two days, and it's bent his mind to cross-examine his past and the self-pity he's carried under a cavalier attitude.

He's about to move on and join Binod in one of the brigade lines when a Nepali girl about Arjun's age runs past him with her long dark hair flowing in the breeze. She's wearing a ragged, soiled white top with little pink panda bears strewn all over it. A pair of denim jeans with holes at the knees hugs her narrow hips. She's barefoot, and as she runs, he hears her melodic voice singing some Nepali children's rhyme. On her heels is a Nepali boy, maybe the same age, with short hair and bright, dark eyes. He's in a plain t-shirt, tattered jeans, and sneakers that are ready for the trash-heap. Suddenly, Lincoln is taken back to the fields behind his home in upstate New York. Before his life was altered forever by the accident. He can see the girl (*what was her name? Octavia, that's it*) he used to play with down the street. The two of them were inseparable until her parents divorced and she moved away. It was his first experience losing someone he cared about.

Binod calls out to him, and the fuzzy memory of his past dissolves. At length, he makes his way over to

Binod and they stride down the road of broken macadam. The last tremor was three hours ago and it only lasted a dozen seconds, if that, but when they come, people freeze. At the moment they're headed to a line forming at the back of a truck delivering sacks of rice, lentils, and vegetables to the camp. Once it's unloaded, they'll look to see where else they can help. Lincoln glances at Binod as they walk. He knows his friend's mind is riveted on his children, so he doesn't bring them up unless Binod does. In any case, he's glad Binod chooses to put his mind to helping people rather than sitting in his tent and spiraling down worrying about things he has no control over. He even smiled this morning, when they helped pull an old woman out from under the collapsed roof of her house.

They get in the supply line and ten minutes later they're ferrying along sacks of rice from person to person. It's not hard work with so many hands, and the truck is unloaded in a matter of a half hour. As they start back to find where else they can help, Lincoln hears voices rising on the next block.

He taps Binod on the arm. "Let's see what up."

They break into a run across the park and fall in with the mob of residents surrounding a mountain of broken brick and concrete. When Lincoln asks what's going on, a man tells him the dogs have found someone trapped under the rubble.

Ahead, a loud voice calls out in Nepali. "We

need two lines and three teams of volunteers to carry large debris to those trucks coming down the road. Don't crowd in, okay? We need space to get equipment through."

At once people form lines and chunks of brick and concrete get passed along and tossed onto the back of the trucks. Lincoln and Binod join a team of men carrying broken timbers and sections of roof. It's a never-ending back and forth under the hot sun, and even though he's tired, sore, and ravenous, he's not complaining. Three hours later, the whine of saws and the rat-a-tat-tat and jackhammers finally go silent. Lincoln looks up, then down the road where an ambulance is slaloming past cars, people, and debris.

They're getting close. He licks chapped lips and spits out gritty dust as the crowd murmurs in anticipation. Then suddenly a jubilant cry goes up and the crowd parts, making way for four firemen carrying a woman on a litter. Lincoln tags Binod on the shoulder and raises his fist in the air. "We did it, Bud!"

Binod's smile is dim. Then he turns and walks away.

APRIL 27, 2015

Binod wakes up next to Sila and the baby. It's been another fitful night of sleep with tremors coming every half hour. He looks up at the top of the tent, thinking about what to do. He's never felt so powerless. It's been two days since the earthquake, and they've been stuck in a hastily erected encampment in a grass field several blocks from where he and Sila live. *Used to live!* They're homeless. Their world has been turned upside down and the last two days have become an exercise in holding their breath, waiting for the next tremor to terrify them. He looks at the blue tarp that shelters them and then at Lincoln, who's across from him. He and Sila and the baby owe the man their lives.

He gets up, careful not to rouse Sila, and steps outside. It's just after dawn, and the cloud bottoms on the horizon are smeared magenta, red, and orange. Below them, the city is in ruins: buildings, homes, shrines, and temples damaged or in total collapse. Everything is gone. He looks off toward the neighborhood that wraps itself around their encampment. It's nothing more than piles of brick and kindling...and death. He swallows, trying to hold back the hopelessness and the rush of emotions that threaten to overtake him. He doesn't know if the earthquake hit his parents' village; he doesn't know if everyone is okay there, if Sunita and Arjun are safe. He takes his phone out and looks at the screen. He and Sila have been calling his brother every half hour since the earthquake until at last they give into sleep. Right now, he'd trade his life for a way to get to Ichok, to pull his family into his arms and hold them.

Behind him, he hears footsteps. It's Lincoln. The man comes out and stands beside him. From the corner of his eye, Binod sees him look off to the wreckage around them. For a moment, Lincoln doesn't say anything, as if he's content just to be in Binod's company—to let him know he's not alone. Finally, the man clears his throat and says in Nepali, "We need find you, Sila, baby place to stay...way from here."

Binod keeps his gaze fixed ahead. "Sila's parents said we can stay with them for a while."

"Good. You hear from Mick?"

Binod nods.

"He, okay?"

"He said he got nicked. I don't know what that means. I assume he's okay."

Lincoln goes quiet again and they stand within the unsettled calm of the camp, watching people emerge from their tents. Finally, Lincoln says, "Where parents live?"

"In Bhaktapur, across town, south of the city."

"No, not Sila parents. Your parents?"

Binod glances back. "Oh! Ichok, north, up in the hills."

Lincoln goes quiet again, and Binod senses the man stirring thoughts around in his head. A minute later, Lincoln asks, "How far?"

The question puzzles Binod. He glances at Lincoln wondering where he's going with this. "Seventy, eighty kilometers. It's a long drive. Why?"

"We need get to them."

If I could, believe me, I would. He turns to Lincoln. Does he really not see what's in front of him? Does he not see no one is going anywhere? He shakes his head, points toward the road clogged with abandoned cars, motorbikes, and trucks. "Lin-ji, I don't have a car, and even if I did, how would I get there? Look at the roads."

Lincoln grabs his arm, and there's a sudden light in the man's blue eyes. "Who said anything about car?"

"What do you mean?" Binod says, furrowing his brow.

Lincoln grins, as if he's just won a lottery. "Chopper!"

Binod almost laughs, then turns to Lincoln. Surely, the man can't be serious? Even if they could manage to get to the airport, Lincoln has to know he doesn't have that kind of money. "Lin-ji, I appreciate you're trying to help, but—"

"No, you no understand. I...umm...ah, I loaded," Lincoln says and his eyes light up again.

Huh? Loaded with what? The Americanism is lost on him. "I don't understand. What do you mean?"

"I have rupee...lots of rupee!"

The way he says it, it's apparent the amount is staggering. Binod is dumbfounded, then over-whelmed, and for a moment he doesn't know what to say. No one has ever offered him a gift like this. If it were for any other reason, he would politely refuse, but this is for his children. Tears come to his eyes. "You would do this for me?"

Lincoln's grin grows on his bearded face. "In heartbeat. Get back hold of Mick. See if he help get chopper."

13

APRIL 27, 2015

*P*alisha has been living out of her clothes since she's been home in her father's house. It was a long three-hour drive to her parents' the night of the earthquake, and she's still exhausted from it. But Mick is alive and that's all that matters. She's going to see him today at Patan Hospital. He was transferred there yesterday. She wonders about his injury. He told her it was nothing, but Mick always plays things down. As she collects her things in her old room, which has been stripped of any traces of her ever having been there, her mother comes to the door.

"I was thinking," she says in Nepali, "we'll get you a proper sari today. What do you think?"

Palisha knows what her mother means by a "proper sari" and she's reluctant. But if she's going to be here for any amount of time, she knows she'll have to give in. It's a strange feeling sleeping under their roof again after so many years, but it's only temporary until she can find something else, and whatever that is will have to come furnished. She has no furniture, nothing! All her clothes and her precious jewelry are gone. Thank Brahmā she still has the necklace Mick gave her. At last, she says, "Maybe tomorrow, Āmā. I'm going to be busy today."

"Busy?" Her mother steps into the room and folds her arms over her breast.

"Yes, I'm going to see a friend in the hospital," Palisha says, pulling on her top.

Her mother frowns. "Who?"

Palisha's hesitant to mention Mick's name, otherwise there'll be more questions. Lots of questions she doesn't want to answer. "A friend."

Her mother purses her lips. "Is it a man?"

Palisha eyes her mother sideways. She doesn't want to lie, but if she tells her the truth, there will be an inquisition. "It's just a guest of the hotel who comes in often. What does it matter? I can't have friends?"

"Of course you can have friends. I was just asking."

It's more than just asking, and they both know it. "I'm sorry. I didn't mean to be abrupt. I'm just stressed. So much has happened."

"I know," her mother says. "When are you going?"

"In a few minutes. I'll be back later."

"When?"

"I don't know. It depends on how long it takes me to get there and back. The roads are a mess and I have to take lots of detours to get there."

"I only ask because I need to know if you'll be here for lunch."

"I wouldn't plan on it," Palisha says. She has no intention of just dropping by to see Mick and then heading right back. "And don't plan on me for dinner, either. I'll get something out."

"Hmm...okay. Make sure you say good-bye to your Bubā before you leave."

"He's still home?"

"Yes, he's working from here the next week."

Wonderful, now I have to deal with his questions too. She steps into her shoes and sighs, knowing it's a lot harder dodging her father when he's suspicious. "Okay." She grabs her purse and follows her mother down the hall to the stairs, rehearsing her answers to her father.

When she comes to the open door of his study, he looks up and she can feel him judging the crisp white top and black slacks she's wearing, but what can she do? It isn't like she's trying to be disrespectful.

"I'm going out," she says.

She can almost hear his thoughts. *Like that?* He says, "Where? It's not safe driving."

"I know, but I have a friend in the hospital I want to see."

He sits back in his leather armchair, sets his reading glasses on his desk, and looks at her speculatively. "What friend?"

"A guest who comes to my hotel who I've known a long time."

He's quiet a moment, and she can see him turning her answer over in his head. Finally, he says, "Is he from out of town?"

Palisha blinks and she knows he's seen her catch her breath. *How does he guess these things?* She swallows and forces a smile. "Yes, he lives in Pokhara. He's a nice man who does business in Kathmandu."

"What kind of business?" her father says, tapping his finger on the armrest of his chair.

This was what she was afraid of, but there's no getting out of this conversation until he's satisfied. "He runs an expedition company up the mountains."

"Does it have a name?"

She hesitates. "High Trails."

"I see," he says as his finger keeps tapping the armrest. He leans forward and fixes her with a meaningful gaze. "Is he married?"

Her heart stops. She's feeling like a little girl and it makes her angry. For the last five years, she's straddled this boundary, trying to balance her needs against those of her parents and their indifference to her stepping out on her own. But not anymore. She steps into the room, bristling, her fists clenched. "Bubā, I'm forty-six, a grown woman, living my own life—"

"Under my roof at the moment," he interjects.

"I didn't ask to be here," she snaps back, "or perhaps you'd rather I live on the street?"

"I will not be disrespected, Polly!"

"Disrespected?" She rolls her eyes, then stares back at him. "Do I not wear the white sari when I'm here? Do I wear jewelry? No! Do I ever embarrass you here? No! I adhere to the old ways here for YOU, because I LOVE YOU. I'm trying, and have been trying for the last five years to be your daughter. Do you remember her? She was the one who went out of her way, everyday, to make you proud. She married the man YOU wanted, gave you your grandchildren, taught them how to be good Nepali men. You talk about respect, what about me? What about my respect?"

Her father drops his jaw as if he's just been slapped across his face.

Palisha feels her heart racing and takes a breath to settle herself. She wants her father to see her as more than a widow living in a white sari. "I want to be part of your and āmā's life more than anything, but I will not be treated like a little girl, nor will I be a ghost, nor an embarrassment to myself. As far as this man in the hospital is concerned, he's a friend, just a friend, who I happen to care about. If that's too much for you, then maybe I should—"

"No, no." He sits back, and she sees his hand trembling on the armrest. "I just want you to be careful. You don't want people thinking more than they should," he says.

It's as close to an apology as she'll get, and she doesn't want to argue anymore. She nods. "Of course. Now, I need to go before the roads get bogged down with traffic."

He picks up his glasses and as she turns away, he adds, "Be careful driving."

"I will, Bubā. Oh, Āmā and I are going out tomorrow to get a sari for me."

Mick is watching Palisha from where he lies in the hospital bed. She's sitting next to him looking off toward the window. He wonders what she's thinking about. After the initial excitement of seeing him and making sure he's okay and telling him about how scared she was for him, she's been quiet.

He glances at the Nepali man in the bed beside him who was transferred to the hospital with him yesterday afternoon, then turns to her. "What's wrong?" he asks in English.

She turns back and smiles, but the smile is betrayed by the sad look in her eyes. "Nothing. I was just daydreaming."

He grabs the controller and raises the head of the bed a little higher. Ignoring the sharp pinch in his side, he says, "About what?"

She looks down at the floor, wrings her hands. "Us."

"What about us?"

"You know," she says, and her voice is just above a whisper. "I should not think such things, but I cannot help it sometimes."

She looks up and brightens her face. She's so beautiful, so introspective and soulful he can barely contain the urge to tell her how deeply he loves her. But he can't say the words because the way they'll come out will be more than just in friendship, and they made a promise in Lukla not to torture each other with dreams that can never manifest into anything more than friendship.

He swallows the hurt she feels. "Me either. So, tell me, where will you stay after things settle down, or will you remain at your parents'?"

"I have not thought that far ahead. But someplace: I cannot live with my parents. Not anymore. I will be okay. You just need to get healed. Have you called your family in...umm?"

"Germany? Yes, I let them know shortly before you got here." He shifts around on the uncomfortable bed, careful to not aggravate the injury, then suddenly realizes he's forgotten all about Alan. "Hey, the guy who was with me at the meeting. You remember him?"

"Yes."

"Is he all right?"

"I do not know. It was insane when everything happened, but as far as I could tell, everyone got out of the building."

"Can you check for me? His name is Alan Forrester."

She reaches into her purse, pulls out a pen, then grabs a napkin from the rolling tray table beside them. As she writes the name down, his phone pings on the table. She reaches over and hands it to him. He wonders if maybe that's Alan right now, until he sees Binod's name flashing on the screen. He spoke with Binod yesterday to make sure he, Sila, and the baby were all right.

"Hey Binod, what's up?" he says in Nepali.

"Hello Mick-ji. I have a question. Umm...can you give me the number of the helicopter company High Trails uses sometimes?"

"Uh...sure. Why?"

"I want to hire them to take me to my parents' village."

It dawns on Mick that Binod's children were left in Ichok with his parents. His brain goes into overdrive, pondering the prospect of High Trails' owner, Karl Ballinger, picking up the tab. "Of course, but chopper rides don't come cheap. Let me see what I can do to get you covered."

"Oh, do not worry, my friend Lin-ji said he'd pay."

Mick blinks. *Really?* "Okay. When we're done here, I'll text you the number." It occurs to him then that the earthquake probably hit up in the foothills where Binod's parents live. His heart thumps. "Are Sunita and Arjun okay, and your mother and father?"

"I don't know. We can't get a hold of anyone. There's no reception up there."

Damn, he must be going nuts. Mick closes his eyes, trying to remember the name of the guy who runs Himalayan Air Adventures. When it comes to him, he says, "Okay, the guy you want to talk to for the chopper is Sandip Sharma. Tell him I sent you. Can you get to the airport, though?"

"We'll get there somehow."

"Who's 'we'?" Mick says, not believing Sila and the baby would go. He looks at Palisha, who's staring back, obviously wondering what's going on.

"Lin-ji and me."

"Oh, okay. All right, I'm hanging up now. Look for my text and let me know if you need anything. Anything at all, got that?"

"Yes, and thanks, Mick-ji. Thank you very much."

Mick hangs up and hands Palisha the phone. "That was Binod. He wants to book a chopper. He can't get a hold of his family in Ichok. Do you know if the quake hit up there? Nobody tells me anything here."

"Yes, there is a lot of damage up there, my father says. Many villages are no more or very bad off. I hope Binod's family is okay. When I get back to my parents', I will see what I can find out."

A knock comes at the door, and they both look over to see the doctor come in. The man pulls the curtain around Mick's roommate and from behind it Mick can hear the doctor talking in Nepali to the man. He ignores their conversation and asks Palisha how her parents are doing and if she's gotten a hold of her boys who are studying in England, then finally, if she's eaten at all. As she tells him she grabbed a bite on the way in, which he doesn't believe, he hears the doctor say, "I'm sorry, we did everything we could," from the other side of the curtain.

He sighs. Even though he doesn't know the man or the loss the man has suffered, he feels for him. More than that, he hurts for the country he lives in. Nepal has been good to him, despite all its problems, and now like a beaten man, it's been kicked again and he's unsure if it can get back to its feet. He shifts in bed, reaching to the tray table for his glass of mango juice.

"Here, I got it," Palisha says.

She hands it to him, and he takes a drink. It's gone warm. He says, "I think they're going to discharge me pretty soon. I'll have to go back to Pokhara, unless the hotel is okay."

"I do not know," Palisha answers. "It did not seem to be badly damaged, but I have not heard anything yet."

Mick nods. He doesn't want to leave Kathmandu, or more to the point, Palisha. She looks fragile to him, lost. "Maybe if not the hotel, there's someplace else? I guess we'll see." He pauses, watches her gaze off into space. "Are you really all right? You seem far away to me."

She turns a smile back on him. "Oh, yes. I am just thinking."

"About what?"

She hesitates, then says, "I do not want to bother you with it."

He gives her an eye roll. "This is me, your best buddy, remember? Out with it!"

"It is just my bubā. We had a...a difference of opinion this morning."

Mick takes another sip. "About what?"

"My choices. To him, I will always be a widow, and you know what that means."

Mick doesn't say anything. He's well aware of it. She's told him how it is when a woman loses a husband in the strict caste of the Nepali world. No red sari, no jewelry, no tika, staying hidden in the family's house like a ghost to be ignored. And if widows go out, people avoid them, going the opposite way when they see them, lest bad luck come upon them.

She shakes her head. "I have tried to be a good daughter, to be sensitive to his wishes, but I am alive! I am a grown woman. I have a right to be more than a widow. I have a right to have friends."

Now he understands all too well what the look in her eyes has been conveying. She's talking about him. "So you told him about me?"

"Not by name, but he knows I have a male friend, and you know how that goes. Widows in his world do not move out, do not go to school, do not have jobs, and we definitely do not have male friends."

The doctor comes around the corner, glances at Palisha and then at Mick. The man, who is a new doctor to him, is in his forties, and he's robust and tall for a Nepali. He pulls his wire-rimmed glasses up to his eyes from where they hang on a slender chain around his neck, and eyes Mick's chart. "Namaste, how are you feeling this morning?" he asks in precise English, pulling the curtain around them.

"A little sore, but I'm doing," Mick says, then notices the doctor smiling at Palisha. There's an unsaid, "You need to leave," coming from the doctor's gaze aimed at her. Mick wants to say, "She can stay, if she wants," but he keeps quiet.

"I'll be right back," Palisha says, and ducks out around the curtain.

The doctor waits until she's gone, then comes beside him, pushes the tray table aside, and peels back the blanket. "Your injury looks like it's healing fine. No discharge that I can see. I need to check under the bandage, though." He grabs a pair of gloves, puts them on, and pries the dressing back, then runs his fingers along the stitches. "You are a lucky man. Had that shard of glass been a centimeter over to the right, you would have bled out before the medics could have done anything."

"So I've been told."

The doctor puts the bandage back into place and pulls the blanket up. "I think you will be able to go home in a day or two. How does that sound?"

"Fine by me," Mick says.

"Okay." The doctor steps away and peels his gloves off. "I will check on you tomorrow. See how you are. You have anyone home to come get you?"

Mick is about to mention Palisha, then censors himself. "Yes, I have a friend."

"Good. All right then, I will leave you to your visitor outside."

Mick watches the doctor leave, then purses his lips, hating that he's had to examine every little thing he's said to the doctor concerning Palisha. And while he knew in the beginning, when his relationship was blooming into something more than friendship with her, that there would be obstacles to overcome, it's becoming abundantly clear he underestimated them. But this is the world Palisha lives in as a widow, and above all, he has to be careful of her heart, and her place in it.

~

It takes all day before Binod finally gets a hold of Sandip. Unfortunately, he and Lincoln have to wait until the end of the week before they can be flown up to Ichok. Himalayan Air's chopper is in high demand, ferrying injured down from the hills up north. The other problem is getting to the airport. They've lost all their transportation, and so far, they haven't been successful in finding replacements. If they don't find anything by Friday, they'll have to walk to the airport, and with the city in shambles, who knows how long that will take. It's only four miles across town, but it could end up being a six- or seven-mile odyssey.

He goes into their tent, leaving Lincoln to start a fire in the ring of bricks they've gathered outside their scanty camp. It's going on 7:00 p.m. and it's been another long day under the sun, moving brick, concrete, and timbers, and he's covered with grit and dust. Inside, the baby is wrapped in a blanket next to Sila, who's sitting on her heels grinding rice into flour with a stone and shaping it into cakes for their evening meal. She looks up at him briefly, pulls a strand of hair over her ear, and goes back to work. Even though she conceded he was right about her going to her parents while he flies to Ichok to get Sunita and Arjun, she isn't happy and hasn't said more than a dozen words to him since their brief argument this afternoon. He hates the silence between them. In all their years together, they've always been able to talk about difficult things, but this time it's different. This is about their children! He wants the days to hurry along, wants transportation, wants it to be Friday, wants the world to right itself, and more than that, wants to feel his children in his arms.

He brushes himself off, sits down beside Sila, and takes Bishal into his arms. The baby yawns, then looks up and holds him with one of his long, searching gazes. It's as if Brahmā is reaching out through the child's dark blue eyes, connecting with him and trying to get his attention. He looks down into those deep wells straddling the worlds and puts his son to his breast, slaking in the unconditional trust and love he needs to feel and believe in.

At last he says, "When are your parents leaving to come get you tomorrow?"

She pounds away at the grains, dashes them into a pot, and pours more rice out of the sack beside her onto a flat rock Lincoln conjured from somewhere in the park. "Sometime in the morning. I'm not sure."

He sits with her answer a minute, unsure how to proceed with his next question. She's a bubble of emotions compressed inside a thin veneer of bravery that's barely holding them in check. He lays the baby back down. "Why are you mad at me? It's not my fault what happened. I'm doing the best I can," he says.

She's in the middle of a downward stroke of the stone in her hand when she comes to a stop. "I'm not mad at you. I'm mad at...at this!" she shouts, waving a free hand around, which sets off Bishal's crying. "I'm mad our children are a hundred miles away and I don't know whether they're okay or not," she cries. "I'm mad we're living in a tent with nothing but the clothes on our backs, I'm mad our baby has to sleep on the ground, that your shirt and pants are filthy, that we have no car, no bike, and that I have to grind rice with a stone and cook in a dirty pot...I'm, I'm...." She drops the grinding stone on the ground between her knees. Her chest is heaving. Her jaw is trembling as she picks up the crying baby and rocks him back and forth.

At last she comes to herself. "I'm sorry. I just...."

"It's okay," Binod says. He leans in and puts his arms around her, letting her distress melt into him, and as he does, the ground shivers. His breath catches and his grip around Sila and the baby tightens until the shaking subsides. Another tremor. It's the umpteenth one they've felt today.

≈

Lincoln scavenges an armful of kindling from the bones of a broken building across the street and brings it back to their tent. Inside, he hears Sila's shrill voice crying out in anger. He tries not to listen as he arranges firewood and twigs within the ring of brick he and Binod built the other day. Above, an army of pewter-stained clouds have chased away the blue sky, and he hopes there's no rain in them. He digs in his pocket for the lighter one of the soldiers gave him and puts the flame to a page of newspaper they keep by the ring. As the fire kindles, he sits to watch the comings and goings of the shaken refugees. The camp is quiet, save for the voices of children playing around the tents.

His mind spins as he remembers pulling three dead little boys and a girl from the wreckage of a house today. Death is winning the game against the survivors with each hour that passes, and it will only get worse, grind him down more. Thank God, Binod wasn't there to see it. His friend doesn't need to have such visions right now, while he worries for his children. More than that, he worries about all of them here in this no-man's land, where the stink of sewage, garbage, and humanity threaten to bring on another insidious catastrophe: typhoid and dysentery. Someone needs to move the latrine tents, fill the cesspools, and dig new ones. He'll make that a priority first thing in the morning. Go looking for a company of soldiers to help.

For now, there's nowhere else to go, and besides, being out in the open is the safest place until the tremors finally end. The last one was an hour ago. It wasn't very long, but long enough to put people on edge. He picks up a stick and stirs the fire, adds more kindling to it and thinks about how much people take for granted, himself included. He gets up every morning assuming there will be enough to eat, a roof over his head, transportation to take him anywhere he needs to go, fresh water to drink and bathe in; the list goes on, and then, THIS. Even with all his money, not that he obsesses about it, here he is, living out of a tent in clothes he hasn't taken off in three days.

It's all an illusion! Bullshit, in the end. Once this clusterfuck is over, I'm going to do something worthwhile with my inheritance.

Then, as if to answer him, the earth trembles.

14

APRIL 30, 2015

*L*incoln sits outside their tent waiting for Binod to get ready for the day. It's mid-morning and the sky is overcast. Here and there, columns of campfire smoke rise up to meet the clouds. The murmur of the milling refuges (most of them women with children and the elderly) is a steady, low hum over the encampment. He wonders how today will go for Binod. Sila and the baby left two days ago with her mother and father for Bhakta-pur. Sila's father, Prabin, had given a worrisome ac-count about the quake. Its epicenter was north of the city, and many of the villages in the hill-lands sus-tained significant damage, which only added to the difficult parting between his friends. There were tears and promises made that everyone knew were tenuous at best. Since then, Binod has busied himself, helping out with rescues and clearing the streets of debris and abandoned cars, many of them crushed or un-drivable, but Lincoln knows he's terrified at what they might find.

At last, Binod comes out and they sling their packs (which are nothing more than cloth sacks) over their shoulders. They'll be walking to the airport, as there's no one to take them, and no one who owns a vehicle is willing to sell them one. Transportation, what there is of it, is like gold, and it's guarded like the last meal on a family's plate. But they're on their way, and if all goes well, they'll be at the airport by early afternoon. The trip to Ichok will only take twenty minutes by chopper, Sandip has said, and he won't be able to take them until after 5:00 p.m. any-way, as he's booked until 4:00 and will have to gas up and have dinner himself, so there's no hurry.

Lincoln tosses Binod a couple of bottled waters and they head away from the squalor of the camp, walking down deserted streets. It's an eerie sensation for Lincoln. Having lived here for over two years, he's used to seeing a sea of humanity pouring over them. He wonders if Binod feels it, too. But Binod doesn't say anything. He just walks, keeping his eyes forward.

Two hours later, they come to the Bishnumati River and the heart of the city across the water. For the most part, the roads have been okay and most of the buildings are still standing. That is, until they look over the bridge toward Dubar Square in the distance. For the first time, Binod comes to a stop, and Lincoln sees his eyes widen as his friend surveys the vast destruction in front of them. Everywhere Lincoln looks, he finds buildings whose masonry skin has been peeled off to expose their insides. Mountainous piles of brick and concrete lie at their feet, along with collapsed shrines and religious statues. Overhead fly hundreds of pigeons, their tiny bodies no more than grains of pepper scattered in the air.

Everything that matters to the people who live in this ancient city has crumbled to the ground. Binod bends over and plants his hands on his knees. The sight is too big for him. In Nepali, he mutters, "Oh, no, *Taleju Temple* is gone, and so is *Dharahara*."

Lincoln has probably seen them before, but he has no idea what they are. He looks over the destruction and sees in the distance the telltale grungy yellow of a backhoe perched high on the mountain of debris. He says, "Dharahara?"

"Yes, it's called *Bhimsen Stambha* now. It was a watchtower used by the army years ago."

"Ah...yes. I know now," Lincoln says, remembering the round-tiered tower that stood over everything around it. "It was tallest building in Kathmandu." Or was, but he doesn't say it.

"Tallest in all of Nepal," Binod says. "But the temple, that's the worst of all. My father will be crushed when he hears about it."

"I sorry," Lincoln says.

Binod straightens. "Let's go. I can't look at this anymore."

They strike off, turning down roads that lead them away from the square, passing shuttered shops, and here and there, shell-shocked city folk walking among dull-eyed foreigners, who seem to be trying to make sense of how their vacations have turned to dust. And then, there's a loud roar of voices several blocks away. Lincoln turns his head toward it as he walks, wondering what's going on, but Binod is on a mission and he keeps going.

When they finally get to the airport, they find a place to sit in the domestic terminal and wait until it's time to look for Sandip at the Himalayan Air counter. As they wait, Lincoln looks up at the TV on the wall. It's showing a British reporter interviewing an Army Emergency man. Behind them is a cheering mob of Nepalis around a fallen building. He gets up to move closer so he can hear what's being said and learns a young boy has been pulled from under the wreckage of a five-story hotel. The boy has been in there for five days, wedged under concrete and steel, and the man being interviewed is the one who risked his life to go in after the boy and pull him out. Miraculously, the boy is barely injured.

The jubilation around the man is infectious, one bright spot in a world of horror. Lincoln smiles, holding on to that vision as he goes back to sit next to

Binod. Certainly, Sunita and Arjun and Binod's family are okay, he tells himself, and he's confident all their fears are for nothing. After everything they've gone through, all the death he's seen, he has to believe that, otherwise he'll lose it.

"You want tea and something to eat?" he asks in Nepali. "I buying."

Binod looks up from his phone and Lincoln sees he's been texting Sila. "Uh, sure. Just tea. I can't eat."

"Okay." Lincoln struts off toward the little café across from them and orders. As he stands waiting, he sees a chopper fly in and land. Out of it jumps a pair of men who reach back into the cab and pull out a stretcher. On it is a young girl with a bloody bandage on her head and a splint on her leg. His first thought goes to Sunita, but he whisks the thought away.

Stop it! She's okay.

When 5:00 p.m. comes around, Lincoln and Binod go to the Himalayan Air counter. There's no one there, though, so Binod pulls his phone out and calls Sandip. After a brief conversation, he hangs up and says, "He'll be right up. He's just finishing dinner."

As Lincoln waits, he watches the people coming and going. The terminal is usually quiet during the afternoon, but it's been busy with the steady stream of injured coming in by chopper. Lincoln is amazed.

Even after five days, they're still pulling people out of the wreckage caused by the quake. Then again, he reminds himself, the injured ones live in remote villages that are hard to get to even when the roads are good, and the roads right now are not good.

A man on a stretcher is being wheeled along in front of him by a pair of medics. The man is immobilized on a flat board on top of the stretcher. His neck is in a brace and his legs are in field splints. Beyond the man, over near the incoming passenger door, are a couple of soldiers smoking cigarettes and talking. Lincoln tells Binod he'll be right back and goes over to them.

"What it like in hills?" he says in Nepali. "Much damage?"

"Yes, it's very bad," one of them says as the other takes a drag of his cigarette.

"Have you been Ichok?"

"Yes, why?" the other man asks.

"My friend over there," Lincoln says, nodding toward Binod, "have family there."

The two soldiers exchange meaningful glances. The first one who answered him says, "I'm sorry, but he might not have family there anymore. It's very bad there."

The hope that was injected into Lincoln earlier flees, and his heart sinks. "So, you bring some people down?" he says, and he's thinking maybe there might be some of Binod's family among them. Those who died, he knows, would be left to the surviving villagers to take care of. Sunita's and Arjun's faces flash before him.

"A few."

"Where take them?"

One of the soldiers drops his cigarette to the floor, blows out a stream of smoke. "Bir Hospital."

"Were there children?"

The two soldiers look at each other. The one who just butted his cigarette shrugs. The other one says, "Not that I know of."

"Okay, thank you," Lincoln says. He walks back to Binod, who's talking to a dark, curly-haired, rotund man wearing a light blue shirt with a helicopter monogram above the breast pocket. He assumes the man is Sandip. "Namaste."

The man looks Lincoln's way as he steps up beside Binod. In Nepali, the man says, "Namaste, you are?"

"Lincoln Webber." Lincoln pulls out his wallet. "You Sandip?"

"Yes." The man turns to his computer, types away, then says, "Okay, almost finished here. Please spell your name for me, and I'll need your credit card."

Lincoln hands his card over and spells his name out for Sandip. A minute later, the printer by the computer spits out a copy of the invoice and Lincoln signs it as the approval comes back from the bank.

Sandip gives his card back. "All right. All set to go. I'll meet you downstairs after you go through security."

Lincoln pats Binod on the shoulder and fifteen minutes later they're ducking under the wash of the rotor blades and climbing into the helicopter cab. It's an old Nardi Hughes 500 model, but it's in good shape. They fasten their belts and take the headphones Sandip passes to them.

"It's a twenty-minute flight to the village," Sandip says over the headphones as he settles into his seat. "Once we get there, I'll drop you off and wait another twenty like we talked about. If you need more time, I'll have to come back, and that'll be an additional charge, okay?"

Lincoln gives him a thumbs up and they're off. As they rise, Lincoln looks down. What he sees below are busy streets and rooftops of undamaged buildings. It's a contradiction to what they've walked through this morning, until he looks west toward Dubar Square. Binod, who sits beside him, keeps his eyes forward as the ground falls away.

The chopper veers left and a minute later they're soaring over the rumpled hills with the ribbon of the Trisuli River flowing down from the mountains. They follow the deep cleft of the river valley for the next ten minutes until suddenly, there it is: the village. It's flattened, as if the foot of God stamped on it. Lincoln glances at Binod, who's looking down, and sees the anguish on his drawn face.

Sandip calls over the headphones, points to a flat, level space of ground. "Ichok. I'll set down over there."

The chopper descends, and the grass below shivers as they pirouette 180 degrees and set down. For a moment, Binod doesn't move. Finally, he unbuckles himself, ducks his head, and climbs out.

The decimated village appears deserted. A few houses, still intact with tarps over their roofs, look down from the hill at the end of the dirt road. A wisp of smoke rises from their flues. In front of the houses, a handful of villagers are gawking at the chopper. The rest of the homes lie in heaps, wood strewn around cracked and crumbling masonry chimneys tilting this way and that, like stakes driven into their hearts. To Lincoln's right, a half dozen black and brown cows graze in a field. Among them are a few black and white goats. But it's the house down the road that holds Binod's gaze. Chickens peck at the soil around its entrails spilled out on the ground.

Lincoln closes his eyes as Binod approaches it and stares over the wreckage, then drops to his knees and cries out, strafing the air with a shriek that drowns the thwapping of the chopper's rotors. The power behind the cry reaches into Lincoln, threatening to rip his chest out. *This can't be happening.* He refuses to believe Sunita and Arjun are dead, that almost everything Binod loves and cherishes has been swept away.

A hand sets on his shoulder. He turns to find Sandip's sad eyes looking back. "I'm sorry for your loss."

Lincoln swallows and looks toward the watching villagers. "I go talk people up there. Be back."

Sandip nods. "I'll wait here a little longer."

"Thanks," Lincoln says, then turns and marches to the three men coming toward him. One of them is an old man using a walking stick. A ragged red robe floats over his bare feet as he walks and a tan Dhaka topi perches on his bony head. When they meet, the man introduces himself as Gokul Sharma. He's frail and thin, with deep-set dark eyes and a large beak nose. Lincoln points to the teeth of the broken house Binod is kneeling next to. "You know what happen family live there?"

The old man peers down the slope, holding Binod in a penetrating, haunting gaze, as if he's looking at a ghost. "Yes. Who are you?"

"I am man friend. He come look for son, daughter. You know?"

The old man drops his jaw and looks to the other two men around him. "I thought they were dead."

"What you mean? Who dead?" Lincoln says.

Gokul looks back, horrified. "Binod and Sila. More government men came up this morning. I saw them talking to Sunita and Arjun, asking questions, I think. I asked them what they were doing, and they said they were here to take them back to Kathmandu.

244

Said their parents died in the earthquake and their other grandparents were taking them in. I thought, okay, this is good, and I was happy to know they were going to be okay."

Oh, my God.

"When they leave?"

Gokul looks to the man beside him. "Around noon, maybe?" The man beside him nods.

Lincoln runs his hand through his hair and tries to think. "Come, we need tell Binod what you tell me."

Binod cannot believe what's in front of him. His heart tries to convince him his parents and children escaped, are staying with someone else, but seeing everything around him, his mind tells him other-wise. He bends down and picks up his father's broken cane, running a trembling finger along the smooth wood. Nearby, peeking out from under a timber, is Sunni's *Harry Potter* book, and beside it is one of his mother's shoes. His heart bleeds, bargains, begs, tries to ignore what he sees. Tries to pretend it's all a dream, that he'll wake up any minute and see Sunni's and Arjun's faces, and his mother's and father's also, feel their arms around him, hear their voices. It's all gone, though, and it's like he's falling head over heels, around and around into a deep black hole from which there's no escape.

"Binod, Binod? Binod!"

He looks up to see Lincoln staring down at him, and beside his American friend is Gokul. Their faces are a blur and they spin around him. They're saying something, but their words are only mumbles in his ears. He wants them to go away, leave him alone, but he also wants them to wrap him up and hold him until darkness sets in and the world goes away.

"Binod, Binod get up, you need to hear what this man Gokul has to say," Lincoln says in English. He puts his hand out and pulls Binod up.

Gokul steps in front of him, his dark eyes glistening, yet stern. In Nepali, he says, "I thought you were dead, I thought both you and Sila were dead."

We are dead!

The old priest grabs his arm. "Your parents died in the earthquake, but your son and daughter are alive, they're alive, do you hear me? And so are your brother and sister. They were taken by helicopter to the hospital in Kathmandu."

Binod blinks, wondering if his ears are cheating him. "What?"

"Your children, Sunita and Arjun, and your brother and sister, they're alive!"

Suddenly, it's like he's been jolted back to the surface. He blinks again, feels his heart lurch. "Where? Where?"

The old priest stares back. "We don't know where right now. There were men this morning, men from the army or police—I don't know—who said you were dead, and that they were sent to take Sunita and Arjun to Kathmandu to live with Sila's parents. But now, seeing you here, I know I made a big mistake... but I didn't know. And they looked official, and they seemed to know about Prabin and Sumi. Oh, Shiva, forgive me. I'm so sorry!"

Binod's breath catches in this carousel of despair, joy, hope, and now fear that's revolving around him. For a moment, he tries to think what to do first: cry for his parents, rejoice that his children are alive, or shudder at the thought of losing them all over again. Sila's face flashes before him. He turns to Lincoln. "We have to find them—we have to find them now!"

"I know," Lincoln says. "They've got a head start on us, though, so we need to get back to Kathmandu and let the police know."

"Yes, yes, okay." He turns to Gokul, presses his palms together. "Thank you, thank you!" he says in Nepali.

"For what?" Gokul says. "I did more harm than good. May Shiva have mercy on me and shine upon you. Now go, and when you get back, I'll perform another burial puja for your parents. Until then, I'll be lighting candles for you every day."

They run back to Sandip and the waiting helicopter, and they're off again, streaking back to Kathmandu. Binod watches the shadowed land slide by, trying to assemble his thoughts on how to tell Sila everything he's found out. He doesn't know where to start. How can he give her children back to her in one sentence only to take them away in the next? How can he bear her fear, her anguish, and the inevitable cry that will stab his heart all over again?

Lincoln taps his arm. "As soon as we touch down, we're going to the police. Tell them what we know."

Binod nods.

Lincoln grabs Binod's arm and looks him dead in the eye. "We'll get them back!"

The American's stern, determined gaze and the power of his words drill into Binod's heart and give him strength. He clenches his fist. "Yes!"

It's 11:00 p.m. and Binod is frustrated, upset, and bleary-eyed as he paces back and forth in the mobbed lobby of the New Baneswor ward of the armed police. Thankfully, the ward was only a fifteen-minute walk from the airport. Lincoln begs him to come sit but he ignores him. He's been waiting here, enduring the dissonance of complaints and cigarette smoke, since he returned from Ichok three hours ago. All he wants to do is speak with someone and file a report. *What's taking so long?* Time is slipping by, and with each minute, his children are slipping away. His phone pings in his pocket, and he takes it out to see Sila's name flashing on the screen again. It's the tenth time she's called in the last three hours. He hates ignoring her, but until he's had a chance to talk with someone in charge, he tells himself he has to hold off.

Lincoln looks up from where he sits, nursing a Styrofoam cup of tea. Binod can see Lincoln is as frustrated and upset as he is. "I'm going for more tea. You want some?" Lincoln asks, tilting his head toward a large Thermos sitting on a beat-down wood countertop.

Binod shakes his head. He's about ready to go back to the reception desk and ask—no, demand— how much longer he has to wait, when he hears his name ring out from an open doorway at the other end of the lobby.

Finally! He waves to Lincoln, who's pouring more tea, then starts toward the open door. The man waiting by it is dressed in a white button-down shirt and navy slacks. A pair of glasses perches on top of his head. He's heavy-set and middle-aged, and he looks as tired as Binod feels. He also appears disinterested, as if he can't wait for the last ten minutes of his shift to end.

"Namaste," the man says, glancing down at the paperwork in his fat, puffy hand. "Go down the hall to the first office on your right. I'll be right with you."

Binod passes him, catching a whiff of stale fruity cologne. A moment later, Lincoln catches up and they walk down the narrow hall to the man's tiny, claustrophobic office. The room's a disheveled mess of overflowing file boxes. Lincoln plunks down in one of the cracked vinyl-upholstered chairs. He doesn't appear impressed.

"I hope his investigative skills are better than his filing," Lincoln says, sweeping his gaze around, "otherwise, I don't know."

Binod worries, too. It's the first time he's ever had anything to do with the police, and from what he sees on the man's desk he wonders if he can even find the phone, let alone two missing children. He takes a seat next to Lincoln in front of the desk, which is buried in stacks of files, overflowing ashtrays, and empty teacups and wrappers, and waits AGAIN until he hears the door shut behind him.

"Okay, what can I can do for you?" the man says in Nepali, rounding his desk.

"My son and daughter are missing and we think they were taken," Binod says, having a hard time not stumbling over his words.

Lincoln speaks up, "Hijacked. And you are?"

"Oh, sorry, Deputy Inspector Magar," he says, then pulls his glasses down onto a thick, bulbous nose. "Okay, where were we?"

"My children."

"Oh, yes, taken against their will," Magar says.

"I left them with my parents in Ichok for a couple weeks. They don't see their grandparents very much, so..." Binod pauses, takes a breath, and goes on, "Anyway, they were there when the earthquake hit, and it...umm, it destroyed the village. My parents died."

Magar leans back in his chair. "I'm sorry to hear that. Go on."

Binod swallows. "We went up to get my children today, and the priest there, Gokul Sharma, said the police, or maybe it was the army, were there this morning, and that they told him my wife and I died in the quake. Said they were supposed to take my son and daughter to their grandparents here in Kathmandu. As you can see, I'm not dead."

"Maybe they, the police or the army, were mistaken about your dying. There's been a lot of miscommunication since the quake. But we can check." He plucks a pen from his pocket and pulls a pad of paper from his desk. "Did you fill out the identifying paperwork for your missing children they handed you at the front desk?"

"Yes," Binod says, getting up. He hands it to the inspector and watches him look it over.

Finally, Magar looks up. "Okay, so when did they leave with the supposed officers this morning?"

"We think around noon."

Magar writes the information down. "Do you have a picture of them I can pass around?"

"Yes," Binod says, taking his phone out. He finds a photo of Sunita and Arjun together, then shows the inspector. "Is this okay?"

"Ah...do you have one of each?"

"Oh, sure. These okay?"

"Yes, those will do fine," Magar says, then gives Binod an e-mail address to send them to. "You might want to check with the army, too. What's your number? I'll send you their information." After Binod tells him, Magar gets up and shoves his glasses back up onto his forehead. Pocketing his pen, he says, "We'll keep in touch and let you know as soon as we know anything. Good luck to you. I hope you find them. I have three of my own, two boys and a girl. I can't imagine losing any of them."

Leaving the inspector, Binod goes out into the night with Lincoln and looks up at a pair of stars blinking down on the city. As the cool breeze buffets his collar, he wonders if it might be a sign Brahmā is looking out for his children. Finally, he pulls his phone out and makes a call he doesn't want to make, because he knows Sila will want to talk to the children, but there are no taxis around and he doesn't want to walk all the way to Sila's parents' place. The one good thing is Lincoln being with him so he can use words like "we" and "us" when she answers.

"Hello, Binod?" Sila says.

Her tone is anxious, and he can see her in his mind's eye chewing her lip, which she does whenever uncertainty of the future comes up. He says, "We're back. Can you have someone come pick us up?"

"Sure, but...how are your parents? Is everything okay there? I've been watching the news. They're saying Gorkha was the epicenter of the quake."

Binod blows out a breath, hesitates, then says, "I'm tired. I'll tell you when I get there, okay?"

There's a long pause on the other end, and he knows where her head is going. Finally, she says, "It's bad in Ichok, isn't it?"

"I'll tell you all about it when I get there. Please, just come get us."

"Okay, where are you, the airport?"

The last thing he wants to tell her is the police station. "Yes, the airport."

He tells her good-bye and ends the call, then goes over to where Lincoln is sitting on the curb with his legs stretched out and hands pinned on his knees. "That was quick," Lincoln says, looking up as Binod joins him. "What did she say?"

"I didn't tell her," Binod answers. He tells himself he's trying to do the right thing, telling her face-to-face, but the truth is he's delaying the inevitable because he's being a coward.

Lincoln nods. "Probably for the best. Well, I have to get back."

"Back where?" Binod says, incredulous, then spreads his hands out toward the city. "Everything is gone."

Lincoln gets to his feet, dusts off his pants legs. "Don't worry. I'll find some digs."

What? "I don't understand."

"Oh...a place to stay," Lincoln says.

Binod shakes his head. "No, you're coming back with me. After everything you've done, I'm not going to have you looking for a place to stay this time of night. Come on, we're getting picked up at the airport in a few minutes."

15

MAY 1, 2015

*S*ila's father, Prabin, pulls up to the curb outside the airport terminal. When Binod gets to the car he's relieved to see Sila has stayed home. He still hasn't figured out how he's going to tell her about the children. When he opens the door, Prabin says, "Where are Sunni and Arjun?"

Binod stares at the accusing eyes looking back. His throat tightens. "I don't know." He's about to say more when Prabin breaks in.

"What do you mean, you don't know?" Prabin snaps.

Binod shakes his head, then tells his father-in-law about what happened to the village. As he fills him in on his parents dying and his brother and sister being flown to the hospital, Prabin's eyes widen more and more, until it comes to the part

255

about the mysterious men whisking the children off under the pretense of bringing them back to Kathmandu.

Lincoln says, "We went police, file report, but think they hijacked. Why they say, Binod, Sila, dead?"

"Yes, I agree. We need to do something," Prabin says, wiping the wetness from the corner of his eye.

"Can we talk about this later?"

Prabin looks back at Binod. "Sure."

"Thanks. Do you mind if Lin-ji stays the night?" Binod says. "He's got no place to go, and it's late."

"Of course he can, get in and let's get home."

The twenty-minute drive to Bhaktapur is done in silence, save for the murmur of the radio. Binod stares out his window into the darkness, watching the ghostly shadows of buildings and trees slip by. A bright full moon is sliding behind a bank of clouds, lighting up their wispy outer fringes. Another wave of guilt pours through him, reminding him he was the one who suggested the children stay with his parents. It's grinding into his gut, burning him, suffocating him. By the time Prabin pulls into the driveway and parks, it's hard to breathe.

At length, he opens the car door and heads up the walk with Lincoln and Prabin following. When he steps onto the stoop, the door opens, and Sila is there with her mother behind her. He sees his wife's eyes search around him for the children. She says,

"Where's Sunni and Arjun? Where are they? You said they were with you."

He didn't say that exactly, but he's not going to argue the point, not with the pleading gaze that's cutting his heart out. "I know. I'm sorry."

Her eyes bulge and her face shrivels. "What do you mean, sorry? Where are my babies?"

"I don't know. We're trying to find them."

For a moment, she stands there looking as if he'd just run a knife into her, then her hands fly to her mouth and a shriek pierces his ears.

Rushing to her, he takes her in his arms, holds her shaking body that's going limp in his grasp, threatening to fall to the ground.

"We're looking for them, and we're going to find them," Prabin says from behind them. "Let's go in."

A half hour later, they're all sitting in a circle in the living room. As Binod tells what he knows, Sila stares into space, her face a blank slate as she listens. His words seem to bounce off her and ricochet around the room.

Finally, Prabin says, "I think it's important we don't get ahead of ourselves here. It might be a miscommunication. The important thing is they're alive."

"He's right," Lincoln says, nodding. "We don't know." But his answer is less than convincing.

In the other room, the baby cries, and Sumi goes to him. Everyone falls silent, and to Binod it feels like they're sitting miles apart in a white room, devoid of all color and furnishing. More than that, it's the separation he feels from Sila. It's as if she's a ghost sitting beside him.

~

When Binod wakes up the next morning, hugging his pillow, the space beside him is cold and empty, as if Sila hadn't slept beside him last night. Through the window across the room, sunshine pours through parted curtains. For a moment he stares at the ceiling, sinking into the gaping hole that *yesterday* left in his life. Downstairs murmuring voices and clacking dishes fill the stilted silence. From what he can tell, Lincoln and Prabin are talking. At last, he peels back the coverlet, drags his pants on, and reaches for his phone. It's 7:06 a.m. He resists the urge to call the armed police to find out if there's been any news and heads for the stairs. When he reaches the bottom, he sees Sila coming toward him with the baby in her arms.

"Do you want to hold your son?" she says, her voice flat and robotic. The ghost that occupied her body last night hasn't left. He nods, and she places his swaddled son in his arms. "My bubā and Lin-ji are in the living room. There's tea in the kitchen. If you want, I can bring you a cup."

"Yes, that would be nice."

She turns, and as he watches her walk down the hall, his heart breaks all over again. He wants his life back, wants his beautiful, vibrant wife back, wants to see her smile, hear her melodic voice singing to the radio like she always does in the morning; and he wants to hear his children squabble over who sits up front on the way to school. So many things he's taken for granted are slinging arrows at him. The baby gurgles in his arms, drawing his gaze down.

Little Bishal is looking up at him, his dark cobalt eyes searching and prodding at Binod's self-inflicted wounds and beaten heart. For a moment, the world fades away.

"He has Sila's eyes," Sumi says, suddenly beside him.

He glances up, then turns back to his son. Brushes his finger over the baby's head, inhales his milky sweet scent and the soft down of his curly dark hair. He wants to ask Sumi if Sila blames him, but that's out of the question. He offers her a tiny smile and puts the child to his shoulder, then walks into the living room. His son is the only thing right now holding him to the world, giving him strength to breathe, to move. He finds a place on the couch beside Lincoln, who looks up as he sits.

"Morning," Lincoln says.

"Morning," he replies, and he leans back into the cushion.

Prabin says, "We've been talking about driving

into the city and going to the different police wards to ask around. We need to make sure everyone knows. Binod, are you listening to me? I know you're suffering, but you have children depending on you."

Binod looks back at his father-in-law's determined expression. He knows he needs to get off this emotional rollercoaster, shutter the voices of doom inside him, and shake the weariness away. "I know, I know!"

Lincoln turns and says, "You not alone, Binod. You have me! And that baby need brother and sister."

Maybe it's what Lincoln says that lights a fire in him, or maybe it's what Prabin said, or maybe it's the baby on his shoulder, whispering unsaid words into his soul; he doesn't know, but suddenly a surge of adrenaline rushes through him.

"Yes, he does," he says, lifting his son from his shoulder and over his head. As he looks up at little Bishal, the baby smiles back. He kisses the baby's brow and brings him to his breast. "When do you want to go?"

"Whenever you're ready," Prabin says.

"Now sounds like a good time!" Binod answers as Sila walks in.

She holds his tea out to him. "Here you go."

"Can you put it in a to-go cup for me?" Binod asks, jumping to his feet. He passes the baby to her. "We're going into the city to start asking around at the wards." Then it hits him that he forgot about the

Army. He digs into his pocket, pulls his phone out, and scrolls through his e-mail. As he pulls up the message from Inspector Magar, a call comes in. His first thought is that it's from the armed police, so he answers it without looking.

"Hey Binod, Mick here," he says in English. "How did things go, everything all right?"

"Oh, Mick. I can't talk right now."

"Why? What's wrong?"

"My children, they're missing."

Mick's voice barrels through the phone. "Missing?"

"Yes. Some men came to the village telling people Sila and I were dead, and that they were taking Sunni and Arjun back to Kathmandu."

"What?"

"I'll tell you more later. I'm sorry, I have to go."

Palisha sips her tea, watching Mick talk on the phone. The architects, engineers, and public safety officers have gone through the hotel and declared it safe to return. There's damage, of course, but it's cosmetic and superficial. That's good news because it'll allow people to return to their rooms instead of taking shelter in tents. It also means she has a place to stay instead of her parents' and Mick won't have to return to Pokhara. She's taken a room on the second floor and Mick has a room down the hall, three doors away.

They've also found out about Mick's colleague, Alan. He was found under a slab of concrete in a collapsed restaurant a few blocks over. Mick had to report it back to the man's family. Even though he didn't know Alan well, Mick took it personally as he struggled to get the words out to the man's wife. It was so like him to get choked up over it. Every day, she sees something new to love about him. From his infectious laughter and humor to his deep sentiments about right and wrong and his feelings for people he barely knows, but more than that, it's how he treats her, how he protects her status and virtue in her world. He's a permanent fixture in her life now, one she can't imagine living without.

Suddenly, his voice rises. "What?"

She looks up to see his face crinkle in alarm. He listens for another moment, then sets his phone down and stares across the café table at her with a dumbfounded expression.

Her heart thumps. "What is wrong?"

"Binod's children," he says in English. "Some men came up to the village saying he and Sila were dead and that they took them back here."

"Who, the army?" She can't imagine who else it would be.

"He didn't say. Why would they say Binod was dead?"

"I do not know." She sets her cup down. She's well aware of her country's sad history concerning inhumanities, but she doesn't want to raise more alarm until they know more. The last thing she wants is for Mick to go charging out aimlessly looking for soldiers until he's well enough to go about doing it.

Tapping his fingers on the table, he says, "Something's wrong, I can feel it."

"It does sound suspicious," she answers, watching him fidget in his chair. "Maybe it is just a misunderstanding."

Mick stops tapping and frowns. "What?"

"A misunderstanding of the army or the armed police, thinking they were dead. We just had an earthquake."

"Yeah, but why would they assume they were dead, and how would they know the kids were up there?"

That she has no answer for.

Mick looks off into space, chews a fingernail. At last he turns to her and there's one of his determined, "I've made up my mind" looks coming back. "We both know what's probably happened, and something's got to be done, and soon, otherwise they'll lose them."

"Mick, before we go running off, let me call my father. I will ask him to make some calls, see if the army has been up to...what is the name of the village?"

"Ichok. Ask him if he can check with the police, too?"

"Let me see," Palisha says, then puts her hand over his. "Just promise me, you will not go running out until we know something for sure. You have just had an operation, and you need to take care of yourself."

"I'm fine."

Palisha takes a breath. "Yes, I am sure you think you are. But you do not want to open your wound. Promise me?" When he nods begrudgingly, she takes her phone from her pocket and scrolls to her father's office number. Touching the send button, she waits for someone to pick up, then says to Mick, "The children, what are their names?"

"Arjun and Sunita Thapa."

She hears someone pick up the call on the other end. "Office of Human Rights," a woman says in Nepali. "How may I help you?"

"Yes, this is Palisha Kc. I'd like to speak to my father, Amir Shrestha."

"Oh, namaste Palisha. This is Bhīma. How are you? Are you okay?"

"I'm fine, thank you," she says, watching Mick stare back. His finger is drumming the table now.

"We were so worried about you."

"Oh, thank you, Bhīma. It was pretty scary," Palisha says, reaching across the table to stop Mick's drumming.

"I bet. So much destruction, so many homeless people now...it's awful." There's a pause on the other end, then Bhīma comes back. "Well, I'll let you go so you can talk to your father. Hold on."

"Hello, Polly?" her father says a moment later. "This is a surprise."

"Hi Bubā. I know. I'm sorry to bother you at work, but I have a favor I need to ask you...if it would be okay?"

There's a short pause. "Go ahead."

"My friend I told you about, he has an employee, Binod, whose two children have gone missing. They were in the village of Ichok visiting their grandparents when the earthquake hit. My friend tells me there were men who came and said the children's parents were dead and that they were bringing them back to Kathmandu. But the parents are still alive, so we're wondering if maybe it was men from the army and there's been a miscommunication. Maybe you could check and find out if they were up in the village?"

"I can make a few calls, but the most I'll find out is whether they were up there. Have the parents checked with the armed police?"

"We don't know. We just found out. We're concerned that—"

"Yes, I know. There's a big spike of it going on right now with all the orphaned children from the earthquake. If that's what's happened, there's little we can do but hope they catch them at the border. How old are they, and when were they taken? And do you have pictures of them?"

Palisha pulls the phone away from her ear, squeezes Mick's hand. "Their ages, and does Binod have pictures?" she asks, breaking into English. "And when were they taken?"

"Umm...Sunita is thirteen or fourteen, I think, and Arjun seven or eight," Mick says. "I assume they have pics, and I think...maybe yesterday?"

She puts the phone back to her ear. "Bubā, the girl is a young teen and the boy, seven or eight. We think they were taken yesterday, and yes, they have pictures."

"Yesterday...hmm..." He pauses again and it's a couple minutes before he comes back. "Okay, tell you what. Get a hold of the parents and see if they can come in for a meeting. Once I hear back from you, I'll arrange for a 3 Angels representative to join us here at my office. By then, I should have some answers. In the meantime, have them keep checking with the armed police. Hurry, though, because if this is what we're thinking, we have maybe a week to get them back."

～

Lincoln shakes his head as they walk out of the Kamalpokhari ward police station. So far they've spent over two hours in just one ward waiting to get some simple answers. At the rate they're going, it'll take two weeks to cover every police ward in the city. Sunita and Arjun don't have that long. He glances furtively at Binod and Prabin, who are walking beside him to the car. It's not hard to see they're getting frustrated as well, and what's worse, a little downhearted.

"I need to eat," Prabin says. "My sugar is dancing."

"Okay," Binod says, but he frowns. "Not too long, though."

"No, not at all," Prabin says, and Lincoln can see Binod's father-in-law biting back a frown of his own.

They get in the car and head toward Baudha ward police station off Boudhanath Sadak. Their plan is to work the north end of the city, where they think might be one of the first places the children would arrive if the police have anything to do with it, but they know they're only guessing. It could be anywhere. Up front, Binod pulls out his phone and tries the Army number Inspector Magar gave him. He gets no answer and ends the call. As he goes to pocket the phone, it pings.

They all jump as Binod puts it to his ear, but a second later his hopeful expression fades. "Oh, hi Mick," he says in English. He listens and a moment later his eyes are darting back and forth, his face lighting up. "Yes, yes, we can do that.... Yes, anytime...1:00 p.m., yes, we'll be there for sure. Thank you, thank you, thank you!" He ends the call with a smile on his face.

"What?" Lincoln and Prabin demand in unison.

"Mick got us in to see the Commissioner of Human Rights in Lalitpur! He's agreed to meet with us and help us clear red tape, whatever that means."

"That unlikely," Lincoln says, raising his fist.

Binod and Prabin glance back and give him a sidelong look. Obviously, he's chosen the wrong word. He chews his lip, then says, "Good."

"Ahh...yes, very good," Binod says, and the outlook in the car is jubilant but cautious.

Prabin says, "Maybe our luck is turning. I have a good feeling about this."

It's certainly fortuitous, but despite his excitement for Binod, Lincoln knows they're still a long way from getting the children back. *No time to rest on our asses, though. We need to keep moving.* He looks out the window as they head down Ring Road, weaving around cars and motorbikes. He never would've guessed Mick is that connected, and he wonders what else he's underestimated about the man.

He pulls out his phone and does a search on the Commissioner of Human Rights in Lalitpur. Amir Shrestha has been with the organization since it was created after the fall of the monarchy some twenty years ago, and he's received several honors and awards for his work concerning human trafficking in the country. Instrumental in upgrading the response to violations by police and other governing authorities as well as building relationships with NGOs regarding the proliferation of human trafficking, he's considered to be the "poor man's" champion. *Just the man we need.* He scrolls further, checking out the NGOs working to combat human trafficking, and clicks on the 3 Angels, which is run by Dr. Rajendra Gautam, an orphan himself who was rescued by another NGO, Asian Aid, and given the chance to be educated in India. Further down the page, he reads about the NGO's tireless fight to save children being trafficked to east Asia, India, and the Middle East; reads testimonies from those who've been saved from a life of servitude and prostitution, and by the time he's finished, he's wiping tears from his eyes.

As he thinks about all that's happened and what he's just read, he reflects on losing his parents in the horrific accident when he was a boy. Remembers being trapped in the car with their bloody bodies lying over him and bleeding out for an hour while he waited for someone to come get him out. That, he will never forget. He's carried that memory around with him like a ball and chain, feeling sorry for himself, taking everything his aunt did for him for granted for too long. What an asshole he was to treat her the way he did when she was dying of cancer, as if she owed him something. Instead of loving her and thanking her for all she did, he begrudged every minute he had to stay home and look after her. It didn't matter back then that she made sure he attended the best schools, had new clothes whenever he needed them, vacations to Florida and Hawaii, a top-of-the-line computer, and a car to take him wherever he wanted, to say nothing about her handling his inheritance, investing it and growing it so he'd never have to worry about money. It was all expected!

His throat tightens, and a voice inside him yells, *get off the God-damned bench, stop carrying that entitled pity-party attitude and that fucking empty water bucket of regret. Do something with your life, if not for you, then for your aunt. Make what she did for you worth it. You have your heritance, put it to use—honor her hard work—make something of yourself!*

16

MAY 2, 2015

*L*incoln piles into the family car the next day with Binod, Sila, and Prabin to go meet with Amir. Sila's mother, Sumi, is staying back with Sila's sisters Amita and Roshika to look after the baby. It's a ten-mile drive to Amir's office in Lalitpur, which is a forty-five-minute excursion through the quake-riven labyrinth of winding, twisting roads. They've left an hour early for the meeting just to be sure they get there in time. Lincoln sits in back with Sila watching cars and motorbikes go by. Traffic is light today and he's glad for it: one less thing to contend with.

Beside him, Sila is biting her nails and fidgeting with her sari, pressing out non-existent wrinkles with constantly moving hands. She's like a mouse that's been caught scampering across the kitchen floor: vulnerable and skittish, a ball of nerves. Then again, they're all nervous, hoping Amir can wave a wand and make the children magically appear, even though Lincoln's pretty sure the best they can hope for is the man's ability to bring more soldiers to the fight against time.

He taps her arm, and when she looks up, he says, "We going find them."

She flashes him a tight smile, then turns her gaze back to her lap.

They turn onto Ring Road and head toward Lalitpur. The highway winds around the south end of the city, passing the Kathmandu University College. Prabin exits at the International Sports Complex, and soon they're passing through Patan Durbar Square's ancient palace, temples, and shrines. The revered square, depicting much of Nepal's storied history, wasn't damaged by the quake. Despite everything that's happened, people are out en masse paying their respects to the deities. He watches them swarm over the old road as Prabin picks his way around them. They come here everyday, young and old, in their red and yellow saris or western attire to light candles and pray for good luck or for blessings. What's missing are the tourists who normally swell the crowds. They're likely back at their hotels, hunkered down, waiting for flights out of the battered city.

Ten minutes later they're making a right at a large stuppa and passing banks, petrol stations, and eateries until at last he sees a sign pointing toward the government office. Prabin makes a left and they trundle down the road a quarter mile to a large gateway that leads into the government quad. Prabin gives their name to the guard manning the gate and after they're confirmed, they're waved in. Amir's office is in an old, broken-down two-story brick and concrete block building. Lincoln's surprised because he expected to see something a little more prominent.

Prabin parks and they all get out of the car and head inside. Amir's office is on the second floor, and the reception space is basic: light blue walls in need of painting, stained and scuffed cream-colored linoleum floors, and an old lay-in ceiling. Tired-looking wood desks and dinted metal file cabinets dot the open office area, and there's a subtle hint of mildew under the veil of disinfectant and fragrant earthy incense. It's staffed by a couple of sari-clad, middle-aged women and a young man who are working at their desks near the back of the room. One of the women looks up from her computer and gets up as they enter.

"Namaste, how can I help you?"

Binod steps ahead and he's about to answer her when a door opens at the back of the room and Mick comes out.

"Back here, Binod," Mick calls, waving him over.

They all give the woman a friendly smile as they file by, and a moment later they're in Amir's office.

Amir is a tall, tan-skinned Nepali with short gray hair clinging to a bony head. A dab of tika is above his dark probing eyes and a wan smile is on his lips. He's dressed in a tailored gray suit with a lime green tie. Binod, Sila, and Prabin greet him with effusive thanks for seeing them. Amir takes their gratitude in stride as they find their seats around his desk. Off to the side, Lincoln spies Mick sitting next to the woman who works at the hotel where they had their trekking meeting. He wonders why she's here, but there's no time to ask questions. He looks back just as Amir comes up to him.

The man loses his smile and says in English, "Namaste, Amir Shrestha. Who are you, and why are you here?"

The tall Nepali, who's maybe in his late sixties, is staring back and Lincoln finds himself startled by his directness. At last, he forces a smile and says, "Lincoln Webber, and namaste to you as well. I'm a friend of Binod and Sila's. I'm here to help in any way I can."

"Okay, hold on and I'll get another chair," Amir says, then calls out to have his staff bring one in. Lincoln wonders why they need another chair. There are two empty seats over by Mick and the woman. *What is her name?* He can't remember.

Amir waves to the tea service on the credenza by the window and breaks into Nepali. "Can I offer anyone tea while we wait?"

"That's very kind of you, but no thank you," Binod says as Amir finds his seat behind his desk. "Umm...there are others coming?"

"Yes, I invited a couple of people from 3 Angels. They're an NGO that works with the orphanages to unite displaced children with prospective parents as well as trying to curb trafficking at the border. They should be here soon."

"What's an NGO?" Binod asks.

"A non-governmental organization that's privately funded. We work with them often," Amir says, then switches to English as one of the staff arrives with a chair. "Ah, your chair, Lincoln."

Lincoln takes it and sits at the other end of the room. Seeing how Amir seems to think he doesn't know Nepali, he decides to keep the fact secret and listens in as Amir slips back into it, ignoring Sila while asking Binod to tell him about himself, where he lives, how long he's been married, where he went to school. As Binod answers the last question, a knock comes at the door.

"Come in," Amir calls.

The door opens and there's a man and a woman behind it. The man has an average build and is dressed in a navy blue suit jacket and a crisp white shirt open at the collar. A tiny red flower button is on his lapel. He's maybe in his late forties and his short black hair is blow-dried and laid back. A sleek pair of stylish glasses on his roman nose and a close-cut goatee beard and mustache gives him a distinguished appearance. The woman behind him is dressed in a print blouse and slacks. She's short and sturdy and wears her long black hair in a French braid. Intense gray eyes look out from a thin face that's seen obvious hardship, yet when she smiles it's like looking at an angel.

Amir gets up and goes to the man, and they embrace. "Namaste Rajendra, thank you for coming."

"Namaste, Amir, and it's my pleasure," Rajendra says in Nepali. He turns to the woman. "This is Kamala, one of my border people. She'll be working with you to hopefully bring the children home. She's the very best at what she does."

Kamala puts her palms together and dips her head to Amir. "Namaste," she says, and her tiny melodic voice is like a drop of honey falling on Lincoln's ears.

"Come, sit. We were just having tea," Amir says.

"Oh, none for me, thank you," Rajendra says. He turns to Binod and Sila, then Prabin, Mick, and the hotel woman, and introduces himself and Kamala. Finally, he notices Lincoln. "Oh, I'm sorry, I didn't see you sitting over there," he says in English.

Lincoln gets up and returns the Nepali greeting, then takes his seat.

As Rajendra and Kamala sit, Amir says in Nepali, "Okay, let's get started." He has Binod repeat the story of how the children were supposedly whisked away under the pretense of him and Sila dying in the earthquake. At this, Rajendra and Kamala dart knowing glances at each other.

When Binod is finished, Amir says, "I checked with the Army, and as far as anyone knows, they weren't up there the day the children were taken. I've also alerted the Special Police Force in charge of trafficking here in the city, and the one in Pokhara. I know they're looking at a number of suspect orphanages right now. Binod, did you check with all the armed police wards?"

"Not all of them yet, but the ones' we have so far know nothing."

Rajendra ponders that a moment, then says, "You said they were taken when?"

"Thursday."

"Two days ago," Rajendra says, more to himself than anyone. He looks to Kamala. "How long do you think we have if they're going to move them out of the country?"

"Two weeks at the most."

"Do you have pictures of the kids?"

"Yes," Binod says, pulling out his phone and showing him.

Rajendra looks at them, then passes Binod's phone to Kamala. "This is very helpful, and in our favor," Rajendra says. "More than likely, the spotters don't know or think we have pictures to show around. Or that you're looking to get them back."

Mick speaks up. "What do you mean? Of course parents want to look for their children, and what are *spotters*?"

"Not necessarily," Kamala answers. "Much of the time, poor people up in the hills sell their children, believing the spotters, who tell them they're putting the children with good families who will offer their kids a chance to go to school and have a better life."

"That's crazy," Mick says.

Lincoln sees the hotel woman shift in her chair, then glance at Mick and Amir. He wonders what that's all about as silence follows, but again, he thinks: *later*.

"It happens," Rajendra says, shrugging, "and if they find out the kids have been rescued from a brothel, they won't take them back. They consider them spoiled and not marriageable." When Kamala hands him back Binod's phone, he adds, "As for spotters, they work with unscrupulous bondsmen who are supposed to place real orphans with real families. But sadly, that's not the case. These men use a network of so-called orphanages as a repository for the kids they steal, and they're almost impossible to catch because they're very careful." At last he turns to Binod. "What are your children's names, and how old are they?"

"Sunita and Arjun. Sunni is fourteen and Arjun, seven."

"Sunita will be their priority," Kamala says to Rajendra, who agrees. She turns to Amir. "We need to get her picture out to as many dress shops as possible, and also to the Special Police and the other wards. Concentrate on the shops around the Gongabu area. If we get a hit, we'll know they're close by."

"Then what?" Prabin says.

"Then we try to ascertain where," Rajendra says. "More than likely it'll be some inconspicuous building masquerading as an orphanage...there's lots of them."

"And once we narrow it down, I'll order a raid on the local so-called orphanages," Amir puts in.

Binod frowns. "I don't understand. Why are we handing photos out to dress shops?"

"Because they'll want to dress your daughter up for a prospective buyer. Make her look grown up and pretty for the brothels or as a toy for some wealthy man to play with," Kamala says, and if Lincoln didn't know better, he'd swear she was going to spit on the floor.

An audible gasp comes from Sila's mouth. Binod puts his arm around her and she leans into him. "What about my son?" Binod asks.

"That depends on whether he remains in Kathmandu or not," Amir says. "A lot of times, they keep kids in these orphanages as emissaries to lure unsuspecting, big-hearted foreigners into making large donations, which they pocket."

"And if they don't remain?" Prabin puts in.

Rajendra and Kamala share glances and Lincoln can see they're trying to figure out how to answer him. He has no idea what could make the two 3 Angels agents hesitate, and he's not sure he wants to know. Finally Rajendra says, "Your son will be fated for a life of servitude if we can't get to him, probably in the Middle East, India, or Southeast Asia."

"You mean, like a slave?" Binod says, and he puts his knuckles to his mouth.

Amir nods, but it's not convincing. "But let's not go there just yet. They might have a bit of a head start on us, but like Rajendra said, we have your son's and daughter's pictures, and that's big. We'll be sharing them with all our border people and the Indian authorities as well as with the airports in Kathmandu and Pokhara."

"What about the other borders?" Prabin says.

"Them too," Amir says, "but their preferred routes are into India. Too much scrutiny and curious guards elsewhere."

"So what are our chances of finding them? What are the odds?" Mick says, leaning forward. "And what can we do?"

"I don't know what the odds are," Rajendra says, "but I know with what we have, they're a lot better than most of the time. As far as what you can do, keep spreading the word, and their pictures."

"Other than that," Kamala adds, "we're afraid all you can do is wait and know we'll be watching everything closely. I promise you, we'll try to get them back with everything we have."

"So that's it, just watching?" Prabin says, frowning.

Rajendra turns to him. "This woman here beside me, she was once taken. She spent three years forced to work in a brothel in India, servicing twenty to thirty men a day. She knows what it's like, how they operate. Believe me when I tell you: if anyone can find your children, it's this woman here, and others like her."

But across the room Mick is staring ahead, and his gaze is burning a hole through the wall behind Lincoln. Lincoln knows exactly what the High Trails coordinator is thinking, and he's totally on board with it. *You're not fucking sitting around, are you, big guy? Well, neither am I! Let them do their thing and we'll do ours.*

The meeting breaks up ten minutes later. Binod, Sila, and Prabin go out and Lincoln is about to follow, but he stops when he sees Mick and the hotel woman drift over to Rajendra and Kamala, who are quietly chatting with Amir. The three of them linger nearby, listening to the ongoing conversation. When the opportunity presents itself, Mick says in Nepali, "Can I ask a question?"

Amir turns to him. "Sure, of course."

Mick turns to Rajendra and Kamala. "What

weren't you telling Binod, when he asked about his son?"

Lincoln moves closer to listen in. The question is on his mind, too.

"What do you mean?" Amir asks, turning a sharp glance at the hotel woman. It's clear he doesn't like Mick's veiled insinuation regarding Rajendra's answer to Binod.

"Well, I noticed people hesitated when he asked about it. Is there more to it than what you told him?" Mick says.

Rajendra glances at Amir, then says to Mick, "You're friends of theirs, I take it?"

"I'm his boss, but yes, we're friends, too."

Rajendra nods. "Yes, there's more, but I didn't see the need to go into detail. They're scared and worried as it is."

"What more?" Mick asks again.

"It's not important. The only thing that matters is we get them back," Rajendra says.

Mick purses his lips and Lincoln sees him draw a breath. "I agree a hundred percent. Look, I don't mean to be difficult, but sooner or later, someone might go digging on the Internet looking for answers, if you get my meaning. Wouldn't it be better hearing it from a friend rather than the web?"

The hotel woman next to Mick darts glances at Amir and Rajendra. She says, "He's got a point."

Amir frowns.

Rajendra puts his hand up. "It's okay, Amir. He's concerned. They're all concerned. I would be, too. And yes, he does have a point." He turns to Mick. "You really want to know?"

"Not really, but I think I should in case Binod and Sila go looking."

"All right," Rajendra says with a sigh. He swallows, as if to get some awful taste out of his mouth, then clears his throat. "The boy could also end up in a brothel or be sold to certain men who have appetites for young boys." He pauses, glances at Kamala beside him, then goes on. "Also...he could be sold on the black market for his organs. There's a big demand for kidneys, livers, eyes, and hearts, and it pays well. Up to half-a-million rupees for a heart."

Mick drops his jaw and the hotel woman gasps. Or is the gasp Lincoln hears coming from himself? He can't believe what he's just heard. Surely he heard wrong. He can't even wrap his mind around such a monstrosity. Who would carve a child up for their organs? *What kind of monsters would do this?* He wants to run out, find and strangle them, beat their faces to a bloody pulp. Across from him, Mick is looking off into space, his eyes wide and glistening as the woman beside him blinks back tears.

At last, Rajendra says, "It's a terrible, wicked thing, but it happens, and way too often. For every child we save, ten or twenty more slip by. But we'll never give up until we put an end to this inhumanity." He puts his hand on Mick's shoulder and looks him in the eye. "Do you understand now, our commitment to bringing these children home?"

Mick nods and Lincoln can see through the blur of his eyes that Mick's fighting to hold back the rage that's also building inside of him.

Palisha follows Mick and Lincoln down the stairs and out to the parking lot, where the family he cares about is huddled around their car talking. She can't imagine what they're going through, doesn't want to imagine it. If anything like this had happened to her boys, she would be out of her mind. She turns and looks up at the window where her father is standing, looking down at them. Today has given her a new appreciation of the things he has to live with in his job. Sheltering her and her mother from it all these years, carrying around the horrors of such atrocities, must have been an unbearable burden. He wouldn't have survived without his intractable demeanor. Suddenly, she loves him in a way she's never expected: sees him as more than the authoritarian figure she grew up with. Sees him as a man of conscience, trying to make life better for those who are pressed to the margins of society. Truly, he's a man deserving of all the love in her heart.

Ahead of her, she sees Rajendra and Kamala get

into their car. It's a sleek black SUV that costs more than most people's homes. Suddenly, she discovers herself making judgments about them, before she remembers her father drives a BMW sedan and lives in a home most people would consider a palace. It's another sobering reminder of all the things she took for granted growing up (and for that matter, even now) while she complained of the unfairness of life. It gives her pause and makes her think she's pretty lucky, and suddenly she wants to give back a generous portion of what's been given to her.

But right now, Mick is the priority. He's shaken and angry, and she's certain he's not going to just sit around and wait. It's not that she doesn't share his sentiment, but what can they do? She has no idea where they'd start, and it's not like they can go running around, demanding everyone stop what they're doing to look for the children. As she comes beside him and Lincoln, she sees a hard, defiant look on his face. She's seen it before. It's the same look Mick had a year ago when a bully in the hotel whacked an unruly child, sending him sprawling to the floor. It didn't turn out well for the bully.

Mick casts a quick look over at Binod, Prabin, and Sila, then turns to her and Lincoln. "So help me, God, if it's the last thing I do, I'm not going to let their children be used and butchered as long as there's breath in me."

"Damn right," Lincoln says.

"What are you going to do, though?" she asks, aching for Mick, wanting to hug him and hold him tight, feel his powerful arms around her.

"I don't know. I need to think," he says, then shuts his eyes tight and grits his teeth.

She grabs his arm. "Are you all right?"

"Yeah, just a pinch. I need to say good-bye, then we should get back to the hotel."

"Okay, I will drive."

Lincoln turns to her. "Hey, you have any more rooms available at your hotel? They've been good to me. I don't want to put them out anymore. By the way, I'm Lincoln, but you can call me Link."

"Palisha Kc. Nice to meet you, Link, and of course, we have a room for you and it will be on the house, as you Americans like to say."

"Oh, that's very kind, but I insist on paying. By the way," he says, glancing back and forth between them, "are you two—"

"Oh, no. Just best friends," Palisha says, and then holds Mick in a loving gaze and adds, "forever."

17

MAY 2, 2015

*P*alisha pulls into the hotel lot and parks. On the way back, Lincoln brought up an idea and she's nervous about it. It's one thing to be passing pictures of the kids around in town, quite another going undercover. Who knows how dangerous these men are, and the thought of something happening to Mick scares the hell out of her. She's kept quiet about it in the car, but once she's alone with Mick she's going to make her feelings known.

Lincoln says, "Once I get settled in, we can meet in my room and go over things."

"Sounds like a plan," Mick says.

Palisha turns the car off and turns to Mick. "I think it would be better if you rested a bit first. You are still healing."

Mick purses his lips and frowns, then breaks into

a crooked grin. He tilts his head back toward Lincoln. "Momma bear up here is putting her foot down."

"I am just looking out for you," she says.

"Not a problem," Lincoln says. "Second thought, it'll give me time to do some research on the net." He leans forward, poking his head between their bucket seats, and looks at her. "Your Wi-Fi's up and running, right?"

"Yes, but it is on and off right now, so you might have problems getting on," she says.

Lincoln sucks his lips. "Okay, I'll just have to deal then, I guess." He turns to Mick. "So, let's say around dinner then? How's that work?"

"Sure," Mick says, then eyes Palisha. "Does the doctor up here have any objections?"

She rolls her eyes and opens the door. "Come on, let's get you up to your room."

They head into the hotel and Palisha gets Lincoln a key for a room on the third floor, then they go to their rooms. While she freshens up, she turns on the TV and listens to the latest news about the quake, but her thoughts remain on Mick and Lincoln's conversation. She's not sure what to make of this American. He seems nice enough, and he certainly cares about the children Mick is fond of, but she doesn't like the ideas he's putting in Mick's head. Hopefully, Mick won't get sucked into Lincoln's plans. There have to be other ways they can feel helpful besides going into that evil, seedy world.

She checks herself in the mirror, reties her hair into a braid, and runs a coat of pink gloss over her lips. Now that she isn't in her father's world, she can wear the necklace Mick gave her, and add a few pretty bangles to her wrists she purchased along with some clothes the other day. Five minutes later, she's out the door going to Mick's room.

"Hello, Mick, can I come in?" she calls softly, knocking on his door. When there's no answer, she knocks again. "Mick, it is me." She waits and waits, then frowns. *Did he sneak off to Lincoln's room? Maybe he's in the bathroom.* She waits another minute, then knocks again. "Mick?"

Again, she waits, and as she does, her heart thumps, and her thoughts fly in several directions. One of them, which she's trying to tamp down, is whispering something's happened to him. Suddenly his wincing on and off from the injury during the meeting, and again in the car on the way home, galvanizes in her head. She's about to start down the hall to get a key card from the office downstairs when she hears him come to the door. He opens it, and his face looks pale when he lets her in.

"Are you all right?"

He nods, but she doesn't believe him. "You need to go lie down." For once, he doesn't argue with her. She goes into the bathroom, washes her hands. "I was worried when you did not answer the door," she calls out to him.

"I was on the throne."

Huh? Oh, the toilet. She snickers, then comes back out. "Take your shirt off, I want to look at the bandage."

He cocks an eye and smirks.

"Oh, please!" But she can't help smiling back as he undoes his buttons. The long bandage under his ribs looks fine, which is a relief, but it's what's under it she wants to make sure of. "Lie back, let me take a look," she says, pushing him back onto the bed. She inserts a fingernail under the tape holding the bandage in place, not sure what she's looking for, but she figures she'll know if something's wrong when she sees it. Lifting it up, she sees the stitched-up laceration is swollen and pink. It's a lot longer than she expected. When she puts her finger to the side of it, he jumps.

"Easy there, Florence."

"What?"

"Never mind. Just be careful. It stings like hell."

"Is it supposed to be warm around the cut?"

"From what I understand, yes, for a few days." She can sense him watching her as she studies the wound. The guilty feelings she has for asking him to fix her sink come rushing back. *If it weren't for me, you'd be okay.* Finally, he says, "Pretty ugly, isn't it?"

She sits on the bed beside him, looking into his pained expression. "I am sorry."

"For what?"

She tilts her head toward the wound. "That! If I had not—"

"Stop it! There's no way you could've known," he says. "And besides, if I hadn't been there, maybe that poor Nepali I helped wouldn't be alive. No one knows why certain things happen, Polly. Let it go. We're here together, alive, and that's all that matters. Well...almost all that matters. We gotta get those kids back." He pats her shoulder. "Mind buttoning me up?"

"Oh, yes." She replaces the bandage, and as she buttons his shirt, she says, "Speaking of the kids, I do not think Lincoln's idea is a good one. We do not know what these people are like. They could be very dangerous."

"That's true, but when things matter, you gotta take chances. Otherwise the bad guys win, and when they win, everyone loses." He pauses. "You know about Hitler, right?"

"I read about him in school, yes," she says, finishing up his last button.

"Then you know what happens when people turn their heads the other way."

"But this is not Hitler, and this is not a war, Mick."

"Really? Think about it, Polly. These men are rounding up children, stealing young women and men, sending them off to be used for sex, or as indentured servants, or carved up as organ donors, and

God knows what else. Sure, they're not the Gestapo, and they're not gassing them, but it's not far off from that, either. If we can save two, maybe we can save more, who knows. But if we look the other way, saying it's too dangerous, I might get hurt, what does that say about who we are? This is your country, your people—your future, Polly. If these were your boys, wouldn't you hope someone would do the same for you? I know you're scared, but I won't turn my head away from this, and I hope you won't either."

Palisha has convinced Mick to order dinner to his room and have Lincoln come there to discuss their plans for digging into the trafficking world. She's had one of her staff bring up a large table. They switch the smaller room table out for it and add a couple of comfortable chairs. At the moment, they're eating: a large bowl of Dehli Chaat with a side dish of *gundruk* for Lincoln, some kabobs and *sandheko* for Mick, and for her, a plate of vegetable momos. Lincoln has scored (his word for it) a bottle of rum, which is being steadily drained by the men. She's sticking with tea.

They're halfway into the meal when Lincoln stabs a ball of deep-fried batter, pops it in his mouth, and says. "I've been reading, and what I've found out will curl your fu..." He glances at Palisha across the table, swallows his food, and smiles, then clears his throat. "Your freaking hair. Apparently, these spotter guys not only look for kids on the street, they trick parents up in the mountains into selling their children by paying other villagers to convince them to do it. Sometimes for as little as fifteen American dollars. Then they whisk the kids into ill-legit orphanages who work with disreputable bondsmen, who then turn around and sell them for up to twenty-five grand."

Mick frowns from where he sits on the bed. "You've got to be kidding me."

Lincoln shakes his head. "Nope, and it gets worse. Most of these orphanages, like Amir said, are ill-legit, run-down, filthy places where kids are forced to work all day in squalor, sleep on pads on concrete floors, eat the dregs no one wants, and this is primo— force girls to sexually abuse the younger boys to get them ready for the brothels."

Palisha blinks, suddenly no longer hungry, and sits back as Mick stops eating mid-bite. "This is sick. This is happening?" she cries out. "I am aware Nepal has an ugly side, I have read and seen a few things regarding prostitution and drugs, but this is...this is..." She looks to Mick, who's staring ahead, the way she saw him do at the meeting.

Lincoln pops another ball of deep-fried batter slathered in yogurt into his mouth, washes it down with a sip of rum, and says, "Disgusting? F'd up? Absolutely." He pulls a folded piece of paper from his shirt pocket, opens it, and reads. "Here's a little stat for you. 'Only 10 percent of children in orphanages are actually abandoned or have lost their parents.'"

Mick downs his rum in one gulp and sets his glass down with a thunk on the bedside table.

Lincoln looks up, his face red, and his deep blue eyes are dark as death. "These guys steal them right out from under their parents' noses, then to avoid suspicion, publish FAKE death certificates. That way the kids won't be found, and they can use them as a meal ticket."

Palisha stares back. "Meal ticket?"

"Umm...preying on the good-natured hearts of volunteers and foreigners, like Amir said," Lincoln says, pushing his plate away. He takes another sip of rum. "And here's another little fun fact. Most of the orphanages in the country are unregistered, and 90 percent of the legit ones fail to meet the minimum standard of care."

"Christ," Mick says. "Why didn't I know this?"

"Why didn't any of us?" Lincoln says, then turns to Palisha. "Your father never told you about this?"

"No, I think he wanted to protect me from what he goes through every day and tries to prevent. This is awful. How could I have been so umm...inexperienced?"

"The word you're looking for is naïve," Mick says. "These poor children. What is wrong with people?"

"It's an ugly world out there, Mick," Lincoln says, and snorts.

"So maybe the kids won't go across the border," Mick says. "That would be in our favor, I would think."

"Maybe. But if the guys who took them are going to move 'em, I think it's going to happen pretty quick," Lincoln says. "Anyway, here's my thought. There's ten legit orphanages here in the city, or at least that's what it looks like according to CCWB—"

"Which is?" Mick asks.

"Central Child Welfare Board," Lincoln says, sitting back in his chair. He refills his rum glass and holds the bottle out for Mick. "They're spaced around the city pretty good, but I think we could get to all of them in one day. I'll use the pretense I'm interested in making a donation, then slip in the fact that my friend, which would be you, Palisha, is looking to adopt, and ask if they could steer us clear of any disreputable bondsmen."

"As opposed to reputable ones?"

"Yeah, it's ass-backwards, I know, but it just might get us started in the right direction."

"Then what?" Palisha says, wondering what Lincoln's hoping to accomplish. She's not sure she likes the idea of her looking to adopt, but it seems safe enough.

"Start asking around on the streets." Lincoln

shrugs. "I know it's a long shot, but it's better than sitting here on our hands."

"And what happens if you find one?" she says.

"Then I pretend I'm looking for what they might have, and ask if they have anything I might be interested in. I'm assuming they'll have pictures."

"And if you find the kids?"

Lincoln smiles, downs another shot of rum, and says, "I'll buy 'em."

"You serious?" Mick says. "You have that kind of money?"

More than you know, big guy. "Don't worry."

Mick pours another glass of rum. "What can I do?"

"Research, and lots of it. We need to know as much as we can about these guys, how they operate, the whole deal."

"We can make the room here like a command center, then," Palisha says, feeling better about Mick remaining in the hotel.

"That works, and I'll check in from the road every hour or so to let you know how things are going," Lincoln says. "Oh, it'd probably be best not to say anything to Binod and Sila about this. We don't want to get their hopes up about this pipe dream unless something comes of it."

MAY 3, 2015

Lincoln's been on the road most of the day and so far he's not had any luck. Two of the orphan-keepers, one at S.O.S. Children's Village and the other at Bal Mandir, were out and couldn't be reached and the other two, Nepal Orphans' Home and Happy Home Orphanage, didn't know anything, or pretended not to. He ended up leaving a small donation at each of them, wary that the money might go into the pockets of people who didn't deserve it.

He pulls into the lot outside the last home for the day, the Lotus Children's Home, and parks. It's a modern-looking brick building with dark bronze trim. A sprawling sward of sheared grass surrounds the building. He's impressed by what he sees and looks over to Palisha.

"This is the last of the so-called legit homes for today. Keep your fingers crossed."

They get out and head toward the front entrance. The lobby, though small, is airy and the walls are painted robin-egg blue with stenciled pictures of lotus flowers and rhododendrons. There's a woman sitting at a wooden desk. She looks up as the door closes behind them. "Can I help you?" she says in Nepali.

"Yes, we hoping see orphan-keeper if he in. My friend, Niru, looking to adopt, and I, maybe make donation to fine orphanage."

"Oh, how nice. Hold on and I'll get him for you," she says, picking up the phone. "Naresh, there's a couple to see you about a child and a donation... Okay?" She hangs up. "He'll be right out."

A minute later, a short, thin man with dark-rimmed glasses and a wide smile on his narrow brown face comes around the corner. He's dressed in a cream-colored tapālan and slacks. There's a slight limp in his walk, which he offsets with a cane in his right hand. He switches it over and puts a hand out to Lincoln. "Namaste. Naresh Parishamee. Nice to meet you," he says in English.

"David Squire, and this is my good friend Niru Gautam. We were hoping you could speak with us, if you have time. Niru is looking to adopt a child and I'm looking to make a contribution to a needy orphanage."

"Of course, of course. Why don't you come with me and I'll show you around? This is a new building for us, funded by our good friends in Kuala Lumpur... all up-to-date facilities. I'm assuming you would like to see the children first? We have so many who need good homes. Right now, they're having dinner in our cafeteria. Are you interested in a girl or a boy?"

"Oh, I think, a girl," Palisha says, glancing at Lincoln, and he can see her mind turning. This orphanage is by far the nicest one they've seen.

As Lincoln walks beside her past the children's bedrooms, he can see they're not going to get the information he's hoping for. The place is so far removed from the world he's read about, there's little chance this guy would have any idea of the type of people he's looking for. But they're here, so it doesn't hurt to try, and he'll feel better knowing any money he gives will likely end up where it's supposed to go.

When they come to the cafeteria, they look in. There are twenty or twenty-five children, ages seven or eight through perhaps sixteen, sitting at tables eating. The food looks freshly cooked and appealing. The kids are dressed in clean clothes: some wearing jeans and short-sleeved pullovers, others in joggers and sweatshirts. They all have footwear in good shape. For show, he points out one of the girls to Palisha, and as he does, one of the boys looks his way. For a moment, he's in quicksand, being pulled down. That boy could've been him, had he lived in Nepal growing up.

"You have a very nice facility here," Lincoln says, doing all he can to look away.

"We like to think so," Naresh says, then turns to Palisha. "What do you think? Her name is Sila. She's twelve and she's been here for three years. Her family passed tragically in a flood that hit Kharapani in 2012."

As if the boy's look, which is a punch to his gut, isn't enough, the mention of the girl's name is like an uppercut.

Palisha says, "What a pretty name."

Naresh smiles. "Why don't we go find out about her? Unless of course you want to see more."

"Maybe after," Palisha says, smiling.

They walk back to Naresh's office and sit. Naresh leans his cane against the wall and takes a seat behind his desk. "I have to say, this is a pleasant surprise. Usually, prospective parents call ahead and make an appointment. I wish I had something here to serve you."

"Oh, that's all right," Palisha says.

"So you usually deal directly with parents, then?" Lincoln says.

"Well, yes. Them, and their bondsmen, of course."

"Of course. That's something we wanted to ask about. Niru will be looking to hire one. Can you let her know the ones to stay away from? We hear there's a lot of disreputable men out there."

"Oh, I'm sure there are. We only deal with the best, though," Naresh says as he logs onto his computer. "Hold on, and I'll get you some names."

Lincoln watches him type and shakes his head furtively. Then again, he didn't expect he'd find out anything.

Palisha leans forward in her chair. "Excuse me, Mr. Naresh."

"Yes?"

"You look like a very honorable man, so please excuse my directness and our pretense, but this is important." She glances at Lincoln, then says, "We are searching for some children who were taken against their will and time is running out for them."

Holy crap, what are you doing?

Naresh frowns. "What is this? Who do you think I am? I think you need to leave," he says, getting up.

Game over! Then again, it was over the minute we walked in.

Palisha pushes on. "I think you are a good man, whom these children are at the mercy of—"

"And whom I'm going to make a generous donation to," Lincoln pipes in, pulling out his checkbook. He tears out a check. "Whether you know anything or not, I'm gonna write out a check here. How many zeroes follow the 'one' is up to you."

Naresh eyes the check in front of Lincoln, then flicks a glance at the both of them. "Is this some scam? What do you want?"

"I assure you it's not. Pull this website up," Lincoln says, snatching a card from Naresh's desk. He writes out the address and shoves it toward him. "It's my bank in the States, and I'll show you."

Naresh sits back down, types in the web address, and brings up the page. Lincoln has him turn the monitor around and enters his password, bringing up his account balances. When he turns the monitor back, Naresh's eyes bulge.

"So?" Lincoln says and sits back.

Naresh is quiet a moment. "These children were stolen, truly?"

Palisha looks back at him, her dark eyes beseeching. "Truly."

Naresh sits with that a moment. Finally, he says, "I know some of the world you speak of."

"At this point we'll take the tiniest bit of info we can get. The parents of these two children," Lincoln says, taking his phone out and showing Naresh their faces, "are going out of their minds."

Naresh presses his lips together, and it's clear he's nervous. Finally, he says, "I can't tell you who any of these disreputable bondsmen are, because no one knows who they are. You must understand, they're everywhere. I wouldn't know if one was standing here right in front of me." He pauses, sucks his lip, then leans forward as if he's afraid someone will hear, and says, "There is a man I've heard about. They call him the Merchandiser or something like that. I can't tell you where to start looking for him, but it's rumored he works the Gongabu district. Apparently he also has a taste for American girls, so maybe Thamel as well." He sits back in his chair. "I'm curious, though, why aren't you working with the police?"

"We are, but we can't just stand by and wait for a miracle."

Naresh nods. "I can understand that." He takes his glasses off and sets them in front of him, then kneads the bridge of his nose with his fingers. "So, if I might ask, what is your plan if you find him? I don't think you will, but if you do?"

"If he has them, buy them back."

Naresh almost laughs. "It's not so easy as that. These guys are very suspicious. You go in like an anxious tourist looking for a souvenir, and he'll think you're the police. Then he'll vanish, and you'll never have a chance of getting the kids back."

"What do you suggest?"

"If I were you, I think I'd approach him like one of his clients."

"Meaning?"

"Rich-looking, and just as suspicious as he is, I would think. Use subtle, indirect language, saying stuff like, 'I have some need of your special services,' and the like." Naresh puts his glasses back on and leans forward again, pinning his dark eyes on Lincoln. "Get rid of that beard and mustache, too, and get a haircut, and some decent clothes—no offense—but you have to look the part."

"Anything else?"

"Yes, get rid of the piece of crap watch you have on and get something expensive. A diamond pinky ring wouldn't hurt, either. And last of all, and this is one thing even I know, never say you're looking to buy a child. Find another term."

"Like merchandise?"

"Something like that. Oh, one more thing, they're gonna check you out on the Internet. You can bet on it, so whatever you tell them, it better match up."

"Right. Thank you, you have been so helpful," says Palisha.

Lincoln grabs his pen. "How does a 5,000 American dollar donation sound?"

"You would give us that much?"

"You're doing good work here, I can see that. The children look healthy and as happy as one could expect," Lincoln says, writing out the check. "If we find these two children we're looking for, I'll be back with more."

"You are too kind," Naresh says, getting up. He smiles at Palisha and gives Lincoln a hopeful glance. "I suppose the adoption is out of consideration then."

"At the moment, yes," Palisha says, "but you never know." And from the corner of Lincoln's eye, he sees her smile.

18

MAY 3, 2015

$\mathcal{B}$inod is in Sila's parents' living room, printing out fliers from the printer he's dragged in from the spare bedroom. Sila's brother, Dibaker, who has taken the day off from his store to come help, is sitting on the floor beside him. The couch next to them is littered with papers, maps, and markers. They've already printed a hundred copies and Binod wonders if that's enough. His plan is to hit every clothing shop he can find in Thamel today, then go to the hospital to see his brother, Galen, and his sister, Anika.

Prabin walks into the room, picks up one of the fliers and looks it over, then says, "Are you sure you want your number on these?"

"What do you mean?" Binod asks.

"Well, you could get a lot of calls that have

nothing to do with Sunita and Arjun. What do they call it, spam."

Binod hadn't thought about that. He looks at Dibaker, who stares back wide-eyed. But how would anyone get a hold of him otherwise? He considers what Prabin says, thinking he should've gotten another phone with a different number, but at this point, it would take most of the morning, and he's already printed out so many fliers, and he's running out of toner...and time. *I'll just have to deal with it.*

"You're right, but it's already 9:00. We need to go. Are you ready?" Binod says, pulling the last twenty copies off the printer tray.

"Anytime you want to leave."

Sila walks in with the baby. She's still in her nightclothes and she's subdued, but at least now she seems to be functioning, and she's talking more. He looks up at her wan face. The empty look in her eyes over the last two days has given way to watchfulness and she's been more attentive to their son, playing peek-a-boo on the couch with him now and then and even smiling on occasion. But he knows she'll never get back to the Sila he knows and loves if they can't find Sunita and Arjun—none of them will. He also knows that it's Sunita she cries for most. Even though she loves both her children equally, Sunita is her heart. The two of them are connected in indefinable ways, a look between them here and there that speaks volumes.

He can't imagine what life would be like if they can't find their children, doesn't want to. He has to find them and get them back. He stacks the fliers in a neat pile and tucks them in a satchel Prabin has dug out of a closet. "We're going now," he says to her, and gets up and goes over to kiss his son on the forehead. The baby wiggles in his mother's arms and sticks a thumb in his mouth.

Sila asks, "When will you be home?"

"I don't know. After I pass all these out, I'm going to see my brother and sister in the hospital."

"Tell them I said hi."

"Of course." He pulls her and the baby to him and holds them. Sila just stands there, no reaction. It cuts him to the bone, and he feels that ugly ripple of guilt run through his body again. Letting go of her, he says, "I'll call you when we're on our way home."

She nods, and he sees a tiny smile come to her face. "Be safe, and if you find out anything, anything at all, let me know."

"You'll be the first to know," he says, and turns to join Prabin and Dibaker at the door.

Outside, the sun is shining through the cracks in the clouds. It's cool out, and there's a hint of rain in the air. They get into Prabin's car and they're off to their first destination, Thamel.

When they get there, they find a place to park and split up. Thamel is perking up after the quake and people are out and about. For the most part, the shops are open, and their owners are standing outside hoping to lure the remaining tourists in. Dibaker has headed south toward Durbar Square as far as he can go. The square is still pretty well cordoned off due to the damage from the quake. Prabin has gone north, toward Amrit College, and Binod is concentrating his efforts in the central part of the district. He goes down the street, ducking into shops. Working in this part of town for Dibaker, he knows quite a few of the owners, and they're receptive to his handing out fliers. Many of them take the time to ask him how he's doing and tell him they'll light candles for him at the temples. He's also having running text conversations with Mick and Lincoln, who are asking him how he and Sila are doing. He tells them they're out passing fliers around and again thanks them for all they're doing.

Around noon, he, Dibaker, and Prabin gather for lunch at Rosemary Kitchen and Coffee Shop. Dibaker has given out most of his fliers and Prabin has maybe a dozen left. Binod surveys the remaining fliers in his satchel and frowns. He has maybe twenty or thirty left. He should've printed more. They order their lunches and eat, talking about their next foray into the district. Prabin thinks maybe they should hit up some of the people going about. Binod isn't sure about that. How would tourists know anything? But Prabin points out that the more people who know about the children, the better their chances, and who knows, they just might get a call.

The waiter comes around with their tab, which Prabin insists on paying. As he digs into his pocket, he says to the man, "Do you mind posting one of these fliers? We're looking for a couple of missing children."

Dibaker hands the man a flier and the man looks at it. "Sure, no problem. What happened?"

"They were taken up north," Prabin says, pointing to the children's faces on the paper, "and we think they're being trafficked through Kathmandu, and then out of the country."

"That's terrible," the man says. "I hear, with the earthquake happening, there's a lot of children being taken right now. We'll definitely keep an eye out for you."

Prabin hands him a pair of thousand-rupee notes. "Thanks."

The waiter starts to go away, then turns around with a thoughtful look on his face. "Have you tried any of the orphanages?"

Binod blinks. *The 3 Angels guy mentioned orphanages. You dummy, Binod. Why didn't you think of that?* He looks at Dibaker and Prabin, feeling like a fool. "No, we haven't."

"You might want to," the waiter says.

"That's very kind, thank you," Binod says. When

the waiter leaves, he says to Prabin, "We need to make more copies and find these orphanages."

"If they'll do anything." Prabin snorts. "They're trying to get rid of what they already have."

Dibaker, who seems to be deep in thought, perks up and says, "No, you don't get it. We don't need 'em."

"Need what?" Prabin and Binod say in unison.

"We don't need fliers," Dibaker says. "They're orphanages. Think about it. They probably hold missing children, too. All we need to do is get in and have a look around. Maybe we'll see Sunita and Arjun in one of them."

It's like a siren has just gone off in Binod's head. "He's right! They let us in and we get to see the children. That's brilliant, Dibaker."

"I don't think it's that simple," Dibaker says, waving a finger. "If they're holding missing children, they're probably working with traffickers, too."

"So what do we do?" Prabin says, frowning.

"We pretend to...to...to be looking to...give a donation, maybe," Dibaker says.

Binod smiles and pats his brother-in-law on the shoulder. "Again, you amaze me," he says, pulling out his phone, and does a search on orphanages. To his dismay, there are hundreds of them all over the city. How are they ever going to get to them all? He looks up and Dibaker is staring back.

"What's wrong?"

Binod shows him the long list of homes, and Dibaker lets out a whistle. "Well, we need to start somewhere, what about this one?" he says, pointing to one across the Bishnumati River.

～

It's going on 6:00 p.m., and so far they've only been to six homes, two of which insisted they come back later. Two others were more than willing to take their money but wouldn't let them in, and the last two they did get into were places Binod wouldn't let a dog live, let alone his children. The kids were in rags, no shoes or socks, and their faces and hair probably hadn't seen soap and water in weeks. But it was their dull, spiritless eyes and tight lips that Binod can't forget. He keeps seeing their empty expressions in his head, overlapping them onto his children. They circle around and around him as Prabin drives him back to Thamel to see his brother and sister.

Prabin says, "I can't believe what I saw. Those little boys and girls. They look so hopeless. And the conditions they live in. They call that a home? It's nothing but a barn. I've seen cleaner outhouses!"

Binod says nothing. Their plans aren't working out the way he hoped. The orphan-keepers (a title they've since learned) are suspicious people. He's also tired of riding this emotional elevator that's tearing him up inside and spitting him out. In fact, he's not sure he can last another day right now. Why is Shiva doing this to him, taking away the only things that matter, turning his world into a black abyss? He looks out the window toward the setting sun staining an army of clouds marching overhead. The deep magenta, yellow, and oranges contrasted against the silhouetted buildings give the brooding city skyline a mournful appearance, as if it were a charred forest clawing at the sky.

Prabin makes a left onto New Road, and it isn't long before he's pulling up outside the front entrance to Bir Hospital. He lets Binod out and goes with Dibaker to find a place to park. Binod goes in and waits in line to find out what rooms Galen and Anika are in, then heads up to the third floor. He's been told his brother is in the neurological ward with a traumatic brain injury and a broken arm, and his sister is in the orthopedic ward with an amputation just above the knee on her right leg. Can this nightmare he's been thrust into get any worse?

He goes to his brother's room first. The room, which obviously is only meant for two, has been arranged to handle three due to the influx of patients pulled out of the earthquake wreckage. It reeks of disinfectant and stale air. A host of monitors stuffed between the patient beds are murmuring, and in the far corner, a small wall-mounted TV is babbling. His brother's bed is closest to the door and when he comes to it, he sees a man he hardly recognizes looking away from him under a swath of bandages covering the right side of his head.

Going up to him, he reaches through the rails and touches Galen's shoulder above the splint. Galen stirs and turns his head toward him. There's an ugly gash on his cheek, which has been sutured, and a dark bruise around his left eye. They look at each other for a minute and Binod doesn't know what to say. Finally, Galen moves his lips and says, "Binod." It's slurred coming out of his mouth.

"I'm here. I'm sorry I haven't been until now."

Galen nods, then says, "Bubā and Āmā, they're okay?"

How does he answer that? How does he tell him they're gone? "They're comfortable, don't you worry." It's not exactly a lie, but close enough that he hates himself for it. "Are you in pain?"

"I hurt, yes, but not too bad. Anika, how is she? No one tells me anything."

"I haven't seen her yet." A half-truth, and again he doesn't like himself. "I'm going to see her right after you. Is there anything you need or want?"

"No, not right now. How are the kids?"

Binod's throat tightens and he looks away. "They're fine."

"Good, good. I've been worried about them. I left them with Gokul. I know he'll look after them. You should go see Anika now. I'll be okay."

"Are you sure?" Binod says, turning back to him.

"Yes, I'm a bit tired anyway. They just gave me my medication. Maybe you can come back tomorrow, and we'll talk more?"

"Sure, okay," Binod says, squeezing his brother's shoulder. He steps back and watches him a moment, wondering what will become of him if he can't farm anymore. It's all Galen knows, and to lose it would destroy him. For that matter, he wonders what will become of all of them. He goes out into the hall, leans against the wall, and the tears come, doubling him over.

"Are you okay?" says a voice suddenly beside him, and he feels a hand on his arm. It's a nurse. He catches his breath and looks up at her through blurred eyes.

"Yes, I'm...I'm all right. Just need to catch my breath."

"Why don't you come over here and sit a minute?" she says, gently tugging him forward. She leads him to a chair by the nurse's station and a moment later, a glass of juice appears in front of him. "Here, have a drink."

He takes a swallow from the glass that shakes in his hand. It's mango juice and it's cool and tart on his tongue. "Thank you."

"You're welcome. Is one of the men in there family?"

He nods, takes another swallow of juice. "Yes, my brother, Galen. He's in the bed by the door." Pausing, he takes a deep breath, then says, "Will he be all right? I mean, he's a farmer in the mountains. It's all he knows. Will he be able to do it when he goes back?"

"I can't say, I'm not a doctor, but I think so. He has a long road ahead of him, though."

It's the first positive thing he's heard in three days. "I hope you're right. Do me a favor?"

"Of course, if I can."

"If he asks about our sister down the hall, don't say anything. They were brought in together, I'm told."

"Okay, who's your sister?"

"Her name's Anika Pande. I'm told she lost part of her leg. I was just going to see her when..."

"Ahh...yes. Why don't you sit here another minute?"

"I'm okay, and thank you for the juice," he says, handing her back the glass. Getting up, he walks down the busy corridor and through the double doors at the end of the ward. He's still feeling a bit shaky, but the juice has helped and he needs to see his sister and then get home. His phone pings with a text from Dibaker letting him know they're sitting in the waiting area off the main lobby downstairs, and to take his time. Binod texts him back, telling him he'll be down in a few, and looks up at the signage to find his sister's ward.

A few minutes later, he's outside Anika's room.

She's talking with the woman in the other bed beside her. He watches her a moment, gathers his courage, and goes in. When she sees him, her tired-looking face brightens. "Binod, I've been so worried about you," she says, patting her bedside. "Are you and Sila okay? Your house didn't get damaged, did it?"

It's so like Anika to put other people's cares before hers. He takes a seat beside her. "Sila and I are okay," he says, "but how are you?"

She glances toward the foot of the bed, then back at him, and shrugs, and he knows she's putting on a brave face. "They had to remove part of my leg. But they said I'm a good candidate for one of these new fake ones."

Which Binod knows she and Kedar can't afford. "That's good."

Anika turns to the woman she was talking to. "This is my bhā'ī, Binod."

"Namaste," the woman says.

Binod returns the greeting and Anika fills him in on what the two of them were just talking about. But he's not really listening. Finally, Anika breaks away from the woman and turns back to him. "So, did you see Galen yet?"

"Yes, I just came from his room. He's pretty banged up, but they think he'll make a full recovery. Are you in pain?"

"Not too much. It comes and goes," she says, snugging the blanket up under her armpits. He sees her take a breath, as if steeling herself for something, and then she puts her hand out to him. For a moment, she just watches him. Finally, she says, "I have something to tell you."

"What's that?"

She squeezes his hand. "Bubā and Āmā, they died in the quake."

He stares back, wondering where she draws the strength he's so lacking in, and says, "I know."

"You do?"

"Yes, I went up to get Sunni and Arjun, and I saw what happened. Gokul says he's taken care of things. Once everything gets back to normal, whatever that is, he'll do another puja for us."

"That's good. Poor Gokul, he was so worried about you. Oh, did you see Kedar? Is he okay?"

"No, I didn't get to see him." He pauses, looking off toward the window at the other end of the room. "There's something you should know."

Alarm comes to her face. "What? Is there something wrong with Kedar?"

"No, not that I know of. It's Sunni and Arjun. They're missing," he says, looking back at her. As her face tightens, he goes on, "Some men, pretending to be police or Army—we don't know—came up and told Gokul that Sila and I had died in the quake and that they were supposed to take them back to Prabin and Sumi."

Anika gasps and her hands go to her mouth. "Oh,

no! No, no, Binod, say it isn't so, please?" When he shakes his head, she digs her nails into his wrist and looks up at the ceiling. He feels her body tremble as she fights to contain the cry caught in her throat. Suddenly, she turns back to him, and her face is pinched. "But wait, how could they know about Sila's parents?"

"We don't know, but we think they might've found out from Sunni and Arjun. They were talking to them just before Gokul showed up to find out what they wanted. We've been looking for them the last three days."

"Have you called the police?"

"Yes, they know, and we also have other people helping us. My boss, Mick-ji, he knows some people who know people in the government, and they're out looking, too. I haven't told Galen this. He needs to get his strength back and doesn't need to hear it right now. I also didn't tell him about Bubā and Āmā." He wants out of this conversation, but it's not fair to Anika. She's been stuck here without her husband for five, maybe six days. "Are you tired? I can come back."

"You're always looking out for me. But I think you're the one who's tired. Why don't you go home, be with Sila. I'm sure she needs you now, more than I do."

19

MAY 4, 2015

*L*incoln gets up and dresses. He thinks it's going to be a long day. So far he hasn't figured out where to start inquiring about this "Merchandiser" man. His first thought is to try the bus station in Gongabu and work out from there, hitting Thamel toward evening. But first he has to take care of a few errands, such as getting a haircut, a shave, and some appropriate clothing, along with a glitzier watch.

Smiling, he looks at the five-thousand-dollar Abyss Chronograph sitting on the table beside him. "Sorry guy, gotta leave you here today." He steps into his boots and laces them up. He'll have to replace these, too, and his feet are already complaining at the thought of being stuffed into a pair of oxfords, that is, if he can find a pair. Palisha has pointed him to a few shops in Lalitpur that might carry what he's looking for.

His first stop will be the barber down the road. The cab he's hired for the day should be outside waiting for him. On the way he'll drop by Mick's room to let him know he's heading out. His esteem of the High Trails expedition coordinator and his pretty best friend, Palisha (whom Lincoln believes is a lot more than just a best friend), has risen exponentially over the last day and a half. If it weren't for them, he's certain he and Binod wouldn't have a chance of finding Sunita and Arjun. He reminds himself they're still a long way off from getting the children back, but at least they have a fighting chance now.

He locks up, goes downstairs and marches down the hall to Mick's door. When the man answers, he says, "Well, I'm off. I'll keep you posted."

"We'll be here digging dirt for ya," Mick says, and around the man's shoulder, Lincoln sees Palisha standing by the window. She's wearing a long bright yellow sari that looks more like a gown, and as the streaming sunlight hits it, he sees a vague outline of her petite body underneath.

Lincoln suppresses a smile. *Best friends...yeah right, sure!* "Wish me luck, we're gonna need it."

"Here's hoping then," Mick says, balling his hand. They fist bump, and a minute later Lincoln's walking out to the waiting cab. Not long after, he's at the barber and looking at himself in the mirror. He doesn't recognize the man looking back, except for the scar that runs over his forehead into his shortened red hair. The beard he's left, but it's trimmed short and he can barely see the other scar running along the jawline. He pays the man and he's off to his next stop to pick up some new clothes and a pair of shoes.

The shop Palisha recommended is an upscale men's clothing store a few miles away, and there's lots to choose from. The problem is, he's tall and much of the clothing here is tailored for Nepalis, who by and large are shorter and less robust than he is. After perusing for twenty minutes, he chooses a merino wool dinner jacket, a couple of cashmere sweaters, a pair of shoes, and three pairs of slacks, which will have to have the cuffs let down. That will set him back a day, but he reminds himself that he probably won't make any connections with the Merchandiser today. At best he'll get a hint of where to find him. Just to make sure he's ready for tomorrow, though, he opens his wallet and, handing the clerk two thousand-rupee notes, tells him to put his tailoring work to the front of the line.

By the time he leaves the clothing shop it's almost noon, and he's hungry. He tells the cabbie, who's a young Nepali with a pencil mustache and light blue eyes, to stop at one of the local cafés, and he buys them both lunch. While he's eating, he checks in with Mick and then calls Binod. He hasn't heard from him since the meeting with Amir.

When Binod answers, he says, "Hey, Binod, how you and Sila? You okay?"

"Oh, Lincoln, how are you?"

"I ask first."

"We're doing okay. It's hard. Sila is very sad."

Understatement of the year! "I wish there more I can do."

"You've already done too much. Did you find a place to stay?"

"Yes. I umm...stay at Mick's friend hotel," Lincoln says, watching his cabbie eat across the table. "What you doing? You keeping busy?"

"Oh, yes. We're out again today passing around fliers of Sunni and Arjun, then going to some more orphanages. We're thinking maybe these men might be using them to hide children. What are you doing? Are you keeping busy, too?"

Lincoln pauses, wondering if they might've crossed paths yesterday. He hadn't thought about just hitting up some of the less reputable orphanages and looking around. Then again, his mission is to find one of these creeps and buy the children back. Maybe Mick and Palisha can work that end of things. He'll bring it up to them when he gets back. At last, he says, "That's good plan. Hey, I no want slow you down, so I go now. Let me know you find anything."

"Sure. Thanks for calling."

Lincoln ends the call, then shoots Mick a text asking him to make a list of as many orphanages as he can. Putting his phone in his pocket, he turns to his cabbie and says in Nepali, "So, what your name?"

"Jiban."

"You like drive cab?"

Jiban takes a sip of his soda and shrugs. "It's okay."

"Must be big trouble with quake."

"It's not bad now," Jiban says and bites a nail. "Just need to know the shortcuts around it. So you live in the hotel?"

"Oh, no," Lincoln says, suppressing a smile. "My apartment collapse, so have stay there 'til find new place. So, what you rather do than cab drive?"

Another shrug. "Don't know. Maybe own a restaurant, something like that."

The kid is directionless, and Lincoln knows the feeling all too well. He's gone from one thing to another all his life with no destination in mind, though he knows what he doesn't want—to be pigeonholed in a nine-to-five job. "You like cook, then?"

"Yeah, it's okay." Jiban takes another sip of soda, wipes his mouth with a napkin, and pushes his plate aside. "Thanks for lunch."

"No problem."

They sit, watching the guests and waitstaff go about them a moment, until Jiban stirs. "Well, where next?"

"The bus station in Gongabu."

Jiban's brow jerks up. "Why? I can take you anywhere you want to go."

How can he explain to Jiban why he wants to go there without looking like some kind of cloak and dagger nutjob? "I do survey for friend."

"Oh, okay," says Jiban, getting up. "I need to go to the washroom. I'll be right back out and we'll go then, okay."

"Sure," Lincoln says. He finishes his tea, and fifteen minutes later they're on their way to the bus station.

It's going on 5:00 p.m., and so far Lincoln's had no luck getting a tip as to where he might find the Merchandiser. He's scoured the bus station, the Kantipur Mall, and streets surrounding the neighborhoods. People just look at him like he's some kind of distorted cartoonish caricature when he makes inquiries, or they just ignore him altogether. He plods back to the cab and gets in, tired and hungry, and debates whether to go to Thamel as he'd planned.

Jiban looks over his shoulder. "So how did the survey go?"

"Not good," Lincoln says, taking out his pocket notebook. He bought it for taking notes, and at present, to pass for show to Jiban.

"Where to next?"

Lincoln sighs. Part of him wants to go back to the hotel, but the larger part reminds him that Sunni's and Arjun's lives are at stake, and what they're enduring is much worse than what he's going through. "Thamel."

Jiban puts the cab in gear and twenty minutes later he's letting Lincoln off outside the lane going down to the Eco Thamel Resort. Lincoln gets out and goes to Jiban's driver-side window. "I meet you back here in two hours, okay?"

As Jiban nods and drives away, Lincoln looks down the busy street. The buildings are draped with signage and prayer flag streamers strung across every thirty or forty yards overhead. He decides to head north among the tourists and hawkers and others who come out of the shadows offering hashish and other opiates. But two hours later, he's back where he started, no closer to finding anyone who might lead him to the Merchandiser. He gets in the cab as another tremor shivers the ground. They both freeze for a second and when it's over, he tells Jiban to take him back to the hotel. Today has been a miserable failure. *What am I doing?* He begins to see the fruitlessness of his plan. He has no idea what he's looking for. Everybody looks the same.

But he can't give up, not as long as there's breath in him. He'll try again tomorrow, maybe have Mick and Palisha do what Binod has started doing, pretending to be a donor to get inside some of the other orphanages in town, the ones that hide in the cracks of the city, pretending to be a safe haven for children.

At length, Jiban drops him off, and he heads inside with his purchases and goes up to Mick's room to tell him of his un-success and to find out what the High Trails coordinator has dug up online. He knocks on the man's door, then glances at the new jewel-encased watch hanging on his wrist. It's going on 9:30 p.m., so he's surprised to find Palisha opening the door. She's still in that yellow sari she had on this morning, and it's wrinkled, as if she's been sleeping in it. She lets him in, and the three of them sit around the table. After several comments about his shortened hair and beard (Mick saying something about him looking almost human again), he gives them his report, telling them about his conversation with Binod and his idea for going into some of the marginal orphanages and doing the same thing. Maybe they might catch a glimpse of the children.

Mick sits back, and as he rubs his beard and looks at Palisha, Lincoln suddenly realizes he's forgotten about the man's injury. He has a good idea she's not going to like what Mick's about to say, and he wants to take the suggestion back and just do it himself. But the reality is, he can't be everywhere at once.

"I'll be careful," Mick finally says to Palisha.

She sighs, looks up at the ceiling. "Fine, but I am driving, and if—"

"I know, we'll come right back," Mick says, and

when he looks at Lincoln, there's a tiny smile on his face. He nods toward Lincoln's watch. "So, how much did you fork over for that little trinket?"

"Enough," Lincoln says, and they chuckle.

After Lincoln leaves, Palisha goes to the window. It's a starless night over the pricking lights of the city beyond. She thinks about the two children they're trying to save and this dark world they're being thrust into. None of them know what they're doing, really. They're out of their element, and they're going to be blindly poking into places that want to be left alone. She feels for these children, but to be honest, she's anxious about it—not only for Mick's safety, but for herself as well. She imagines her and Mick on the wrong end of a knife, disappearing into a river or a lonely alley to be found dead a week later. The thought of never seeing her sons or parents again presses down on her desire to do the right thing, to support the man she loves.

She glances back at him. He's busy writing something on the pad of paper he's been using to take notes on all day. So far, they've made a list of nine orphanages around the city besides the ones she and Lincoln went to. But these orphanages aren't like the Lotus Children's Home, she's sure. They're way down the list on the search engine page with no websites, and they're located in neighborhoods no respectful Nepali would go to.

Mick looks up. "Okay, I have a plan," he says, and he tells her how they'll go in looking like one of the NGOs Amir was talking about—but a German NGO because he knows the language.

She raises a brow. "I do not know German!"

"You don't have to. I'll speak in broken English, using a few German words here and there that you can help me put into the right words."

"Okay. But why do you want to do this? I do not understand."

He motions for her to sit by him on the bed, and when she does, he takes her hand. "Because it'll make it look authentic, and also, if they use Nepali it'll give me a chance to listen in on them without their knowing, and I'll know what they're saying."

"But if I am with you—"

"Not if you make an excuse to call someone. You'll think of something."

She shrugs. "Okay, but are we not just looking for the kids? Why do you want to spy on them? I do not get it."

"Because I want to know if they're doing what we think they're doing," Mick says. "And if they are, we'll let your father know, so he can keep an eye on them."

"I do not know, Mick. This is getting complicated. I do not mean to be difficult, but..."

He looks at her with those pleading dark eyes that are impossible for her to say no to. "Look, I know you're scared, I am, too. But we can do this. Be a light, save some children's lives, give them a better future."

She shakes her head and takes the pad of paper from him. Once again, he's defeated her, but she knows what he says is right. Looking down, she reads the plan he's written out.

"All you really need to do is help me when I pretend not to know an English word," he says.

She nods. "I guess. We should practice what we are going to say, though, so we do not make mistakes."

Mick smiles. "Thank you. Everything will be okay, you'll see," he says. "I need to lie down. Would you like to join me?"

There's nothing she would rather do, but she knows what her body would eventually want, and it takes everything she has to bite back the urge. "I think I will just sit next to you, if that is okay. I do not want to fall asleep while we are practicing."

He looks back, and she knows that he knows why she's refrained.

MAY 5, 2015

The next morning, Lincoln is off again with Jiban. It's unseasonably warm and the molten sun is shining down with a vengeance. After he picks up his tailored slacks, he tells Jiban they're going to a different section of town this time to do his supposed survey. He wants to work the streets in and around the Dallu neighborhoods he thinks might be productive. In the meantime, Palisha and Mick are making their rounds at some of the orphanages Mick found online yesterday. One of them is right outside the Kalimati neighborhood where he lived before the earthquake. How did he not know about that? So many things happening right under his nose, all the time, and he never sees them. Has he always been this blind, just going about his business, seeing things and not thinking twice about them? Then he reminds himself, isn't this the way of the world? How many people go through life, never really looking around themselves, at both the beauty and the ugliness? Unless, of course, it touches them directly where it matters. This is especially true in America, he thinks, but then he has to admit he's prejudiced when it comes to consumerism.

Jiban pulls over and lets him out near the Monkey Temple. As always, the great mound west of the city is crowded. The earthquake has had little impact on the masses coming here. The hill on which the great Buddhist temple sits looks out over the whole of Kathmandu Valley, and at night, no matter where someone is, they can see the illuminated white stuppa shining out over the city. He remembers the first time he saw the Buddhist temple back in 2011. He and Collins spent the afternoon here under the countless prayer flag streamers tangled with the tree branches, perusing the shops selling all manner of Nepali jewelry, singing bowls, artwork, candles, and offerings to give to the Hindu gods. He smiles as he remembers one of the populous temple monkeys stealing an ice cream cone right out of his hand and scampering into a tree to enjoy its ill-gotten treat.

Joining the crowd, he marches up the long stairs, keeping his eyes open for any individual he might think could lead him to the Merchandiser, but like yesterday, he sees no one vaguely close to what he thinks he's looking for. Then again, this is a temple.

An hour later, he's out working the streets as the tremors come every thirty or forty minutes. And again, two hours later, he ends up with nothing but a sunburn. He'll pick up some sunscreen when he takes Jiban for lunch at the nearby coffeehouse. After that, he'll check in on Mick and Palisha to see where they're at with the orphanages, then head out to another section of town. Maybe he'll try the area around the airport—didn't Amir say something about kids being trafficked through it? At this point, he's ready to try anything, even a monastery!

They arrive at the airport around 3:00 p.m. and Lincoln gets out of the car. He tells Jiban to wait in the parking lot while he goes to mingle with the crowds standing outside the terminal. It's a semi-ordered confusion around the front doors where friends and relatives are calling out to incoming travelers. Mixed in with them are those who are waiting in disjointed lines to be admitted indoors for outgoing flights. He stands off to the side, making himself as inconspicuous as possible, and watches and listens for anyone who might not be who they appear to be.

An hour goes by, and then another. Once more, all the faces look the same, except for incoming foreign tourists and the occasional red-robed Buddhist monk. He's about ready to go back to the cab when he sees one of the airport security guards coming toward him. The tall Nepali guard comes to a stop and waves him forward with the flick of his hand.

"What are you doing?" he says in English as Lincoln walks up to him.

Lincoln's heart thumps as he peers back at the uniformed man, who's casually fingering his baton. The last thing he wants is to find himself being hauled inside and interrogated. "Waiting for a passenger."

The man cocks a brow. "Hmm...for almost two hours?"

Christ, he's been clocking me. Think fast. "I mean, fare."

"You're supposed to wait in your car. Where is it?"

"Over there," Lincoln says, and points to Jiban's cab.

"It belongs over there, by the curb," the guard says.

"Oh, I didn't know," says Lincoln, forcing a smile. "I'm new at this. I'll take care of it right away."

"You do that," he says and waves Lincoln away.

Lincoln hoofs it back to Jiban, taking a deep breath as he goes. *Whew, that was close.* Getting into the car, he tells Jiban to find a place for dinner before they head back to Thamel again. As Jiban drives, Lincoln opens his pocket notebook and goes through his notes, then to keep up appearances, pretends to scribble in it.

"How's this place?" Jiban says, pointing ahead.

Lincoln peers over Jiban's shoulder down the Bag Bazar Sadak. A sign on the corner with an arrow points to the right, reading *Bhojan Griha*. "Sure, whatever."

Jiban turns down the lane and they park near the restaurant's front entrance. Lincoln gets out and takes in the three-story colonnaded façade. Buttery cream-colored walls with bronze trim on the columns and arched openings give it a distinctly European flair. Beyond the arched openings are backlit balconies, and below them is a courtyard of paved stone with wrought iron tables and chairs. Presently, the place is humming with a cacophony of Slavic, Israeli, American, German, and some other languages he can't make out. But it's the heady aroma of garlic and basil permeating the air that trumps all the senses. If he didn't know better, he'd think he was in Italy.

"Good job," he says to Jiban. "Let's find a table, I'm starved."

Twenty minutes later, Lincoln is digging into a plate of lasagna alla bolognese and texting Mick and Binod for updates on their progress. It's hit and miss getting past the orphan-keepers to see what's going on behind closed doors, and what they've seen so far is often heart-rending. They're pretty sure the places they've gotten into are hiding things, despite the excuses and/or rules the orphan-keepers tell them. Mick is keeping a list of those places, which Palisha intends on showing to her father. As for Binod, Lincoln is sensing he's losing hope, and he aches for the man. They need some good news, anything to give him something to hang onto.

He puts his phone away, finishes his dinner, and looks around. Watches people eating their dinners, sipping wine, laughing and conversing. One wouldn't know there had been an earthquake here less than two weeks ago. He wonders how people can be so indifferent from such a tragedy, as if they lived in an insulated bubble of normality. Then he reminds himself, even though he'd been a first responder and then an ER doctor, he'd once lived in that same bubble. He'd go home after working twelve- or sixteen-hour shifts in the ER or pulling someone out of a wreck, and slide into bed and sleep like a baby, as if it was just another day. But now, something is different inside him. This new way of thinking, of seeing things, is like waking up to discover he's been sleepwalking most of his life, going from one thing to the next on auto-pilot.

As he considers this, he finds himself drawn back again to the accident that took his parents' life, how it shaped his world, his thoughts, projecting him into this long search to find meaning for what had happened, what he had been responsible for by horsing around, causing his father to take his eyes off the road, and for the first time he understands he's been trying to balance the scales of guilt and innocence by launching into the world of healing people, when in reality he should've been healing himself. Is he doing it again, projecting himself into Binod's tragedy and ignoring the root of this battle he's been fighting for the last twenty-five years? He doesn't like to think so, and what's more, his heart suddenly feels something he's never felt before—passion!

He turns to Jiban, who's just finishing his spaghetti and meatballs. "I need go washroom. Be back and we go, okay?"

Jiban nods as he lays down three thousand-rupee notes on the table for the bill.

It's 6:30 p.m. when Jiban drops him off in Thamel, and like the day before, he'll meet him back here at the Eco Thamel Resort. Lincoln watches Jiban drive off, weaving around the people going into shops and restaurants, then starts walking. He plans on covering the west end of the old part of the city tonight, and unlike the night before, he'll venture out to some of the outlier lanes less traveled by the tourists, and for good reason. For the moment, though, he keeps to the main streets, stopping here and there to look into store windows or peruse goods set out on tables.

An hour and a half later, he's turning down another lane, passing beggars and hawking store owners, and he's halfway back to where he's supposed to meet up with Jiban, when out of nowhere, a man comes out of a shadowy doorway and approaches him. He's a swarthy-looking character and he moves his sinewy body with a cautious yet forward stealthy motion.

"Namaste!" the man says, looking around as if he's hiding from something or someone. He offers in faltering English, "You like hashish, I have."

Lincoln is about to decline when it hits him: maybe! "Yeah, yeah, I like."

The man motions him over to the side, out of view of the passing people. "How much you want?"

"I don't know. How much do you have?"

The man pulls a plastic bag from his pocket and shows him. "It very good. You will like."

"How much?"

"Two thousand rupee."

Lincoln digs his wallet out, plucks two notes from

it, and hands it over to the man. "By the way, I'm looking for some special product from a man who goes by the name of the Merchandiser. Maybe you know him?"

The man eyes him suspiciously, but when he digs out five more thousand-rupee notes and hands them to him, his eyes light up. "I might know someone who knows someone."

Lincoln's heart is racing and he has to tamp his hopes down. "Will you ask for me?"

"Sure."

"When?"

"You come back tomorrow, same place, same time, and I'll let you know. You want more hashish then, too?"

Lincoln nods. "Maybe, we'll see. Tomorrow then?"

"Tomorrow," the man says, and he slips away into the shadows as if he was never there.

20

MAY 5, 2015

*M*ick peers out the window of Palisha's car as they arrive at the Compassionate Heart Children's Home, which is their third stop this morning. He's lived in this country for over twenty years, and he's seen a lot. There's immense poverty in this world he calls home, people living on the streets or in old broken-down hovels and buildings, eking out a life selling produce and flowers, anything they can to survive living at the fringes of humanity. Until today, he's never really looked at it hard, never paid much attention to this struggle to exist. He's suddenly appalled at himself for ignoring these places, and others like them, after living in this country for so long.

Stepping out of the car, he ignores the pain in his side and casts a long, sweeping critical look at the tall, crumbling concrete wall stretching around the old brick three-story building. Here and there, rambling ivy roams on the building's exterior, clambering about small, dark windows that peer down at what he presumes is a courtyard beyond. A gnarled, withered tree pokes a leafless branch over the wall. The broad black barn door in front of him is cheerless: basic, with no ornaments, no frills, no glass. It gives him the impression of a prison gate meant to keep people in. He glances over at Palisha.

"Well, this place certainly has possibilities," he says, but he hates the taste of the sour words coming out of his mouth, because like the other two orphanages they've visited this morning, he's pretty sure the kids inside aren't getting any better care than the sad-faced children they've already seen.

Palisha looks on, but she doesn't say anything. She's been quiet since they came out of the first orphanage. Then again, she hasn't had to say anything. The shame and disdained judgment in her eyes says it all. Each of them, for different reasons, has been blind or chose not to look at this world that's been right in front of them for years. More and more over the last week, he feels small, an imposter. A fraud who pretends to revere the Sherpa, who eke out their lives in the mountains, and the struggling Nepali community he says he loves because it's easier to pay lip-service than to face up to the fact he's used to eating in the best restaurants, living in nice apartments, flying around the country like some important businessman.

He's also beginning to understand who Frank Kincaid really was, and why Sarah Madden, the Sherpa and Nepali people loved the man. The mountaineer, who came to this land as a boy and died saving others, never tried to change it, to make *it* his own by reaping the rewards of others. Instead, Frank gave back in the currency of respect, honor, and with his time, helping people make their lives a little better. Now, Mick is feeling the baton being passed to him, and he's not sure he's worthy of it, but he's going to take it and do the best he can.

"You ready?" he says to her. When Palisha nods, they approach the door and press a button on a scuffed-up keypad. While they wait, they quickly go over the plan. A few minutes later, he hears someone come up to the door on the other side. As the bolt-latch clanks back, he winks at her.

The door slides open and they're greeted by a bony, dark Nepali dressed in a pressed white tapālan with red, green, and yellow embroidery on the collar. He looks out at them with a half smile and keen, dark eyes that are both welcoming and cautious. "Namaste, can I help you?" he says in English, darting a glance back and forth between them.

"It further like, I help you?" Mick says in pretentious, stilted English, and smiles back. He turns to Palisha, then back to the Nepali. "My American is not all that good and my Nepali not umm...suitable. She will help me find right American words, okay?" When the man nods, Mick looks at Palisha, and says, "Guten morgen. I am Mick Hanson. I am with NGO from Deutschland. We hear of Nepal's orphan... umm...what is word?"

"Outpouring," Palisha puts in.

"Ah...outpour, yes, after earthquake, so we here help support need for local orphanage in Kathmandu with grants up to three thousand euros." He hands the man a card they made this morning at a local office shop, then steps back.

The man looks at the card, then back at them. The cautious welcoming smile grows broad and toothy. He puts his hand out toward the courtyard beyond. "Of course, come in. By the way, I'm Anup," he says.

They follow him in and look around. The courtyard is better than Mick expected. There are wood benches placed around a greensward surrounded by planters of marigold and lilies in the middle, and an old swing set is off to one side. A small sunk-in reading area is in one corner. He spies a couple of young girls inside, then glances at Palisha. Maybe he misjudged this place, but he's skeptical all the same.

Anup leads them across the yard into the main building. Inside, the halls are drab and the pale linoleum floors are scuffed and yellowed. A couple of old pictures of the mountains hang on walls that haven't seen paint in years. "Please excuse the appearance. We just bought the building and it's old and needs a lot of work. We've been trying to concentrate on the children's rooms and play areas first," he says, walking to a doorway that leads into the main office. Inside, it's stuffy and the dark blue carpeting is frayed and faded. A pair of old wood desks stacked with files sit near the doorway and a large beaten wood table with chairs is behind them. He goes over to it, clears a stack of papers to one side, and has them sit.

"Can I get you a refreshment, perhaps tea or soda?" Anup says.

Mick shakes his head.

Anup sits across from them. "What would you like to know about us?"

Mick says, "Whatever you want tell."

The man leans forward and tells them how he and his brother started the home three years ago with money they saved portering in the mountains to fill the need they saw. They have a big plan to completely renovate the building and to provide high-quality care and experiences such as music and art, math and science for the children. As Anup speaks, Mick is thinking he's never seen these men on the mountain before, and he's seen a lot of porters over the years.

"So you porter in mountains. Where? Everest?"

"Yes, many times," says Anup, nodding. "It's beautiful up there."

Yes, I know! "Ah...I used know a man in Khum Jung. Maybe you know. Frank Kincaid," Mick says, leaning back in his chair.

"Hmm...the name does not sound familiar."

Gotcha! "Just wondered. So many people up there," Mick says and smiles at Palisha.

"So, you umm...register with CCWB?"

"Not yet, but the paperwork is in. We expect to get it back any day now."

My ass. "Good, it will make much easy for me to...umm..."

"Convince?" Palisha says.

"Yes, convince my partners to donate for you. Can we look around?"

Anup smiles, but Mick thinks it's a nervous smile. "Sure. Why don't you wait here while I get someone to take you around? I'll be right back."

Mick watches him walk out, certain he's going to make sure everything looks on the up and up on their tour, then turns to Palisha and says, "Everyone who porters for Everest Base Camp knows Frank Kincaid."

"So, he's never been up there?"

"No, he's lying, and you can bet he has no intention of renovating this place, let alone registering it. When we go on the tour, find an opportunity to hang back and make a call or something so I can hear what this tour guy might be saying to the kids."

"He is probably dressing them up, too," Palisha says. "You know we never discussed what would happen if we saw the kids in one of these places. They do not know you, right?"

"A little. They've seen me a couple of times."

Palisha's brow goes up. "What if they call your name out? Or come running to you? What would you do then? The people here would know we are not who we say we are. Oh, Mick, this would not be good."

Why didn't he think of that? How could he have been so stupid? While Sunita might know enough to keep her mouth shut, Arjun wouldn't. He'd come running right up to Mick. But it's too late now. He nibbles a fingernail, trying to come up with a solution. Could he keep a straight face and deny he's ever seen them before? Maybe, but the bigger problem would be if Arjun called him out by name. That would be too much of a coincidence. And what of Palisha? She'd be in as much danger as him if things went south. Maybe they should make an excuse and beg out of the tour, but how would that look? No, they're just going to have to go through with it, and take their chances.

Finally, he says, "Tell you what, you've seen Sunita's and Arjun's faces. I'll make sure to stay out of direct line of sight. Or maybe better yet, you pretend to make an excuse that you forgot something and have to go to the car. I'll do the tour without you."

"I am not leaving you alone," she says, with a look that's defiant and non-negotiable.

He looks at his watch. It's been almost fifteen minutes since Anup left. They're definitely doing some house cleaning, and with every passing minute, he feels his gut tighten, pulling on his wound. He shifts to one side and grits his teeth.

"Is that what I think it is?"

He knows what she's getting at. "It's okay. Don't look at me like that. I'm fine."

She looks away as she taps her nails on the table-top. "After we leave here, we are going back to the hotel. It is not a request."

At length, Anup comes back and his ever-present smile is still on his face. "Ah, I'm sorry it took so long. We've gathered the children outside. It will be much easier that way to see them. If you're ready, we can go."

Of course you did. "Sure. But what about look at rooms?"

"Oh, we can do that afterward," says Anup.

They get up and follow the man outside. The children are lined up in the courtyard with one of the staff on each side, looking on with pretentious smiles. The kids are dressed in good clothes and their hair is combed or put up in ponytails, but their faces are not exactly smiling. Sunita and Arjun aren't among them. He's both relieved and disappointed. Going up to them, he greets each one, gauging their age. Most of them he thinks are between six and fifteen years old. The younger kids avert their eyes to the ground while the older kids, who are mostly boys, look back at him with suspicion. A few of them have scrapes on their arms, and one of the older boys has a fading shiner on his right eye. He wonders how that got there and how many of them have been taken against their will to be used as a commodity to lure well-meaning foreigners into giving money that will end up in Anup's pockets, or worse yet, sent to the border.

Anup says, "Shall we go inside again so you can see their rooms?"

Mick nods and he and Palisha follow the man to another door in the far corner of the yard. Inside, the hall is dim and there's an odor of mildew permeating the air. When they come to the end of the short corridor, Anup leads them past the children's rooms, whose doors are swung wide. In each room the two twin beds, if you want to call them that, are made and there's a tiny dresser with a lamp between them. There's no carpet, just a stained linoleum floor. A tiny window in each room is barred from the outside, and the doors all have bolt latches facing the hallway.

Palisha shoots him a wary look and he sees her take a furtive breath of disgust. She taps him on the arm, then turns to Anup. "I have to use the bathroom. Is there one around here?"

"Yes, down the hall," Anup says. "Last door on the right."

Mick watches her leave and gestures to Anup to go on with the tour. The man's gaze strays down the hall where Palisha is walking, but then he turns into another hall on their left. At the end of it they come to a large room used for recreation. Spidery cracks run down the plastered walls. Ratty wall-to-wall blue carpeting covers the floor, and there are large round tables with chairs, along with a row of bookcases crammed with broken toys, dusty boxes of puzzles, and games. A small portable TV sits on a white plastic table at one end of the room. It's not plugged in.

Mick's seen enough, and he says, "I thought you say, rooms been renovated."

"Oh, ongoing," Anup says. "We just started."

Mick nods and they back out and head to another room, which Anup says is the dining room. Like the recreation room, it suffers the same fate, and there's a distinct odor of spoiled greens being blown around by a pair of ancient ceiling paddle fans. Anup shrugs. "We just fed the children lunch."

Again Mick nods and as they get ready to leave, one of the staff comes rushing up. He pulls Anup to the side and in Nepali, says in a low voice, "Thakur is fighting again."

Anup flashes Mick a tight smile, then turns back to his employee. "Put him in the 'box' for now and I'll deal with him after our guests leave."

The man dips his head to Anup and scurries off.

Mick watches the man turn the corner. He has a good idea what this "box" is.

"So," Anup says, "This is pretty much it. But soon, we'll be looking much better, especially with your generous donation."

Mick smiles. "There's second and third floor. What about them?"

"Oh, the second floor is where we live and the third is empty," says Anup. "We use it for storage right now, but eventually, my brother and I, along with our staff, will move to the third floor and expand the orphanage to the second."

"Oh! All right. Well, we certain to look very hard here," Mick says as Palisha heads toward them. "Maybe here, we give more. We see. Now we must go. I have meeting with partners."

Anup's eyes light up. "That would be very helpful. Very helpful indeed, and I know the children would be so grateful. Come, I'll walk you out."

Don't you worry, we're going to take good care of them, and put you in a box with bars around it.

∾

Palisha opens Mick's hotel room door and helps him to the bed. He's overdone it today, which is no surprise. He's almost as stubborn as her father. As he lies down, she goes into the bathroom to wash her face and freshen up. She's seen more than she wanted to see today, and she's angry and heartbroken. She stares at the mirror, looking at herself straight on. Sees a tightened jaw and condemning eyes. Those lost children, those throw-aways in the orphanages could have been hers, in another life. She wonders if their parents are still alive, looking for them, or maybe as her father and Rajendra said, have given them away and forgotten about them already. She can't imagine giving away a child, or worse yet, forgetting about them, as if they never were. How do people do that, sell their children? She can't fathom it.

Suddenly, she has to hear her sons' voices. It doesn't matter that she talked with them a week ago after they called to see if she was okay after the quake. She pulls her phone from her pocket and enters her oldest son's number, not bothering to look at the time. When Milan answers, she closes her eyes. It's like coming up for air after being underwater all morning. At last, she says, "Milan, it's me, Āmā. How are you?"

"I'm good, Āmā. Is everything all right? You sound sad."

"I'm okay. I just had to hear your voice again," she says, turning away from the vanity.

"Okay."

She hears a swooshing sound coming through the phone, as if he's in traffic. "What are you doing?"

"Walking to class."

"What time is it?"

"A little past seven. You sure everything's okay?"

"Yes, yes, I'm fine," she says, and smiles, feeling like her doting mother. How did that happen? "It's just your Āmā missing you. How's school?"

"School's fine. Hey look, can I call you back later? I need to hurry along here. I'm running late."

"Oh, sure. Have a good day, okay?"

"Of course, bye."

The line goes dead and she ends the call. Her other son, Nugah, is probably already in class. She sighs and puts her phone away, but at least she was able to talk with one of them, even though it was only for a couple minutes. She opens the door to find Mick sound asleep, droning like a beehive. Smiling, she walks over and looks down at him, remembering the night up on the Namche ridge looking up at the stars. It seems like a lifetime ago. She would've given herself to him that night, but he was more concerned with her heart and the world she was bound to. Such an honorable man he is, she thinks: a man deserving of so much more than what she's been giving him. Pulling the blanket up around him, she leans over and brushes his cheek with a kiss, then slips out of the room.

As she goes to the office to catch up on work she's missed over the last few days, she thinks about whether she should call her father and tell him what she saw. He'll more than likely scold her for putting her nose into things she doesn't know about. But she knows what she saw, and it disturbs her to the core. All her life, she's been sheltered from the world she and Mick have just seen, and now that she's seen it, she can't ignore it. Her thoughts return to her sons, and she knows she can't keep silent.

Going into her office, she shuts the door and sifts though invoices and receipts that need to be entered into the computer. On the desk in front of her is a picture of her family, taken a few years back before the boys left for university in England. There's also another photo of her and Mick up in the mountains. They're standing near the Hillary Bridge. As she enters data on the spreadsheet, she glances at it, remembering her trepidation about crossing the cable-stayed expanse over the river far below. But she gathered her courage and stepped out onto it.

Now there's a different bridge in front of her, and though she doesn't know where it leads, she feels compelled to find out, despite what it could mean. Her children have grown, making new lives for themselves, and she's heading toward fifty. While she's come a long way since losing her husband and living as a widow in her parents' home, she still hasn't taken the final step and left the proverbial nest. Maybe it's time to do it and trust that love will become the tie that binds her life to theirs.

She sits back and looks out the window, contemplating the future she's considering. There's no scenario she can see where Mick isn't part of it. And while he isn't Nepali, and they come from different worlds, one thing is immutable: she's in love with him, and so far as she can tell, it's mutual. And where Mick goes, she knows she will go too, if push comes to shove. She takes her phone out, scrolls to her father's number, and hits send.

"Hello?"

"Hi Bubā, do you have a minute?"

"Oh, Polly. Yes, what is it?"

Palisha takes a deep breath to steady her nerves. "I want to alert you to something I saw today. And please let me finish before you say anything."

"Okay."

Here goes. "I was at an orphanage this morning in Gongabu, helping to look for the children of my friend. I believe they're trafficking children there. You should have seen it. They have bars on the windows in the children's rooms and locks on the doors to keep them in like animals. And it was filthy and it stank and—"

"Stop right there! What are you thinking, going to a place like that? I told you all to wait and let us do our jobs. Do you know the danger you put yourself in? The people who run these homes, they are not to be fooled with."

"But—"

"But nothing! You will not go to another one. Do you understand me? I will not have my daughter in such places. That is my final word!"

She knew this rebuke was coming, expected it, but what she didn't expect was her reaction. Once again, she feels like a little girl, wanting to get back in her father's good graces, and it takes all her might to push that feeling down. "Bubā, I'm sorry, but in this you cannot stop me. If you do not wish to do anything about this, I will call the police and work with them."

Silence roars through the phone for a moment, then Amir says, "Why do you torment me? Hmm?"

She grits her teeth. "I do not mean to torment you."

"Yet you do, every time I turn around."

"That's not true, Bubā, and you know it! I love you."

"Then do as I ask."

"I'm sorry, I can't. If you're not going to help, then—"

"Do you think I don't already know about these places? Of course I know about them. All of them, and so do the police, but I cannot suggest they raid one of these homes based on your feelings."

"Then what? Just let them go on doing what they're doing?"

"You exhaust me." She hears him take a breath. "Fine, what is the name of this place?"

"The Compassionate Heart Children's Home."

"I'll look into it, okay? Is there anything else you wish to torture me with?"

Palisha shakes her head and rolls her eyes. "No. Like I said, I love you."

"Then stay away from these places, before you make me a grieving father."

His plea grasps her by the throat, and for a minute she can't breathe.

21

MAY 6, 2015

*B*inod pulls his buff up over his nose and wipes the sweat and dust out of his eyes as he walks past broken buildings. It's mid-morning and the sun is beating down on the streets, lanes, and tented fields around Chamati. The stink of garbage is everywhere, and the birds are having a feast. He's passing out fliers today to the earthquake refugees who are rummaging around the rubble for household items, personal effects, and scattered clothing. He looks at them as he walks, watching them trying to put their lives back together. It's depressing; an overwhelming, grim struggle to reclaim what the quake has taken from them.

What it has taken from him!

Lately, he wonders what's the point of life when everything can be ripped away in a moment.

In the next district over, his brother-in-law Dibaker is handing out fliers in shops and stores that still stand in Naya Bazaar; Prabin is making for the rest of the armed police wards they haven't gotten to. Binod texts them both to see how they're doing and to find out where they'll meet for lunch. As he types, he notices two little boys, maybe five or six, down the road stacking broken bricks on top of each other. A small white dog is bouncing around them, wagging his tail. For a moment, Binod's heart skips as he stares at them, breathless: but no, neither of them is his son. This trick of the eye, wanting to see what it wants to see around each corner is taunting him, leading him to think every little boy is Arjun.

He finishes his text, turns down another dusty street, and follows the broken macadam, passing more damaged buildings. A few lean to one side, propped up by timbers to keep them from falling over. The grunting of unseen heavy machinery on a mountain of wreckage behind them thrums in his ears. Ahead, a group of locals, mostly men, is standing in front of a little marketplace that has miraculously managed to escape the earthquake's wrath. Most of them are probably in the clothes they had on two weeks ago, and they reek of body odor. At the moment, they're looking at him like he's just walked out of a cloud like some kind of deity into this mangled world.

He pulls his buff down and goes up to them,

greeting them with a smile and a friendly hello. Handing them a flier, he asks, "Have any of you seen these two children? Some men stole them up in the mountains. I'm their bubā and I'm looking for them. If you know anything at all, I'll be forever in your debt."

They pass the flier around, each of them looking it over. They shake their heads. Well, what did he expect? He thanks them for their time and continues on the road as it bends to his left until he comes to a wall of rubble and timber that forces him to make another left. Ten minutes later, he's back on the street where the boys were playing. They're gone now, but something white amid the wreckage nearby catches his eye. Curious, he goes to it, and when he gets close, he puts a hand to his chest. The little white dog is lying bludgeoned and bleeding on the ground, and beside it is a child's ratty sneaker.

He whips his head around, looking up and down the road. In the distance, he sees a tall, dark figure walking with two small figures on either side. Suddenly, he knows what's going on, and he's damned if two more boys are going to be snatched away. In an instant, he's running after them, unsure what he's going to do when he catches up to whoever it is. But one thing's for sure: those two little boys aren't going anywhere, except back to their parents.

When he's close, he yells, "Where are you taking my boys?"

The man wheels around and lets go of the boys' hands. His long, swarthy face is in shock. For a moment, he looks back at Binod as if deciding whether to contest him or run. Binod bends down and picks up a piece of broken timber, and when he looks up, the man is bolting away.

Bastard! Dropping the chunk of wood, he runs up to the children. One of the boys is crying and the other flinches when he comes near. He bends down on a knee and says, "It's okay. I'm not a bad man. Where are your parents?"

The hesitant child points back down the road.

"Let's go find them," he says. He stands and gestures back the way they came. As he walks beside them, he asks their names.

The hesitant boy says, "Gokul."

"I know a priest in the mountains named Gokul. That's a lordly name! And what's your name?" he says to the child who's wiping his eyes.

"He killed my dog."

"I know, and I'm sorry about that," Binod says. "We'll do a puja for him. What was his name?"

"It was a she, and her name was Pressie."

"Ah, what a pretty name. And what's yours?"
"Rajan."

"Well Gokul, Rajan, I'm Binod, and I'm going to take you home. Do you want to take my hand or would you rather walk on your own?"

Neither one offers their hand to him. That's all

right with Binod. "Do you know," he says, "I have a little boy, not much older than you?"

Gokul looks up. "What's his name?"

"Arjun, and he's lost, so I'm looking for him. He's a good boy like you." He's about to tell them how Arjun loves to draw like his sister, then realizes it's too painful to talk about, so he pauses and asks, "Is your house okay?"

"It fell down," Gokul says. "My bubā is trying to fix it. He says it'll be done soon, but right now we have to live in a tent. Maybe you could come help him."

"Oh, I'd love to," Binod says as they near where the little dog lies. He puts himself between them and the dog in the rubble, and a moment later they're walking up to the edge of a field of tents. He's about to ask which one is theirs when a woman comes running toward them holding her skirt up, calling the boys' names. They run to her and she wraps them tight to the folds of her generous body.

Binod smiles as the woman's brown eyes look back at him suspiciously. "I found them being led off by a man. Be careful not to let them play in the streets alone." The woman's eyes grow large and she sends the boys to their tent with a sharp reprimand. When the boys are out of earshot, he adds, "The dog: she's dead back there in the rubble. I'm sorry."

"You saved my boys. Thank you, thank you!" she says, working her lips. She turns her head back to the tented field and he can see she's distressed about something. Finally, she turns back. "We have nothing to repay you with, except our daughter. She's sixteen, a good hard worker, and will make you a good wife. Come, take a look."

"Oh, no, I'm already married, thank you, but you can pass this around for me," he says, handing her a flier. "My son and daughter. They were stolen up in the mountains and we think they're here in the city somewhere."

She studies the picture and looks up at him. "Such beautiful children," she says. "Of course we'll help you with everything we have."

"Thank you," Binod says, pressing his palms together prayerfully and dipping his head.

She returns the gesture, then looks up. "May Brahmā bless you."

"And you also."

When Binod returns home that night, he's tired and sore from walking all day. But saving those two boys has raised his spirits. He didn't say anything to Dibaker or Prabin about it and he's not sure why, except for some reason, he wants to keep it to himself—a ray of sunshine he can hold onto in the darkness that has pervaded his world. He listens to the conversation Prabin and Dibaker are having about their search today while Sila, Sumi, and Dibaker's wife, Sabita, linger by the table. The baby is down for a nap and Dibaker's kids are in the other room playing. Binod looks over at Sila, who's sitting next to Sabita. Her face is like a blank sheet of paper as Sabita prattles on about something little Bishal did during a change of diapers that made her laugh. He hates to see Sila this way, so he turns back to Dibaker, who's swirling lentil soup into a mound of rice with his fingers.

His brother-in-law looks up. "I can't help tomorrow, I'm sorry, Binod. I need to get back to the Singing Bowl and open up. It's been almost two weeks and I need to start making money again."

"It's okay," Binod says, and takes a sip of tea. "You've been so helpful."

Dibaker nods. "Maybe Saturday I can help again?"

Again the selfless deed Binod did this morning washes over him, lifting up his wounded spirit. He sees the little boys' faces in his mind's eye, and the gratitude of their mother. Is his stumbling upon them a sign from Shiva? Some kind of test of his heart, to put aside his despair and do the right thing when so much is at stake for Sunni and Arjun? There's a feeling he has about it that won't let go, that something is going to go his way.

Finally, he says, "Maybe you won't have to. I think something good is going to happen."

Dibaker and Prabin are about to scoop a handful of supper into their mouths, but they stop. Dibaker says, "Oh? Something happen you didn't tell us about?"

Prabin looks on with expectation, and Binod can sense Sila stirring behind him. He says, "No, just a feeling, I can't explain it."

They all go quiet then and focus on their dinners.

Should he have said anything? He wonders about it as he picks at the steamed broccoli on his plate. But he couldn't help keeping his mouth shut. Unlike all the other times when sudden hope rushed through him only to abandon him an hour later, this new optimism feels rooted deep inside.

An hour later, Dibaker and Sabita are packing the kids up to go home. He follows them to the front door with Prabin, Sumi, and Sila trailing behind. As they go out, Binod bids them safe travels, then looks up at the black of night. Above, a bright star is shining directly down on him. He watches it flicker and feels his heart lift again, answering back to whatever it's saying in a language he has no words for. The only thing he knows is that wherever Sunni and Arjun are, it's looking down at them as well and whispering the same secret into their hearts.

He turns to Sila and pulls her aside, out of earshot of her parents. "We're going to find them. I need you to believe that, because there's no other acceptable answer. I know it's hard, but our son upstairs needs you right now. I need you."

She looks back and he sees the dark abyss in her heart staring up at him, threatening to swallow them up. "I'm trying, but..."

"I know, but try harder. Raise that tiger in you and fight."

That brings a dim smile. "You never liked her before."

He smiles back, takes her hand and squeezes it. "That's because the tiger was snarling at me."

She presses into him, putting her head on his shoulder. "You promise we'll find them?"

He knows promises can be broken, but in this, there's no brooking it, not as long as there's a breath in his body. "I promise you."

Lincoln gets out of Jiban's cab in Thamel outside the Eco Resort and tells him to meet him back there in an hour unless he texts him before then. He looks down at his watch, checking the time. It's a little past 7:00 p.m. He's early for this meeting with the street dealer, but that's okay. He wants to make sure he's where he needs to be on time. He heads down the street with his heart pumping. Should he have told Mick about this meeting? Probably, but it's too late now. He turns left at the fork in the road and walks down the lane. The old part of the city is busy tonight. Tourists trapped by the devastating earthquake are out and about shopping for souvenirs and patronizing the local restaurants that are still operating. The beggars and hawkers are out as well. One wouldn't know there's a section of town littered with crumbling buildings and shrines not a half mile away.

He stops to look in a shop window, pretending to peruse the outfitter apparel, to blend in with the crowds swarming around him. The place where he met the man the other night is a couple of doors away. He glances back and forth at the shadowed recesses around him, looking for the man, trying to remember what he looks like. The clerk in the shop beside him notices him, but he's busy with a customer, so he doesn't come out to see what Lincoln wants.

Thirty-five minutes later, Lincoln is still waiting. The man is fifteen minutes late and Lincoln has looked into almost every window, pretending to shop to keep up appearances. It's getting harder not to look conspicuous, and the shop owners are casting suspicious glances at him. If the guy doesn't show up in ten minutes, he'll cut his losses and go back to the hotel. He's about to text Jiban when he hears a whistle. When he looks up, the man is waving him over.

Finally!

Lincoln crosses the street, weaving through the surging crowd. "You said to meet you here at the same time. I've been waiting for over fifteen minutes."

The man is indifferent to Lincoln's annoyance. "You like my hashish. It very good...right?"

"It was fine," Lincoln says. "Did you find out what I asked you to?"

It takes a moment for the question to click in the man's head. "Oh, yes."

"And?"

"Someone will be coming soon." He pulls out another bag of hashish. "So, you want more?"

Lincoln digs into his pocket and pulls out a few notes. He suspects this man would tell him anything for a chance at another sale. But he's the only game in town at the moment, so he hands him the money and says, "If you want to continue doing business with me, you better be right about this someone."

"Oh, he will come. You no worry," he says, taking Lincoln's money and handing over the bag. They linger there a minute until finally the man's phone chimes in his pocket. He takes it out and looks down, then says, "Follow me."

A couple minutes later, they're standing in a dark narrow alley several feet away from the main street. Lincoln looks around, feeling stupid and vulnerable, wishing he had a knife in his pocket. This isn't his brightest hour. The man reaches into his breast pocket, pulls out a pack of cigarettes, and offers him one. Lincoln gave the habit up a long time ago, but he takes it anyway. After the man lights up, he takes a puff and offers his lighter to Lincoln.

"Ah, here he comes," says the man. Lincoln lights his cigarette and follows his swarthy companion's gaze to a shadow coming at them from the other end of the alley.

Whoever it is, they're tall and lean and they're approaching like a cat sneaking up on a mouse. The shadow stops a few feet away, and a moment later a bright light is blinding Lincoln's eyes.

"Why you want to see the man?"

The voice is male and it's low, menacing, demanding. "I hear he has a product I'm interested in," Lincoln says, shading his eyes from the light.

"And what product would that be?"

"That's my business," Lincoln says, taking a drag. It takes all his resolve to keep his cool. "Do you know him or not?"

The noise in the street beyond suddenly fades in Lincoln's ears, and it's replaced with a long, palpable silence descending over the alleyway, gripping his chest and making it hard to breathe. Finally, the man says, "I might. You have a number?"

"Sure."

Lincoln wedges the cigarette between his lips and goes to take out a business card from his jacket pocket when he hears a click.

"Nice and slow," the man says.

Lincoln swallows, plucks the card out, and holds

it, hoping his trembling fingers don't betray him. The man takes it and averts the light to the card. "What kind of name is Lincoln?"

"It's English," Lincoln says.

"Says here you're a doctor." The light averts back to Lincoln's face. "What kind of doctor?"

"Emergency Room doctor," Lincoln says, blowing out a ring of smoke. "What difference does it make?"

"A lot of difference," the man says. Lincoln hears him flick the card with a finger. At length, he slips the card away and puts his hand out, palm up. "Carrying charge."

Lincoln parks his cigarette back between his lips and reaches into his pants pocket to dig out a roll of thousand-rupee notes. As he goes to hand five of them over, the man says, "If you want first-class, you'll need to do better than that."

"How do I know you'll even pass this along?" Lincoln says, peeling another five notes into the man's hand.

The hand snatches the money away. "You don't."

"When, then?"

"He'll be in touch if he's interested." The light disappears from Lincoln's face, and a moment later he's alone in the alley. Apparently, the go-between man had other business to take care of. He flicks the burnt cigarette to the ground, buts it with his heel and walks back to the street, taking a deep breath to calm his jittery nerves. He's glad he didn't have a heavy supper, otherwise he's pretty sure he'd be losing it right now.

∼

It's going on 9:30 when Lincoln gets back to the hotel. He flips Jiban a few thousand-rupee notes and gets out. He's a bit calmer now, but his head is aching because he realizes he might be in over his head. But it's done. Now he has to wait. He wonders for how long, and whether he should finally tell Mick of his progress. If the expedition leader knew of the danger he was putting himself in, Lincoln's pretty sure he'd demand to get involved. Palisha wouldn't like that one bit.

He goes up to his room, picks up the bottle of rum he keeps on the dresser, and pours a good stiff drink. He's more than a little nervous about where things are going, but he's going to see it through. The question is, will this all be in vain? There's no guarantee this man has the children, and if he doesn't, what then? And what interest would his being a doctor be to this Merchandiser? He ponders that for a minute, then realizes it probably has everything to do with the black market that sells organs, mainly kidneys. That will mean it won't make any difference to him what the kids look like. A kidney is a kidney. The only thing that matters is blood type, and it's not like the guy's gonna let him go in and draw blood from any of the children he's holding. Or maybe this guy already knows their blood types. How can he finesse it so he can see the children's faces? He needs to think about this, but not right now.

He sips his rum and sits back, looking out the window, wondering if Sunita and Arjun are okay. What if they're already gone? He shudders at the thought, tries to believe what his heart is telling him, what the 3 Angels reps said about watching the border for them. Faith and luck is all they have left; that, and the good will of God, wherever he is in all this. Lincoln hasn't talked to Him since He dumped that ration of shit on a little boy riding home with his parents. He drains the rest of his rum and sets the glass down with a thunk.

All right, I'll try this one more time. If You're up there, now would be good a time to lend a hand.

22

MAY 8, 2015

*M*ick is getting dressed when a knock comes at his door. He buckles his belt and zips up, then goes to answer it. Palisha is on the other side with breakfast. She's in her hotel work clothes, a pressed white button-down blouse and a pair of dark slacks. His birthday present is around her neck and it's radiating a buttery glow against her smooth tan skin. They spent most of yesterday on the road checking the orphanages on their list, then hunting for others online back in his room until they ran out of gas. The last he remembered, she was lying in his arms on the bed, talking about what they saw and how sad and angry it's making them feel. He doesn't remember her leaving.

"Namaste, I hope you are hungry," she says. Her smile is like sunshine as she passes him and sets the tray on the table. Breakfast is scrambled eggs with seasoned garlic-fried potatoes and sliced mangos. A few slices of roti bread and a cup of coffee round out the fare. "I have to work today," she says, turning back to him. "Namu has been doing so much, and she needs a break. How are you this morning?"

"Better now," Mick says, drawing her into his arms. "How's my best friend?"

"She is okay. A little tired," she says, wiggling out of his embrace. When she steps back, there's a look in her eyes he can't place, as if something has changed between them. He wonders if it has to do with the dark world they've been seeing the last week, or is it something else? Did he say something wrong last night? They'd both been dipping pretty good into the bottle of rum he bought, pouring out their thoughts and feelings about this new world they were being thrust into as they danced around the proverbial elephant in the room. Did something happen when they were lying together? Should he say anything? Suddenly his breath leaves him.

"Hey, what's wrong?"

"What do you mean?"

He pauses, trying to put words to what he's thinking. Finally, he says, "You seem different, like...I don't know, like you're wanting to get away from me. Did I do something last night when we were—" He nods toward the bed.

She laughs, but he senses it's a nervous laugh.

She shakes her head. "Oh no, you were perfect. I just...it is just hard sometimes being close to you...and our situation."

"I'm sorry."

"Do not be. It is just something I have to work out...and I am," she says, coming back to him. "I have to get back down to the office. See you later?"

"Of course."

"Do not worry, okay? And behave yourself. You are still not 100 percent," she says, patting him on the chest. She reaches up on tiptoes and pecks him on the cheek. "If there is anything you need, let me know."

As the door shuts behind her, Mick wonders what this thing is she has to work out. He senses she's wrestling with a decision about them and it sets his nerves on edge. The thought of her extracting herself from his life is overwhelming. But how can he press her to stay if she wants to distance herself from him? He blows out a breath, trying to shove the thought out of his mind, and pulls a chair up to his breakfast.

As he picks at it, his thoughts go back to Germany and Vivian. They'd met in middle school, grew up together, and fell in love. She'd become such an integral part of his life, so connected to his thoughts, his feelings, his dreams, that when she died, it was like half of him was gone. He didn't know himself, and it took everything he had to rebuild a semblance of himself, to fill the gaping hole she left and start living again.

For the first couple years, he bounced around like a ping pong ball, going from day to day working odd jobs with no direction until a co-worker at a restaurant where he served bar announced he was going to Nepal. He'd landed a position in one of the expedition companies on Everest. That was when Mick knew he had to leave home, get away from all the places he and Vivian had made memories, memories that taunted him day and night. And so he left and never looked back, save for yearly trips home during the summer treks, the holidays, and to see family and a few friends. He's been here twenty-five, or is it twenty-six years now, living a solitary life, and he's been content with it, for the most part. That he would ever fall in love again was never in his wildest dreams, yet that's exactly was has happened and he has no idea what to do about it.

He finishes his breakfast, leaving a third of it on the plate, and grabs his key card. He's been meaning to buy some more clothes and to check in with Ken Wentworth at High Trails to see what's going on. He's pretty sure all the treks have been put on hiatus for the time being, but he wants to make sure. There's also the matter of getting paid. He's been living out of his wallet for the last month, and funds are beginning to dwindle. There's also the matter of rent for his apartment in Pokhara, and probably a pile of mail waiting to be opened in his pox-box. But he can't leave right now, not with Binod's kids in the wind.

He grabs the room-service tray and is on his way down to the elevator. When the door opens, Lincoln is inside. "Hey, we missed you yesterday."

"Yeah, I've been pounding the streets," Lincoln says, but he seems distracted, as if something's pressing on his mind.

"Us, too. We ticked off a few more orphanages from our list. So where you off to today?"

"Gonna grab some breakfast downstairs right now, then back to the streets. You?"

"Shopping for some clothes. Hopefully, I find something for this flabby body of mine. Their idea of large is lacking."

Lincoln smiles. "You think?"

They're quiet as the elevator chugs down to the first floor. Mick is wondering what has Lincoln so preoccupied, so when the door opens, he says, "Gotta drop this tray off down there. Mind if I join ya?"

"Not at all," Lincoln says.

They walk down the hall and go into the café. Mick hands his tray off to one of the wait staff and follows Lincoln to a table near the window. They sit looking at the menus and when the waiter comes around, Lincoln orders. Mick opts for a cup of tea and sits back. When Lincoln gives him a puzzled look, he says, "Had breakfast up in my room."

"Oh."

Mick taps his finger on the table. "So, want to tell me what's nibbling at you?"

Lincoln looks away, then turns back. "I need your word on something."

Mick stops tapping and leans forward, ignoring the twitch in his side. He has a feeling he's not going to like this. "Okay."

"Promise?"

"Yeah."

"Okay. You need to keep your mouth shut until I know for sure if this is going to happen, and that means everyone, including Palisha. No one needs to know what I'm going to tell you."

It's becoming clear to Mick now. "You connected, didn't you?"

Lincoln nods. "I'm waiting for a call."

"Then what?"

"I don't know," Lincoln says as the waiter comes with their tea. After the man drops it off, Lincoln looks over Mick's shoulder, then casts a glance around the café. "I'll tell you this, though; these guys mean business, and I don't want you all involved, understand? One of us sticking his neck out is enough."

Mick sits back, blows out a breath. "Boy, what are we getting ourselves into?"

"I've asked myself the same question, believe me," Lincoln sighs. "But right now, the kids are all I can think of. They're what's important to me, and if I can do something to get them back, then that's what I'm gonna do."

"Right. But there must be something I can do. Tell me, and I'll do it."

Lincoln doctors his tea with honey and stirs it in. "I'm not sure what it would be. If I think of something, I'll let you know. Remember, not a word to anyone."

In this, Mick knows Lincoln's right. There's no need for Binod, Sila, or Palisha to know. Hopefully, it won't come down to lying to them.

Lincoln's sitting on his bed watching TV. It's been almost two days since he met that man in the alley, and so far not a peep. He stares at the phone in his hand. It's like a ticking time-bomb. The question is, will it go off or remain silent, a dud taunting him with false hope? Right now, he's doing everything he can to keep his mind from spiraling down into things he has no control of. The show on the TV is one of the inane reality Nepali shows that cram the cable-connected world. He watches the couple on the screen, who are in a heated argument about some stupid slight one of them did to the other. It's American TV with a Nepali twist. He's about to grab the remote and turn the channel when his phone pings. He jerks up and looks at the number. He doesn't recognize it, and it's not like he's been getting a lot of calls these days.

Heart thumping, he accepts the call. "Hello?"

"I hear you're looking for something?"

The male Nepali voice is monotone and his English is precise. Lincoln turns off the TV and swallows. "I am."

"And what makes you think I have it?"

"Word on the street."

"You're lying. I don't do business on the street. Good-bye."

"Wait, wait, I'm sorry," Lincoln says, rushing in. "You know I'm a doctor, I'm sure."

"I do."

Lincoln's thoughts race as he tries to think of anything that will keep the man on the line. "Well then, you know I have certain needs, and the money to pay handsomely for them."

There's a moment of silence, until finally he hears, "Go on."

"I'll make it well worth your while, I assure you, just hear me out," he says. Holding his breath, he prays the man on the other end stays on.

"Like I said, go on."

Now what?

He tries to think of an answer that will satisfy the man. His first thought goes to the obvious, that he's a doctor and what else would a doctor be looking for. But he doesn't want to go there.

Fuck it. "Not over the phone. Like I said, I have money, and lots of it. Take it or leave it."

There's a long pause, and Lincoln closes his eyes. Finally the voice comes back. "Okay, I'll tell you what. I'll send you a text with a time and place. Come alone, and don't be late."

Three hours later, Lincoln is looking down at the text he's just received. He's nervous about this meeting and the tightening in his gut is letting him know it. The address the text gives is a bus park in the Naya Bazaar district. He's supposed to be there at 9:00 p.m. sharp. The text also reminds him to come alone. He's already called Mick and asked him to ask Palisha if he could borrow her car. While he waits for an answer, he showers, trims his beard, splashes on some cologne, and puts on his new sweater and slacks. The story Mick will give Palisha is that Lincoln's meeting a woman friend who's come in from out of town, and that he doesn't want to stuff her in a cab. The story jives well with the way he's dressed. Hopefully she won't question it.

He slips his new watch on and looks at the time. It's 7:48. He's done a Google search on the bus park, and it's only fifteen minutes away from the hotel, but he knows it'll take longer than that to negotiate the detours the quake has created. He figures he should leave at 8:30 at a minimum. Right now, he needs a drink. He pours himself a glass of rum and tosses a couple of ice cubes in. In the background, the TV is babbling. Some movie he's been ignoring for the last hour and a half. It's just for the noise that fills the room, distracting him from the tangled thoughts swirling around in his head. He picks up his pocket notebook, looks at the notes he's been scribbling over the last couple days. He doesn't feel prepared, despite writing down several thoughts of what he would answer should this Merchandiser ask why he wants to see pictures of the kids. As he reads them back to himself, none of them seem to work. It's all nonsense, and right now, he can't afford nonsense, nor does he want to venture down the path to the black market. He's betting the Merchandiser will be, though. Lincoln's a doctor, what else could he want the kids for?

Mick told him to just be up front, and maybe that's the best advice. The more lies he tells, the easier it will be to get tripped up. The danger with that, though, is it makes him look like someone he isn't, a pedophile. The word is like vomit in his mouth.

His phone pings and he picks it up. It's Mick and he tells Lincoln everything's all set with his ride and to stop by his room to pick up Palisha's keys. He checks himself in the mirror one last time, steps into his new shoes, and laces them up. For a brief instant, he considers packing a knife, but dismisses it. If the man has a gun, what good would it do? It would create a major problem if it was found, and at the moment, another problem is the last thing he needs. He slips his dinner jacket on, stuffing his phone and credit card wallet in the interior pocket. The tightening in his gut is exerting itself more and his legs feel a bit wobbly underneath him. He blows out a breath, steels himself, locks up, and walks out.

Ten minutes later, he's in Palisha's car. He turns it on and pulls onto Ring Road. As he drives his heart is pumping a hundred miles a minute. He's also remembering the click he heard in the alley, which isn't helping. *Chill. You don't want to look like a stupid American in front of this guy.* He comes to a light and his first detour. This will take him down a maze of roads until it cuts back and connects with another road heading north. He checks his watch. It's 8:45. He's doing okay. He makes a right and follows the road, then turns left at a detour, then right at another detour, and another right after that, then finally a left. At last he comes to Chamati Bishnumati Road and here he makes a left. The bus park is right up the road about a quarter mile.

Lincoln follows the river on his right and slows down as he comes to the parking lot. It's deserted. He checks his watch. It's 8:55.

Twenty minutes later, he's bristling. No one's coming. He's been stood up. Shaking his head, he slams his palms down on the steering wheel. "God damnit! FUCK!" Now what? He puts his hand to his head, raking his fingers through his hair, trying to think—checks the text message that was sent to him three hours before. This has all been for nothing, he thinks, and he feels his throat tighten.

He's about to put the car in gear when there's a tap on his window. He looks over to see two men standing outside. It's dark and he can't make out their faces. But they're well-built from what he can see. Despite his relief, he's pissed as he rolls the window down. "You're late."

"You need to leave car here, come with us," says the man who tapped on his window.

For the first time, Lincoln sees the banged-up black SUV in his rearview window. He's not comfortable with this new wrinkle. "Where?"

"You want talk to him, or not?" the man says.

Lincoln thinks about it, but there's really nothing to decide. He gets out of the car, and the other man comes forward. He has a stern, hard face, and his dark eyes are like black buttons. "Put hands up," he barks, and when Lincoln does, he pats him down, then nods to the other man. "Your phone. Where is?"

Lincoln hands it to him and he takes it. "I want it back."

"You will get later," the man says, and swipes his finger across the screen of Lincoln's phone. What he's typing on it, Lincoln has no idea, and when the man is done, he slips it into his pocket. "Come with us."

He follows them to the SUV, and they put him in the back seat. A minute later, they're driving, and it seems like they're going in circles, turning here and there, as if they're lost and looking for a sign or something. By the time they finally come to a stop fifteen minutes later, Lincoln has no idea where he is. He eyes the two-story brick building with dark glass outside his window. It looks like it belongs in one of the Italian boroughs on the island along the shores of the Hudson. He opens his door and the driver, who was the one who patted him down, waves him out.

"Follow us," he says.

Lincoln is led to a door around the side of the building and once inside, up a flight of stairs and down a narrow, dimly lit hall. At the end of it, they go in another door. The room is long and wide and it's cluttered with broken-down desks, wood cabinets, and dusty, over-stuffed bankers boxes that are stacked three and four tiers high. Above is a stained lay-in ceiling with recessed fluorescent fixtures that flicker down on the tired hardwood floor. They snake their way around a bank of file cabinets and suddenly, the clutter melts into an organized, spacious expanse with a bank of windows looking out over the street. Lincoln takes in the fine-crafted mahogany casework and leather chairs as they approach a man sitting behind a broad desk reading paperwork in a folder held in his hand. The man has thinning dark hair and he's in a solid navy-blue suit and red tie. A pair of black-rimmed glasses is perched on a narrow hawk nose and a thin, dark mustache rides over his mouth. He's maybe in his late fifties, and his buttery complexion blends in with the pressed cream-colored shirt. Without looking up, he waves them in.

"Have a seat, I'll be right with you."

Lincoln finds a chair in front of the desk and sits, furtively glancing around the rest of the room. Finally, the man puts the folder down on his desk and turns his way. He points to the file and smiles solicitously. "So, Lincoln Webber, is it? You have quite a history. EMT, doctor, mountaineer. Hmm.... And now you're here in front of me, looking for product. I'm very curious about you. Talk to me. Oh, but wait a minute. Can I get you a refreshment? Tea, perhaps?"

"I'm good."

"All right. So, what brings you here?"

"Business. I'm looking for something you carry."

"What makes you think I have what you're looking for?" he asks, taking off his glasses and leaning forward.

Lincoln tries to ignore the presence of the men behind him. "I was told by a friend of a friend you might have it."

"Who?" the Merchandiser says, leveling a direct, probing gaze at him.

Lincoln crosses his legs, tamping down the urge to make something up. He smiles. Having been in tight spaces before, he knows how important body language is. "Why does it matter?"

"Because I want to know who's got a big mouth," the man says, his tone threatening.

Lincoln pauses. How he answers this question will determine how he leaves this building. "I don't know him, and I didn't get a name."

There's a long silence as the Merchandiser considers his answer. Finally, he sits back and nods. "Okay." He picks his glasses up, twirls them around by the stem between his fingers. "Let's say I do have what you're looking for. What do you want it for?"

"That's my business," Lincoln says. *Hurdle number one done.* "Do you have it or not?"

"I might. It all depends. You say you have money, show me."

"I need my phone."

The Merchandiser nods to one of his men, and his phone is placed in his hand. He brings up his bank's website, signs into his account, and shows the Merchandiser his balance. The man smiles and says, "So, it appears you're serious. Okay. How many you want?"

"Two...one of each. You have pictures?"

The man scratches his chin. "I might."

"Well, I'd like to see what I'm buying," Lincoln says, laying his phone on the desk.

"Okay." The Merchandiser drags a phone beside

Lincoln's folder over to him, types something in, and shows him a picture of a young girl.

Lincoln nods. "Very nice. Can I see more?"

"Sure." He reaches over and hands him the phone, and Lincoln scrolls through the pictures. None of them are of Sunita or Arjun. "You have any more?"

The man pauses, and Lincoln can see him debating. "Maybe."

He gives the man back his phone. "Can I see?"

The Merchandiser takes it and taps the screen. Putting the phone to his ear, he says, "It's me. I need some pictures of our new arrivals. Send them to me now." He ends the call and puts the phone down. "It'll be a few minutes. Sure I can't get you some tea?"

"Thanks, but I'm fine."

The man sits back, studying Lincoln. "You know, I usually don't do business with people I don't know, especially Americans. What brings you to Nepal, if I might ask?"

"Business."

"Well, I hope your business doesn't conflict with mine," he says, and the way he says it lets Lincoln know he's persona non grata if it does.

"I assure you, it doesn't."

"Good, see it stays that way." His phone pings. "Ah, they're here." He picks it up, taps the screen, and hands Lincoln the phone again.

Lincoln scrolls through the new pictures. No luck. He presses his lips together. "That's it?"

"Afraid so. Don't see what you like, or maybe..." he stares hard at Lincoln from over the top of his desk, "...you're looking for something specific? Like maybe a couple of items that belong to a friend of yours?"

Lincoln's heart thuds. He was afraid of this. "No, I was just hoping for a certain look. Let me look again." He scrolls through until he comes to a girl of around thirteen. She has long jet hair and dark almond-shaped eyes that look back mournfully. He holds the phone up to the Merchandiser. "This one will do." When the man nods, he turns the phone around and scrolls some more until he comes to a light tan-skinned boy of around eight or nine. The boy's gaze into the camera is like that of a trapped animal. "This one, too."

"Okay." The man takes a sip of his tea. "When do you want them?"

"Tomorrow?"

"Well, that will depend on when I have your remittance," he says, putting his elbows on the desk and steepling his manicured fingers in front of him. "I require funds up front."

Lincoln figured on this and re-crosses his legs, folding his hands in his lap. "How do I know you'll deliver?"

"You don't, but I have a reputation to uphold."

Lincoln sucks his lips. "Okay." He picks up his phone and brings up his account again. "How much?"

"Two million rupee...each."

"I'll give you three."

The Merchandiser laughs. "You think you're haggling on the street? It doesn't work that way here, American. Five million for both. If you want to keep haggling, I can keep going up."

"No, no, that's all right," Lincoln says and forces a smile. "Five then?"

The Merchandiser nods. "I thought so, and yes, five."

Lincoln types in the amount and hands the man his phone. "I need your routing number. Don't worry, it's encrypted."

"I'm sure it is," the Merchandiser says. He types his numbers in and hands the phone back.

Lincoln checks to make sure the man didn't fiddle with the amount, then hits transfer. "The money'll be in your account tomorrow. Where can I pick them up?"

"As soon as I confirm it, I'll send you a text with their location. Make sure you get there at the specified time. I can't guarantee it won't spoil if you're late."

"I'll be there."

The man gets up and puts his hand out. "It's

been a pleasure doing business with you, Mr. Webber. Maybe I can help you again sometime."

"I'm sure you will," Lincoln says, getting up and shaking his hand. It's warm and dry as snakeskin.

"My staff will see you back to your car. Have a good night. Oh, and do be careful around that bus lot. I hear there's a lot of—how do you Americans say—seedy people around there. Wouldn't want to see you get mugged—is that the word?"

"Yes, and don't worry, I'll be careful." He turns and follows the men out.

23

MAY 9, 2015

*M*ick is looking at the revised trekking schedule Ken Wentworth sent him this morning. With the earthquake and the monsoon approaching in the next month, everything has been put off until the fall season. In the meantime, they want him to return to Germany in a couple weeks to run an Alps trek in Switzerland. This is something he's done most years, going different places like Spain, France, and Italy to run treks during the summer months. He chews his lip. Leaving Polly now is the last thing he wants to do. How can he get out of it?

He brings up his checking balance on the computer. After the deposit High Trails made yesterday, he has 2,500 euros. Between rent (which the company usually pays) and other expenditures, he could probably eke it out. The question is, would Ken let him take a season off, and would he still have his position, or for that matter, any job, when the fall season comes back around?

He's been with High Trails for over ten years now, and he's well liked (at least that's what he assumes), but business is business, and it doesn't exist in a void. If he loses his job, he'll have to dip into his savings until he finds another gig. The problem with that is a lot of companies on the mountains are going through tough times, too. So if not another gig, he'd be starting on the bottom rung. He sits back, rubbing his chin, gazing out the window at the slate sky, and hears Frank's voice in his head: one day at a time. The man always had a way of putting things into perspective. Mick smiles. *Yeah, I know, don't get ahead of myself.* At length, he looks down at his watch. It's 10:30 a.m., too early to call Ken. Instead, he texts him, letting him know he wants to have a chat. Just as he finishes, a knock comes at his door. He gets up to answer it and finds Lincoln on the other side.

Lincoln had stopped by last night after he got back to let Mick know he was still alive and to drop off Polly's car keys. He didn't say how things went, only that he'd let Mick know in the morning. Mick lets the American in and shuts the door behind them. Lincoln takes a seat at the table and for a moment nobody says anything. At last, Mick sits down and studies the troubled expression on Lincoln's face.

"Everything all right?"

"Yeah," Lincoln mutters. But the pinched expression on his face says otherwise. He nibbles a fingernail and stares into space.

An ill feeling rushes over Mick. His stomach tightens as he braces for bad news. "So, talk to me. What happened?"

"Nothing...and everything," Lincoln says, shaking his head.

Mick frowns and sits back. "What's that supposed to mean?"

Lincoln turns to him. "He doesn't have them!"

"Damn."

"There's more," Lincoln says, looking away again.

"What do you mean?"

Lincoln rakes his fingers through his hair, tilts his head back to Mick, and eyes him askance. "I bought two kids."

For a second, Mick isn't sure he heard him right. "Say again?"

"I bought two kids!" Lincoln shrugs. "I was put in a spot, and I...uh...bought two kids."

"Christ," Mick says, dumbfounded. He tries to process the thought, but he can't wrap his mind around it. Finally, he says, "Where are they?"

"I'm waiting to hear when to pick them up, and I know...I know, what you're thinking," he says with a shrug, "but it is what it is. I'll figure something out. At least they're not going to end up in some brothel...or worse."

Mick can't argue with Lincoln's motives, but he wonders where they're going to put two kids. It's not like bringing home a couple of stray cats. And who's going to watch over them? Beyond that, a million questions are flying at him he can't begin to answer. "So where are you going to put them after you get them?"

"With me, I suppose."

"In your room?" Mick asks, raising a brow.

Lincoln jerks his shoulders up. "Unless you have a better suggestion."

"Right." Mick shakes his head and looks back out the window. *As if things aren't crazy enough, now this?* He wants to do the right thing, God knows he does, but he's not sure taking kids in is a good idea with everything else that's going on. He turns back to Lincoln. "What about Sunita and Arjun? Are you giving up on them?"

"Of course not."

"So...let me understand this. You're going to have them living in your room, while you're out hunting for Binod's kids. How does that work? Where do they sleep? You can't keep them locked up, attached to a TV and room service for days on end."

"I don't know. I don't know!" Lincoln snaps, tossing his arms up in the air. "But I'm not taking them to some orphanage that might put them right back where they were." He pauses, shakes his head. "Maybe I'll adopt them."

Mick has all he can do to stifle the laugher in his throat. "Okay, okay, let's settle down here and think." He scratches his head and a moment later, Palisha's face flashes before him. He can just imagine her dropped jaw, the wide-eyed stunned look; can hear her making every objection he just made and more when she finds out. "Umm...there's another thing we're forgetting," Mick says, sitting back.

"What's that?"

"Palisha. She'll be compelled to tell her father, and who knows what he'll do."

He sees Lincoln turning that over in his head. "Maybe we don't tell her."

At this, Mick can't help laughing. "Right. What world are you living in? Of course she's going to find out."

Lincoln nods. "I suppose. Let's not say anything until she sees them, though, if you don't mind."

"Why's that? You think her seeing them is going to sway her? Make her say, 'Ah, look at them. They're so beautiful, of course we'll take them in,'" Mick says. He leans forward and holds Lincoln with a pene-trating gaze. "I can assure you, it's going to take more than that. She has a good heart, but you have to re-member the position she'll be in. I'm not sure what the laws are concerning all this, but whatever they are she'll be bound to follow them, and here's another thing, what happens if there's police around? You'll look damned suspicious dragging two Nepali children behind you, especially if they're reluctant."

"Shit, you're right. Damn, I didn't think about that," Lincoln says, and chews his lip. He shrugs. "I'll just have to take my chances."

Mick puts his hand on Lincoln's shoulder. "I have a better idea."

"What's that?" Lincoln says, looking up.

"We'll bring her with us. She can get the kids."

Lincoln stares back, then shakes his head. "You think she'll do that?"

"After she drills us a new one for lying to her, yes," Mick says, but already he's dreading the look he'll get from her. *Hopefully I won't be put in solitary for too long.*

"She doesn't know what they look like."

"You'll go with her. Once you spot 'em, let her know, and she'll take it from there."

Lincoln's phone pings and he fishes it out of his pocket. "The kids will be at the Monkey Temple on the steps near the main Buddhas at the front at noon."

"It's 11:15. They don't leave you a lot of time." Mick gets up, walks to the dresser, and pockets his phone. "We better get a move on it."

398

~

Bright sunshine rains in through the living room window as Binod looks out. Snuggled against his shoulder is his son. The baby is gumming the burp towel slung over his father's shoulder, and his little legs are digging into Binod's shirt. Tiny hands claw at the towel. Binod inhales the milky scent radiating off his son as he thinks about his plans to scout the Nardevi section of town. He drifts over to the coffee table and picks up a map of the district he printed out this morning. It's basically a residential area with a few restaurants and stores scattered about. It's also an area hard hit by the earthquake. Is he wasting his time there, he wonders? He's tempted to change his mind and skip it and look north to the Khusibun section, but then he reminds himself to stick with the plan. Start south and work his way north.

Sila walks in and announces breakfast is ready. She's been better since the night he begged her to find the tiger in her, but he knows it'll only last so long. They need some good news, anything that'll reenforce her struggling spirit. He hands her the baby, and as he starts for the dining room, his phone pings. He's been getting lots of calls since passing out the fliers, but from all the wrong people trying to solicit business from him. He's been letting them go to voicemail. Where once he would've been jumping to answer every call, now he's more inclined to deal with them all at once. He comes around the corner, taking a seat at the table across from Prabin, and the two of them eat in silence while Sumi and her daughters busy themselves in the kitchen.

Ten minutes later, Prabin pushes his bowl away, takes a drink of tea, and says, "I need to take care of mail and make a couple of calls. As soon as you're ready, let me know."

"Okay, probably in a half hour or so," Binod says as his phone pings again. It's the second call he's gotten since he sat down to eat.

"Are you going to answer that?" Prabin asks, getting up.

Binod dunks a slice of roti bread into his porridge, takes a bite, and looks up. His father-in-law is looking at him with an expectant expression on his puffy face. Binod swallows. "I'll look at it before we go. It's probably just another person trying to sell me something."

"Okay, I'll be in the other room. Come get me when you're ready."

Binod watches him leave. His father-in-law's shoulders have been sagging more and more over the last two days. The man is losing hope and Binod's worried it will be contagious. He'll light a candle for him to *Pārvati* at one of the temples today to give him strength. For himself, he holds onto the belief that he passed the test Shiva threw down at him the other day. Why would Shiva do it otherwise?

Sumi walks in with a watchful look in her eyes as she collects her husband's bowl and cup.

"You want more roti for your porridge?" she asks.

"Oh, no. It's fine." He scoops up another helping of breakfast with the bread, pops it in his mouth, and pushes his bowl away. As Sumi picks it up, he plucks his phone out his pocket, wakes it up, and scrolls down the numbers. He starts with the oldest one first, the one that came in on his way to breakfast.

"Namaste. This is Inspector Magar calling for Mr. Thapa. Please call me back at this number. We believe we have your son, Arjun, in our custody. At the moment we're...."

Binod jerks up and he almost tips his chair over. For a moment he can hardly breathe, hardly hear Inspector Magar's voice telling him they're questioning the men who were holding Arjun on the other end, or Sumi's alarmed voice right next to him. At last, he puts his hand to his face. He's overwhelmed and he's shaking. Turning to Sumi, he grabs her arm and cries out, "They found them! They found them! They found them!"

The dishes in Sumi's hands crash to the floor and seconds later, her daughters come rushing into the room, followed by Sila and Prabin. Everyone's talking over each other, asking what's going on. Binod tosses his phone on the table, rushes to Sila, drags her into his arms, and dances her around.

"They found them," Sumi says.

"Who found them?" Prabin says.

"I don't know!"

"They found them," Binod says into Sila's ear, and as he does, her arms tighten around him and she cries out. It's the sweetest sound he's ever heard. He pulls back to look at her, wipes the tears streaming down her face away with his finger.

Prabin tugs Binod's arm. "Who found them?"

"The armed police," Binod says. "Oh, I got to call them back." He lets go of Sila and grabs his phone.

Palisha's busy with a guest at the front desk when she looks up to see Mick and Lincoln heading her way. From the way they're walking, they're on a mission. She runs the guest's credit card through the reader and prints out the invoice for them to sign, then tosses Mick and Lincoln a smile, but they don't return it. Instead the look coming back is that of a pair of restless teens chomping to get out of the house. When the guest leaves, Mick rushes forward.

"Hey, I know you're busy, but we got a big favor to ask, and we don't have much time," he says.

She's never seen Mick this anxious, and her thoughts fly in several directions. "Sure, what?"

"We need you to come with us. We'll fill you in on the way."

"Mick. you are scaring me," she says.

"Sorry, Polly, it's just we don't have a lot of time."

"We're picking up the kids," Lincoln chimes in over Mick's shoulder. When Mick turns and frowns at him, Lincoln adds, "Well, it's the truth."

Palisha blinks. *He got the kids back!* "Wait, when did all this happen?" she asks, flustered. "And why do you need me?"

"We just do," Mick says, pressing the point. "You know I wouldn't ask you if it wasn't important."

"Oh, okay. Let me get Rajan up here," she says, picking up the phone.

Five minutes later they're walking out the door toward her car. On the way, she listens to Mick sugar-coat the lie he told her the night before concerning Lincoln's need for her car. When they all get in, she turns to Mick. She's not only disappointed and sur-prised he'd lie to her, she's hurt.

"You could not trust me to know this?"

"I'm sorry, Polly. I should've told you. I just...I don't why I didn't."

"It's my fault," Lincoln says. "I should've kept my mouth shut."

She turns to Lincoln in the back seat. "Yes, it is! You put my best friend in a spot. Him, I forgive...you, not so much." She turns the car on and they pull out of the lot. "So, where are we going?"

"Swayambhu Temple," Mick says, and she can see him from the corner of her eye glancing at her furtively. "Am I really forgiven?"

Shifting into fourth, she gives the car gas, then swats him on the arm. "Yes, but do not ever lie to me again, about anything." She looks into the rearview mirror at Lincoln, who's tapping his finger on his knee. "Now tell me, how are they? Are they okay?"

Lincoln clears his throat. "Umm...well, yes and no."

"What do you mean?" When she sees Mick shift in his seat beside her, she gets a bad feeling. "Mick?"

Mick looks straight ahead. "Tell her, Link."

"Yeah, sure. Umm...the kids we're getting aren't Sunita and Arjun. They're a couple of other kids. I was put in a tight spot and I..."

Palisha can't believe what she's just heard. She pushes down on the brake and comes to a stop in bumper-to-bumper traffic. "You bought two kids? Are you crazy? Do you know how much trouble you have just put yourself in? If someone suspects you are trying to steal them, like a cop for example, you can go to jail for a long time."

"I was forced into it...sort of. And that's why you're here."

Palisha drops her jaw and turns to Mick. A horn beeps behind her. "Was this your idea?"

Mick stammers, "I just thought...."

"You just thought?" she shrieks, not wanting to believe it. She shakes her head, hears more beeping, and starts moving. "Why would you put me in this position? Huh?"

"I didn't know what else to do."

"Right! What we ought to be doing is calling the police and having them get the kids. In fact, as soon as we get them, we are going to the police ward and dropping them off."

"Hey, I'm not putting those kids in an orphanage to be sold off again after getting them away from those creeps," Lincoln says.

"Oh, and where would you put them? Hmm?"

"They'd stay with me," Lincoln says. "I have money, I'll adopt them."

Palisha bursts out laughing. "You Americans, you think you can buy everything!"

"That's not fair," Lincoln says. "Because obviously I can, and I just did."

She can't argue with that, and to be truthful, she has to admit that were she in Lincoln's shoes, she might be thinking the same thing. But there's one big difference. Lincoln isn't Nepali. She pulls up behind some cars waiting for a light, composes herself, and says, "Lincoln, I get it, and I feel the same way you do. But you have no idea how things work in Nepal. Can you teach and bring them up Nepali? No, you cannot, because you cannot begin to understand Nepali ways. You cannot even speak Nepali fluently. And what if their parents are alive and looking for them, just like your two friends, hmm? I am sorry, I do not mean to sound cruel and heartless, but what you are thinking is a fantasy."

She looks out the window at the temple mount ahead. The bright white conical stuppa at the top of the hill is peering over the Kathmandu Valley like a beacon for the Hindi and Buddhist faithful. Beside her, crowds of her colorfully clad countrymen and women are thickening as they walk on the side of the road. Rickshaws draped with leis of marigold garlands trundle along beside them. Outside her window is the incessant beeping of horns, lyrical Nepali chatter, and the cacophony of Nepali rock and folk music.

She peers back at Lincoln and sees his stiffened chin and defeated gaze. "This is my Nepali, Lincoln," she says, nodding toward the crowds passing by them. "Can you be that for them? I do not think so, no matter how hard you try."

"Then what?" Lincoln says. "Are you saying I don't belong here?"

"Not at all. What I am saying is, there are other ways to be Nepali. There is a saying we have here. Maybe you have heard it. 'Never ending peace and love.' N.E.P.A.L. To be Nepali is to have that in your heart at all times. And I believe you do, just like this man next to me. Now let us go find these kids."

∼

Binod picks up the phone and calls Inspector Magar as Sila and the rest of the family crowd around him.

As it rings, his heart races. His promise to Sila won't be broken. Shiva has rewarded him, given him and Sila back their children. Binod will never forget this lesson, to look after others even in distress, even if the world is falling apart around him.

A voice answers. "New Baneswor ward."

"Hello, this is Binod Thapa. I'm returning a call I got from Inspector Magar this morning."

"Hold on."

There's a long pause and Binod chews a fingernail as he waits.

Sila says, "Put it on speaker."

"Oh, yes." He presses a button on the side of the phone, sets it on the table, and they wait some more. *What's taking so long?* The minutes pass and he feels like he's about to turn inside out. He's not the only one feeling this way. Sila's gripping his arm, and with every second that passes, her fingers dig a little deeper. He wonders if they lost the connection. Maybe he should call again. He's about to pick the phone up when a voice rings out on the other end.

"Inspector Magar."

"Inspector, this is Binod Thapa. You called me about my children this morning."

"Ah, yes. We believe we have your son in custody at the Metro Circle ward. He was found during a raid this morning at umm...the Himalayan Children's Home."

Sila asks, "Is he all right, and what about his sister, Sunita?"

"He's okay," Magar says, then pauses, "but his sister wasn't with him. Apparently, your children were split up when they were brought to Kathmandu. Metro is questioning the perpetrators who had your son as we speak. I don't know what, if anything, they've discovered, but I'm sure they're leaning on them pretty hard." Magar pauses again, then says, "I'm sorry, I know this isn't what you hoped for, but no one's giving up, and neither should you. Anyway, your son is waiting for you. Should I let Metro Circle know you're on your way?"

"Yes, of course," Binod says, "and thank you." He doesn't know what else to say. He feels Sila's trembling body beside him, senses her anguish. Feels the arrow piercing her heart because it's piercing his, too.

Sumi comes beside her daughter. "Have strength, Sila, for your son. He needs you," she says softly, just above a whisper.

"Don't give up hope, Mr. Thapa. Have courage," Magar repeats. "People are looking for your daughter and we won't give up until we find her. I'll stay in touch."

Prabin speaks up, "Inspector, we've been talking to an organization called 3 Angels. You know them?"

"Yes, we work with them all the time in these cases."

"So, you'll let them know what's going on?"

"Oh, yes, I'm sure they've been contacted, but I'll let Metro know to double check. Okay, I'll let you go now so you can get your son."

The call ends and everyone stares at the phone, as if they don't know how to feel. It's like being kissed by Brahmā, then kicked in the stomach by Yama.

24

MAY 9, 2015

*B*inod sits up front with Prabin, looking out the window at the passing buildings with people milling about them. Sumi and Sila sit in back as they drive to the armed police ward in silence. Little Bishal is home with Sila's sisters. Ever since the call from Magar, everyone has been trying to come to terms with Sunita still being in the wind. These conflicting feelings of happiness for Arjun and despair for Sunita are grinding Binod up. But he has to be present for Arjun, so he swallows the bitter pill of longing for his daughter.

Prabin turns right onto Putali Sadak off of Sinamangal Road, which they've been on for the last twenty minutes. From here to the Metropolitan Circle Station it'll be a zigzag route around the old city. Binod peers down at his phone, debating if he

411

should text Mick and Lincoln about the news. After all they've done, they'd want to know. But he just can't find the strength to do it and then see their happy responses and congratulations.

At length, Prabin looks over at him, then up at the rearview mirror. "We need to put this...this gloom aside. I know it's hard, but the boy needs us to be strong. And like the inspector said, this isn't over. They found Arjun; they'll find Sunni! So smile. We're getting our boy back!"

He's right, of course. Binod knows it. He glances back at Sila, who's staring out the window. She's like spun sugar, brittle and fragile. It isn't hard to see this new emotional up and down is gnawing at the last few strands keeping her from falling apart. Her mother reaches over, puts her hand over her daughter's. As she does, he sees Sila clutch it.

Ten minutes later, they see the four-story police station ahead. It's a modern design, clad in gray panels with a prominent sky-blue extruded façade. A tall strip of dark glass runs up the center of it. Prabin pulls their car into the parking lot, and they all get out and go in through the front door. The lobby is bright and airy, the polished granite floors gleaming under their feet.

They give their names to an officer at the front counter, and a few minutes later they're led down a hall into a large conference room. The officer tells them to take a seat at a long oval table and asks if they'd like a refreshment while they wait for the station commander. They decline, and when the door shuts, they're left to wait again. It seems like all they do is wait, Binod thinks, and he's so tired of it. All he wants right now is to see his son, feel him in his arms, hold him tight and never let him go. Then he wants to know what they're doing to find Sunita. Have the monsters they've arrested said anything?

The ticking wall clock fills the silence, the minutes sliding by, sucking air out of the room, until finally the door opens and the suited commander walks in. He's a tall, robust man, maybe in his mid-fifties, and a hint of white dusts his dark hair. Sharp, intelligent, all-seeing gray eyes look upon them. A gentle smile rests on a tan, experienced face.

They all stand to greet him.

"Namaste," he says, waving them back down. "Please, please sit. First of all, I'm Commander Banjara, and I know you must all be anxious to see your son. But before I bring this boy in, I must verify you're his parents. I hope you understand. I don't want to raise false hopes. Who would be the father?"

"That would be me," Binod says.

"Mr. Thapa, right?" Banjara says, taking a seat.

"Yes."

Banjara pulls a small pad from his suit pocket and flips it open. Looking down at it, he says, "Now, the boy has told us his birthday and where he lives, so I'll need to ask you to tell me the same things, and if your answers match, I'll bring him in and we'll all celebrate."

"My son's birthday is July 27 and he lived at Bijaya Marge," Binod says, then adds, "Our apartment was destroyed in the earthquake."

Banjara's smile spreads and he balls his fist. "Wonderful, wonderful." He stands and extends his hand to Binod, then to Prabin, and they all shake on the happy confirmation while Sumi pulls Sila into her arms. "Now, before I bring your son in, let's talk about your daughter," Banjara says, sitting back down. "From what we've gotten out of the two guys we've arrested, she was sold to a man named Anup. They say they don't know the man's last name or where he holes up, but we're guessing he might run one of the so-called orphanages in the city.

"Also, the fact that he bought your daughter tells us he's planning on selling her to someone else, probably someone with lots of money, and soon. Your daughter is a pretty girl, and pardon my saying this, he'll get a good price for her and more than likely it'll come from someone across the border. Inspector Magar has told me you're working with the 3 Angels. That's good. They know what to look for. In the meantime, we'll be looking more into this Mr. Anup. I'm sorry I can't tell you more."

"You've already done so much," Sumi says.

"Yes, of course," Binod and Prabin echo.

"Okay, let me go get your son," Banjara says.

Binod watches him walk out, then gets up, takes a deep breath, and braces himself for when Arjun comes flying in. But he's not prepared for what he sees when his son comes to the door. His beautiful boy looks back as if he doesn't recognize him. There's also an angry scrape on the side of his perfect head and his face is gaunt, as if he hasn't eaten in days. Accentuating this is the Ama Dablam t-shirt that's hanging off his slender shoulders like a dirty rag. Sila gasps and comes beside Binod. Bending to her knees, she puts her arms out to her child. For a moment Arjun stands gaping at her with his large brown eyes, until suddenly he breaks down crying and runs into her arms.

Palisha parks outside the temple mount and gets out of the car. Mick will stay back while she and Lincoln go up to find the kids. She waits for the American to join her and surveys the crowds climbing the long concrete stairway to the great Buddhist stuppa beyond the trees. Before her, a mangy dog is roaming around the surging crowd, looking for handouts. Pigeons flock around two giant Buddha statues sitting on either side of the stair. A lanky monkey sits in one of the Buddhas' laps, pawing himself. What she's interested in, though, are the police. While she's pretty sure she won't be questioned if they see her with two

Nepali children tagging along, she's wary all the same.

When Lincoln joins her, she asks, "Where are they supposed to be?"

"On the second tier, over there somewhere," he says, pointing to an area near the long flight to the top. "They're supposed to be sitting on a stone wall."

"You know what they look like, right?"

"Of course," he says.

"Okay, stay back from me going up, and when you see them, text me and let me know. Better yet, after you text me, go back to the car." When she sees his reluctant frown, she adds, "Do not worry, I know what I am doing." Which isn't exactly the truth, but the last thing she wants is to have him lingering around, adding another layer of conspicuousness to this whole crazy affair.

The two of them blend into the crowd and start climbing. The first flight leads to the level of the Buddha statues, and so far she's seen no police. But when she comes to the second flight, there's a temple mount guard over to the side, nibbling on an ice cream bar and talking to a Nepali man. She glances over her shoulder to see Lincoln a little closer than she likes. Waving him back, she sneaks up the steps to the second-tier landing and walks to one of the vendors selling candy and ice cream. After purchasing a couple of bars, she drifts off, pretending to take pictures with her phone. Lincoln's text comes a minute later, with a picture of a girl and boy attached. They're not more than ten meters away.

She texts him, telling him to leave, then meanders over to the children. The boy is dressed in a clean tie-dye t-shirt and faded jeans. His hair is combed and his face is freshly washed, but that's as far as it goes concerning his wellbeing. The girl beside him is sitting crossed-legged in a short skirt showing a lot of leg. A printed blouse with the top two buttons undone hugs her thin body. On her feet is a pair of sky-high heels. Palisha watches the girl finger a thick lock of dark hair that's draped over her shoulder. Palisha shakes her head. The girl can't be more than thirteen.

But it's the vacant look of abandonment in their listless dark eyes that bothers her more. They're like a pair of baby rabbits caught out in an open field with no den to hide in, and when they flick a look at her, she can see the fight for survival is nearly gone. It's all she can do to keep from reaching out and pulling them into her arms. She surveys the area around them, wondering if their captors are nearby watching, then takes a last furtive glance to see where the guard is. When she sees the man involved in another conversation, she slides in next to them on the wall.

"Namaste," she says, breaking into a friendly smile.

They don't say anything.

"I'm Palisha, what are your names?"

The girl stirs, but doesn't look back. "Are you our new owner?"

Palisha closes her eyes, gathering her resolve. "No, I'm here to take you home."

"I don't have a home," the girl says.

"No parents?"

"They gave me away. They don't want me anymore."

Suddenly, Palisha's throat tightens. She swallows the ache, not wanting to believe a mother could just give her child away. "Well, you have a home now, if you want it." There's no answer, and this is killing her. She gets up, squats before them, and looks them in the eye, and before she knows it, words are spilling out of her mouth. "What if I told you I want you?"

The minute she says it, she wants to take it back, not because she doesn't mean it, but because she knows the impossibility of it. The boy looks up and holds her with an apathetic gaze, as if he knows she can't deliver.

The girl says, "So where are we going?"

"Someplace safe. Come," she says, getting up and putting her hand out to the boy. "Are you hungry? I have a couple of candy bars until we get where we're going."

The girl shakes her head, but the boy nods. She hands him the Snickers bar and after he takes it, they all get up and head for the stairs. As they walk, the girl struggles to keep her balance in her heels. Palisha turns and tells her to remove them, then dumps them in a nearby trashcan. When she looks back, the girl who's standing before her barefoot and dressed beyond her years is suddenly a child again. She grits her teeth, wondering at the evils of men, how they can find this grotesque aberration of feminine sexuality attractive.

"Better?" she says to the girl.

When the girl nods, she smiles, then ushers her and the boy ahead, acting as natural as she can. As they pass the guard, she can't help feeling his eyes upon her. She shakes the feeling and leads them to the car. As the kids get in back, Lincoln tells her if they must go to the police, then they should take them to the New Baneswor ward. He knows the inspector there.

As Lincoln buckles them in, she turns to Mick. His sympathetic gaze looks as if he's feeling the same things she is, and for a moment it's all she can do to keep her mixed emotions of sadness, anger, and revulsion in check.

Twenty minutes later, Palisha pulls into the New Baneswor ward. It's been a quiet ride, save for Lincoln questioning the children in Nepali, asking their names and where they live. The girl finally tells them her name is Pratima and that she lives in Helambu up in the mountains. The boy pays strict attention to his candy bar and remains silent. As for how long Pratima has been with the traffickers, the girl doesn't know.

Palisha parks and they all get out. The ward is quiet at the moment and not many people are in the waiting area. While the children stay back with her and Mick, Lincoln goes to the counter to ask for the inspector.

Pratima looks up at Palisha. There's a questioning look in her eyes.

Palisha says, "We're going to find you a home, someplace safe, and the police are going to help. Let's go sit over there while we wait."

Mick and the boy follow her and Pratima over to a bank of chairs near an old wooden table with a coffee-urn and cups on top. A vending machine offering packaged pastries and snacks stands beside it. As they sit, Mick turns to the boy.

He gestures to it. "You want something in there?" he says in Nepali.

The boy looks up and nods.

"Well, let's go take a look." Mick puts out his hand, and to Palisha's surprise, the boy takes it. Mick glances back, surprised, and smiles as Lincoln comes and sits.

"Shouldn't be long," Lincoln says in English. "I hope you're right about this. I mean, about them going to a good home. Back in the States, we call *it*

420

the *system*, and once kids are in it, it's like a black hole; one home after another, never really feeling like they have roots, that they're wanted."

Palisha doesn't know about the States, and to be truthful, she doesn't know how the *system* works here in Nepal, but she has to believe she's doing the right thing, that the kids will be looked after and cared for. There's one thing that will be missing for Pratima, though, and that's the love of a mother, and it bothers her. At last she says, "What other choice do we have, really? Be honest with yourself, Lincoln. You are not in any position to take a child in, let alone two. And like I said, how can you educate them to follow Nepali ways, when you have no idea what those ways are? They will be..." she pauses, searching for the American idiomatic phrase, "a duck out of water."

"Fish out of water," Lincoln says, and sighs. "I know you're right, it's just...I don't know...it feels so cold to just dump them after getting them away from that monster."

"I know," Palisha says.

"Lincoln Webber," a man calls out.

Lincoln looks up. "That's us."

He gets up, and Palisha follows him with Pratima at her side. Mick and the boy tag along after them. The man standing by the door is heavy-set and mid-dle-aged, and when he sees Lincoln, he points and says in English, "I remember you. You came in a couple weeks ago with Mr. Thapa."

"That's right," Lincoln says.

"You must be happy hearing the news."

Lincoln pinches his brow. "What news?"

"We found Mr. Thapa's son. Didn't he tell you?"

Lincoln's eyes light up. "No, no, he didn't. That's fantastic. Oh my God, we've been going so crazy worrying about them. When?"

"Just this morning. But I'm confused, if you didn't know, why are you here?"

Lincoln turns to the children standing beside Palisha and Mick. "We, I...umm...rescued these two from a trafficker."

The inspector blinks and his brows leap up. "You what?"

"We sort of did our own undercover operation," Lincoln says.

"No, *you* did," Palisha corrects.

When the inspector looks to her, Lincoln says, "This is Palisha Kc and that's my friend Mick Hanson, who's Binod's boss."

"Oh, okay." He nods to Mick, then Palisha, and then glancing at the children says, "Let's go back and sort this whole thing out. If you don't mind my asking—"

"You don't want to know," Lincoln says.

"No, I suppose not, but you'll tell me anyway."

25

The meeting with Magar goes into the late afternoon, and by the time they're done, Lincoln is feeling a bit better about the kids, especially after Magar agreed to call Mr. Naresh at the Lotus Home. He'll pay whatever the cost is to take the kids in, and Palisha has donated money for appropriate clothes, especially for Pratima. The boy, who remains silent, will be a challenge. If he was stolen, Magar had said, then finding his parents will be difficult, unless he opens up and starts talking. He'll make a call to Next Generation Nepal, an NGO that specializes in re-unifying children with their families.

After the kids were fed lunch, they were led out by a woman for a physical at Bir Hospital, and then they were transferred to Mr. Naresh. What followed was a long conversation about the Merchandiser.

Magar had heard of the man, but until now, he was just a rumor, a ghost working in the dark margins of the city. Lincoln told him all he knew and gave a description of the man, which was the first tangible evidence that he even existed. When he finished, Magar warned him against trying any more stupid stunts in the future, then thanked him.

Lincoln sits in the back seat as Palisha drives them back to the hotel, thinking about the long road the children have ahead of them, then reminds himself again how lucky he was growing up. More and more he finds himself gravitating toward something he can't quite put his finger on, but he knows it'll end up having something to do with the lost children of Nepal.

Right now, Mick is on the phone talking with Binod, and it's clear from Mick's frown that all is not as well as they believed. Palisha taps Mick's arm as she drives. "Hey, what is wrong?"

Mick pulls the phone away from his ear and holds it out. "I just put you on speaker. Say again, Binod."

"They split up Arjun and Sunita, and took her somewhere else. We don't know. Some guy named Anup bought her. The commander thinks they're heading for the border, but he's not sure."

"Christ," Lincoln says, crestfallen.

Mick perks up and says, "Say again, Binod?"

"They split up Arjun and Sunita, and took her somewhere else."

"No, the guy's name who bought her."

"Anup, why?"

Mick turns to Palisha, and they share a knowing *what-if* look.

Lincoln says, "What?"

Mick mutes the phone. "When we were out checking the local orphanages, there was a guy with that name in one of them. I didn't like the look of him, either," Mick says, then turns around and puts the phone to his ear. "Hey, Binod, can I call you back?" After he ends the call, he says to Palisha, "You think your father would be willing to check on this guy?"

"He is already doing it," Palisha says. "I called him the other day."

"Really? How come you didn't tell me?"

"I forgot. I am sorry."

"We have to work on this communication thing," Mick says, eyeing her sideways. But there's a grin on his face.

Lincoln leans forward and taps Palisha's shoulder. "What did your father say? Did he tell you when?"

Palisha shakes her head. "I do not know, I assume sometime this week."

"Can you call him again and ask him to light a fire under someone?"

"Light a fire?"

"Urge someone to move faster," Mick says.

"Oh, yes, of course. I will give him a call as soon as we get back."

~

Twenty minutes later, they're back in Mick's room sitting around the table. Mick and Lincoln are watching her as she scrolls to her father's work number. She's a little apprehensive about calling him again about this, but she knows it needs to be done. When a male voice comes on the line, she asks for her father and waits. Mick is doing his finger-tapping thing on the table beside her and Lincoln is chewing his lip. She puts her hand over Mick's, quelling his anxious anticipation. He's making her nervous. Finally, her father picks up. He sounds tired.

"Bubā, it's me," she says in Nepali. "Sorry to bother you again, but I have some additional news to give you concerning what we talked about the other day. It's very important."

Lincoln gestures to her, and she guesses he wants her to put the call on speaker so they can all hear.

Her father says, "Go on."

"I'm going to put you on speaker so my friend Mick and the American you met at the meeting can hear. Is that okay?"

"Sure."

Mick and Lincoln introduce themselves, and after her father greets them back, she explains the situation and the developments concerning Binod's daughter. "I know you're looking into this man named Anup," she says, "but can you have someone look into him sooner, today or tomorrow at the latest?"

Her father clears his throat. "I've called the CCWB and alerted them, and they're looking into it. I believe they have a surprise inspection planned for this Compassionate Heart Children's Home, but I don't know when, and I'm not sure if they can put a team together this soon."

"What about having the police go in?" Mick says.

"They won't go in unless they have probable cause," Amir says. "The best I can do is alert them to this new information and let them know what you suspect."

Lincoln rakes his hair and Palisha can hear him tapping his foot on the floor. Suddenly, he says in Nepali, "And what that do?"

"Ah, Mr. Webber, I see you speak Nepali after all. Not very well, though," Amir says.

"Bubā, please?"

"Very well," Amir says. Palisha hears a sigh. "What that will mean, Mr. Webber, is that they'll keep an eye on the comings and goings of people in and out of the orphanage. Just to be clear, do not mistake what I'm saying for my not caring. I care very

427

much what happens to this girl, just as I care for every child who is being trafficked, but there's only so much I can do legally. I'll give the CCWB another call and see if they can move things up.

"One last thing you all need to understand, the CCWB has limited authority to search this home, but they do have the power to shut it down immediately if they feel there's something going on there. If Anup refuses to show them the whole building—all the rooms—they can bring the police in and have the children they know of taken away and the building locked up. If the girl is still there and hidden away, we'd find her as soon as the proper paperwork could be forwarded for a warrant."

"How long could that take?" Mick says.

"A couple days at the most. So? Okay? I'll do the best I can. Polly, take me off speaker now. I want to talk."

Palisha picks up the phone. "I'm here."

"I trust your part in this affair will be over now?"

"I think so, but I don't know, Bubā."

"Why doesn't that surprise me? You exhaust me; you know that? And these new friends of yours, be careful you don't get too close. Their world is not ours, okay?"

But I'm already close, Bubā. Maybe their world is different, but is that so bad? I could do worse, a lot worse.

"I know, Bubā. Don't worry."

"Hmm...anyway, call your āmā, she's wondering how you're doing."

The call ends and she sits back. "I guess we have to wait," she says in English. "But my father is a man of his word, and I trust him. If she is still here in the city, he will find her."

"And if she's across the border?" Lincoln says, staring back.

"My father has many connections with authorities across the border, Lincoln. They will be looking too, trust me."

"I do, it's chance I don't trust," he says, getting up. "I'm gonna head up. You guys want to meet for dinner later?"

Mick glances at Palisha. She'd rather have dinner alone with Mick, but she doesn't want to be rude. "Sure." She watches him go to the door and when he's gone, she turns to Mick and in Nepali, says, "I want to talk about us."

Mick blinks and she sees him swallow. "Okay."

"I've been thinking about our friendship, about what I want. All my life, I'm always doing what others expect of me. I don't want that anymore, Mick. I've seen the man you are, the goodness and pain in your heart. Of all the men I've met in my life, you are the most honorable, deserving man I've ever known. You understand what I'm saying?"

She sees him spinning that around in his mind. At last, he says, "I think so."

"I hope so, because what I have to say is very hard for me. I love my parents, and I would do just about anything for them, but in this...US...I will no longer compromise."

He takes that in and again, spins it around. "What about your sons?"

"Yes, my sons. I have thought a lot about them and I have to believe they would accept my decisions. They are not like my father. They are more progressive, and I am pretty sure they only want me to be happy. You want that, too?"

A smile spreads on his face, and she wants to kiss him right now. "With all my heart."

"Then, show me. Be more than my best friend."

He gets up and pulls her into his arms. Kisses her. It's gentle, soft and caressing at first, then more urgent. He pulls back to look at her. His gaze is intense, searching; yet it's also fragile and vulnerable. He whispers, "Are you sure about this?"

"Never more in my life."

Binod gets out of the car. The ride home from the police station was quiet. Arjun clung to his mother, falling asleep in her arms. After being reunited with his son, Binod doesn't know what to say to him. He has so many questions about what happened, but he knows it's too soon to ask them, and he's not sure if he should even ask them at all. The boy wakes up, rubs his eyes, and looks out at his grandparents' house. There's a look of confusion on his face. Binod puts his hand out to his son and helps him out of the car.

"Our home was destroyed in the earthquake," he says to him, then picks him up. He's so light in his arms, and bony. Binod forces a smile. "We're staying with your hajurabubā."

Arjun takes that in, then says, "For good?"

"Only until we can find another place. Are you hungry?" Arjun nods as his mother steps beside them. No one says anything for a moment, and the only sound is the car doors shutting. Prabin and Sumi walk up behind them.

Sumi reaches over and runs her fingers through the boy's hair. She says to Arjun, "Your brother is waiting for you inside. You want to go see him?"

Again, Arjun nods.

"Let's go then," Sumi says, and she strikes off behind Prabin for the front door.

When they step onto the porch, the door opens and Sila's sisters, Amita and Roshika, come out with little Bishal wriggling in Roshika's arms. "I just fed him," Roshika says to Sila and hands the baby to her. To Arjun, she says, "We've missed you so much. I'm so glad to see you're okay."

But Binod knows Arjun isn't okay. There's a shadow lurking behind his son's solemn expression. He puts Arjun down, and they all remove their shoes and go in. The house is alive; afternoon sunlight pours in through the large picture window in the living room, vibrant Nepali music floats in from another room, and the aroma of garlic, curry, and herbs wafts around him.

Amita says, "Dibaker will be over soon with Sabita and the kids. We've prepared dinner in the kitchen. Arjun, you want something to drink?"

The boy looks up at his mother. Sila switches the baby over in her arms. "Go ahead. It's all right."

Binod watches Amita take his son's hand and lead him into the other room as Sumi and Prabin go off in different directions. When he's alone with Sila, he says, "He's so different, so quiet. It's like he's another person." And as he says this, he's thinking of Sunita, what she'll be like if they get her back...*when we get her back*, he chides himself.

"I know," Sila says, looking on. "The woman who deals with stolen children cases at the station said it's to be expected for a while."

"Oh, when was this?"

"When you were with the commander," Sila says, patting the baby's back. "She said not to worry just yet, let him adjust for a couple weeks, and to also get him in to see a therapist."

Binod wonders how they're going to pay for that. They have nothing right now. "I guess we just have to be patient then," he says. He sighs and when he turns to go wash up for dinner, he catches Sila looking out into space. He knows who's on her mind, because she's on his mind, too.

Dibaker and his family show up ten minutes later and the homecoming for Arjun turns into a big party. After dinner, Amita and Roshika gather the kids together and play board games while Binod fills Dibaker and Sabita in on how Arjun was found and what the police are doing to find Sunita. One thing that bothers him, but that he doesn't mention, is Arjun's not asking about his sister. The commander said they'd asked him about Sunita, but when they did, he went silent and looked away. What secrets does his son hide behind the fragile armor he's wrapped around him? Binod shudders to think what they could be. The councilor at the station said not to press him about it, to let it come out naturally. Except they don't have time.

Around eight, they all gather around the TV to watch a movie that Arjun has picked out from Amita's collection of DVDs. It's a Disney movie: *Aladdin*, one of Arjun's favorites. He sits cross-legged on the floor with his cousins, immersed in it. For a moment, Binod watches him, and as he does, he sees the vibrant boy he remembers and hears the sweet sound of his laughter. But there's a giant hole in this room and until it's filled, everything will be gray and subdued. Pulling out his phone, he stares at the picture of Sunita he's uploaded for wallpaper, willing the phone to ping, to hear the voice of the commander telling him they found Sunita. It's silly doing this, but he can't help himself.

Two hours later, the movie is finished, and Dibaker and his family have left. Sila takes Arjun up to bed while Binod talks to Prabin and Sumi about what more they can do in their search for Sunita. They're just finishing up and getting ready to go to bed when a loud cry comes strafing down from upstairs. They all look up, startled, and when another one comes, Binod runs up to see what's wrong. He rushes into Arjun's room to find his son's head buried in his mother's shoulder. As Sila rocks her crying son in her arms, Binod asks, "What's wrong?"

"I don't know. When I turned out the light, he screamed. I told him it was time for bed, but..."

Binod goes in and sits on the bed beside them. "Arjun, what's wrong?"

The boy raises his head, and the look in his eyes is one of terror. For a minute he doesn't say anything. Finally, he swallows and rubs his eyes. "I want the light on."

"It's okay, you're home with us now. It's time to go to bed, we need to turn the light out," Binod says.

But Arjun breaks into more tears. "Please, Āmā, Bubā, don't turn it off. I'm scared."

Sila and Binod look at each other, puzzled. Arjun has never been afraid of the dark before. Binod caresses his son's cheek with his hand, then shrugs. "Okay, we'll leave the light on, then."

Sila rubs her son's back. "Whatever you want, baby." Nodding toward the door, she says, "I'll be down in a minute."

"Okay," he says, then kisses his son on the forehead and goes back down to find Sumi and Prabin waiting at the foot of the stairs. "He's scared of the dark, so we're going to leave the light on in his room, if that's okay."

"No problem," Sumi says.

"He's never been scared of the dark before," Prabin adds.

Binod shrugs. "I know."

"It probably has something to do with what happened," Sumi says, shaking her head. "The poor child: such an awful thing to have happen to anyone. I hope they put those bastards away for a long time."

26

MAY 10, 2015

The sound of the alarm wakes Palisha up. She leans over and shuts it off as Mick snores beside her, then remembers yesterday and her taking him inside her. She had been nervous and anxious, unsure of what to expect because it had been so long since she was with a man. But it was more than she could've hoped for, and last night had been even better. Her intuition about him was spot on. He was everything she wanted—gentle, attentive, but also strong and needful, taking control of her shuddering body that longed for him. She snuggles close to him, draping her leg over his. The scent of their love-making lingers in the room and she inhales it. It makes her want more and she considers rousing him for another round when her phone goes off. She sighs, then turns and picks it off the nightstand. It's her father. She wrinkles her brow, wondering why he's calling. He rarely calls unless it's urgent. Sitting up, she answers it.

Mick stirs beside her. She taps his arm, then puts her finger to her lips. "Hello?"

"It's me. I pulled some strings, and they're going to raid the home this morning. I hope you're right about this, otherwise we're going to look stupid."

Palisha is astonished and excited. "I'm sure of it."

"I'll keep you posted," he says, and then ends the call.

"Who was that?" Mick asks, sitting up beside her.

"My father. He says they're going to raid Anup's home this morning."

His jaw drops. "Really?"

"Yes, let's hope we're right. My father is going out on a limb here," she says, setting the phone on the nightstand. Turning back to him, she nestles into the warmth of his arms again. "I have a good feeling about this."

"I do, too." He's quiet a moment, and she can hear his heartbeat. At last, he says, "Do you regret last night and yesterday?"

"No, not at all. Do you?"

"No. You were beautiful," he says. "I just don't want anything to ever ruin how we feel about each other, because first and foremost, like I keep telling you, you're my best friend."

"Nothing could ever ruin that."

"My friend Frank used to say, 'never say never, and never promise anything except the truth.'" He squeezes her shoulder and when she looks up, he says, "I love you. I've loved you almost since I met you."

His words are like cool water after searching for happiness in an emotional desert for the last twenty-five years, and she drinks them greedily. "Say that again. I want to hear them again and again."

"I love you, I love you, I love you."

Burying her head into his shoulder, she savors this perfect moment, never wanting to leave it, and says, "And I love you, Mick Hanson."

His arms clasp around her. "Your father's not going to be happy about that."

"Probably not, but this is my life, and I choose you. Maybe I should take the day off, and we just stay right here, what do you think?"

She senses his smile coming back. He says, "I think you're going to kill me if we do that."

"Well, we wouldn't want that," she says, lifting her head and winking at him.

"No, we wouldn't," he says. "I want to have many years with you, so I can explore every inch of that beautiful body of yours."

"Starting right now, straight through the summer. It will give us lots to do during all these rainy days coming up."

"Yes, umm..."

"What?"

He pauses, then taps her shoulder. "I was going to wait awhile, but now, I think it's best I tell you about a few things I need to decide on...or rather we should decide on."

The cautious way he says it makes Palisha's heart skip. She sits up and looks him in the eye. "Okay."

Mick clears his throat. "High Trails wants me to come back to Germany to run a few treks during the summer, like I've done before. If I refuse, I can get pulled from the Himalayan rotation, and worse, I could lose my job, although I don't think that would happen."

"I see. When did you find this out?"

"Yesterday morning. I've been wrestling with it ever since. And now after last night, and what we just said to each other, I know what I want."

She's pretty sure she knows what his answer is, but she needs to hear it, to know that he meant what he said. "And what's that?"

"You, of course. I don't want to be anywhere you're not. But I need to be able to support myself, and High Trails won't pay my rent here if I'm not working."

She stares back, her mind reeling. Why didn't he tell her this before? Except, now that she thinks of it, he has left Nepal every summer. If she'd remembered that, or better yet, if he'd told her before yesterday happened, would it have made a difference? She's not sure, and she's also not sure if she's mad at him or hurt, or missing him already. She swallows the tightness in her throat.

She's about to ask him what he's going to do, when he says, "I know what you're thinking, and I'm not thinking that at all. What I want to know is, do you want to come with me? You wouldn't be that far from your sons. You could go see them, spend time with them while I'm away? I know your father will hate me and do everything he can to dissuade you, but I love you, and being away from you would drive me crazy."

Suddenly all her uncertainty vanishes. The thought of joining him never occurred to her. She throws her arms around him as the last of his plea dribbles away in her ear. "Of course I'll come!"

Lincoln has decided he's going to go see Mr. Naresh at the Lotus Home and make sure the kids have gotten settled there. He looks out his hotel window and sees Jiban outside waiting for him in his cab. Collecting his wallet, he locks up and is out the door.

It's an overcast day and cool for May. He hoofs it to the cab and gets in. "Namaste," he says to Jiban in Nepali. "We go Lotus Home in Budhanikantha. You know where is?"

"Oh, yes," Jiban says, pulling away from the curb. "How are you?"

"Okay," he says, but that's the furthest thing from the truth. He's anxious for Sunita. Amir has said he'll look into having the CCWB pay this Compassionate Heart Home a visit, but who knows how long that will take. With every minute that passes, Sunita's fate dims. But sitting in his room at the hotel vacillating on the what-ifs would drive him nuts, so he's doing something to take his mind off it.

As Jiban drives through traffic on Ring Road, Lincoln scrolls through his phone, checking messages, but there's only a few come-ons from people trying to sell him things he doesn't need. He puts his phone away, settles in for the forty-minute drive, and says, "How things with you?"

"Okay. You doing some more survey work today?"

"Something like that," Lincoln says, looking out the window. He's trying to collect his thoughts, but they're all over the place. He worries about Sunita. Is she okay? Is she still in the city, or has she been taken across the border, put in some brothel, forced to give up her innocence to the evil machinations of men, or worse? Then there's Pratima and the boy. What will happen to them, and will they be able to find the boy's parents, if they even want him back?

Lincoln shakes his head. How can anyone give up a child without a second thought? Finally, there's the matter of where he'll live after the dust settles and what he'll do. He's finally discovered what his heart has been screaming for, what it's always wanted, but there are only so many places it can go and the need is great. Should he opt for the 3 Angels, or Save the Children, or the other NGO, Maiti Nepal? And what about the orphanages? There's lots of work to do there. Maybe he'll even create his own NGO.

He watches the buildings slip past his window. The highway around the city is busy this morning, as always; cars and motorbikes, trucks and rickshaws weave in and out ahead. As he looks on, he realizes his life so far has been just like this mindless, tangled swarm of traffic, always searching for daylight and clear sailing ahead, never thinking things through. Every hasty decision has ended up wide of the mark. This time, he has to make sure he's not making the same mistakes he's always made. He has to make it count, not only for himself, but for those who deserve nothing less than his full attention.

Jiban turns off Ring Road and they head into the dense maze of neighborhoods that meander every which way through the Kathmandu Valley. The route they're on is like that of a ball going through a pinball machine, left-right-right-left and left and so on and so on. Funny, he didn't notice it the first time he came here with Palisha; then again, he'd been too focused on their mission to track down the Merchandiser. They cross a river he has no name for on a one-lane bridge that looks like it's about to crumble underneath them when his phone pings. He looks at the number. It's Mick.

"Yeah?" he says.

"Guess what? Palisha got a call from her father this morning. They're doing a raid on that children's home today. Where are you, anyway? I went to your room and you weren't there."

"I'm going to the Lotus Home to check on the kids, and that's great," Lincoln says, brightening. "Let me know the minute you hear anything."

"Will do. Keep your fingers crossed."

"Hopefully they'll find her, or will know where she is," Lincoln says. "You haven't said anything to Binod yet, have you? I think it's best we keep this to ourselves until we know anything."

"No, I haven't, and I agree. Okay, gonna get off the phone here so I don't miss a call."

Lincoln puts his phone away. He's encouraged and delighted that Palisha's father is pushing buttons and pulling strings. Maybe today will be a great day, he thinks as Jiban turns into the Lotus Home parking lot. He gets out and pays him, then says, "Can you hang awhile?"

Jiban takes the money and stares back.

"Umm...stay here sometime?"

"Oh, okay. How long do you think it'll be?"

"I do not know, maybe hour?"

Jiban shrugs. "I'll be over there, then," he says, nodding to a space under the shade of an acacia tree.

Lincoln thanks him and marches to the front door. As he goes, he sees a group of boys kicking a soccer ball around in the fenced-off yard next to the building. A couple of girls are off to the side watching them. He recognizes the girl who reminded him of Sunita the last time he was here. Pratima isn't with them, nor is the boy.

He goes in and finds Mr. Naresh in his office. The man gets up, grabs his cane, and comes around his desk. "Namaste, Mr. Webber," he says in English. "This is a surprise. How are you?"

Lincoln greets him prayerfully. "I'm good, thank you."

"I assume you're here to see the children we took in for you yesterday."

"I am. How are they doing?"

Naresh shrugs. "They're adjusting. It'll take time, the boy especially. He refused to sleep in the bed last night, preferring the floor instead. Not sure what that's about. I have a counselor assigned to him." He turns his head and coughs. "By the way," he says, and clears his throat, "thank you for that additional donation yesterday. It'll go a long way in providing books and materials for the children's classrooms. Can I get you a refreshment?"

"Oh, no thank you."

"Very well, shall we take a walk, then?"

445

Lincoln nods and follows him out of the office and down the corridor. As they walk side by side, Lincoln notices the ongoing artwork on the walls, colorful crudely drawn pictures of birds, flowers, and Disney characters such as Aladdin and Mulan. Naresh tells him he got the idea of having the kids decorate the walls from his daughter.

"I hope you don't mind our using some of the money you donated to buy paint and brushes for the kids," he says, pointing at the pictures.

Lincoln smiles. He made the right decision about the kids coming here.

When they come to Pratima's room, Lincoln finds her sitting on her bed, cross-legged, leafing through a picture book on her lap. She's wearing new jeans and a pretty pink short-sleeved top. Her long dark hair is pulled back in a ponytail and the gaudy nail polish that was on her nails yesterday has been removed. She looks up, studies Lincoln a moment, then turns back to the book.

"Pratima," Naresh says, "aren't you going to say hi?"

She glances back up. "Hi."

"What you reading?" Lincoln says.

She holds the book up. It's *The Lion King*.

"That a great story," Lincoln says.

She shrugs, then drops the book to her lap and turns a page.

Naresh leans in close to Lincoln and whispers in

his ear, "The doctors suspect she's been sodomized, but we're not sure. Lots of times before the spotters or bondsmen sell them to the brothels, they have a little fun, oral sex and the like." When he pulls back there's a look of disgust and anger on his face. He breaks into Nepali, and says to the girl, "Lunch is pretty soon, okay. We're having pizza. You like pizza?"

Another shrug.

Naresh glances at Lincoln, shakes his head, and returns to English as he walks off. "She didn't hardly eat anything yesterday. Hopefully her appetite will return soon. She's already too thin."

"Good-bye, Pratima," Lincoln says, and his heart is crashing for the girl. "I be back soon, I promise." It takes all his strength to pull himself away from the door and follow Naresh.

When he catches up to him, Naresh says, "So, you really found this guy, this Merchandiser?"

"Yeah. And if I never see him again outside a prison cell, it'll be too soon."

"Hmm...what does he look like? It'd be nice to know so I don't make a mistake and send a child off with him."

Lincoln gives Naresh a thumbnail description, then says, "I doubt he'd come to you in person. He likes hiding behind his desk and letting others do his dirty work. By the way, you were right about being careful how I asked about the children."

"It was just a guess, that and rumors from others about him." Naresh comes to a stop by a door and pushes it open. "Namaste," he calls in.

There's no reply. Naresh gestures Lincoln to follow him in. When Lincoln comes to the door, he sighs. The boy is dressed in jeans and a plain t-shirt, and he's sitting with his back against the wall and his knees pulled to his chest, with his head down. "How are you doing?" Naresh says to the boy in Nepali, approaching him with a cautious stride. "There's someone here to see you, won't you look up and say hi?"

The boy stirs and peeks up through a thick curtain of bangs hanging over his eyes. There's a spark of recognition and then it's gone. Lincoln follows Naresh over and squats before the child. "You remember me?" he says, and smiles. "I was one in car with friends. Kind woman who gave candy bar and big guy who bought donut from machine. His name, Mick, remember him?"

A barely perceptible nod comes back.

"Would you like see Mick again? I can bring him sometime I come?"

Another nod, this one a little more direct.

"Okay then, I bring him back." Lincoln gets up and takes a deep breath, suddenly realizing how much he doesn't know about reaching out to these kids. If he's going to work in this world, he's going to have to educate himself.

~

Binod is eating lunch alone when Sila comes into the kitchen with Bishal in her arms. He looks up to see a constrained frown on her face. "What's wrong?" he says.

"I just came from Arjun's room. He wet the bed last night," she says. "He's never done that before."

Binod blinks, wondering if he heard her wrong. "Did you say anything to him?"

"No."

"Maybe it's just a one-time thing," he says, but he knows he's deceiving himself. After what happened last night with Arjun shrieking over the lights being turned out in his room, Binod's pretty sure it has to do with his son's ordeal. *What did they do to my boy?* He's not hungry anymore. He pushes the plate of chaat and roti bread away. Fire courses through his veins, and he wants to reach out and strangle the men who took his son, crush them in his hands, kill them. "Where is he?"

"In Roshika's room, watching TV with her," Sila says, switching the baby to her other arm. "He hid his wet pajamas in the closet. I didn't make a big deal out of it."

"Good, there's no need to upset him," Binod says, staring out the window, trying to contain the rage bubbling up inside him. He's not sure how much more of this he can take.

"I want my baby back, both of them," she says.

He's about to say, "I know. So do I," when his phone pings on the table, startling him. He picks it up. He doesn't recognize the number, but decides to answer it. The last time he waited, it was the Metro police calling. He won't make that mistake again. "Hello?"

"Is this Binod Thapa?"

"Yes."

"Commander Banjara here. Hey, I'm wondering if you can come down to the station."

Binod almost jumps out of his chair, making little Bishal cry. "Sure. Did you find her? Did you find my daughter?"

"I have news of her," Banjara says. "If you can just come down, okay?"

Binod's heart thuds. He doesn't like the implications behind Banjara's evasive statement. He's also afraid to look at Sila and let her see the sudden fear coursing through him.

"What?" Sila cries, aggravating the baby's bawling. She paws at his arm. "What's he saying?"

He puts his hand up to shush her, but it's more to give him time, to put off seeing the contorted gaze of hope, terror, and dread coming back. To Banjara he says, "Yes, we'll be right there."

"Good. Take your time," the commander says.

Binod ends the call and sets the phone down. He's trying to breathe, trying not to go down a dark hole, to believe he's just jumping to wrong conclusions. At last he turns to his wife and looks at her with a steady, sure gaze that's taking every ounce in him to maintain so she won't unravel before him. "They want us to come down to the station. They have news of Sunni."

Sila's eyes bulge as Bishal wails and flails against her. "What news? Binod, tell me!"

"I don't know!" Binod says. "They just want us to come down."

Sumi and Prabin come rushing into the room, alarmed. Sumi asks, "What's wrong?"

"The commander at the station just called," Binod says. "They want us to come down."

"They find her?" Prabin says, as Sumi clutches her husband's arm.

"I don't know, they didn't say. We need to go," Binod says.

"They lost her. They lost my baby, I know they did," Sila wails, her face crumpling.

Binod grabs her shoulder and looks at her hard, defiant. "Don't! We don't know anything. Understand?"

She stares back at him, panting, and nods.

"Now we need to go," he says, and rushes out of the room. He calls up to Roshika, asks her to come down and take the baby. When she comes to the landing, Arjun is with her. His son stares down, his penetrating gaze passing through Binod to someplace

Binod doesn't know. For a moment as he looks back at his son, it's like peering at a shadow: there, but not really there. A shiver runs through Binod as Roshika comes down to get the crying baby from Sila. With a force of will, Binod shakes off Arjun's unsettling gaze and heads for the front door.

～

Thirty minutes later, they're getting out of the car in the Metro parking lot and rushing into the building. The officer at the front desk leads Binod and the rest of them back to the conference room, and when the man opens the door, Binod sees Mick, Palisha, and Lincoln at the table. Also, there next to the commander is Amir.

What? How...why are they here? Oh, no...no!

He feels his legs turn to jelly as he looks at their sober expressions that thrust his worst fears and thoughts back at him, bouncing them back and forth, crashing them into each other. They all get up as he walks in with Sila and her parents. The commander comes forward.

"You have a lot of friends who care an awful lot about you," Banjara says to Binod and his family in Nepali. Binod knows the commander is trying to lighten the mood, relax them, but it's not working. The commander clears his throat, loses the dim smile on his face, and continues, "Also, here with us on conference call is Kamala Gautam from 3 Angels. I believe you know her?"

A second later, her voice comes through the speaker. "Namaste!"

Banjara waves them to their chairs. "Can I get anyone something to drink? We have tea or coffee, or perhaps a soda."

Binod shakes his head and sits.

Banjara presses his lips together and takes his seat next to Amir. "Okay then, I called you all down here to go over some new developments regarding your daughter. This morning we raided an orphanage here in the Metro area at the request of Commissioner Shrestha. The home, which has been running uncertified for some time, was known to us, but until today we didn't have enough evidence to move on them."

"Binod, Sunita was there," Lincoln says, leaning forward. "They had her!"

Had? Oh, no, it's true then. She's gone over the border...my Sunni's gone!

The room closes in around Binod. He knows Sila is sitting by him, but he doesn't sense her there anymore. Her shriek is like a distant echo in his ears, and the faces in front of him are a kaleidoscope of distorted shapes.

Banjara waves his hands, palms down. "Mr. Webber, please," he says, then turns back to Binod. "It's true they had her, however, after interrogating the owner, Mr. Silwal, we now have a very good idea where she's been taken."

"The guy named Anup," Mick says, clarifying.

Binod blinks, snapping out of his miasma.

"What? You do?"

"Yes," Amir says, piping up. He leans toward the phone on the table. "Kamala, can you please repeat what you told us a few moments ago for Mr. Thapa?"

"Sure. Mr. Thapa, I believe they've taken her to Patna," she says. "I've already been in contact with the Indian authorities there and have had Sunita's picture passed around in the surrounding areas, police and the like. Patna would be the first place they'd take her before moving her further. I'm sure of it, that is, unless one of the local brothels bought her, then she'd remain there, which would be good, believe it or not. The police will be keeping a close eye on things in the area, and if she's there, we'll find her."

"So, she's in India?" Prabin says.

"Yes," Banjara says. "She was transported across the border four days ago, or so Mr. Silwal says."

Sila cries out.

Binod reaches over and takes her hand, and she seizes it. "How do you know he's telling the truth?"

Banjara clears his throat. "I assure you he is. His future depends upon it."

Amir says, "The route Silwal said they were using to take Sunita across the border goes through Raxaul, unless they switched up and went through

Gaur or Sonbarsa. In any event, we're pretty sure your daughter is in Patna." Amir takes his glasses off, then looks directly at Binod and Sila. "All is not lost. Do not give up hope. Your friends here have not given up, nor has Kamala. They've worked hard for you, and it's because of them we have an excellent chance of getting your daughter back. Also, I can't tell you how many young girls and boys we've gotten back because of 3 Angels in the last year. They never give up, and neither should you."

Amir sits back, and as he does, Binod laments. More waiting. It feels like he's been waiting forever, trying to keep his head above water, and he's not sure how long he can keep treading in this whirlpool of hope and despair. He closes his eyes, trying to hold on, and feels Sila's grip on his hand fade away. He wants to be here for her, wants to be strong, to let her know he hasn't given up, that she's not alone in her misery, but he's so exhausted.

Suddenly, there's a powerful hand on his shoulder, and when he looks up, he sees Lincoln standing behind him. There's a determined expression on the man's long, sturdy face, a strength and defiance in Lincoln's eyes and clenched jaw that rouses Binod's battered spirit. "We're going to get her back," Lincoln says in English, "even if I have to spend every last fucking dollar of my inheritance."

27

MAY 12, 2015

*B*inod opens his eyes to cool gray light filtering in through the curtains. The space beside him in the bed is empty. It's been empty a lot lately when he wakes up. He clutches his pillow and hugs it as the comforting arms of sleep slip away. The oblivion of unremembered dreams is the only peace he's known the last two weeks. He supposes he should get up, get around and start the day, except he's trapped in this Sunni-less world and he doesn't know how to live in this new normal. Already the sweet sound of his daughter's voice is like a distant murmur in his ear, fading more and more every day. It horrifies him to think he might forget her voice, never hear her call him Bubā again.

How has everything gone from the perfect life he had six weeks ago to a world of sullen shadows creeping over everything he holds dear, blotting out the beauty that surrounded him? How easily it was swept away the moment he took his eye off it. And now, all that's left is the scattered rubble of a life that lies barren before him like the rubble in the city beyond. How does he put it all back together when there are so many missing pieces? Will it end up looking like some grotesque reconstruction with misplaced pieces forced into misshapen holes? Will he and Sila become empty shells, moving on and forgetting because remembering is too hard, or will they wrap themselves in armor, keeping each other out while they nurse their guilt and anger against each other?

At last he gets up. Somehow, he's got to figure out where they're going to live. They can't stay here forever, cluttering Prabin and Sumi's life. And then what to do about money? With the trekking season in the trash, the money he depends on to make ends meet isn't there. He'd thought about driving a cab part-time while Sila was on maternity leave, except driving a cab is the last thing he wants to do full-time. What's more, he doesn't have a vehicle, and he doesn't have the money to get one. Maybe construction, he thinks. Certainly there'll be opportunities there, except again, he's not a mason or a carpenter. At best, he'll get a laborer's job, which means doing all the things no one else wants to do. They need clothes, too. They've been living out of Prabin and

Sumi's closet since they got here, and that can't continue. So many things they need: furniture for an apartment, a bassinet for the baby, a crib. Where does it all come from?

Suddenly, he's exhausted. Just thinking about all this is overwhelming. He feels that his life is like one of the damaged buildings in the city, leaning to one side, ready to come crashing down at any minute.

Sila walks in with the baby. She's still in her pajamas and her hair is a tangled mess. She lays the child on the bed and goes to the dresser, pulling out a pair of jeans and a top. Since the meeting at the station, she hasn't said more than a dozen words. Just moves from place to place, doing this and that as if she's some kind of robot. He watches her dress, then brush her hair. Her face is wan and expressionless, her body stiff and purposeful.

He says, "I'm going to start looking for work today. We need money."

She doesn't answer.

"Did you hear me?"

She turns, considers him a moment. "Whatever you think."

"You blame me, don't you? If it wasn't for my suggestion to leave the kids with my parents, they'd still be with us."

For the first time in two days he gets a reaction. "Why do you think it's all about you, all the time?"

Binod's jaw drops. He's confused. "I didn't say it was about me."

"Didn't you? If you feel guilty, go cry on someone else's shoulder." She picks the baby up and goes out, leaving him baffled and hurt. Never has she spoken like this to him in all the long years of their marriage. He tries to console himself that she's just upset, but he knows it's more than that. It's clear she's harbored that feeling for a while, but never said anything about it. What else is she harboring against him? He tamps down the urge to follow her and defend himself, but changes his mind and finishes dressing. It's best he gets out of the house today, puts some space between them: between the hurt, anger, and disappointment.

Lincoln paces around his room. He's tired of watching TV, tired of looking at road maps of India, of making phones calls to Kamala, Binod, and the authorities in Patna. He's been doing it for almost two days. Waiting has never been one of his strong suits, and now with all that's happened, it's actually painful. He shuts his laptop and lies on his bed thinking of Sunita, then of Binod and Sila. They've gone through so much. And now with Arjun's difficulty adjusting to life back home, it's only getting harder. He thinks about what Binod told him: how

Arjun needs the light on at night, his sudden bedwet-
ting, and his avoidance of talking about his sister.

What the hell happened to him?

He rakes his hair with his fingers, thinks about
the vibrant little boy, and the beautiful, talented, cre-
ative girl. Considers renting a car and driving to
Patna: he's been mulling it over the last two days. But
once he gets there, then what? It's not like he knows
Hindi. He barely has a grasp of Nepali. He'd be
thrashing around, going in circles, getting nowhere.
And then there's the road to Patna. From what he's
read on the web, India's highway NH27 is one of the
most dangerous roads in the world, and he'd be on it
for 265 kilometers; 177 miles. Seven hours of hell,
not to mention another five hours from Kathmandu
to the border.

He picks up his phone from the nightstand. It's
just after 9:15. They're serving breakfast downstairs
in the café now. He's not really hungry, but he supposes he ought to eat, and it won't hurt to get out of
the room and be around people. Then what? He
could call the Lotus Home, see if there's anything
they need, maybe spend some time with the kids. But
he was just there yesterday, and he doesn't want to
make a nuisance of himself, except he has to do something, anything to get his mind off Sunita; off visions
of her being forced to give her body up to men willing
to pay a few rupees to slake their wanton needs. The

thought of it makes his blood boil as he collects his wallet and steps into his boots.

Down in the café, he runs into Mick and the two of them share a table. The expedition leader tells him he'll be going back to Germany in a couple weeks to run the summer treks. It's something he does every year during the monsoon. But there's an odd expression on Mick's face that Lincoln can't quite place. It's as if Mick's looking forward to it, and then reluctant at the same time. The reluctance, Lincoln understands, but the looking-forward-to-it look raises Lincoln's curiosity.

"Somebody back in Germany waiting for you?" Lincoln says between mouthfuls of eggs.

Mick sets his fork down and looks up. "Nope, just the opposite. I'll be bringing someone back with me this time."

"Palisha?"

Mick nods, and it's obvious he's happy about it. "Hopefully, we'll get Binod's daughter back before we leave. I hate the thought of going with her still in the wind."

"I know."

"What about you?" Mick says. "I assume you're gonna stick pretty close to Binod."

"Yes. He and Sila are gonna need the support if this thing goes on for any amount of time," Lincoln says. He takes a sip of tea. "In the meantime, I'm thinking of volunteering at the orphanage where we took Pratima and the boy. It'll give me a chance to get to know them as well as keep me out of trouble. You know how I like to get into that."

"All too well," Mick says, grinning.

Lincoln pops the last of his breakfast in his mouth and swallows. "So, just best friends, huh?"

"Who?" Mick says, wiping his lips and sitting back.

"You and Palisha," Lincoln replies, then winks at him.

Mick averts his gaze and rounds his shoulders. "Oh, umm...that...ah, things have sort of—"

"Grown between you two?" Lincoln says, suppressing a smirk. When Mick's face colors, Lincoln knows he hit the bulls-eye. "You know, from what I've seen of Amir, he looks to be a proper old-world type. Her telling him she's going to Germany with you must've been a conversation for the ages."

"She hasn't told him yet," Mick answers.

Lincoln snorts, thankful he didn't have anything in his mouth, or he would've spit it all over the table. He leans back in his chair, leering at Mick. "Oh!" Lincoln says, then clears his throat for emphasis, "You know...you might want to consider getting out of town before that happens?"

"I've thought about it, believe me," Mick says, and gets up. "Well, I got to get busy and write a few e-mails. Talk later, and oh...by the way, Palisha coming with me is just between the two of us, okay?"

"Sure, and hey, I'm happy for ya." He watches Mick drift over to the cashier, then picks up his phone and calls Naresh, asking if he could drop by, see the kids and maybe talk about what more he can do to help the orphanage. Maybe donate some time there, providing medical skills for the home until he figures out where to put his energies concerning the lost children of Nepal.

Naresh is more than happy to welcome him back. The kids will probably be busy with their brushes when he arrives, working on their pictures in the main corridor. In his mind's eye, Lincoln can see their blue, red, and yellow paint-streaked faces. He smiles, telling Naresh he'll be over within the hour, then calls Jiban for a ride.

Jiban drops Lincoln at the Lotus Home around 11:15 a.m. As he drives away, Lincoln heads inside, where he hears the echoing laughter and screeches of children. The receptionist looks up from behind her desk. She's gotten to know him now, so she waves him on toward Naresh's office.

"Namaste," he says, tapping on the orphan-keeper's door.

"Ah, come in, come in," Naresh says, looking up from his computer. "Have a seat. Can I get you a refreshment?"

"Oh, no, thank you," Lincoln says, finding a chair. "Thanks for letting me drop by. I've been going nuts back at my hotel."

"They still haven't found the girl, I take it?" Naresh says.

"No, and what's more, she's been taken over the border."

"Oh, no. That's terrible."

"Yeah. We think they've hauled her off to Patna. The 3 Angels rep thinks she's there, anyway, so they're spreading pictures of her around the city. Kamala, the rep, believes we have a chance of getting her back, but I don't know. India's a big country. She could be anywhere."

"I'm so sorry to hear this," Naresh says, "but never give up hope, no?"

"No. It's just the waiting and not knowing."

"I know. I will light candles for her to Lakshmi tonight. If there's anything I can do, please don't hesitate to ask."

"Thanks." Lincoln pauses. "Any changes with Pratima and the boy?"

"No, not yet. It takes time, and from what I've seen so far, it's going to take quite a while before they start opening up, the boy especially."

"He sleep on the floor again?"

Naresh nods and loses his smile. "I have my suspicions why he does, though."

"What's that?"

465

"Shut the door, please," Naresh says. Lincoln gets up and pulls it closed. The friendly old man takes his glasses off and rubs the bridge of his nose. "My guess is he was raped on a bed, so he associates any bed with the experience."

"Jesus, he's only seven or eight," Lincoln says, and again anger roils inside him.

"I know. It's awful," Naresh says. "Hopefully, the therapist you hired for him will help. It's way beyond our skill here."

"What about Pratima?"

"She's doing a little better. She came out of her room this morning and did a little exploring."

"You think she was..."

Naresh shakes his head. "Sodomized probably, but not the other. They would want to keep her virtue intact for a big-time client."

Lincoln doesn't know whether to be thankful or angry for a moment, then decides he's angry. "I'd like to cut their nuts off."

"So wouldn't we all."

"How do you deal with this? Doesn't it ever get to you?"

"Oh, yes, but I can't let it get in the way of my kids. They need smiling faces, hope, and a feeling of security and trust."

Lincoln chews on Naresh's answer a moment. Can he put aside his anger like Naresh? Be there for the kids in spirit? Or is he better suited to work with an NGO, where he can be on the front lines? Until now, he hasn't given much thought into what goes into working face-to-face, hand-to-hand with children. Again, he pushes away his urge to dive into something without thinking it over first, but it's hard. He's always been a man of action, striking out on ledges without looking down.

"Well, shall we see what the children are up to?" Naresh says.

"Yes, let's," answers Lincoln, getting up.

Naresh grabs his cane and they go out. Around the corner, down the hall, Lincoln hears children talking and the clicking and clacking of brushes against (he assumes) jars of paint. A radio murmurs a current lively Nepali tune.

"Sounds like they're having fun," Lincoln says. "How often do you get offers for adoption?"

Naresh shakes his head, turning his lips down. "Not often enough. Maybe once or twice a year: usually a foreign national, and more often than not, they want a younger child. I'm grateful for any placement, don't get me wrong, but it's sad to see the older ones always left behind. And the child they do take loses so much of what it means to be Nepali. The foreigners promise to be sensitive to the child's heritage, but it's not the same."

"And the older ones?" Lincoln asks as they come around the corner. In front of him, a dozen boys and girls of varying ages, brushes in hand, are paying attention to their artwork. A couple of the older girls are helping the younger ones as a staff member lingers nearby. Lincoln doesn't see Pratima or the boy, though. *They're probably in their rooms.* A vision of Sunita painting beside the kids flashes before him. He blinks and it's gone.

Naresh continues, "People don't want to deal with their problems, and they have many, despite what you see here. They may appear adjusted and content, but underneath there's anger, hurt, and knowing they'll probably spend their life here until they're able to go out on their own. So this is their family, and it's not nearly enough. Then there's the difficult transition into the real world and making a life for themselves. Even educating them the best we can, they're at a disadvantage when they leave. I fear many of them will end up in poverty or worse yet, working the brothels."

Suddenly, a memory of arguing with his aunt about one of her rules flashes before Lincoln. The distant echo of his berating the widow who took him in after his parents died roars in his ears. *You're not my mother. You can't tell me what to do. I can't wait until I get out of here away from you, on my own.* He looks away, embarrassed.

"Something the matter?" Naresh says.

Lincoln collects himself. "No, just thinking." He swallows the knot in his throat, then drifts toward the children to watch them paint.

Behind him, he hears Naresh say, "I'll leave you to enjoy your time with them. Lunch will be in an hour. We're having chatamari today. Will you be joining us?"

"I'd love to."

"Very well. I'll see you then."

After Naresh leaves, Lincoln joins one of the young boys who's slapping streaks of blue paint on the wall. In Nepali, he asks, "So what you painting?"

The boy, who's maybe Arjun's age, looks up at him. His heart-shaped bronzed face is speckled with paint. "Genie from *Aladdin!*" He dips his brush in the jar, then adds another stroke on the wall that Lincoln assumes is supposed to be the Genie's head.

"Why you like Genie?" Lincoln says, bending down and sitting on his heels beside him.

The boy focuses on his painting, drawing the brush around to form the Genie's jaw. Over his shoulder, he says, "Because he has magic and can make anything come true."

Lincoln ignores the impulse to ask the obvious. "What your name?"

"Binod."

Lincoln smiles. "I have good friend name Binod."

"You do?"

"Yeah. How old you?"

"Six, going on seven," he says as his brush goes back for more paint.

"You been here long?"

The boy shrugs. "Since I was a little boy."

"You like paint?"

"It's okay. I like drawing better."

"Maybe show me drawing you do later?"

"Okay." He turns to Lincoln and holds him with a steady, sober gaze. "Are you here to take one of us home with you?"

Lincoln's throat tightens and he has to take a deep breath. "No, Binod. I here so make life better for children in home. Maybe I work here sometime, help out, play game with everyone. What you think?"

"Okay." He hands Lincoln his brush. "You want to paint with me? You can if you want."

"I love to, but this your painting."

"It's okay. I don't mind," he says, shrugging.

Lincoln dips the brush in the paint jar and adds a stroke to the top of the Genie's head, then hands the brush back. "We need give eyes too. You have white paint?"

Binod nods, squats down, and pulls another jar of paint over, and as he does, Lincoln feels his mind being made up about where he'll devote his future.

An hour later, Lincoln is in the lunchroom sitting next to Naresh and four of the older children. At the next table is another group of children and Binod and Pratima are with them. Pratima sits stiffly, watchful as she nibbles her lunch, her dark eyes panning the room like a cat. The boy Lincoln brought in yesterday is sitting with a group of seven- and eight-year-olds beyond. He sits quietly, his head down, paying attention to his lunch as the other kids eat and talk.

Naresh taps Lincoln's arm and says in English, "How's your chatamari?"

"It's good," Lincoln says. He takes another bite, and as he does, he feels a tremor ripple through the building. Another aftershock, he tells himself. He hasn't felt one in a while, so he's a little surprised. He waits for the shaking underfoot to subside but it doesn't. It's getting stronger! Naresh looks up with sudden alarm in his eyes. When a second jolt hits, the kids stop eating and their eyes bulge. Lincoln jumps to his feet.

"Everyone outside!" he yells in Nepali.

All at once there's a stampeding of feet rushing for the door. Plates fly off tables, crashing to the floor. The paddle fans above wave back and forth. Lincoln ushers Naresh ahead along with a couple of straggling children who've frozen in their seats.

They all run outside and Lincoln looks around as the ground rolls beneath them. At the edge of the lot, trees sway back and forth, but they aren't what he's concerned about. *Has everyone gotten out? Except I don't know everyone.* He eyes the boy named, Binod, and Pratima, and then the children he painted with this morning.

Where's the boy? Lincoln ushered him out of the lunchroom, he's sure he did. *Where is he?*

Fear leaps into his throat as another jolt slams into him, almost knocking him off his feet. Suddenly, he's running into the building, ignoring Naresh's cries to come back. Inside, broken ceiling tiles and shards of light bulbs lie scattered on the floor. A flickering light winks back from the other end of the corridor. For a second, he freezes, then a thought clicks and he's racing down the dormitory hall. When he comes to the boy's room, he finds him hiding in the corner with his back against the wall.

"I got you," he says, running over and covering the boy's head as dust and debris rain down. A moment later, he's dodging falling ceiling tiles in the darkened hall, running for daylight with the boy over his shoulder. He rounds the corner as another jolt barrels into the building, sending him flying against the wall. The sharp pain ripping through his shoulder takes his breath away. But the commanding voice in his head refuses to give in. He yanks himself from the wall, and a second later he's running through the exit door to the terrified children and staff in the quaking lot. As he joins them, the ground goes still. For a moment everyone looks around, waiting for the next jolt, but it doesn't come. After a few minutes, Lincoln senses the collective sigh.

Naresh and one of the staff, standing a few yards away, head toward him. "Are you okay?" Naresh asks.

Settling the boy on his feet, Lincoln bends over with his hands on his knees. Spits grit out, then nods toward the boy. "He ran and hid in his room. Guess he panicked." Finally, he looks up at Naresh. His shoulder hurts like hell, but he's sure he didn't break anything.

The woman beside Naresh says in Nepali, "What do we do about the children? They can't go back in there."

"No," Naresh says. "We'll have to get some tents or tarps from somewhere. Is your phone working?"

The woman nods.

Lincoln spits more grit and looks back at the building. He says to Naresh in English, "Most of the damage is superficial, I think. If the authorities clear it, you should be able to go back in by the end of the week. The important thing is everyone's out, right...RIGHT?"

Naresh looks to the woman and repeats Lincoln's question. When she nods, Lincoln says, "What did you do the last time?"

"It was just a little shaking here, so it didn't affect us." As Naresh says this, Binod's and Sila's faces flash before Lincoln.

Jesus, no! He digs his phone from his pocket, scrolls to Binod's number, and holds his breath as the phone rings on the other end. *Pick up, pick up...*

"Hello?"

"Binod, you okay?"

473

"Oh, yes. Lots of shaking here, but no damage. Everyone is okay. What about you and Mick? I just tried calling him, but he isn't answering."

Oh-oh. That can't be good. "I'm sure he's okay. I'm over visiting the orphan home I gave money to. Going to be here for some time, I think. The building has some damage, so I'm going to help out. I'll call Mick, too. If I hear anything, I'll let you know. Be safe, and remember, if you hear anything at all about Sunita, let me know, okay?"

"Okay. Will do."

Lincoln ends the call. He's seen Mick with his phone. The man lives on it. He hits his number and listens as it rings until it goes to voicemail. "Hey big guy, call me back, ASAP. Don't make me wait too long. I'm worried, and you know me when I worry, I do stupid stuff, like forgetting secrets I'm supposed to keep."

He ends the call, trying to ignore the bad feeling in his gut.

28

MAY 12, 2015

*M*ick is sitting with Palisha in the café talking about her coming back with him to Germany while he does his summer treks there. He's excited to have her join him, and he's wondering how his family will receive her. They're pretty open-minded, but he's a bit nervous all the same. His sister Lind can be a little judging, especially when it comes to his choices. She was never a fan of his coming to Nepal, especially over the last few years with their parents getting older. He can still hear her deriding him the last time he was home. *You should be here with them instead of gallivanting all over the world.*

As for his parents, he's sure his mother will be happy with Palisha. She's always wanted him to get married and have a family. It's a little late for children, but he knows she'll be pleased he has someone to love. His father will be his usual self, quiet and watchful, asking pointed questions of Palisha from time to time—what her family is like, are they educated, what do they do, and what is their opinion of his son.

"You'll love Berlin," Mick says. He pops a momo into his mouth, chews, and swallows. "There's lots to see and do there: museums, the Berlin Memorial Wall, the Reichstag Building, maybe a ride down the Spree River, or maybe we'll go to a couple of castles. There's one in Rhineland outside a pretty little town called Beilstein I know you would like. It's called Eltz Castle. It's a full day's ride in the car to get there, but it's well worth it. We can get a room in a B and B for the weekend—"

"What is a B and B?" Palisha asks.

"A Bed and Breakfast. An overnight inn, like a teahouse with guest rooms for visitors. They serve breakfast, too—a little different than what you're used to. We Germans like our 'meats and cheeses.'" He smiles. "Boy, but I miss good old-fashioned German fare and beer. It's the best! Wait 'til you try it."

"I will look forward to it," Palisha says, watching him deer-eyed.

It's clear he's overwhelming her, so he checks his excitement. "Sorry, I'm a little pumped here."

"It is okay." She takes a bite of her lunch, dabs her lips with a napkin, then is quiet a moment. He wonders what she's thinking. Finally, she says, "So, where will I be staying while you are out on trek?"

"With my parents if you want, or maybe my sister."

"Oh, I do not want to be any trouble. Maybe a hotel would be better?"

"Nonsense," Mick says, looking at her hard. "They'll love you, and I don't want you to feel like a tourist while you're there. You're part of my family now."

"Okay, if you are sure."

"I am." His phone rings and he pulls it out of his pocket. It's Binod and he's wondering if High Trails has anything going on over the summer he can do. Mick presses his lips together, wishing he could tell him there's a trek, but they both know that's not the case. He asks Binod if he needs money. He knows he's lost everything. As Binod makes a feeble excuse that he's fine, Mick sees Palisha wrinkle her brow. He looks at her, wondering what's wrong.

She gets up. "I think I left my phone in the room. I will be right back."

He watches her wend her way through the café and out the door. "By the way, how are you and Sila doing?"

There's a pause, then, "Okay."

Mick nods. He knows there's nothing okay about what Binod and Sila are enduring. "Hang in there, guy. Remember you've got friends here pulling for you."

"I know."

"Okay, I'll check back later," Mick says and ends the call. For a moment, he sits there staring into space, thinking about what Binod is going through, and he feels powerless to help. At last, he comes to himself, and as he reaches for his glass for a gulp of juice, he feels a tremor shiver under the building. He's gotten used to them over the last two and a half weeks, so he pays it no mind. But when another one comes, jolting the building a little harder, his eyes widen. He looks up to see the hanging swag lamps swing back and forth. The next jolt rocks the building, and now the walls are shaking.

Oh, shit, here we go again!

Suddenly, people jump up from their chairs, overturning tables, knocking plates and glasses to the floor. A second later, he's up and running with them, heading for the exit beside the café. Behind him, he hears crashing and banging, the shattering of glass, and a low, menacing groan from the building. As he weaves back and forth around the tables, avoiding falling ceiling tiles and debris, the memory of running out of Palisha's apartment flashes before him. But unlike last time, there's no stairs to fumble down and no one he has to carry doing it.

He staggers around the corner, and a moment later he's outside, standing in the middle of a rolling parking lot with a crowd of terrified hotel guests. As people pour out of the building, he runs around to the front, searches the gathered mob standing some ways back on the drive going out to Ring Road. He expects to see Palisha there, but she isn't, and his heart thuds. Turning back to the building, he stares at the front doors, watching more people run out.

Where are you? Come on, where are you, come on!

But she doesn't come, and the quake is intensifying. A long narrow crack is zigzagging through the lot, unzipping the macadam and flipping it over like a bed sheet. A second later, a loud pop jerks his gaze upward just in time to see shattering glass rain down on the surrounding lawn. Screams and cries bounce off him as he turns back to the crowd, searching again for her, thinking he missed seeing her come out. As the reality of her still being inside galvanizes, his breath leaves him, and a moment later, he's running into the dark mouth of the waving building.

The stairway is down the corridor off the main lobby. As he picks his way to it through the heavy haze, avoiding chunks of ceiling tile and drywall lying helter-skelter on the floor, his gaze flits back and forth, searching and wary. A severed metal conduit backlit by the amber glow of an emergency light waves back and forth above. The stairwell is right under it. He pulls the door open, and as he starts up, he realizes the earth has stopped moving. For a moment, he's not sure if he's imagining it. He stops, grips the railing, looks upward, and waits.

"Are ya done yet? 'Cause I really need to be somewhere right now."

As if in answer, a guttural moan comes from above. *Palisha!* He rushes up to find a man lying on the landing with his leg turned at an unnatural angle. Bending over him, Mick looks down and sees a small pool of blood under the break. "Do you hurt anywhere else?"

The man winces, shakes his head.

"Okay, you have a compound fracture. Keep still. Try not to move. I'll be right back." He hates leaving the man there, but he has to find Palisha. He runs over, pulls on the door. It doesn't want to open. The frame is racked. He yanks hard, and it inches back little by little, the bottom scraping the floor, until finally he can slide through.

The hallway is dark, save for the amber glow from the emergency light across from him. His room is four doors down. There's a slab of ceiling leaning against the wall in front of him. He steps around it and rushes ahead, his boots crunching glass and drywall. When he goes to open his door, it won't open. The card reader doesn't work—the power is out.

He pounds on the door. "Polly, Polly, you in there? The lock isn't working! Open up. It's me."

He puts his ear to the door, but there's only silence. *Maybe she's not in there, but where would she be?* He calls her again, but there's no answer. *Did she go to the other room?* He runs down the hall, pounds on the door to her old room, calls her name. Nothing. What did she say? He tries to remember what it was before she left the table. It was their room, he's sure of it! Rushing back to the room, he steps back and tries to kick the door open, but he might as well be trying to kick down the door to *Shambhala.*

He glances around, looking for something to use as a battering ram. Sees the door to a janitor's closet and rips it open, paws around inside, tossing boxes off the shelves. He's at a complete loss when he comes out, and he's sure an aftershock will be coming soon. Suddenly the doom of losing someone he loves again descends on him. *No, no...this isn't happening again. Please no, God!*

He runs back to the door, kicks it again and again. Rams his shoulder into it. He's exhausted, his lungs burn, and his body aches. "Open up, you son-of-a-bitch!" he cries, slamming his shoulder into it again. When he backs up for another shot, he catches a glimpse of a fire extinguisher on the wall beyond. He stops and stares at it.

A moment later, he's ripping it away from the wall and carrying it back. Smashes the end of it into the card reader, again and again, until finally the lock gives in and the door cracks open. Another kick and a ram of his shoulder, and he's blinking into bright pale sunlight pouring in through the waving curtains. He tosses the extinguisher aside, peers over the battered room. Stares at the arm poking out from under a large chunk of fallen ceiling lying on the floor.

The next thing he knows, he's breaking pieces of it away, throwing them aside until she's free. There's a streak of blood running down the side of her face and a small pool staining the carpet. He bends down and turns her over gently, closes his eyes and checks for a pulse. When he feels it, he lets out a sigh.

"Come on, let's get you out of here," he mutters, picking her up. As he cradles her in his arms, her lids flicker open for a second. "I got you, don't you worry. Mick's going to get you out of here." He kicks a chunk of drywall aside and carries her out into the dark corridor and down the hall. When he comes to the stairwell, he meets a couple of firemen who are mobilizing the injured man's leg. They look up, surprised, and one of them puts his hands out, offering to take Palisha, but there's no way he's letting go of her until they're safe outside.

"I got her," Mick tells him in Nepali, "but she's going to need medical attention. Is there an ambulance outside?"

"There's one on the way, yes," says the one working on the man.

The other one looks to his partner, and when he gets a nod, says to Mick, "Follow me."

They go down the stairs, out through the lobby, and across the lot to the lawn on the other side. Gently, Mick lays Palisha on the grass and bends over her as people gather around him. He bends and pulls a lock of blood-matted hair back from her face and sees the open wound that stretches up under her hairline. It's deep and there's a hint of bone below. The fireman bends down beside him, checking it over, then calls for one of the medics who've just arrived.

"She's got a fractured skull," he says, looking up at Mick, then goes about checking for other injuries as the medic arrives.

The man's words ricochet in Mick's head as his phone pings in his pocket. All he can think of is life without her.

May 14, 2015

Palisha wakes up and blinks into bright light raining down on her. She's in a hospital bed and her head hurts. The last thing she remembers is Mick carrying her out of the hotel. The crashing ceiling coming down in her room flashes before her and then the memory of the building shaking and the shattering of glass. She tries to reach up and touch her head, but the sharp pain in her shoulder takes her breath away. Suddenly Mick is looking down at her.

"Hey, hey, take it easy there," he says in English.

"What happened?"

"Another quake. You were in the room when it happened and took a shot to the head."

She blinks again, tries to get comfortable. "Another quake?" Her thoughts go to the hotel, and she shudders. "Namu, Rajan, Kesab, my staff—"

"They're okay. Everyone got out. A few people were injured, but not bad. Couple of broken bones, scrapes, and cuts. You got it the worst."

"What about the hotel?"

"Still standing, but no one can go in yet."

She takes that in, mulls it around. "What about you? You are okay, right?"

"Better now that you're okay. You gave me a hell of a scare."

She looks up to his smiling face, sees exhaustion and fear behind his loving gaze. "What are you not you telling me?"

"Nothing," he says.

She stares at him hard. "Remember what I told you about lying to me?"

He rolls his eyes. "Yes, I remember very well." He pulls her blanket up a little. "You're okay, everything's okay, I promise."

"Hmm...then why does my head hurt so?"

"Your head hurts because you have a fractured skull. The doctors say you'll be fine, though," he says. "You want something to drink?"

But the way he looks at her makes her wonder if he really believes what he says. "You are sure?"

"You're persistent, just like your father says."

"My father! Oh, I need to call him," she says, jerking up. For a second, her head feels like it's going to explode and her eyes roll back.

"Easy there," he says, laying his hand on her shoulder. "He already knows. Your parents were here most of the afternoon. They left a little while ago."

She gasps as the blinding ache fades. Finally, she says, "They were here?"

"Yes, I called them," he answers. "Lie back down."

"How come you did not wake me up?"

"Wasn't up to me. You had to wake up on your own. Concussion, fractured skull, you know?" he says, tapping his finger on his head.

She mulls that over. Suddenly she feels unmoored. "How long have I been here?"

"Two days. Since Monday afternoon," he says, pouring a glass of juice. He sticks a straw in it and puts it to her lips. "Drink."

"You are bossy."

"I'm picking up a few tips from your father," he says, and grins.

"You did not tell him, did you? About us?"

Mick shakes his head. "No. I'll leave that to you. Drink."

She takes a sip, watches him. "How long have you been here?"

"Since you came in."

"Two days? Where did you sleep?"

When he nods toward the chair next to the window, it occurs to her they no longer have a place to stay after she's released. She doesn't like the thought of going back to her parents and being separated from him.

"Don't you worry about that...we'll figure it out later. Right now the only thing that matters is you. Have another sip."

She shakes her head, winces, and sighs. Just when she thought things were beginning to come together, this happens, and for a fleeting moment, she wonders if this is karma punishing her for walking out on her parents, putting her needs above the honor of her father and family. But no, it's a silly thought. She has a right to live her own life. Except now, she doesn't know what that life looks like. Will she really be all right, or will she end up with a disability? She doesn't need to be told brain injuries are tricky. What if she has seizures or worse, cognitive impairments? How could she put Mick through that, ask him to give up his life to take care of her? How can she live without him, though? She muses on their plans to go to Germany, grieving the lost opportunity of seeing his world through his eyes, then the loss of her apartment, the treasures from her sons, her clothes, her jewelry, and now the hotel. How can it all be replaced? Where will the money come from? Not from her parents: she won't allow that.

"What's wrong?" Mick says.

She doesn't want to burden him with these self-incriminating and mournful musings. But the way he looks at her is so tender and caring, she can't help from being overcome.

"Hey, hey there," he says, wiping her tears away. "Everything's going to be all right. You'll see. We got each other, right?"

She nods, but a little voice in her head wonders if that's enough.

MAY 15, 2015

Binod is in the bathroom shaving. He's going to go help Dibaker clean up the earthquake damage at the Singing Bowl today. He's glad for the distraction that'll take him away from his machinations about his daughter. It doesn't hurt that he'll be away from Sila. They haven't said more than a few words since her rebuke the other day. He wonders if this is the beginning of the end between them. Never in his wildest imagination could he ever have believed it, but now, he's not so sure. He stares in the mirror. He's lost his parents, his home, his daughter, and now maybe his wife. It would be so easy to run the straight razor over his neck and be done with it.

"Bubā, you have a call," Arjun says, running in with his phone.

"Oh, thank you, Arjun. Put the phone on Āmā

and Bubā's dresser and I'll call whoever it is when I'm done."

"Okay."

He watches his son run out of the room. He should be happy to have him back, but he wants more. He wants his daughter back too; wants the life he had to return to him. He finishes up his shave, and as he wipes his face, he hears his phone ping again.

Hold on, I'm coming.

A moment later, he's in his room picking it up. "Hello?"

"Namaste. Is this Binod Thapa?"

The voice sounds familiar, but he can't place it. "Yes, can I help you?"

"It's Kamala from 3 Angels. Are you sitting down?"

There's an urgent tone in her voice. He sits on the bed. "Yes, what is it?"

"I got a call this morning. A girl was pulled from the wreckage of a building in Bihar, which is not far from Patna. She's been taken to the hospital down there with a broken leg and a few scrapes. You know, we circulated pictures of your daughter down there? Anyway, one of the firemen who pulled her out believes this girl is your daughter. They asked her for her name and she told them Sunita."

For a moment, Binod sits, dumbstruck. Is he imagining this, is this some cruel trick of his mind?

"Binod, you still there?"

Finally, he comes to himself. "Yes, yes," he cries. "Is it really her?"

"I think so. I'm looking at the picture they sent back for verification, and to me, it's your daughter! I'm going to send it to you after I hang up. Take a good look, and get right back to me."

"Yes, yes." He ends the call and runs out of the room and down the stairs. "Sila, Sila! Come here, hurry!"

She comes around the corner, wiping her hands on a towel. "What?"

"They think they found Sunni! She was rescued from a fallen building in Bihar." His phone pings in his hand. "They're sending pictures right now." He opens the text message, watches the picture load on the screen, and when it comes up, Sila screeches. He pulls his wife into his arms, swings her around. Sudden tears flood his eyes. He can't believe it. "That's her, that's her!"

Roshika, Amita, and Arjun come to the top of the stairs. Sumi and Prabin rush out of the kitchen. "What is it, what's wrong?" Sumi says, running up.

"Nothing! They found Sunni!" Binod cries, showing Sumi the picture on the phone. He redials Kamala's number, tells her that the picture is definitely Sunita. Kamala tells him she'll get back to the hospital and let them know Sunita's parents are on their way.

Prabin runs and gets his keys. Says to Sila and

Sumi, "I'll get the car gassed up while you finish up here, and we'll leave as soon as I get back. Binod, you get directions to the hospital while I'm gone." Prabin clenches his fist. There are tears in his eyes. "We're going to get our baby back."

~

Palisha is just finishing breakfast when Mick and Lincoln come to the door of her hospital room. She's feeling better emotionally today. The dark thoughts that have been taunting her the last two days seem to have gone back to where they belong: locked away in a dark vault where hope is the jailor. Maybe it's the sunshine coming through the window, but in her heart she knows it's because of Mick. His beautiful smile simply refuses to let her spiral down.

She introduces Lincoln to her roommate, a young woman who sustained a broken arm and a lacerated spleen. As Lincoln greets the woman, Palisha fills her in on how he saved a young girl and boy from a life of servitude or worse. When she elaborates, telling her just how he did it, the woman's eyes nearly pop out of her head. That gets a good laugh out of the tall redhead.

"He's a bit headstrong," Palisha says to her room-mate in Nepali, "but we love him anyway."

"I am problem child," Lincoln says with a grin. "I like trouble."

Mick comes beside Palisha, plants a kiss on her forehead. "How's my gal today?"

"I'm fine," she says. She glances at the two of them. They look rested and Mick has changed out of the clothes he's been wearing over the last two days into new jeans and a tan sweater that clings to his generous body. When he finally agreed to leave her yesterday afternoon, she made him promise to find a place and get some rest. For once, he seems to have followed her wishes. "I like your sweater."

"Do you, now?" Mick says, appraising it. "It's a little tight around the chest, don't you think?"

She drains the last of her mango juice and smiles at him. "I do not know. I kind of like what I see." Lincoln snickers and Mick's face colors. "So where are you two staying?"

"We holed up in hotel near Lalitpur," Lincoln says as Mick's phone pings.

He pulls it from his pocket and looks down at the number. "Hey Binod...ah-huh...really?" His eyes suddenly light up.

Palisha taps his arm, wondering what's happening. The way he's acting, it's something good, and she has an idea what it is. She puts a knuckle to her mouth, hoping she's right.

Mick raises his finger as he listens. "You're kidding me. That's fantastic. Where are you? Ah-huh... okay, yes, I'll let everyone know. I'm so happy for you. This is such great news. Drive safe, okay, and keep us

491

posted. I want to know the minute you see her." He ends the call. "They've found Sunita. She's in Bihar."

Lincoln lets out a big whoop and punches the air.

Palisha closes her eyes as joy courses through her for Mick and Lincoln. They've done so much for their friend, putting themselves in harm's way. And then there's Binod and Sila. She doesn't know them all that well, but there's a connection there all the same. Suddenly, she feels like she's gaining another family, a new family created out of the rubble of so much pain.

A knock comes to the door and she looks over to see her parents. Her father nods to Mick as her mother comes to her bedside.

Lincoln steps back to give them space. "I go get breakfast downstair. Let you all be awhile." As he backs out of the room, she sees him wink at Mick. She wonders what that's all about.

Her mother takes a seat next to her, introduces herself to Palisha's roommate, then asks how she's doing. But Palisha is darting her eyes toward her father and Mick, who are standing by the window talking. She can't hear what they're saying, and she's nervous. Beside her mother and sons, these two men are the most important people in her life, and their getting along is critical to her happiness. When she sees her father smile at something Mick says, a cautious ray of hope shines in her heart. Finally, the two of them come to the other side of the bed.

"Hi Bubā," she says. The two of them hold each other in a probing gaze, as he stands stiff-backed beside her. She longs to feel his arms around her, but she knows it's a fool's hope. It's not what he does. He's never been very affectionate toward his kids, even when they were very little.

Finally, he reaches out and grabs hold of the bed rail. Puts his trembling hand to her shoulder. "How's my girl?"

"Much better, now that you're here. How are you? Did the house have any damage?"

"No. Just a bit of shaking. A couple of pictures fell down. So, I hear you know about the girl."

"Yes, they called Mick this morning. They're on their way down there right now."

Mick says, "I'm gonna let you have some time with your parents and go join the problem child downstairs. Be back in a while."

After he's gone, Palisha turns to her father. "Thank you."

"For what?"

"All you did to help."

He shrugs. "It's my job."

"I know, but still. It means so much to my friends, Mick especially."

Her father nods and looks over at her mother, as if conferring about something they've already discussed. Finally, he says, "He's not bad. It's too bad he isn't Nepali. I think he would be good for you."

"He is good for me."

"As a friend, yes, I can see that. But he wants more. I can see it in his eyes, how he talks about you. I hope you know what you're doing. It can never—"

"No, Bubā. No more," Palisha says. She darts a glance at her mother, daring her to open her mouth, then turns back to her father. "If you want me and my love, you need to accept my choices now."

Her father sighs, and not for the first time, Palisha sees the weight of their long indifference to her decisions bearing down on him. "So, we come to an ultimatum?"

"I'd like to think of it as you loving me enough to be happy for me."

"Of course, I want you to have happiness."

"Well, then? He makes me happy. And you yourself just said he would be good for me."

"If he were Nepali."

"What difference does it make, Bubā?"

"Will you marry him?"

"I don't know, maybe."

"I see. Well, I guess if you've made your mind up, there's nothing I can do."

"You can be my Bubā," Palisha says, and takes his hand, holding it in hers.

Again, he looks to her mother and sighs. "How is it you always know what to say to bring me to my knees? Lord Shiva, save me from an impertinent child." He shakes his head. "Very well then, seeing how you're determined, I will say this to you: if he's the man you say he is, then he must marry you. Do not accept less. I won't have a whore for a daughter."

It's been over ten hours since they left Kathmandu this morning. Despite his excitement at seeing his daughter and having her back in his arms, Binod is wiped out. The road to Bihar seems to go on forever, passing through town after town. Every time they have a clear road ahead of them, ten minutes later they run into road construction or a traffic jam. He looks out the window. The bloodshot sun is low, hovering amid the streaking magenta clouds that roll over an undulating gray horizon. A sign on the road says fifteen kilometers to Patna and the clock on the dashboard reads 7:09 p.m. Prabin has been at the wheel for the last four hours, and he looks like he could use a break. The two of them have been swapping driving duties while Sila and Sumi sit in back. The two women are both leaning against each other, asleep at the moment.

"You want me to drive for a while?" Binod asks.

Prabin rubs the bridge of his nose, looks down at the gauges, then blinks. "We need gas in a bit, so maybe when we stop in Patna for it we can switch."

Binod nods, then looks at the passing trees shrouding a river he has no name for. They've been following it for the last hour. He picks his phone out of his pocket and scrolls through pictures of Sunni, studying each one in detail. Her smiling face, the shine in her dark eyes, the tiny dimples at the corners of her petal lips as she stands next to her pencil drawing of their neighborhood that won a citation in a school art contest. Then another one where she's wearing a bright red sari during the festival of lights. She looks so grown up in it with her hennaed face, long dark lashes, soulful eyes, and thick black hair pulled back in a braid. She has so much of her mother in her. He smiles, and for a moment, he doesn't feel the tear trailing down his cheek. Wiping it away, he closes his eyes.

Twenty minutes later, he's opening them to see a broad dun river passing below and a daunting urban sprawl ahead. The powerful tang of the river seeps in through the crack of his window, wrinkling his nose. He rolls it up tight as Prabin negotiates a stop-and-go path through the weaving motorbikes and cars on the bridge. When they approach the end of the expanse, Prabin points to a fuel station ahead. "We'll gas up there and you can drive the rest of the way."

"Okay," Binod says, looking down over the dark, brooding waters, hoping he doesn't lose their way through this far-reaching sea of humanity. Hopefully, his phone will guide them through it. In back, he hears the women stir and sit up.

"Are we there yet?" Sila asks, her voice low and sleepy.

Prabin says, "No, not yet. This is Patna. We're going to get gas, and Binod will take us the rest of the way. Is anyone hungry? We can stop and get something to eat, too, if you want."

"No, no. I want to keep going," Sila says. "How much farther, do you think?"

Binod brings up his GPS and maps it out. "Another hour and a half, it says. Maybe we just get something to go." He eyes Prabin and they share a knowing glance. "I think your bubā's hungry."

"Okay," Sila says.

Sumi peers out her window. "Wow, such a big city! I hope we don't get lost."

"We'll be okay," Prabin says as he pulls into the station.

They all get out and stretch their legs, peering around them at the swarming crowds and the endless line of traffic surging in and out of the city. At length, Sila and Sumi go inside to get snacks while Prabin stands beside Binod as he fills the tank.

Prabin says, "You think they did to anything to her?"

Binod knows exactly what he's talking about, and he doesn't want to go there, to imagine his daughter being forced to give up her virtue. "I don't know. All I know is, I want her back in my arms."

Prabin nods. "I shouldn't be thinking about such things. Sorry."

"It's okay. It's been on my mind, too." The lever on the gas handle pops, and he pulls the nozzle out and replaces it on the pump.

"I'll go in and pay, see what the women are up to, then be right back."

Binod watches him go, thinking about what his father-in-law said. Years ago, a woman who lost her virtue before marriage would be doomed, and even though things have progressed since then, it would still be hard for Sunni. Men want their wives to be pure and clean when they marry, and it doesn't matter whether the girl lost her virtue willingly or not. He gets in the car, pulls up to the front of the station and waits, trying hard to drive the unwanted thought out of his mind.

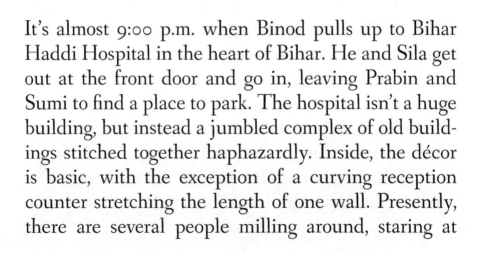

It's almost 9:00 p.m. when Binod pulls up to Bihar Haddi Hospital in the heart of Bihar. He and Sila get out at the front door and go in, leaving Prabin and Sumi to find a place to park. The hospital isn't a huge building, but instead a jumbled complex of old build-ings stitched together haphazardly. Inside, the décor is basic, with the exception of a curving reception counter stretching the length of one wall. Presently, there are several people milling around, staring at their phones or reading while they wait for whatever they're there for. A couple of security guards stand talking off to one side. Binod and Sila file in behind a short line in front of the desk.

As they wait, Binod's heart is racing, wishing people would hurry up. Seconds drag into minutes and the longer he waits, the more impatient he's getting. He doesn't need to look at Sila to see she's feeling the same way. Her hand is squeezing tight around his knuckles. Finally the person in front of them leaves and he rushes up with Sila and breathlessly asks the man staring at his broad computer monitor for Sunita's room number.

The man looks up. "What is your name?"

"Binod Thapa, and this is my wife, Sila. We're here to get our daughter, Sunita. She was in the earthquake and was admitted yesterday with a broken leg."

There's a puzzled look on the man's face after Binod finishes. "You're her father?"

"Yes," Binod says and pulls out his phone to show him the picture Kamala sent him. "See, that's her."

The man's expression turns wary and he waves to one of the security guards. Binod is wondering what's going on, and suddenly fear wells up inside him. "What?"

Sila gasps, and her grip tightens around his fingers. "What's wrong? Is there something wrong with my baby? Someone, say something!"

The receptionist ignores her as the guard walks up. He says to the man, "I think we have a problem upstairs." He glances at Binod and Sila. "The girl who was brought in yesterday, you remember her?"

"Yeah," the guard says, eyeing Binod with a speculative gaze.

"Well, these two here say they're her parents. Problem is, there's a man upstairs with the girl who says he's her father."

Binod's eyes almost pop out of his head, and Sila shrieks. "Who? I'm her father! See?" He shows the guard Sunita's picture, then scrolls to one after the other, many of them showing Sunita with him, Sila, and Arjun.

The guard looks back to the receptionist, suddenly alarmed. "Call upstairs. Tell them what's going on, but not to say anything more until we get there." He calls the other guard over and tells him what he just found out, then sends him off running. "Okay, you two stay here until I call back," he says to Binod and Sila, then rushes off behind the other guard.

The receptionist says, "Why don't you come over here and sit by me, until we get this all straightened out."

But sitting is the last thing Binod wants to do. Who is this man claiming to be Sunita's father? Is it one of those monsters? His gut churns and he's going to explode at any minute if he doesn't find out. Beside him, Sila is shaking. He sucks a breath and puts his arm around her, anything to keep himself from going up and grabbing this imposter by the throat and punching him in the face.

He looks up just as Prabin and Sumi come in. They pan their gazes over the lobby until they see him and Sila. Binod gets up and waves them over, and when they get there, he fills them in on what's going on. Sumi's eyes widen and Prabin grits his teeth.

"What are we doing here? We need to be upstairs!" Prabin says.

"No, we can't go yet, not until they come back down."

"Who's they?"

"The guards."

"What are they doing?"

The receptionist says, "Arresting the man, I would presume. That's why they want you to wait here. They want to do it quietly." The desk phone rings and he picks it up. Binod watches him talk to the person on the other end, sees him nod. When he hangs up, he says, "They just took him into custody and will be taking him out the back way. You can go up now."

Binod jumps to his feet and everyone is three feet behind him until he realizes he never got Sunni's room number. He stops and turns around.

"What?" Sila says.

"We never got her room number." He runs back,

gets it, and three minutes later they're on the third floor, rushing toward Sunni's room.

On the way, one of the doctors stops them. "You're Sunita's parents, I assume?"

"Yes," Binod says. "She's okay, right?"

"Yes, she's fine. A bit banged up, but she'll recover. In light of what just happened, after you see her, come see me, okay? I want to talk about some things."

"What things?" Sila says, alarm once again coming to her face.

The doctor waves his hands, palms down. "Not to worry, I just want to have a talk." He pauses and shakes his head. "You know, it's a good thing you got here when you did. I was prepared, Lord Shiva save me, to release her to that man tomorrow. Anyway, go see your daughter. I'm sure she'll be overcome to have her real parents beside her."

"It's okay, you didn't know. How could anyone? Thank you," Binod says, and when he turns to Sila beside him, she's gone, running up the corridor with her mother trailing behind, checking room numbers as she goes. When he sees her stop in front of a door, he knows she's found Sunni. He waves to the doctor and runs up with Prabin. When he gets to the door, he hears sobs of happiness coming out of the room. Inside, his daughter is lying on the bed, grasping at her mother. He walks up to her, passing the cast on her leg, and eyes the long sutured cut running along her jaw. For a moment he holds his daughter in his gaze.

"Bubā?"

There's a moment between them where he doesn't believe what his eyes are telling him, and then unfathomable happiness reaches into Binod's heart, waking up a spirit that had almost withered away.

He reaches over the bed's bar and pulls his daughter into his arms, holding her tight, and as he does, his throat tightens and his eyes blur. The long dark night lifts and the feeling of her arms around him is like clouds suddenly parting, and her weeping is like sunshine pouring over him from the heavens.

Wiping his eyes, Binod pulls back and watches his wife wrap her arms around her daughter, the two of them shedding tears of happiness held for too long, of finally finding each other again. He has his precious daughter back, and no matter what the future holds, this is all that matters.

Dear reader,

We hope you enjoyed reading *Out Of The Rubble*. Please take a moment to leave a review, even if it's a short one. Your opinion is important to us.

Discover more books by Ronald Bagliere at

https://www.nextchapter.pub/authors/ronald-bagliere-author-new-york

Want to know when one of our books is free or discounted? Join the newsletter at

http://eepurl.com/bqqB3H

Best regards,

Ronald Bagliere and the Next Chapter Team

ABOUT THE AUTHOR

Ron is a retired architect living in upstate New York. An avid hiker and photographer, he has traveled to Nepal, New Zealand and throughout the United States, Alaska and Hawaii collecting ideas for character-driven stories of romance and adventure. Other novels by Ron are:

Loving Neil – Published by Next Chapter, 2017 (Also available on Audio through Amazon)

Starting over - Published by Next Chapter, 2018. (Also available on Audio through Amazon)

Beyond the Veil – Published by Next Chapter, 2017.

The Lion of Khum Jung – Published by Next Chapter, 2017 (Also available on Audio through Amazon)

On My Way to You - Published by Next Chapter, 2019. (Also available on Audio through Amazon)

The Himalayan - Published by Next Chapter, 2020. (Also available on Audio through Amazon)

Connect with Ron via Facebook at R.J. Bagliere or on the web at: www.rjbagliere.com

Out Of The Rubble
ISBN: 978-4-86745-836-5
Large Print

Published by
Next Chapter
1-60-20 Minami-Otsuka
170-0005 Toshima-Ku, Tokyo
+818035793528

27th April 2021